THE ADVENTURESS

BOOKS BY SANTHA RAMA RAU

The Adventuress
Gifts of Passage
My Russian Journey
View to the Southeast
Remember the House
This Is India
East of Home
Home to India

The
ADVENTURESS

A NOVEL BY

SANTHA RAMA RAU

Harper & Row, Publishers

New York, Evanston, and London

TO MY SISTER, PREMILA WAGLÉ

Contents

1

I   SOFTLY

78

II   IN THE HOUSE OF STRANGERS

143

III THE WIDE MOSQUITO NET

225

IV   BEAUTY, REASON, VIRTUE

PART I

Softly

The summer of 1947 was unrelentingly hot in Tokyo. There were, besides, a couple of other factors that made it unusually tiresome for the Occupation personnel. For one thing, a good many members of foreign diplomatic missions had arrived. Houses and cars had to be requisitioned for them, and the already over-crowded living conditions of the city were further strained. For another, "dependents" were arriving in force from America to bedevil numbers of men who had, in the course of two years of Occupation life, worked out pleasant, exotic, and thoroughly satisfactory arrangements with Japanese women.

Many of the men had arrived in Tokyo after the war expecting to find the Japanese at least plain, if not positively repellent. They scarcely noticed the moment at which their eye changed and that subtle pliability of infinite power, a birth-right of Japanese women, undermined their preconceptions. It was the moment at which their own women seemed both domineering and colorless. Later, they were astonished when newcomers commented on the ill-proportioned stature of the Japanese, or the broad features and flaming cheeks of the country girls who had come into Tokyo to find work, or the thick legs and seedy clothes of the pompom girls who loitered about under the railway bridges in the center of town or paraded beside the bombed-out lots and shattered factories near army billets. Often the newcomers would mimic the sad little pompom girls' refrain. "Harro, harro, G.I., prease. How much, you say, long time? Short time?" And the veteran members of the Occupation would look embarrassed and change the subject.

That summer, in any bar in any American billet, there would be the familiar quota of men sitting alone, sipping whiskey and glumly considering how they would tell some Japanese girl that a wife (or mother, or daughter—anyway, a dependent) was arriving and that life would be different from now on. They were the men with a Personal Problem—a P.P., as it came to be called, or, as some musically minded wag had insisted, a Softly. There would be brief exchanges of this sort:

"What's the trouble, Dick?"

"The usual," Dick would reply. "A Softly."

"Yeah," his friend would say sympathetically. "A Softly does it, all right."

Looking at Charles Beaver, sitting alone in the bar of the Imperial Hotel, one could easily have supposed him to be a Softly victim—a civilian government employee, scowling over a letter that was evidently hard to write when he should have been back in his office. The last of the late-leavers from the bar, a young colleague who had decided, as he often did, to drink his lunch, stopped by Beaver's table on his way out. "Boy, you sure look solemn," he remarked in half-drunken friendliness.

"Yeah," Beaver said, scarcely bothering to look up.

"A Softly, I guess. A Softly always does it."

"A *what?*" Beaver asked, startled out of his absent-minded-ness.

"A Softly, Mac. You know, a Personal Problem . . ."

"Look, either you're drunk or I'm—"

"A *Personal Problem*—a P.P. Get it? Didn't you ever have to take music lessons?—a *pp.*"

"Yeah, *pp*, a Personal Problem, pianissimo. Yeah, I get it."

"So it's called a Softly. We all have them."

"Well, sure—"

"Hardest letter I ever had to write. To little Fumi-san. Telling her my wife was coming out. Couldn't bear to tell her in person. Waited till the last moment—"

"Listen. It isn't that kind of a Softly—"

"Any kind is murder—"

"I'm writing to my wife."

"Don't do it, Beaver. Take my advice. We gotta go back to the States after all this is over. A Softly is a Softly—don't louse up your future for it."

Beaver said patiently, "I'm writing to my wife asking her to come to Japan with our children. I'm not in love with some pompom girl. I just *like* the damn country."

"O.K., O.K. Jesus, though, you had me worried there for a moment. Some of these nuts really do wreck it all just for . . . But they sure are accommodating, you have to ad-mit—"

"Yeah," said Beaver, "they're trained to be." He returned to his letter with an air of dismissal, and his friend went reeling off happily, leaving the older man to the emptiness of the bar.

Beaver was drinking Coca-Cola, not whiskey, and actually

he *was* writing to his wife urging her to come to Tokyo. He had fallen in love, not with a Japanese girl but with Japan— a much more difficult thing to explain in a letter.

"To you, of all people," he had written, "I should be able to say all this so it makes sense. But all I seem to repeat is that if you came out here you would understand—not the Japanese, necessarily (and I couldn't blame you), but why I want to stay on after my regular tour of duty is over." He stopped to reread his words in all their hopeful falsity, and imagined Susan opening the letter over breakfast in the tiny dining room of their Georgetown house. The house had been Susan's idea soon after they were married; an extravagance before the war, a remarkably good investment ever since. She would be wearing what she called a brunch coat, her hair neatly brushed, but no lipstick. First thing in the morning it makes a woman look hard, she had told him once. His two daughters, equally tidy, would be finishing breakfast. Susan, in a very fair tone, would say, "Your father writes that he's fine. He's enjoying himself in Japan. He says it's very hot, though I guess it's no hotter than Washington right now." She would put the letter away for prolonged consideration later, after the rest of the mail had been dealt with, after the house and the girls had been organized for the day.

"I wish I could give you some really cogent reasons—why I feel so strongly about this. It is an extraordinary privilege, at our age, to find the opportunity of exploring a foreign and a deeply rewarding culture." He stopped again to stare at the clumsy, stilted phrase. The fact was that he couldn't write, "I love the place. For the first time, my life seems to hold something unpredictable." In the years during and since the war, he and Susan had exchanged many letters, from army camps in America, from Australia, from New Guinea, from Japan.

She had soon worked out a formula. She used to keep a diary which she mailed to him once a week. In it she recorded her daily activities, the health of the girls, items of news about friends. Each installment ended, "We all love you and miss you." He had soon fallen into the pattern, thinking it wise of her to save them from easy emotionalism. He, in turn, described his food and living conditions and tried to add a bit of interest to his letters by putting in a few facts about the country in which he found himself: Australian sheep farmers, in their vast isolation, get medical advice by radio, or New Guinea natives eat wallabies—that sort of thing. He always closed with "I think of you and the girls all the time."

It was too late now to change the tone of his writing. He should, he thought, have started long ago when he first began to feel the excitement of Japan in small things, the elegance with which they wrapped a parcel, the most ordinary parcel, for instance. Or the sound of a flight of ducks over the lake in Ueno Park: a sudden whisper of wings on a cold evening and there were the ducks, wheeling black against a rose-pink sky.

"To be practical," he wrote, "you should have no trouble renting the house—Barret will always help you. I'm pretty certain I can wangle us a good house here, if you don't mind living a bit out of town, and Japanese servants are excellent. Actually, I'm entitled to it—as you know, they still grade us according to our army equivalents, so I'm a civilian colonel. The girls can go to the American school here. It's run on the same system as the ones back home, so they won't be missing anything academically. I don't think they'll be lonely here, as there are plenty of American families in Tokyo by now. Besides, they are at the age when travel really can broaden the mind instead of simply confirming one in one's prejudices."

Beaver looked up from his letter when the door of the Imperial bar swung open. Usually, he could count on having the bar to himself at this hour—too early for the after-office whiskey, too late for even the most long-drawn-out lunchtime martini. He could have stayed in his room to write his letter, but the bar was air-conditioned, and his cramped room, with its narrow windows outlined in an ugly brownish volcanic stone, was not. With vague resentment he saw a girl come into the bar. She wore a white silk suit, startling against her deep sun tan.

She held an enormous white handbag, almost as big as a briefcase, and since she was both short and slender, it gave her a look of slightly ludicrous importance. With only mild interest, Beaver wondered who was the lucky bastard that could claim her as a dependent. He thought she looked vaguely Latin. Spanish, perhaps.

"As it happens," he wrote, "there is another advantage. You know that living here is very cheap, so what we could get in rent from the house would cover..."

The girl held herself very straight, and walked across the room with an air compounded of grace and defiance. She couldn't have been more than twenty-three or -four. She took a table near Beaver's and for a couple of minutes stared down the length of the room toward the bar where one of the bartenders was hunched over a ledger illuminated by a gooseneck lamp, holding the pages down with his left hand while his right flicked the beads of an abacus. The other bartender was gazing out of the window at the desultory activity of the car park, the coming and going of jeeps and occasional diplomatic limousines. At last, she said, in a high, clear voice, *"Ano ne!"*

The bartender turned, sidled out from behind the bar, and

came over to her table. With a quick glance at Beaver's drink, she said, "I would like a Coca-Cola, please, with plenty of ice."

The thing that made Beaver look at her sharply was that she said it in Japanese. A simple enough sentence, certainly, but after two years of studying Japanese, Beaver knew that a particular authority and intonation that a phrase book could never give came with experience and fluency. He continued to watch her as the drink was poured out and set before her. Then she reached in her huge handbag and brought out some Japanese money. The waiter smiled at her rather wearily, and explained that he couldn't accept Japanese money.

"If you prefer military scrip ..." the girl said.

The bartender shook his head, still smiling.

On an impulse, Beaver leaned across his table. "You need chits," he said, holding up a little white book.

A look of defeat crossed the girl's face. "Chits?" she repeated, as though it were the end of the world.

"Didn't anyone tell you?" Beaver asked. "You can buy them at the desk in the lobby—"

The girl got to her feet.

"—if you're a resident in the hotel."

The girl turned to him with a distress quite out of proportion to the insignificance of the incident. "But I'm not. I was supposed to meet somebody here. What shall I do? I was supposed—"

"Well, don't get excited," Beaver said. "I'll pay for your Coke. It's only a nickel. Your friend will probably turn up before you've finished it." He smiled at her encouragingly and handed the bartender the slip of perforated paper.

"I didn't know about chits," the girl said, and didn't add

the "thank you" that would have ended the matter. "You live here, I suppose?"

"For my sins."

"But it's a very nice place. The best. The best of Western style, that is."

"Mm. I'd rather live in a Japanese house."

She turned her full attention on him for the first time, and he noticed that she had wide dark eyes, clear features, and an anxious expression. "Do you like the Japanese?" she asked, as if she seriously wanted to know.

"I suppose I do," he replied, equally seriously. "Anyway, I like Japan."

"Is that fashionable now?"

Unaccountably irritated, he said, "I wouldn't know." After a pause, he added, "Damn it, the war's been over some time. Any fool ought to know they aren't all monsters. I suppose you don't trust them?"

"I know them very well," she said noncommittally.

"That's a rash statement. B.I.J., I take it?"

"What? B.I.J.?"

"Born in Japan—missionaries' children and that sort of thing. If you had been, you'd know B.I.J."

"No, not B.I.J."

"Then how come you know them so well?"

"I've lived here." She was clearly not going to pursue this remark.

"I see. Well, at least you don't find them inscrutable. Most dependents do, and that's a bad way to begin because you can't unscrew the inscrutable."

She hesitated for a moment, and then decided that this was a joke. She gave a sudden clear peal of laughter that made the bartenders look across in surprise from the other end of the room. Beaver thought she looked quite beautiful when she laughed, the white teeth against the brown skin, the head, with its heavy knot of straight black hair, tilted back. He was certain that she couldn't be American, not only because of her accent, but because he thought an American woman's laughter would not be so released. He tried to think of something funny to say, and meanwhile, in the silence, she poked at the ice in her glass with a straw, and his eyes returned to his letter. "... what we could get in rent from the house would cover ..."

She was the one to break the silence, and with some amusement Beaver heard her offer that sturdy gambit of pickups, "Could you give me a cigarette? I seem to have come out without any." She hadn't opened her bag since she had produced the Japanese money to pay for her Coke.

"I don't smoke. I'm sorry."

"Can one buy them here?"

"Not *here*. At the PX, of course, and—"

"Never mind. It's probably good for me not to smoke."

"Not if it's a real pleasure to you. I just don't happen to, but—"

"But it ruins your sense of smell, and that is important. There is a moment of the year—autumn, in the mountains— when the country is twice as beautiful if you can smell it. And moss. Do you know that moss has a scent?"

"Damp and sort of moldy, you mean?" Beaver asked, smiling at her gravity, and remembering that most of the foreigners found that the country smelled of night soil and the city of pickled daikon.

"No, no! Beyond that. Very faint, very delicate, but lovely. And certain fruit woods, when you burn them ... You are laughing at me. Still, here it is an art to use your nose."

"Here what isn't an art?" Beaver got up from his table.
"You're going?" the girl asked quickly.
"Back in a moment." He arranged his papers and an air-mail envelope addressed to his wife face downward on the table as a guarantee of good faith. He left the bar, conscious that the girl was watching him, and straightened up from the normal slouch of a sedentary life as he went. In the steamy corridor outside, he didn't pause to wonder why he was doing this but walked across the dark landing to the small cur-tained reception room that was used as an auxiliary PX for the convenience of generals, colonels, diplomats, top civil-ians who lived at the Imperial. He did work out in his mind, while he was waiting for his carton of cigarettes, that if she wasn't American, she also wasn't a member of one of the foreign diplomatic missions—in that case she would have had access to embassy stores. If she were Japanese (in spite of her looks), she shouldn't be in the Imperial at all. Japanese were not permitted in the public rooms of army billets. He considered with some curiosity which of his fellow-residents at the Imperial might have made a date with her.

She, meanwhile, had been flicking through the papers on his table. When he returned to the bar, he stood in front of her table with his hands behind his back. A glance at his own table showed him that his papers had been disturbed and not very neatly replaced. He dropped the carton of cigarettes in front of her. "Go ahead and ruin your sense of smell," he said cheerfully.

She stared at the carton for a long time in silence. At last, she said, "One always hears that Americans are very gener-ous."

"Generous, or guilty, or eager to be liked," he said. He called the bartender over and, while he ordered two more

Coca-Colas, moved his papers over to her table. "Unless you prefer something stronger?" he asked, as an afterthought.

"I don't drink alcohol," she replied, still staring at the cigarettes.

He shoved the box toward her. "Go ahead," he said. "They're tax free." He sat down next to her. She took one package out of the carton and put it on the table. The rest she slipped into her bag. When the bartender returned with the drinks, he put a box of matches next to the cigarettes without being asked.

From five o'clock the bar started to fill up. Civilians and army officers stopped in on their way from work, often without going to their rooms first, for a breath of air conditioning and a drink. Later, the dependents would join them or replace them, women in summery cocktail dresses, powdered and scented for the evening. Many of them would carry Japanese fans, some would have flat gold brocade bags made from *obi* material, all would have a recognizable air of conquest.

Beaver and the girl talked about Kyoto. She seemed to know the city pretty well. ("I used to stay with friends there," she told him, and did not elaborate), so they discussed palaces and gardens, selecting their favorites and explaining why. Beaver found himself remembering Kyoto with enthusiasm, though during his one visit there he had been, if not disappointed, at least uncomfortable, sometimes bored, and always a foreigner trapped in a foreign life. The previous spring he had taken a week's leave to spend in Kyoto, traveling down by the day train for the short glimpse of Mount Fuji through the carriage window. His excitement mounted as he saw the familiar outline of the volcano, all blue, almost perfectly symmetrical, its peak showing above thin horizontal bars of cloud, like a painting one has loved from childhood.

In Kyoto, however, his mood had changed. He had a cold Western-style room at the Miyako Hotel because the Japanese inns were not open to Occupation personnel. Since the restaurants, too, were closed to foreigners, he had to eat his meals at the Miyako—the same army rations that he swallowed without noticing in Tokyo—and that first night, looking around the dining room, he realized with a sense of depression that his tours of the city, his attempts at sightseeing, would be accompanied, dogged, by scores of dependents. Some were escorted by their men, some had come in parties of their own. The one thing they all knew to be worth seeing in Japan was spring in Kyoto, the cherry blossoms and the brightly dressed girls in the processions. He turned out to be quite right. Later, when he thought about the many lovely things he had seen in Kyoto, his memories were laced with the avid chatter of the dependents, their unfailing amusement and fuss at having to take off their shoes before they entered a palace or a teahouse, their predictable doubts about the cleanliness of the felt slippers provided. Even his solitary walks through the city took him past antique stores and silk shops where greedy voices were buying, buying, buying—bartering PX goods for a celadon bowl, or paying in illicit yen for a length of brocade, a ceremonial kimono.

Now he recalled one or two other moments and told the girl about them with an eagerness that surprised him. Once, at the Katsura Summer Palace, he had been left alone for a few minutes in one of the rooms while the rest of the sightseeing party wandered after the guide. He had pulled back the sliding screen across a window, and had stood staring out at that perfect garden, the little lake, the carefully casual trees, all blurred by the spring rain. "I even wrote a poem," he said without embarrassment, "in my head, I mean."

She nodded. "Very proper," she remarked approvingly.

"But of all the places I think the one I liked best was Ryuanji. Most of the others couldn't see it as a garden—it just looked like a mess of gravel and rocks to them."

"They probably didn't stay long enough. You have to wait until you hear the sound of the sea in the trees. Then the gravel turns to water, and the rocks become islands, and there you are, looking down from a long distance at the ocean."

He was halted by the certainty in her voice. "Well, I guess I didn't really see it, either. At least not like that. I just liked it as an abstract."

"An abstract what?"

"Well, I don't know. An abstract design, I suppose."

"I always prefer things to have a story."

"Listen—" he began, and then noticed that she had reached down for her bag, and was pushing her chair back from the table. He hurried on, holding her with the pleading in his voice, to tell her of an evening after dinner when he had walked all the way from the Miyako to Gion, the geisha section of Kyoto. As it happened, he had not gone into any of the geisha houses (though he hadn't planned to describe this part), not solely because they were off limits, more because his Japanese wasn't good enough to conduct an evening of banter or elegant conversation with geishas, and he was too timid to try anything else with them. He had been to occasional geisha parties with Japanese businessmen whom he had to meet in the course of his work in the Economic Section in Tokyo. They were elaborate affairs with beautifully arranged food and wine and presents afterward, but the geishas were always quiet and discreet, recognizing the occasion for what it was, a business dinner. In Kyoto, he had hoped to sample something gayer, but the sight of those shuttered doors, the unobtrusive signs with the names of the houses, the thought of the distant, secret life behind the exquisite wooden façades had, in the end, defeated him. He had wandered (and this was the part he emphasized) through the crosshatching of narrow charming alleys, aware, with relief, that there wasn't a sign of bomb damage and that the darkness hid the evidences of the tight war and postwar life. Somewhere near the river, he had paused under a lighted upstairs window and listened to the sound of a samisen accompanying the sharp wail of a Japanese song. It was at that moment, alone on the nighttime street, that Japanese music had become music to him, moving and intimate, not simply a meaningless (even humorous) twanging of ill-tuned strings. He didn't get much of a response from her to all this because she stood up and remarked briskly, "I must go now."

"You haven't even smoked a cigarette," he said.

"I'm saving the pleasure for when I can give it my full attention. I haven't smoked an American cigarette for a long time." She picked up the package from the table and put it with the others in her bag.

"Your date seems to have stood you up?" She said nothing. So Beaver asked her straight out, "Whom were you meeting?"

"Colonel Peterson. Do you know him?"

"We meet occasionally. Transport, isn't he?"

"I believe so."

Beaver looked around the room, at the tables along the walls and under the windows, almost all occupied by now. He stared for a long moment at a table by the door. He turned back to the girl thoughtfully. "If you really must go..." he said.

"I'm afraid so."

"May I call you—tomorrow? Soon?"

"I'll call you."

"But you don't even—"

"Charles Beaver, Economic Section, SCAP. Or Imperial Hotel," she recited rapidly. "I looked at the return address on the letter to your wife. While you were getting the cigarettes. You don't mind, do you? I was curious."

Beaver said slowly, and not really meaning it, "I don't mind. But I'm willing to bet you won't call."

"Tomorrow. You'll see. Goodbye."

Like just about everyone else in the room, Beaver watched the girl walking straight and easily to the door. If we ever dance together, he thought, I shall look grotesquely tall next to her.

The girl walked along the street outside the Imperial toward the Dai Ichi Building. She walked quite fast and the heat didn't seem to bother her. At the second big intersection, she paused on the sidewalk and for a few moments watched the traffic go by. It was the height of the rush hour and the buses and tramcars were dangerously crowded, with people standing on the steps and platforms, clinging insecurely to handrails or to other passengers. At every stop, a tangle of men and women would fight to get on, several would get pushed off, others would find an invisible foothold in the shift of passengers. It seemed a miracle that the babies strapped to their mothers' back were not smothered in the crush. There were not yet nearly enough trams and buses back in operation to meet the needs of the city, and the Japanese were not allowed to ride on Occupation transport. There were pitifully few private cars among the Japanese, but there were some taxis on the streets, many of them converted to run on charcoal instead of petrol. They carried clumsy metal stoves riveted to their rear fenders, with rattling pipes puffing out heat and smoke. In the middle of it all, on a giant pillbox, an American MP, directing the traffic, performed a fantastic kind of ballet, waving his arms, stamping, swinging his body around in movements of exaggerated precision.

The girl waited for his signal that pedestrians might cross, and then joined the queue at the bus stop. Jammed in with the other patient queue members, she still caused a small flurry of attention. She was the only person dressed in white. The others mostly wore practical dark clothes that didn't show the dirt—kimonos, dresses, business suits—often still in the ersatz materials of the war years. She appeared to be unaware of the scrutiny.

In the Imperial Hotel bar, Beaver got up, shuffled his papers, collected his belongings, and walked to the door. After a moment's hesitation, he stopped at the table near the door and remarked to its sole occupant, "How are things, Colonel Peterson? I thought you'd left the Imperial."

"I have," replied the middle-aged man in uniform. "My wife and family arrived two weeks ago, and we moved into our new house."

"I hadn't expected to see you here," Beaver said carefully.

"I stop in every now and again, after work, for old times' sake. It was good in those days—"

"What was good?" Beaver asked.

"Tokyo, Japan, whatever—"

"Before the dependents arrived, you mean?"

"Well. Not that I'm not—"

"—devoted to your family. But you had a Softly?"

The Colonel looked up sharply, and began to bluster. "No, no, of course not. Nothing like that, but now it's 'What about the stove?' and 'You *must* requisition some new living-room chairs,' and—well—you know—"

"I soon will. I've just been writing my wife to come out to Tokyo. I had hoped it would be better living in a Japanese house than in the hotel." Beaver sounded thoughtful.

The Colonel said uncertainly, "Yes, sure. Why, sure it is. . . ."

"Well, I must be going. I expect you were meeting someone?"

"No," said the Colonel sadly. "No, I'm expected home for dinner."

Three buses passed without space for more than the most aggressive of the front line of passengers. At last, the girl found herself pushed onto the rear platform, wedged in with the solid crowd, traveling in silence like the rest, until she could squirm her way out again at Shibuya, half an hour later.

Nowadays the main streets in Tokyo had clearly marked names given them by the Occupation—A Avenue, or B Street, or Meiji Road—but the Japanese, accepting this innovation without rancor, continued to give an address or find their way about by the old landmarks: a bus stop, a police station, a famous building, the name of a ward or subdistrict. The girl soon turned off the main street from the Shibuya bus stop into a smaller one (without a name), and from there into an alley (without a name), and finally into a cul-de-sac known only as the turning between the Ichi Riki *sushi* shop and the greengrocers'. Halfway down the lane, there was a long wooden fence, recently mended in places, cut by a gate which carried a very new board painted with the name "Col. F. R. Peterson." According to the tradesmen, Colonel Peterson had moved into the house behind the fence only two weeks before, when his wife had arrived from America. They had hired a local man to get their garden back into shape, and the daughter of the Ichi Riki proprietor as a maid. The neighborhood was interested and, so far, pretty well pleased with the Petersons, although they had seen very little of them because either the heat or the problems of getting settled in an unfamiliar house kept them indoors.

There was still a Japanese man mending the final slat in the fence. He bowed to the girl as she passed. She returned the greeting and hesitated before she walked on. *"Konnichi wa,"* she said, smiling. "You are working so late?"

"The Colonel-san, too. He isn't home yet."

For a second she looked alarmed. "Really? I heard that they spent every evening at home."

"Yes, yes. They do. There is still much to be done in the house and garden, his wife says. She says that after it is all in order, then will be the time to go out."

"Then why isn't he here?"

"Sometimes he works late at the office. The Ojo-san tells me, so I know."

"I see," she said, with a note of relief in her voice. "I must be getting home."

"Your husband is better?"

"Yes. Much better, thank you."

"My respects to all your family."

"My respects to yours." They both bowed again.

The girl walked to the far end of the lane, where, on the right, she pushed open a gate and stepped into a tiny garden and from there to the sliding wooden doors of a modest house. In the foyer, she slipped off her high-heeled pumps, padded barefoot to the inner screens, and called softly, *"Tadaima!"* (I'm back.)

Instantly the reply came, *"O-kaeri nasai,"* which has the sense, if not the meaning, of "Welcome home." An elderly woman in a gray kimono and white cotton socks came into the narrow passage. "We have been waiting for you," she said, in a gentle, accusing voice.

"I'm sorry. The buses seemed unusually crowded."

The woman nodded. "These days will pass—"

"Eventually, I suppose they will. Meanwhile ..."

"Meanwhile, was it all right? Are you—"

"Yes, I'm all right. And it went quite well. For a beginning."

"You look tired, child. Please go in and see him now. He has been anxious." Without a pause, she raised her voice to call out pleasantly, calmly, "Keiko-chan is here!"

The girl walked through the house to a room at the far end of the corridor. There a very thin man looked up when she entered. He was sitting cross-legged on the floor. On the low table in front of him was a neat pile of flimsy paper, a bottle of ink, and a steel-nibbed pen.

"Are you writing a letter, too?" the girl asked. "To the military authorities again?"

"No. No, I have no claim on them. It is not a war wound—"

"But it's because of the war that—"

"Keiko. We know all the arguments." He smiled as though it hurt him. "Now, tell me what happened this afternoon."

"Then why are you wasting your energy writing letters?"

"Takahashi's wife came in to see my mother. It seems that

she knows of a sanitarium, in the mountains, that has space. Her daughter lives in that village, so the information is reliable. Also, she will give my letter to the superintendent personally."

"A private sanitarium?"

"Yes, that's the drawback." He looked away with an expression that Kay thought was partly fatigue and partly embarrassment. Where the *shoji* were drawn back, they could see a dusty gardenia bush growing against the wooden fence, with a strip of paved path separating it from the house. She knelt on a square flat cushion, across the table from him.

"Well, it needn't be so much of a drawback now." She opened her big white bag and started piling cigarettes on the table, while he watched in silence.

"Ten packages of American cigarettes," he said at last. "Where did you get them?"

"In the Imperial Hotel bar. An American gave them to me."

"Just like that? A stranger gave them to you?"

"They are very soft-hearted. Anyway, he doesn't smoke."

"That isn't a reason." He was beginning to look frightened.

"For him it's a reason. I am to telephone him tomorrow. There will be more things, I am sure of it. Perhaps not cigarettes, but still things with value."

"All for kindness? This fortune?" When she didn't reply, he continued painfully (and, unexpectedly, in the most formal manner of speech), "I must express my profound gratitude to you."

"Oh, listen," she said, with tears in her voice, "you should be in bed. I can't think why you're up. I can't think why you speak to me in that way." She stood up in a quick movement.

"Your mother can write the letter. You must rest. You're feverish. I can tell by your color."

"It's the heat."

"Even if it's the heat . . ." She walked to the sliding doors of the cupboard opposite the window and began to pull out thin mattresses covered in faded silk. In a few moments, she had arranged them in front of the window and, with a kind of angry efficiency, tied the tapes that fastened the sheets to the quilts, spread the coverings, and placed at the head of the bed a hard little pillow stuffed with pine needles and covered with coarse cotton. She looked up only when the old woman came in with a tray of tea things, and said, "Thank you very much, Oba-san."

The man said nothing at all. He seemed to be quite unconscious of the activity around him. But both he and his mother, one sitting almost motionless, the other busy with the small fussy business of setting out teacups, kept glancing toward the untidy stack of American cigarettes.

"Mr. Beaver? Good morning."

"Hello? Oh, it's you—"

"You didn't think I would call."

"I was afraid you wouldn't. Which is rather different." He heard her laugh, and imagined her, for a moment, sitting with her head tipped back in the Imperial bar. "Well . . ." he said hesitantly. He hadn't had an occasion in years to ask a girl for a date.

"Well," Kay said, with laughter still in her tone. "You are in your office, I suppose, and can't talk because your secretary is sitting at her desk in the corner, and although she pretends to be typing or reading or something, she is really listening to your conversation?"

Beaver joined her mood cheerfully. "As it happens, I'm alone. A poor office, but my own. My stenographer—who isn't really mine, I share her with two other people—works in an immense room called the secretarial pool."

"It sounds like an aquarium."

"Lord knows there are some pretty queer fish in it."

"I've always wondered—"

Beaver took a deep breath and interrupted her. "Look, when can we meet? Are you free for dinner tonight?"

"Yes."

"Yes?" he repeated anxiously, and then, with enormous relief, said, "Fine. Where shall I pick you up?"

"I'll meet you outside the Ernie Pyle cinema at seven."

"Good Lord, why the Ernie Pyle?"

"I thought it would be convenient. It's so near the Imperial."

"I can easily fetch you. I have a jeep."

"No," she said slowly. "You see, I'm staying with some people who wouldn't understand."

Then he remembered something that *he* didn't understand. "You know," he said, in a cautiously offhand voice, "your date didn't stand you up yesterday."

"My date?"

"Colonel Peterson. He was there all the time—at least, not *all* the time. He must have come in sometime after five, I suppose. I'm astonished you didn't see him."

After a pause, she said, "You sound as though you are demanding an explanation."

"It's none of my business—"

"You will think me very silly. And vain. I'm very short-sighted and I hardly ever wear my glasses."

"He was sitting right next to the door as you went out."

"I don't walk around staring at all the men I pass."

"I see."

"And I *didn't* see," she said, laughing again. "In a way it's lucky, isn't it?"

When she had hung up the receiver and paid the proprietor of the Ichi Riki for the use of his telephone, she produced the ten packages of American cigarettes.

"Any use to you?" she asked, as though it meant nothing.

His expression was greedy, though he said lightly, "Yes, I can use them; who can't? These days."

"A price."

"Of course," he said, but he was already scribbling on a piece of paper. He handed the paper to her and she looked at it resignedly. "Yes," she said, "it will do. It will have to do."

"Nothing else?" he asked calmly.

"Not just yet. Later, I hope."

"I hope."

"Domo, kyoshuku de gozaimashita," she said, bowing.

"Taihen arigato gozaimasu," he replied, bowing.

She collected the money he handed her and, with a look of distaste, returned to her house.

The old woman hurried to the door when she heard Kay's voice calling, *"Tadaima!"*

" *O-kaeri nasai.* Did you speak to him?"

"I am to dine with him tonight."

"Alone?"

"Of course alone. Don't worry, Oba-san. It is quite proper among Americans."

"Perhaps he will have enough tact to invite some others."

"If he does, it won't be from tact. It will be because I told him a lie and now he doesn't trust me. I told him I was meeting Colonel Peterson yesterday."

"But you don't know him."

"Exactly. But I had to explain my presence. I thought Colonel Peterson would be safe because the Ojo-san from the Ichi Riki says they never go out."

"So. It was a wise choice."

"By some mischance, yesterday he was in the bar."

"*Ara!*" the woman cried, accepting disaster at once. "And you were forced to confess."

"I told him that I do not see well, and when I walk I do not look at men."

"Then he will admire you for your modesty. Where should your eyes rest except on the ground before you?"

Kay said in exasperation, "Even if he believed me, it will not be long before he wonders why, in that case, Colonel Peterson didn't recognize *me*. Surely you understand that?"

The old woman seemed to have caught only the tone, not the meaning of Kay's words. Very correctly she said, "However all this may turn out, Keiko-san, we will always realize how much you have tried to do for us."

Kay gestured toward the closed doors at the end of the passage. "You talk like him," she said bitterly. "What is the matter with you people? Can you never accept anything simply? Please make no mistake. I am doing all this for myself."

"It is only politeness that makes you say so," the woman replied.

That evening, Charles Beaver had to wait only about five minutes outside the Ernie Pyle (which used to be the Takarazuka Theatre and was now, with wartime memories embedded in its new name, reserved for Occupation personnel). He stood rather awkwardly watching the stream of G.I.s walking through the swing doors or loitering in the lobby, the small gang of American teen-agers with their blue jeans and checked shirts and candy bars, the dependents in their pastel cotton dresses, the soldiers strolling in pairs along the sidewalk, heading for the Ginza, looking for a girl, or a good time, or a way of spending the money in their pockets. It occurred to him that he was considerably older than most of the people around him, and he thought it absurd that a man of forty, wearing the new Palm Beach suit that his wife had sent him, should be waiting on a street corner for a girl he had picked up in a bar, a girl who told silly lies. Japan—or the girl—had brought out this unaccustomed boldness in him. A couple of wolf whistles made him turn, and with a rush of pleasure he saw her walking toward him. She was wearing a narrow, sleeveless dress made from *yukata* material, a stylized blue design of flying birds on a white ground, distinctly different from the look of the Occupation girls, fresh, and carrying, in the way she walked, some impalpable air of excitement. Less Latin than last time he saw her? More Oriental, perhaps? Anyway, Beaver hadn't time to analyze it, for she was standing before him saying, "Good evening. Am I late?"

"I was early. I usually am. The result of inner tension, I expect."

"Of what?"

"Oh, I don't know. Anxiety. Giving too much importance to details and to . . . You look very nice."

"So do you," she said, smiling.

"Well . . ."

"Well."

"Well, let's go and get a drink." He gripped her elbow to take her across the street. "We can get in through the side entrance over there."

"Not to the Imperial," she said, stopping abruptly.

"We can go to the Dai Ichi if you prefer. I have a friend
there and we sometimes trade chits. Just for a change of
scene."

"I thought we might go to a Japanese restaurant."

Beaver tried, with no success, to read her expression.
"They're off limits, you know. For us."

She said reassuringly, "Don't worry, Mr. Beaver. You will
be visiting the home of a Japanese friend."

"Even that—" he began, and then decided the hell with it.
"Don't call me Mr. Beaver. My name is Charles."

"All right, Charles. I am Kay."

"Kay anything?"

"Just Kay will do for the moment."

"Anything you say, Kay. O.K. Oh, Kay." And they both
laughed.

They walked to where Beaver's jeep was parked, and for
the next few minutes he concentrated on Kay's directions,
and on watching roads made treacherous by potholes and
scars from the raids. At last, Kay said, "You can park here."

"Where?"

"Anywhere here. Then we'll walk to the restaurant. In case
the MPs spot your jeep," she went on, "you can always say
you wanted to take a walk. They won't know where to look for
you until you come back to the jeep."

"You think of everything."

"One learns to be careful."

The proprietress of the restaurant bowed low to them
when they entered, but showed no surprise at their furtive
appearance. She ushered them into a small room, bowed
again, and left, closing the doors behind her. The first time
that Beaver had been in a Japanese room, he had had the odd
but pleasing sensation of stepping into a cigar box. By now,

the quiet contrasts of color, beige and tan and sand, were familiar to him, and he noticed with satisfaction the flawless proportions of the room—almost any Japanese room—and the subtle juxtaposition of texture, the woven reeds of the *tatami* covering the floor, the grain of wooden beams and pillars, the translucent rice paper of the *shoji* opened to a small garden partly obscured by the gathering darkness outside. The only furniture was a low table in the middle of the room, and the only decoration a scroll painting of a masked figure, set in an alcove with a bamboo vase of flowers before it.

Watching Beaver's appreciative scrutiny of the room, Kay said, "This used to be a famous restaurant before the war. Actors came here a lot."

"You were here before the war?"

"And ever since," she said briskly. "The *kakemono* is a scene from a Noh play—a ghost. Very appropriate for summer. It's supposed to chill you."

"Don't change the subject. What on earth were you doing—"

"A student. I was caught here when the war broke out."

Beaver said softly, feeling ashamed of his urge to pry, "No fun. Prison camp, I suppose? I'm sorry—don't talk about it if you'd rather not. In retrospect, it seems I had a very comfortable war. At the time, I felt sorry for myself."

"As long as one survives," Kay said. She rubbed her finger on the polished surface of the table. "I should have been interned like the rest of the Filipinos. As it happened—"

The proprietress came into the room with tea and cold damp towels on little lacquer trays. She knelt beside Beaver and began to set things out on the table.

Kay said, "I think perhaps I had better order the meal. A

lot depends on what they have been able to get in the market," and after the long, courteous exchange between the two women, there seemed no occasion to return to the earlier conversation. Instead, Kay and Beaver talked about trivial things and found that they were enjoying themselves very much. A small joke, a passing individual observation or expression received a heightened response; in that quiet room with the lamplight spilling into the shadowy garden, there were no distractions. As the succession of fastidiously assembled courses began to arrive—the raw fish with its sharp, vinegary sauce, the grilled eel, the rice, the tiny pickled eggplants and cucumbers—Kay instructed him in matters of eating etiquette. Always pick up your *sake* cup when someone is about to serve you, but never with your left hand—that is the sign of a drunkard, a "left-handed drinker" who is so eager to have his cup filled that he uses the hand nearest the maid instead of showing a decorous reluctance. But never pick up your teacup to have it filled—you could scald your fingers, and besides a slight bow of the head is sufficient acknowledgment of the service. Never leave your chopsticks in your rice —this is done only in an offering to the dead. Never "dirty" your rice with sauces or fragments of food (in the vulgar manner of the Chinese), and always leave your rice bowl clean, so that it doesn't seem to have been used at all. Never touch a dish unless you are going to eat it all—food has always been precious in Japan. And on and on.

Beaver was enchanted. These fragments of information gave detail to his picture of the elegances of Japanese life, and he was pleased that Kay offered them as a kind of game. At one point, she came around the table to his side and, kneeling on the *tatami* on his left, gave an imitation of a geisha, slightly drunk, flirting with a client, and acquiring yet more elaborate turns of speech and gesture with each shared cup of *sake*. The proprietress came into the room in the middle of this performance, and the three of them laughed together. "One day," the woman said to Beaver, "if you come back here, you must hire a real geisha. We need only a day's notice."

Beaver was so pleased at having understood her words that he agreed enthusiastically. In a moment, however, he was suddenly serious.

"Something's the matter," Kay said, her expression immediately matching his.

"It's just occurred to me. I haven't any yen—I never thought to change any. And it's against regulations to pay the Japanese in dollars."

"Is that all?" Kay said, sitting back on her heels. "You will be my guest tonight."

"No, no. I asked you to dinner—"

"Well, tomorrow's just as good. I've known her a long time. She won't mind." Kay turned to look out of the window. "Or, if you want to do something really nice for her—she has two grandchildren, war babies—if you wanted to—well, what they need is powdered milk, vitamins, things like that—I mean, she can't buy them. . . . Not if you'd rather not, of course—it's just . . . those kids have never even tasted *chocolate*. Though I don't suppose that matters. During the war, people used to make a sort of sticky mess out of maize flour and molasses—it was the closest most kids came to candy—"

"I'll see what I can find at the PX."

"You don't have to—" Kay said quickly, made uneasy by his expression.

"I'd like to." In fact, Beaver was frowning because although he knew perfectly well that day-to-day living for the Japanese was complicated by shortages, rationing, and the shockingly high prices of things on the black market, he had somehow managed to keep from relating this knowledge to a specific individual. Certainly the few Japanese businessmen and economists whom he met in his work never mentioned such matters, and he had no Japanese friends. Reflecting rather sourly that Americans justly had the reputation for being sentimental about children, he still realized that it was the thought of those grandchildren, to whom corn flour and molasses was a treat, that had disturbed him. The older of the two neat little girls in the Georgetown house had, some time before, touched him very much by telling him in a letter that she had decided to eat less candy. "Chocolate," she had written, "is *very* bad for the teeth. We learned that in Hygiene."

Before Beaver had finished his after-dinner tea, Kay stood up. She said she would explain the situation to the proprietress. It would be more tactful that way—one never discussed payments with the person immediately involved, particularly a transaction as unorthodox as this one. However, their conversation seemed to be as speedy as it was delicate, and Kay soon reappeared, smiling and a little excited. She and Beaver drank a final cup of tea in an atmosphere of assured friendliness.

When they left the restaurant, they walked slowly in the summer night toward the jeep. "I can't remember how long it's been since I had such a nice evening," Kay said.

Beaver stopped to peer down at her in the darkness. "There'll be others," he said, surprised to find himself whispering. He held her bare arm above the elbow to pull her toward him. The deserted aspect of the alley and the quiet gave them so great a sense of isolation that they turned, guilty as lovers, when a child stepped out of the deeper shadow of the jeep, smiling at them hopefully. "Harro, Joe, harro," he began in the usual way, and then made the familiar request for cigarettes and chewing gum.

Beaver, in an expansive mood, smiled at the child. Kay said, "We have none. Leave us alone."

The child retreated against the shuttered doors of a house. Beaver took his hand away from Kay's arm, and the two of them walked stiffly and in silence the few yards to the jeep. As Kay stepped up to her seat, Beaver said, with outrage in his voice, "You could have given him a cigarette. It's not much, is it? Or did you come without any—again?"

"I came out without any."

He climbed into the driver's seat. "Well, where to?"

"Could you take me home? Shibuya station."

"O.K. Shibuya station it is."

The side streets continued to be empty and ill-lit until they reached the main road leading to Shibuya. There, as though the passing lights and the sight of people on the sidewalks had brought her back to life, Kay said, "I suppose I should tell you. It is true that I have no cigarettes with me. I gave them away." In a clear, conversational voice, and without hesitations, Kay told her story. Beaver, listening, turned from time to time to look at her face, alternately shadowed and illuminated as they drove by bomb sites or clusters of newly built, active shops. He felt he was out of his depth with her and waited for deceit.

"It's odd, isn't it—out of all the people you know, the ones that actually help you? Accident? Circumstances? A sort of universal kindness? I don't know what makes them decide to protect you. They are seldom your closest friends. I knew such a girl—well, actually it was her mother more than the girl herself that I'm talking about."

"What are you talking about?"

"The cigarettes. The cigarettes, and a friend of mine, Sakiko's mother. Sakiko and I were fellow-students. She was not a very clever girl, and we hadn't even very much in common. I was an art student—Japanese art teachers are, for very good reason, famous—and she was taking the general course in college. But I liked her because in those months before the war, foreigners—English-speaking foreigners, that is—were not very popular. Most of the students were polite, but wary. Sakiko's manner never changed. They had stopped teaching English in the colleges by then. It was German instead. But Sakiko, for some reason, wanted to keep up her English—it was one of her best subjects, perhaps that's why. Sometimes I used to give her lessons in the hostel where I stayed. Sometimes she would take me to her house for tea or a meal. She was a dull girl, you understand, but in the circumstances I liked her.

"I was at her house on the day of Pearl Harbor. She and her mother and I all listened to the radio together. Afterward, the mother said, 'What will you do?' and I said, 'I don't know. What do you think?' She said, 'I don't know.'

"Of course, both of us knew. For the first time, I really looked at Sakiko's mother and saw that she was my friend, not simply an old person who lived in the house. I couldn't, you see, think of myself as a 'colonial.' There were other foreign students—Filipinos, Indonesians, Indians—who were bitter about the West. They had nothing to fear. But I had never thought much about it—the student talk, the debates, the freedom of Asia—I wanted to be an artist. Most especially I wanted to study and learn *sumi-e*."

"Learn what?"

"*Sumi-e.* It's a special technique of Japanese painting, perhaps the most exciting, disciplined yet lucid form. However, you do not want to hear about the theories of Japanese art."

"Not that it isn't interesting."

Kay heard both the chill and the disappointment in his voice. With a deep sigh, she continued, "Looking back on it, it seems that the students were eternally talking, discussing, making anti-imperialist or anti-American speeches. If I talked, I talked openly, and approving or criticizing—I no longer remember the details. I suppose I was pro-American. Anyway, the idea of America excited me—as a Filipino, that was not unnatural—and I hadn't been cautious in the way I spoke.

"We stayed up until late that night listening to news bulletins as they were broadcast. When I got up to leave, the mother said, as though it were all arranged, 'You will stay the night in Sakiko's room.' We all knew it would be more than one night.

"In the next few days, we learned things from the newspapers, from the neighbors, the radio, gossip. Tokyo was full of rumors. Months before, we had all started to carry our papers with us, so there was no reason to return to the hostel, and after a while I thought it strange that I had ever suggested it.

"I won't bore you with all the lies and tricks of those months, the visit of the police, the discretion of the neighbors. The fact is, they sheltered me for more than two years. At first, it was only a question of hiding. Later, it was a question of food. Of course, I had no ration card. Sometimes I used to stand at night in the little garden and think, It is one prison or another; and even though I tried to make myself useful in the house, the mother would get angry with me, and I would become resentful. You can thank people for small things, you know, but not for your life.

"Sakiko had given up her studies—she never much cared for them. She was doing war work. I used to see her in the mornings, in her *mompei*—do you know those funny overalls? Sort of baggy trousers? It was practically a uniform for the girls doing war work—even the schoolchildren. She looked happy, she had a boyfriend, her first. The war brought its liberties, too, for some people.

"In the end, it brought me a kind of liberty as well. The raids started. We, like so many others, used to hide in the subway stations during the bombings. I'll never forget the look of those frightened women and children crouched against the frivolous pink and yellow tiles of the walls, their neat bundles of food or warm clothing tied up in patterned *furoshikis*. Tokyo subways are so shallow that we could hear the noise of the raids outside. Afterward we walked home by circuitous routes, followed by the sound of the fires crackling through the houses, 'like the sound of dry leaves blowing along an autumn street,' Sakiko once said. I daresay it was the only poetic thing she ever said. Once we had grasped the extent of the bombings, the recurring confusions and fires, the lost homes and the dead, we—the mother and I, that is, —decided to kill me, too. It was surprisingly easy; there were so many burned, unrecognizable bodies. We charred my papers and passport—quite elated at the thought of *doing* something. After that, we had only to bribe the fishmonger's wife to turn them in to the police, to say she had found them in a pile of rubble, the debris of a burned house. I was dead.

"Life is different—in this case easier, but different without an identity. They managed to smuggle me to Kyoto, where

Sakiko had an old uncle, a good many years older than her mother. He was old, a retired professor, and he asked no questions. He lived on the edge of the city and I was to keep house for him. I had only to be silent, and for the local tradesmen I was a distant relative, badly shocked in a raid." She touched her temple lightly. "Not quite . . . you know."

For the first time since Beaver had started the jeep, she turned to look at him, at the sharp conventional profile against the blur of the passing street. "I'm afraid this is a long story," she said.

"I'm listening."

"Oh, well, there were a lot of things in Kyoto—the quiet, and the blackouts, and the anxious faces. I had my ups and downs. Some of it required ingenuity. Mostly we were left alone. People had their own troubles. Nearly everyone had someone—a relative, a friend, someone—staying with them; they didn't ask too much, and in any case the old professor was a solitary, people took that for granted. He was indulged, his eccentricities and everything. And I was part of them, or accepted as such. In his absent way, he took care of me, somehow gave me an assurance that another, invincible layer of life continued beyond the war and the dying and the chaos around us. He was the one that took me to the gardens—you remember? Ryuanji, and the sound of the sea? Well, that was him.

"Then the rest, when the war was over. I had expected a reprieve, or something of the kind—I don't know why. By any standard, I had been lucky. But I was tired and much older. At first, when the Japanese were winning the war, it had all gone much faster. It took a long, long time when they started to lose. With them, I saw the victory as a defeat—it's all in how it's put to you. By then, they were my people, sort of.

Still, I expected a kind of reprieve, though I'm not sure just what I meant by that.

"I came back to Tokyo, and went at once to see Sakiko and her mother. We wrote no letters, of course, and the old professor never gave me their news—if he knew it himself. And this is where it really begins—my explanation, I mean. Sakiko had married and she lives in Nagoya. The mother was alone, though she lived with friends—hired a room, that is— her house was bombed. She was—is—very ill. I didn't realize it at first, though I noticed she looked frail, but I thought that was only time and the war. I stayed with her. It didn't occur to either of us that there should be a different arrangement. I wanted to take care of her. It wasn't long before the people in the house where she lodges told me that she had tuber-culosis.

"I thought I would get a job. She needed money, of course, and treatment. Sakiko could send us only very little. It's quite difficult to get a job without papers, but peace—or, rather, defeat—had brought me advantages. It was suddenly very useful to know English. I found pupils and gave lessons—I am not proud, so I have a number of pupils of all classes. The most recent was the girl from the *sushi* shop on our corner. She wanted to get a job with an Occupation family.

"Now we manage, but it is still not enough. The old lady must go to the mountains. She must have proper care. You can see that I must do my best for her."

Beaver said, "We are almost at Shibuya. What do you want me to do?"

"Stop anywhere," Kay said sadly. "I'll walk home from here."

Beaver pulled up with a jerk at the sidewalk. He lifted his hand from the wheel to touch her shoulder. "You never thought of going to the Embassy? To some authority?"

"What would be the point?"

"You might get help. At least you could get your passport back—your papers—"

"I'm scared to try. After all, I'm not really alive. And if I am, I'm probably a war criminal or something—"

"But surely—"

"Well, a collaborator, anyway. No, no, I just want to get her settled. I can manage by myself later." She took a deep breath. "Just so I can get her settled."

"Kay, look, I'm sorry—"

"Oh, for God's sake," she said impatiently. "It's a long way of explaining about the cigarettes, but there it is. I sold them on the black market, to the proprietor of the *sushi* shop—he'll probably sell them for even more—still, there it is, and now you know. And now I'd better be going."

She felt the pressure of his hand tighten on her shoulder. "I want to help you," he said.

She shook her shoulder free. "It's the old lady who needs help."

"However you want to put it. Will I see you again?"

"And I told you another lie."

"I know—"

"About Colonel Peterson. I don't know him, and I had no date with him at the Imperial."

"I know. What were you doing in the bar?"

"Looking for you. Or someone like you. It sounds awful, doesn't it?"

"An easy touch, you mean?"

"No. I hadn't expected your generosity with the cigarettes. I just wanted advice. I wanted to see if I could get some Occupation jobs."

"Why didn't you apply to the regular SCAP agency? Each section has its translators' pool, you know."

"Without papers?" Smiling, she added, "Even the smallest fish in your aquariums need papers. I was thinking of people who might want to practice their Japanese, or even women who need someone to go shopping with them—that sort of thing. You can see that their dollars, or things from the PX, would help Sakiko's mother much more, and much sooner, than the few yen I earn. But anyway it doesn't matter. I'll think of something. I just wanted to tell you that bit of it, since anyway I was telling you so much. I'll say good night now, and," she finished, like a well-behaved child leaving a party, "thank you very much for a lovely dinner."

Beaver, who had been wanting for some time to kiss her, climbed down from the jeep so that she could wriggle out on the side away from the traffic. He helped her onto the sidewalk but kept hold of her hand. "I think I'm old enough," he said, "to ask whether I may kiss you good night. Without offending you, I mean."

Almost before he had finished, she reached up and held his face between her hands. Stooping toward her, he remarked, "We'd never be able to dance cheek to cheek—not comfortably, that is—" Later, he said happily, "Anyway, I'll have to see you tomorrow to give you the stuff for that restaurant woman. I don't think for a moment I'd be able to find my way back there."

"Till tomorrow."

"Six o'clock? In my room? I can't very well carry cans of things around—"

"Yes, in your room."

Beaver watched her walking swiftly into the crowd in front of Shibuya station. In a minute, her small figure and purposeful bearing were hidden by the dark clothes of the pedestrians and the dark of the summer night.

The next evening, when Kay came to his hotel room, Beaver had, at first, been embarrassed by the idea of barter. Money seemed to him a cleaner, more impersonal way of paying for things. But Kay had been so matter-of-fact about the procedure, assuring him that he had chosen exactly the right cans and boxes, tying them expertly in a printed purple *furoshiki*, slipping the candy bars and vitamin pills into her handbag with such open satisfaction, that he hardly asked himself whether he was infringing regulations. When she looked up at him, smiling and easy, he handed her, rather awkwardly, five ten-dollar bills.

"What's this for?" She sounded only puzzled.

"Well, you said you wanted a job as a sort of general interpreter. I'm your first customer." He noticed with some alarm her suddenly withdrawn look and asked quickly, "Is that all right? I hope it's all right."

"Yes," she said. "Oh, *yes*—it's just that it seems like too much. And *dollars!*"

"Why not?" he said, relieved. "I'm allowed to give you dollars—you're not Japanese."

"I'm not anything," she replied.

"So you see?" He felt he'd won some kind of obscure victory. "Your duties start immediately. Where shall we go for a drink?"

Late that night, in the Shibuya house, Kay woke up to the half-heard sound of her name. "What is it? Nobuo-chan? What is it?"

"A dream . . ." His whisper hardly disturbed the quiet. "I don't sleep well in this heat."

"I'm glad you're awake. I wanted to tell you we can send you to the mountains. As soon as the hospital can take you."

To his silence she replied, "I have got a job. With that American, Mr. Beaver, whom I met in the Imperial. His wife is coming out to Tokyo very soon. They have three small children—the youngest only a baby—so he has hired me to help him set up his household here before they arrive."

Nobuo still said nothing, and Kay hurried on, "You can understand he doesn't want them to stay in the hotel. And with the children to look after, she would not be able to attend to the functioning of their place immediately. So I am to hire the servants, the gardener. See that whatever repairs are necessary are made. Arrange with the florist. That kind of thing. Get the place running. He pays me in dollars. Afterward, if she is satisfied, I am sure there will be other similar jobs. You know how many of them are coming to Tokyo now."

"Keiko," he said wearily, "don't tell me lies."

"I'm not telling lies. I'll introduce her to you when she arrives, if you like."

"No, no—"

"Then believe me. Or trust your mother; she will help me with all this—I couldn't do it alone."

"Go to sleep," he said. "It's too hot to argue."

"In the mountains it will be cool and dry. You can lie outdoors all day. It's not for long. You will soon be well. And the autumn will come, and winter. Snow and sun. It won't be long."

"Go to sleep," he whispered.

Kay closed her eyes on the darkness, reminding herself that in the morning she must take the PX things to the proprietor of the Ichi Riki. Out of the money she would get—

certainly far more than the restaurant bill—she must also keep aside enough for some new clothes.

During the weeks that followed, Beaver and Kay saw each other almost every day. They did many things that Beaver had counted as pleasures even before he knew Kay—walks in the Tokyo parks; visits to museums, temples, gardens; long idle pauses on one of the bridges across the Sumida, watching the languid pace of the river traffic below. Once, on such an occasion, Kay had told him a story that stayed in his mind. A courtesan—beautiful, of course, much desired, of course—floated with her *samurai* lover on a boat down the Sumida when the cherry blossoms were in bloom and the falling petals scattered like pink snow across the water. As they sailed, she sang to him, the most beautiful love songs. But he was jealous of her loveliness and convinced that she was really singing the songs to some secret lover. He killed her in his passion of love and suspicion, and learned only later that she had, in fact, been entirely true to him. "So now," Kay told Beaver, "in the springtime, when the trees along the banks flower, you can often see young girls standing on the bridge, their eyes filled with tears, dreaming of love and death. They claim that sometimes you can still hear that sweet singing floating down the river."

Beaver said, with a rare lack of embarrassment, "Kay, you bring the entire city to life." For "life" he had almost said "love."

With Kay beside him, talking, explaining, often laughing, he felt that at last he was no longer an observer in Japan. He thought he was getting under the skin of the country, and he was aware of a sense of superiority to his colleagues in the Economic Section.

Often Kay took him to Japanese restaurants—this one famous for *ayu*, the tiny trout, served whole with their tails curled high; that one for its view over the river and the moving lights on the black water; yet another where she insisted that he eat iced noodles to counteract the dense heat of the city. He always allowed her to make the arrangements, and became quite used to paying for their meals with candy, cigarettes, tinned food, and was even rather moved when Kay conveyed to him the profound thanks of the various proprietors.

One morning, a letter from Susan arrived for him, the reply to his efforts in the Imperial Hotel bar during what seemed, by then, an excursion into some distant past. Actually, it had been only three weeks. Susan had read his letter very painstakingly several times, and had felt it worthy of a special answer, written in the middle of the week, not just included in her usual diary posted on Saturdays. She could quite understand that Japan must be "a fascinating experience." But to consider renting the house, uprooting the children for what might turn out to be only a passing enthusiasm, "that *really* requires more thought." Beaver, who was not given to rash and transient enthusiasms, felt helplessly that, quite simply, he hadn't got his point across. He couldn't blame Susan. He knew he was just no good with words. "In any case," she concluded, "you are due for home leave in November—just think, a real American Christmas at home with all the family! It will be our first in five years!" Plenty of time then to discuss the matter seriously and in person, she suggested. "Your perspective will probably change when you get back home—you'll see."

Beaver mentally shrugged his shoulders and thought, Oh, well, I *did* try. What's more, I meant it at the time.

With Kay, on some Saturday or Sunday afternoons, he drove out to Kamakura or to Kawane, finding in both places too great a concentration of foreigners, and occasional unnerving confrontations with his acquaintances.

They explored further, driving one weekend along the coast of the Izu peninsula, a shoreline scalloped with coves, painted in the familiar design of Japanese landscapes, the angular, tormented pine trees growing from dark seamed boulders against the grayish glitter of the sea. They spent that night in a village hotel, high on the cliffs, and from Beaver's room he could see the flares of the men searching for crayfish far below on the rocks.

He stood for quite a long time at the window, staring down. He was remembering the drive down with Kay, quiet most of the way, and how he had been relieved that she didn't, like so many women, feel she had to make continual little exclamations—"Oh, how pretty!" "Just look at that view!"—although she was constantly, acutely alert to the passing countryside.

"You really live in your eyes, don't you?" he had remarked.

"As much as I live anywhere," she had replied, more seriously than he had expected.

He reconstructed, too, the picture of the wayside *sushi* shop where they had stopped to eat, since neither of them was hungry enough for a proper dinner. They sat at a counter and Kay had picked out the *sushi* for him, small, vinegary rice cakes with a fancifully cut sliver of bamboo leaf or a radish the shape of a snowflake.

"They say that a really expert *sushi*-maker puts exactly the same number of rice grains in each cake."

"Has anyone ever counted them?" (As always, delighted by these absurd bits of information.)

"Oh, I hope not! That would ruin the whole fantasy of the idea."

In fact, what Beaver was doing, standing gazing out at the soft summer darkness, was trying to keep his mind from formulating his thoughts too clearly. He was surprised to notice that he had, at some point, clenched his fists so tightly that now his knuckles stood out fierce and white. At last, he turned toward the room. In his socks he padded quickly across the *tatami*, down the wood-floored corridor, and knocked gently on Kay's door.

"O-kaeri nasai." Her voice was light, impersonal, as if she were expecting, perhaps, the maid.

"It's me. May I come in?"

She came to the door. Barefoot, wearing a cotton kimono, she had apparently been unpinning her hair. A couple of long strands fell across one shoulder, the rest was half uncoiled on her neck. "Is anything wrong?" She pulled the kimono tight across her waist. "I was about to go to sleep."

"I just wanted you to see something—"

"What kind of 'something'?"

"The kind of thing you like." He beckoned her in silence to his room and she followed, a question still on her face. He told her to close her eyes, led her to the window, and then, like a triumphant conjurer, said, "All right. Now, look!"

She glanced down at the rocks and the spasmodic, moving flares for a moment before bursting into sudden, irrepressible laughter.

"Isn't it beautiful? Don't you like it?" He sounded anxious.

"It's lovely, and I love it." She faced him with knowing eyes, laughter bubbling in her voice. "I have identically the same view from my window."

Only then did he allow himself to smile. "I know you do,"

he said before he pulled her into his arms and took the last two pins out of her hair.

Early the next morning, while the first chill was still in the air, they climbed down the cliff path to swim. Stepping carefully over the patches of wet lichen on the rocks near the edge of the water, Kay suddenly stooped to pick up an iridescent bubble of thick glass that must have floated away from one of the nets and was miraculously preserved in a crevice. It was washed by the sea and reflected the pale colors of the morning, and she held it out to Beaver with an air of wonder that he remembered for a long time afterward. It was the only present she ever gave him, and even after it had dried to a pale dull green, he kept it, took it with him back to Tokyo, where he hid it carefully in the drawer containing his socks and handkerchiefs as if it had enclosed forever Kay's expression of unguarded pleasure and some fragment of the happiness of that morning.

However, it was the Chiba coast rather than the Izu peninsula that came to be their favorite. On one of their long drives north from Tokyo, they had come upon a fishing village, a scatter of huts, nothing very impressive, but there was a charming inn, practically on the beach, which appealed to Beaver at once. He felt secluded there, far from Tokyo and the Occupation, and he preferred the flat expanse of sea and sand to the more admired and picturesque Izu landscape.

Every weekend through high summer and into early September, they drove to Chiba, and the fact that the whole area was off limits to Occupation personnel gave each trip a fresh sense of adventure. With an intoxicating consciousness of daring, Beaver had worked out an obscure route along unsurfaced beach roads to avoid the roadblocks and the MPs, and on Saturdays at noon he and Kay would set off in the jeep, a package of egg-salad sandwiches ordered from the Imperial Hotel bar between them, and bottles of Coca-Cola and beer under Kay's feet. When they were beyond the straggling, ramshackle suburbs of the city, and had reached the manicured landscape of rice fields and compact villages breathless in the heat of midafternoon, they would stop to kiss, to picnic. Both of them, in their minds, were already smelling the sea, feeling the cool wind off the Pacific, half present in the jeep in the shade on the side of some road, half arrived in Chiba.

The inn itself was as unpretentious as the village, a typically Japanese house except for the stone-walled side that protected it from the sea winds. The soil was too coarse to grow anything but the tough dune grasses and the scrubbiest of bushes, so the front garden was made from rocks and neatly swept sand that seemed to Beaver a faint reminder of Ryuanji. Feathery tamarisks grew against the wooden fence, and a stone lantern stood by the entrance at the curve of the gravel path leading to the porch.

Inside, there were only four guest rooms, all, of course, Japanese in style. The rest of the house was occupied by the innkeeper and his family. He had come to expect them in the early gilded evening. They brought him presents of food and sometimes a bottle of whiskey. He, in turn, had the bath ready for them (an expensive courtesy in those days), gave them his best room, restless with the sound of the surf, and left them to themselves. In Chiba, Beaver had so marked a feeling of well-being that he assumed it was love, and he wanted to do everything in the world for Kay.

On one occasion, he told her so—the part about doing everything in the world for her, that is—and, to his bewilderment, noticed that all at once her eyes filled with tears.

"Kay! Oh, my baby—what's the matter?"

"Nothing. It's just that—" She held her eyes wide open, as though she hoped in that way to dry them off.

"What *is* it?"

"It's just that ... nobody ever ... Oh, damn!" Weeping quietly in his arms, she whispered, "You really meant that."

He comforted her as he would a child. "Hush," he said. "Hush. Whatever it is, it's all right."

"You did, didn't you?"

"Of course I did."

"That's all." After a minute, she asked for a handkerchief, blew her nose briskly, and said, "I'm superstitious. One mustn't comment on ... on good fortune. It's like casting the evil eye."

"Idiot."

"It's true. The wicked spirits get jealous."

"And suddenly you are Cinderella in her rags sitting on her stool being tormented by a wicked stepmother—"

"Shh!" She put her hand over his mouth and, as he kissed it, said, "Just don't ever talk like that."

One evening, walking along the beach, they had been drawn to a small crowd of villagers near a fishing boat, and with the rest had peered into the big baskets that held the catch, each a miniature earthquake of fish, scarlet, silver, and blue, slithering and jerking about. On the spot, they had bought some, choosing by color and not caring if the price they paid was fair. They carried them, wrapped in seaweed, back to the inn, where the cook shook her head in amusement but managed to make something out of the fish for dinner. After that, they often bought fish on the beach, learning to be choosier, finding that they enjoyed bargaining about the price.

Once, on a night of brilliant moonlight (both of them wearing the blue-and-white kimonos provided by the inn for after-bath or informal lounging about), Kay and Beaver raced along the sands and arrived laughing and excited, as if they had just escaped a storm, at a point of the beach where they had dimly seen an eddy of activity. To the inflexible beat of a chant, somewhere between panting and singing, the fishermen, naked except for G-strings, and their bare-breasted women were pulling on ropes that gradually hauled the fishing boat onto the beach. The lacquer of moonlight on wet skin, the presence of Kay beside him, her hair loose on her shoulders, the slow movement of the hulk of the boat, the gasping chant, and the slapping waves—all fused into one impression in Beaver's mind. This is the first time in my life, he thought, that I have felt free.

Later, he and one of the fishermen fetched beer from the inn, and all of them sat on the sand drinking from the bottles and passing them around. There was an air of hilarity over everything, though Kay could catch and translate only a little of their fast, humorous patois. The woman next to Beaver pulled on his sleeve and asked if he found the night so cold that he needed to keep his kimono on. She gestured toward the rest of the men, but since Beaver did not understand her, he thought she wanted a drink. He handed her a bottle of beer with the only toast he knew, *"Kampai!"* As he said it, he remembered that it meant, "Empty your cup," a ridiculous phrase under the circumstances, but she laughed as though he had said something witty, and he laughed with her, pleased by her pleasure, the night, the mood, and even the pervasive smell of fish.

At the inn, Beaver didn't need to turn on the lamp in their room. The moon and the reflected light from the sea filled the place with an almost theatrical radiance. Embracing Kay, he said, "It's more than just you—"

"It's the moon," she said. "Everyone gets a little crazy."

He hadn't the words to explain his moment of liberation on the beach, or the neat irony of the fact that in the same moment he saw himself trapped, enmeshed by Japan and Kay.

Late in August, Kay skipped one of their weekends. She had to go to the mountains, she explained to Beaver, to the sanitarium. "She has been writing to me," she said in a particularly measured tone which she used when she spoke of the old lady, a tone that indicated worry and affection but left no room for sympathy. She didn't, she gave the impression, want to discuss the matter, but there were certain loyalties that she couldn't abandon. "She is much better, but she is lonely. There is a difference between the good care that professionals give and the other sort of caring from other people—you know what I'm talking about." Beaver, feeling quite desolate, had given her some extra money for the trip and wondered what to do with the weekend.

He returned without enthusiasm to the old pattern of his days, indifferent meals eaten indifferently in the hotel dining room, solitary evening walks along the moat enclosing the palace grounds, a long tepid letter home written guiltily with the hope that its length would make up for its triviality. He was, by now, out of the habit of telephoning an acquaintance or a colleague to meet for a drink, and the few Occupation families that had before invited him for dinner, or for a lazy American Sunday spent with the children in the suburban atmosphere of the Jackson Heights or Washington Heights housing projects (re-creations in both name and amenities of places back home), had slipped from his life entirely. They had been put off too frequently with transparent excuses. In short, Beaver was recognized as a man with a Softly.

He, however, did not, in all honesty, come to the same conclusion until the following Friday, when the letter from his wife was waiting for him on his return from the office. He knew only that he missed Kay, that he was disconsolate, that the Occupation life (which had never pleased or engaged him) was now unbearable, that even the things that had first appealed to him about Japan lost some of their color without her presence. Now he felt the distance between himself and his colleagues not only because of his appreciation of aspects of Japan that seemed to them only a bore, but because Kay had given him an intimacy with the life of the country and its people. He was growing more confident every day and, when he was alone, often contrasted in his mind the Japanese grace in their manner of doing things with the coarser American way. It was not surprising that on the Monday afternoon after that weekend he greeted the sound of Kay's voice on the telephone with the uncritical joy of a prisoner released from solitary confinement.

"You're back!"

"Naturally I'm back. You sound as if I'd gone away forever."

"It felt like that. Look," he hurried on, "I'll try and get out of here as early as possible. I think I can swing it by five or so. Can you come to the Imperial about—" He checked himself, abruptly worried. "Or are you too tired to meet me this evening?"

"I am. But I'll meet you anyway. The bar?"

"No. My room. You can rest there."

"That's *exactly* what I can do there." He heard the smile in her voice and kept it like a secret talisman at the back of his mind while he hurried through the papers and files on his desk.

In his hotel room, he washed his hands, splashed cold water on his face, changed his shirt, and then stood looking critically around him. There wasn't much to see. It was simply a hotel room, like a hundred others, in the Imperial. Twin beds, covered with mud-brown spreads, divided by a night table and lamp. A narrow writing desk with some hotel stationery and a few letters on it. A chest of drawers holding a photograph of Susan and the girls in a folding leather frame. A traveling clock he had received from them one Christmas which he, out of habit, wound and corrected each morning (it consistently gained four minutes a day). An upholstered armchair. The stenciled army sign on the back of the door: "No Smoking in Bed." It occurred to him that there was almost no impress of personality on the room—his or anyone else's. He waited for Kay to bring life to the room.

In response to her knock, he said, *"O-kaeri nasai."*

She entered frowning. "You don't need to say '*nasai*.' Only women have to be so polite. For you, '*O-kaeri*' is enough.

"*O-kaeri*, darling. Is that better?"

"Much." She flopped into the armchair, leaning her head back and stretching out her legs in a movement both peaceful and fatigued. "Did you have a horrid weekend?"

"Horrid."

"Good."

He laughed. "And you?"

"Oh, well. You know how it is in hospitals—one feels so isolated. Poor old lady. She was so touchingly happy to see someone from 'home.' We sat out in the sunshine and I peeled fruit for her. Persimmons. She has a hankering for persimmons."

Beaver, crouching beside her, started to say "We'll send her all the persimmons she can eat" as he pulled off one of Kay's shoes.

She jumped up, almost knocking him over. "Don't do that!" To his look of alarm, she explained, "Take off my shoes, I mean. We're in Japan. It isn't proper for you to—"

"To take off my girl's shoes when she's tired? The Japanese can damn well keep their sense of propriety. This particular patch of rather shabby carpeting happens to be *my* domain."

"An American's hotel room is his castle?"

"I'll say." Very tenderly he pushed her back into the chair and took off her other shoe.

"You do this ... all this ... just because I am tired?"

Shaken by the incredulity in her tone, he replied very simply, "Because I love you," and as the sentence hung in the air, echoless, but with some continuing, independent existence of its own, Beaver felt a spreading feeling of confidence and contentment—a contentment that settled, but did not diminish, in their subsequent meetings that week.

It was not until Friday, after he had read his wife's letter, that Beaver was, at last, forced to admit fully to himself that he was in the commonplace, almost comic position of the man with a Personal Problem. He was distressed but not really confused and upset. There are, after all, relatively few changes to be rung on the Pinkerton-Butterfly situation, and Beaver, with Kay's absence still fresh in his mind, saw the resolution of his Softly as already determined. He was pleased (he felt it saved his self-respect), and he set himself apart from the agonizings of other American men in the same position. Consequently, it didn't occur to him to change his plans for spending the weekend with Kay in Chiba.

Susan, it turned out, was not wholly without intuition. Beaver had, in his letters, always insisted he was enjoying himself in Japan. Now he sounded happy, and that was quite another matter. (Not, of course, that she put it to him as flatly as that.) She wrote to say that she had thought the whole thing over and was now convinced that since he felt so strongly about Japan, she and the children would join him in Tokyo. "We have always tried to share everything," she ended. "It has been one of the best things about our marriage. If I seemed to hesitate before, it was mostly worry about the girls. I'm still apt to think of them as babies, but I ought to realize that they are old enough to have their horizons widened. But more than anything, the reason is that we miss you and love you. . . ."

Walking along the Chiba beach hand in hand with Kay, Beaver broke a longish, easy silence to say, "Kay, I have something to tell you and something to ask you."

"Oh, why *now*?" she said pettishly. "Just when I'm looking forward to buying the fish. All shiny and pretty and slipping about—"

"There's never an exactly right time. This is as good as any. But it can wait, if you'd rather."

"Silly to put it off now, and have you fretting for the next hour." She smiled at him disarmingly. "You won't have your mind on the fish."

"Well, then." He paused. He hadn't really planned how to begin, only how it would all end. They stopped walking, looking at each other warily, like duelists.

"I suppose you are going to tell me that your wife has decided to come to Japan. What else could there be in that

letter you carry around so importantly? Reading it over and
over when you think I'm not watching. And what did you want
to ask me? What we are going to do now? Whether we can
go on this way? Well, the answer is of course we can't. You
will have no time and it will all be too complicated. You have
no talent for explanations. Anyway, I doubt if you'll want to.
More likely, you'll wonder how in the world you ever came to
be involved in this. The first sight of her—and the children
—will probably be enough, but certainly after a week or two
you will ask yourself, 'What could I have been thinking of?'
A summer lunacy. Now come along, shall we go and buy the
fish?"

Beaver walked on beside her and, looking straight ahead,
said, "You're wrong. I wasn't going to ask that. I was going
to ask if you would marry me."

"No, no!" Kay said explosively. "How can I marry you? No,
no—it's impossible. Don't speak about it."

"Kay, please—"

"No, no! Don't go on—"

"Kay," Beaver said, hoping for some kind of control,
"it can all be worked out. I'm sure Susan will be reasonable—heaven knows, I'm not the sort of person people fight
over—"

"I can't marry you," Kay said with finality. "Anyway, I'm
married."

Beaver, who had expected problems and discussions, even
tears, was not prepared for drama. "What?" he said."What?"
as if he were deaf.

"What an awful moment to start this," Kay said gloomily.
"I didn't tell you before because I didn't think it was any of
your business. By the time it *was* your business, I didn't want
you to know—I was afraid—"

"How long could that have gone on?"

"I don't know. Until just such a letter arrived, I suppose. I tried not to think about it. I'm quite good at that. It's been a long time now that I've tried not to think about my marriage." She stared angrily out to sea, and Beaver could only see the back of her dark head, tilted up arrogantly, and hear the light, distinct voice that was threaded through his days and nights, saying, "I suppose you'll want to know who to. Sakiko has a brother. I'm married to him. It explains a lot, doesn't it?"

"You'll have to tell me what it explains."

"Oh, why Sakiko used to take me home with her from college so often. Nobuo had something of a crush on me; he used to make her invite me. And why their mother protected me. And why the police left me alone after that first visit to the house—everyone had to be registered with the local police station in those days, and there were frequent checks and searches. They couldn't really have hidden me very long—there is not much privacy in Japan, the houses are open, the walls are thin—any extra person automatically broadcasts his presence. One of the neighbors would have talked. There would have been—I don't know—trouble, anyway, possibly internment, prison camps, the rest. I don't know, but certainly *something*. You have no idea what those days were like. But never forget, they *did* protect me. In the only way they knew how.

"We were supposed to be engaged, Nobuo and I—you can see how useful that was, how much protection it meant for me. Whatever I'd said before, the rash talk, the lack of enthusiasm about the New Asia—well, it was all excused as youthful foolishness now that I'd committed myself to a Japanese, a Japanese soldier. If anything, I was a heroine. Can you understand that I thought myself remarkably fortunate? There was a lot of fear at that time, and I'm not very brave."

"But you *married* him," Beaver said incredulously. "You, who are so good at explanations—unlike me—you can surely pull something out of the hat for that one. Come on, Kay, let's not—"

"Dear God! How American you are. You don't understand —do you? The moment of no hope, a defeat. When you know"—she turned to stare directly at him—"when you *know* there is no future for you. I married him in that hysteria before he was sent overseas because he wanted me to. I didn't care, and he thought he was going to die."

"And you didn't care if he died?"

"That's not what I said, but in fact I didn't. It was the old professor in Kyoto—after the house in Tokyo was bombed and I moved there—he brought me back to a sense of life, I mean a sense of what life is like beyond violence. Well, Nobuo wasn't killed, and I was even glad about that—"

"I bet you were—"

"Because I thought that now we could settle everything honorably and leave each other. We had, after all, served a certain need in each other's lives." With immense dignity, Kay said, "That isn't how it turned out."

Beaver said, "Look, baby. I can't believe that this is the way things happen. Whatever it is, however it turned out, you can get a divorce. I can, too. It has to work—*I want to marry you.*"

"Oh, my darling," Kay said, and she seldom used endearments, "let's just go on for—for however long it is, and forget about the rest. Nobuo won't divorce me. He's very Japanese. Like the rest, he's greedy for impossible contests, the kind no one can win. He knows I want to leave him. That is enough reason for him. And he knows about you—well, not that it's *you*, but that there's someone. It's not hard to check. I tell him that I'm visiting his mother in the mountains or that I'm working. He can't argue because he couldn't afford to help his mother, and he's glad that I don't ask him for money. Mostly we live in a terrible silence. I think the silence will only be broken when he wants to marry someone else. That is what I had waited for, and it didn't seem too bad. But then I hadn't expected to meet you."

"Kay, just tell me. Do you *want* to—"

"Marry you? No. Or, rather, yes, if it were this minute. But with all the fuss in between, no. I just want to go home— home to the Philippines, I mean. We have a house near Baguio—not big. But the hills are very cool, and misty, and bright green in the rain. It's too large an ambition to think about."

Touched by her look—the lost and bewildered look of a child caught in some inexplicable grown-up situation—and struck by the pathos of her dream, Beaver said gently, "Please, Kay—I know the world hasn't given you any reason to believe this—but there has to be—"

"A way out? Yes. Oh, yes." She stared at him with something like hatred in her face. "Yes. Money."

Startled, he said, "Money?"

"Disgusting word, isn't it?" She sounded mocking. "And you thought we were talking about love."

"You mean you can *buy* him off?"

"Come. We've said enough. Let's go. It will be too late for the fish."

"The hell with the fish." With rising agitation, calculating in his head, grabbing her arm, he jabbered on, "Look, we can manage it. An economist doesn't earn much, but then again, for years I haven't spent much—"

"Alimony," she interrupted harshly.

"Oh, Susan will have the Georgetown house—it's an excellent investment—and besides Susan will be—"

"Will be reasonable. Good old reasonable Susan. Really, Mr. Charles Beaver, SCAP economist, sometimes I am so much older than you."

She smiled and, knowing he had won, Beaver said joyfully, "You'll see. I'll write to her tonight. Tomorrow I'll go to the bank."

"There's still the old lady to think of—"

"We'll think of her, too." Undaunted, and riding high on his exuberance, he held Kay close and said, "You won't mind being poor—for quite a while—with me—"

"I have been poor all my life," she replied, and Beaver saw that she was crying.

Beaver fulfilled all his promises. He wrote to his wife, extracted all his savings from the bank, handed over the fat envelope to Kay, and sadly-happily heard her say that she must go to the mountains for the weekend to say her farewells to the old lady and pay up the hospital expenses. He tried to work that weekend, but his excitement was too acute. Sunday evening, in an agreeably wistful mood, a sentimental end-of-summer loneliness for Kay, he drove his jeep aimlessly around the city streets for a while, and then attempted to find his way back to the restaurant where he and Kay had dined the first time he took her out. He was feeling a little reckless, parked his jeep at the door, and brazenly knocked, ignoring the usual precautions. Happiness breeds courage, and he was happy.

At his knock, the door was opened by the shriveled figure

of the proprietress. She bowed low, as before, but peered at him in the half darkness without recognition. He explained himself clumsily, partly in English, partly in Japanese, reminding her of the last time they had met, trying to describe Kay. She seemed to understand, but Beaver, to impress the occasion on her memory, asked, "Did your grandchildren like the candy?"

"Grandchildren?" she repeated.

Thinking that he had used the wrong word, he rephrased the question. "The children. Keiko-san came back. She brought things for you. Sweets for the children."

The woman smiled and bowed and invited him in. She said, "Yes. Keiko-san returned. She brought me the money."

"And the food? The sweets?"

"Everything you ate was paid for. Please do not worry. A day's delay in payment is nothing."

In bewilderment, Beaver said goodbye to the proprietress and walked back to his jeep. He was never certain how much of his conversation the woman had grasped or how much of her comments he had understood.

Faintly uneasy, he drove about the streets once more, almost unaware of the fact that he was heading for Shibuya. From occasional references by Kay, he knew the general locality of the house in which she lived and remembered the name of the *sushi* shop. At last he found it, and after inquiring there from the owner, who spoke a certain amount of broken English, he walked down to the house at the end of the alley, not quite certain why he was doing this, hoping perhaps to meet Kay's husband and confront his unsuspected but surely not invincible adversary.

His entrance was welcomed by the old lady. Recognizing him at once as the kind American who had helped them all, she tried very hard to understand him and made all kinds of formal acknowledgments in Japanese. But since he seemed to be repeatedly asking something of great urgency, with many gestures, she finally decided that the moment was important enough to lead him to the *sushi* shop on the corner where the owner or his daughter could act as interpreter.

There, with relentless clarity, Beaver learned a number of things: one, that it was Nobuo, not the old lady, who was in the mountain sanitarium; two, that the old lady had no daughter—Sakiko did not exist, nor was there an old relative —the professor—living in Kyoto; three, that Nobuo expected to marry Kay as soon as he was well; four, that he, Beaver, had been made use of to further this end. It was all said with the greatest deference, the most penetrating subtlety, the lightest innuendo. It was all obviously, and most agonizingly, true.

In the blue light and the sharp air of early evening in the mountains, Kay talked to Nobuo. "I feel much better about leaving you this time," she was saying. "The improvement is so great. It shows even in your voice."

"Tonight?" he asked.

"Yes, I'll have to take the late train."

"If you left tomorrow—"

"I have to be at work tomorrow morning."

"The same people?" He looked down at his thin hands crossed on the quilt that covered him.

"No. That job is finished, but Mrs. Beaver seems to have been pleased with me. She recommended me to friends, and now—"

"Kay," he said, still not meeting her untroubled gaze, "you have done too much for me."

"I owe you a lot," she replied, as though she were thanking a stranger. "You got me out of that internment camp—"

"At a price."

"It was no price."

"And we were happy together. Were we happy together?"

In exasperation she answered, "You ask such silly questions—for heaven's sake—yes, we were happy. For a while. While it mattered. Surely we can talk about this another time."

"Don't you ever think of Kyoto?"

"The quiet, yes. Away from the bombing."

"The quiet shared? The gardens shared?"

"Just the quiet."

"Kay, if you would marry me?"

"I cannot marry you. We would never even have been together had it not been for the war, and the internment camp. And—and your help."

"Help?" He gave her an acid smile.

She looked away and said quickly, "Call it what you want. You risked your position. . . . I do not forget that. But"—she sounded almost pleading—"it has all been over a long time, the war and—everything. Why do you now—"

"Remember this, if you save a man's life you are responsible for him forever."

"I'm not!" she said, her voice rising in alarm.

"When you give a man back to the world—to sorrow, perhaps, or misfortune—you accept his life and what happens to him. You are responsible and he has claims on you."

"Not on me! I won't accept—"

"That is why you help me, why we will always be together."

"Don't you see? I'm *buying* my way out of indebtedness." She sprang up from her chair. "I'm *buying* my freedom."

"It can't be bought."

"I'll prove you wrong," she said shrilly. "You'll see! For the first time in my life, I'm in love—"

"Beaver," he said quietly.

"Yes, Beaver." She was both defiant and determined. "And I won't be cheated of—"

"I thought it was only the money."

"At first it was. But now—"

"Kay. Don't argue with me. There is only one ending."

"I'm not listening," she said. "I don't want to hear about —about *destiny*." She made it sound like a ridiculous word. Reaching into her bag, she pulled out Beaver's fat envelope and handed it to him. "Here," she said. "For you and your mother. With gratitude."

As soon as Kay got back to Tokyo, she went directly to Beaver's room. "I came straight here," she said, laughing. "I couldn't wait. Isn't it absurd?"

"How was the old lady?" Beaver asked.

"Better—so much better."

"And she was glad to see you, of course?"

"Well, of course. And so relieved that the hospital bills are all paid up. Sometime I'll find a way of telling you—how much I owe to you!" She was busily doing all the small arrival things, setting her bag down in a corner, smoothing her hair in front of Beaver's mirror, kicking off her shoes, settling wearily in a chair. "All because of you—and at last I could really help her, and what's more—"

"You told her our plans?"

"Oh, yes—and she promised to make it all right. The least she could do, she said. Your generosity, with a bow." Kay got up to make a funny, silly, serious Japanese formal bow.

"She's going to—well, *pull rank* with Nobuo." Kay was in very high spirits. "Parents, you know, have a lot of authority here."

"I know."

"So it's set—it's all set—"

"Or would be, if—"

"It's going to be a glorious life—we're going to—"

In an exhausted voice, Beaver stopped her by saying, "I know just what we're going to do. What *I* am going to do, that is. I talked to her myself, you see."

Kay knew at that moment that defeat had overtaken her rapid words. She tried very hard to salvage something. "Let me tell you the story," she said. "Please—my darling—please let me tell you—"

"I've heard enough stories."

"No, this time it's the truth—"

"Don't tell me," he said as unemotionally as he knew how. "*Don't* tell me that you're in love. It can all be explained—as usual." In a rather false voice, he recited, "At the beginning, it was different. But now—but *now*, for Christsake, you're in love, in love for the first time in your life. You see? I can tell your stories for you."

"Yes, you can," she said humbly. "Yes. That is what I was going to say."

"Poor Kay," he remarked, not meaning it.

"Still, it *is* true—"

"Yes, indeed," he said.

"But you wrote to her, didn't you? Your wife, I mean—"

"I did. I'll have to face that particular bit of idiocy by myself." Theatrically, he added, "Shall I tell her, in your phrase, 'a summer lunacy'?"

"Better tell her the truth."

For a moment, he looked at her in astonishment, and then began laughing helplessly.

He handed her the overnight bag, and while she put on her shoes he opened the door and stood with his hand on the doorknob.

"Poor Kay," she repeated as she left.

There was really nowhere to go. Not back to the Shibuya house certainly. A hotel? But then there was the question of money. She couldn't waste any of the money she had kept aside from Beaver's envelope for what, until that conversation, would have been a carefully planned trousseau and, in addition, some original and splendid wedding gift for him. Now it would have to provide her retreat—by any standard, she had been engaged in a battle, bravely fought, perhaps, but unquestionably lost. Some time would have to pass before she would be able to see the ending of that summer with Beaver in any other way.

She walked through the deserted nighttime streets of the city to the bridge over the Sumida River, and stood there, bag in hand, thinking. It was too early to weep and she couldn't yet summon up any jauntiness. So she leaned against the railing, for all the world like one of the sentimental springtime girls. A G.I. tried to pick her up, but she snapped at him and, startled, he went on to more accommodating company. Kay stayed where she was, looking down at the black and greasy water.

Through the night, which was cool now with the approach of autumn, Kay, standing on the bridge in Tokyo, had considered and rejected several plans. She thought them through with great concentration, as much to obliterate the painfully clear details of her final exchange with Beaver in his hotel room as to ensure some measure of success for her own determination to get out of Japan. At last, she walked through the early-morning stirring of the city to the railway station. Even at that hour, it was crowded with travelers waiting for trains that might not arrive until midday or afternoon. By being near the front of the lines, they would have a better chance of squeezing into the second- and third-class carriages to Kyoto, Kobe, Yokohama—whatever their destination happened to be. First-class carriages were reserved for SCAP personnel. For the Japanese, no reservations were permitted and, as with buses and subways, whoever managed to push his way into the sadly limited accommodation traveled. The others waited hours, even days, for the next opportunity.

Kay found her way to the ladies' room, where she washed and tidied herself as much as she could. She then returned to the waiting room, established a small space for herself against one wall, and sat on her weekend case and waited for offices to open.

The small concrete building where a number of different consulates and foreign chancelleries had their offices was not far from the huge Dai Ichi block that was SCAP headquarters. There Kay asked directions to the representative of the Philippines, and, still looking moderately composed and trim in her white silk suit, carrying her suitcase and handbag, she took the elevator to the third floor. A secretary in the outer office asked her name and the nature of her business. "Catalina García," Kay replied, as if she were speaking of a stranger. "I wish to return to the Philippines."

"You are a citizen of the Philippine Republic?"

"Yes."

"You will have to go to the transport division of SCAP. They will stamp your passport with the necessary exit permit and will instruct you about army transport facilities. As you know, there are no commercial airlines flying yet between Tokyo and Manila."

"I have no passport."

The young man at first looked only puzzled; gradually he became worried.

"You have lost your passport?"

"No. The American passport I had when I came to Japan was destroyed, along with my other possessions, during the air raids. Now I haven't even got any identification papers."

"Miss García." The secretary began to sound ruffled, almost hostile. "You will have to explain this to me in further detail."

"May I see the Minister?"

"I'm sorry. I will need more information from you before *I* take the matter up with the Minister."

"Very well," Kay said, with no rancor in her tone. "May I sit down? I had only hoped not to bore you with a rather tedious story."

Caught a little off guard by Kay's air of casual assurance, the young man pulled up a chair for her, muttering, "Excuse me. Please be seated."

"It's not really very complicated, but I'm afraid I've been rather thoughtless. Perhaps you can help me sort things out." She smiled disarmingly. "I'm very ignorant about official matters." She arranged herself, unhurried, in the wooden chair while the secretary returned to his place behind the desk and fiddled uneasily with a pencil.

A small deprecating gesture of her hand, and then she began her minutely rehearsed account. "You see, I was caught in Tokyo at the time of the Japanese attack on Pearl Harbor. I didn't really understand what had happened. I was only a student on my way to college in America. The University of California. I was so looking forward to going there—the pictures were so splendid in the brochure!" She allowed a note of wistfulness. "I don't suppose I shall ever see it now." A brief pause, and then she resumed, steadying her voice to a neutral recital. "Anyway, that is in the past. I was traveling on a Japanese freighter—I would have liked to go on the Clipper, but my family couldn't afford it. The freighters were very slow, of course, but so much cheaper, and I didn't mind because they stopped at various ports. I had never traveled before. Naturally, I looked forward to seeing something of the world.

"There were several of us students on the boat, and we were delighted when we were told that passengers would be permitted to leave the freighter in Tokyo, where, evidently, there was a good deal of shipping business to transact, that we could spend a week of sightseeing in Japan, and then rejoin the boat at its next port of call, Kobe. We made up a party amongst ourselves and disembarked in Tokyo, leaving most of our luggage and possessions in our cabins, taking only our passports and what clothing we would need for a brief stay.

"Well, that was the week of Pearl Harbor. It was all so sudden. We—there were four of us—we had no idea what to do. We were told to leave the youth hostel where we were staying. We couldn't return to the boat. At last, one of us suggested that we go to the American Embassy to make inquiries from the official in charge of Filipino affairs.

"As you can imagine, we found everything in considerable confusion at the Embassy. The Japanese had already taken over. The members of the diplomatic corps had been placed under house arrest. The rest of us who held American passports were sent off first to interrogation centers and later to internment camps. I expect you were at home at that time. You cannot, I'm sure, imagine the complete disorganization and fright of those early days." Kay had been speaking very evenly, without a trace of accusation in her voice. However, the young man shifted uneasily in his chair.

"Yes, I was at home." He added quickly, "Until I joined the guerrillas, that is."

Kay nodded. "The guerrillas and internment camps. Probably we would both do better to forget those days."

"They cannot be forgotten," the young man said with sullen, searing bitterness. "Nor can the Japanese be forgiven. You have not been back since the war? You will see—and hear when you return."

"I have heard enough already. You see, I tried to reach my family after we—those Filipinos that were still alive—were released from the internment camp. I wanted, if it was possible, to go home. The letters were returned to me. Addressee unknown."

Kay sat silent for a while, staring at the young man's fingers still turning the pencil over and over. Awkwardly, he began, "I'm sorry—" but she interrupted, refusing any kind of formal condolence. "I was not, by any means, the only one to lose a family. But it did leave me very alone, as if I had no real existence. I am not entirely clear in my mind about those days. They put me in a hospital—I think it was a hospital—for some time. I cannot tell you exactly how long."

"All this must have been after the Philippine surrender, when the puppet government was set up in Manila—"

"—and the puppet embassy here. I remember we were all urged to cooperate with the Japanese, now that we were part of the Greater East-Asia Co-Prosperity Sphere."

"We—many of us—continued to fight in the mountains of Luzon. But there were also many collaborators in the Philippines." He looked at Kay appraisingly. "Here, in Japan also, there were many Filipino collaborators."

"So I understand," she said, without much apparent interest. "After the war I read about the people's courts that were set up in Manila to try the war criminals."

"And the collaborators."

Kay nodded, but said nothing further. The young man was frowning. He seemed unsure how to proceed, to be turning over in his mind a story that appeared possible, even plausible, but somehow suspect. He couldn't decide whether it was the manner of the telling or the account itself that was troubling him. At last, since Kay evidently had no more to add, he said, "There is another question I must ask you, Miss García. Why did you not apply for repatriation papers after the peace treaty was signed, after the Occupation was set up? Or even last year, when we became an independent republic, you could, like the other Filipinos, have applied for a passport."

Kay was quiet for a long time, a silence that had not so much a quality of suspense as of rather painful consideration. At last she looked directly at him. "All right. I suppose it is your job to ask, and I suppose it is necessary for me to reply. You see, I fell in love. It's not a very suitable—I mean *officially* suitable reason, is it? However, it is true. I met an American —he works in the SCAP administration—and I fell in love with him. He loved me, too." She halted. "Yes, I'm sure he loved me. Anyway, I thought we would be married and when I left Japan it would be with him, as his wife. There seemed no reason to make other plans. Until last night, that is."

Abruptly, Kay's even tone and decorous manner broke

down. She got up from her chair, scraping it harshly against the floor, and turned away from the secretary with every sign of distress. Holding tightly to the back of the chair, she whispered, "Please forgive me. . . . I hadn't expected to—I mean, I didn't realize you would have to know all this—"

The young man had stood up, too, and leaned anxiously across his desk. "Miss García. Do please sit down. You needn't—"

"Goodness knows, it's commonplace enough as a story—"

"You needn't continue. Just sit down for a—"

"I learned that, of course, he is married," Kay said rapidly. "His wife and children are coming out to Japan." Almost inaudibly, she finished, "I want to go home."

"Believe me, I will do my best to help you. Here is a form you will have to fill out. You may take it with you, if you prefer, and complete it at your leisure."

Kay turned to face him. "No, I'd rather do it now. May I borrow your pen?" She pulled the chair close to his desk, sat down, and began to write. Almost immediately, she stopped. "Address," she said, as though the word were a death sentence. "I have no address any longer in the Philippines."

"No friends? Nobody who knew your family?"

"I don't know where any of them live now. I could give you the name of the convent where I went to school. Perhaps there are still some sisters there who would remember me."

"That will do. And your address in Tokyo?"

Kay shook her head, her whole attitude limp and vanquished. "None. You see, until—well, until last night I was staying with him."

"But how will we reach you here?"

"I'll have to be in touch with you." She completed the form, pausing at only one other point to ask whether internment counted as having a prison record, signed and dated it, and handed it across the desk to the young man. "I'm afraid I can't remember the number of the passport I used to have."

"That doesn't matter too much. It will be in the records. We will, in any case, have to look up your file."

"My file? Why would there be a file on me?"

"The Swiss took care of all American property after Pearl Harbor. They were very careful and very thorough. Both the Embassy and the Consular records were preserved. And then we have also the records kept by the Japanese."

"I see." After a few moments, she picked up her bag. "I suppose that's all for now? Shall I come in again this afternoon?"

"I think we'll need more time than that."

"But, please, I must—"

"Miss García. I know you want to leave Japan as soon as possible. We will do our best. If you get in touch with me tomorrow at three o'clock, I should have some information for you by then."

"Very well," Kay said. "And thank you for your help."

The young man watched the girl leave his office, a spruce but oddly forlorn figure, and wondered just what she *had* actually been up to during the past years in Japan. In the course of his job in Tokyo, he had learned to acknowledge the fact that the aftermath of war threw up some very strange stories indeed. Something about her general bearing continued to nag at him, poised yet clearly under considerable strain, emotional yet almost defiantly impersonal. But those conflicting impressions were not, he decided, what really bothered him. He had the puzzling feeling that somehow she hadn't existed before she walked into his office, as if she had

been born, fully grown, at that moment, that she had no
background, no past at all—and possibly no future. He didn't
notice that he shook his head to clear it of these uncharacteristic meanderings. More prosaically, he told himself that perhaps it was nothing more than an indication that she had
been telling him lies. Well, there was one simple and logical
way to find out. He got up from his desk, holding Kay's form,
and knocked on the crinkled glass of the door leading to the
Minister's office. Inside, in a correct official voice, he reminded the Minister of a meeting with members of the War
Reparations Committee called for eleven-thirty. He paused a
moment and then said, "I wonder, sir, if I might take up
another matter with you now, if you can give me the time? It
is a question of repatriation of one of our nationals. . . ."

Kay, meanwhile, continued doggedly with the schedule she
had mapped out for herself. At the SCAP offices of the Transport Section, she was told that Colonel Peterson was in conference at the moment and would probably not be free until
lunchtime. Would she care to make an appointment? She
said she would rather wait, on the off chance that Colonel
Peterson might be able to spare her a few minutes after his
conference.

The G.I. who seemed to be acting as both receptionist and
switchboard operator shrugged, indicated a wooden bench
against the wall, and said, "I'll leave a message that you're
here, ma'am."

From the orderly rows of desks and filing cabinets, men in
uniform and a few girls in civilian summer clothes had
looked over briefly to the slight diversion Kay's entrance had
caused. Now as she sat, without fidgeting, staring across the
long, drab, strictly utilitarian room, she seemed to create a

sort of island of timeless isolation around her, and the employees of the Transport Section returned to their papers and typewriters and memo pads. People hurried in and out all morning carrying files, manifest sheets, official forms, sometimes stopping at one of the desks, sometimes vanishing through one of the inner doors. But it wasn't until nearly twelve-thirty that Colonel Peterson came out and walked purposefully toward the swing doors next to Kay.

"Excuse me, sir." The G.I. at the switchboard stood up. "This is the young lady waiting to see you."

The Colonel, his hand on the door, swung around impatiently. The girl looked elusively familiar, the way she sat so straight on the bench, a posture both timid and determined. "I wondered if I could talk to you for a few minutes?" she said. "Charles Beaver suggested you would be the best person to see."

Ah, of course, Beaver's girl. Beaver's Softly, in fact. "I'm afraid I have a lunch date at the Imperial. Perhaps you could—"

"It won't take long," Kay interrupted. "Really, it won't."

Colonel Peterson hesitated a moment, then motioned Kay to precede him through the swing doors. "Ride over to the Imperial with me. You can tell me on the way."

In the car, he hardly listened to Kay's short, flat sentences. He was thinking of his own Softly, now fairly remote in both time and memory. Last spring, and it had been raining, and the thing that had touched him most had been her terrible, unquestioning resignation. No arguments, no reproaches, no pleading. Just *"Iroiro osewa ni narimashita ...,"* a phrase that he had come to know, through many repetitions in the previous months, had the rather stately meaning "I am beholden to you in many ways. ..." His goodbye present of shoes and two American dresses from the PX had remained unopened on the torn *tatami* of the shabby little Japanese room. She had bowed very formally when he left.

Kay was saying, "You understand that I cannot remain here. He suggested that you might, perhaps, be able to—well, expedite things for me." The white handbag on her lap looked absurdly businesslike under the grip of her childishly small brown hands. It contained all the money, Japanese and American, that she possessed. "I can pay for the flight. Also, fortunately, I'm a Philippine national."

Well, Beaver was being wise. And, apparently, generous. Poor girl, Colonel Peterson thought. Poor Beaver. Best thing all round, probably. He said, "You're very young," surprising both Kay and himself. "Yes." He cleared his throat with unnecessary vigor. "Yes, I'll check our flight schedules to Manila this afternoon. There's a weekly supply run, but that usually carries a maximum load. I'll see what else we have."

"Shall I call you?"

"Do that. Anytime after two-thirty." He put his hand briefly on her arm, hardly more than a pat. "There's bound to be something. We'll work something out."

Kay kept her face turned toward the window. "You're very kind," she said, and asked to be let out of the car at the big intersection before the driveway to the Imperial.

Walking slowly through the lunch-hour crowds, Kay allowed her attention to focus on nothing but the mechanical details of getting through the next two hours. She must make herself eat, and whatever she ate must be cheap. She must find a place to rest. She must be near a telephone. She counted out in her mind exactly how many yen she had left in her purse (keeping intact, of course, the envelope containing Beaver's precious American dollars).

In one of the alleys near the Sukiabashi, she found the kind of restaurant she wanted, scarcely more than a snack bar, really, where clerks and other minor office workers from the neighborhood stopped in for a quick meal and tea. She appeared not to notice that she was the only girl there or that a small eddy of silence followed her progress to the scrubbed wooden table surrounded by plain, square stools. She was about to order noodles, knowing this to be the least expensive dish, when a vivid, unwanted recollection filled her head with the plaintive little tune that the *soba* vendor played on his flute to attract passers-by. For a moment she was in Kyoto, walking beside Nobuo in his army uniform, during his home leave long ago. The road still held the blurred purple shadows of evening and Nobuo had been laughing about something when they heard the notes of the flute. He had hurried her forward to the *soba* stall, and together they had stood, each holding a small basket of thin noodles, using their chopsticks to dip them into the porcelain bowl of sauce. The *soba* vendor had been so respectful to the uniform with its array of decorations, and at Nobuo's request had repeated his brief special melody again and again for them.

With more asperity than she intended, Kay ordered *udon*, which had no plaguing associations entwined in its thick spaghetti. It cost a little more, because it was cooked in a watery broth with fragments of vegetable and egg. She ate it extremely slowly, counting each mouthful, as if she were engaged in some ritualistic discipline. Afterward, she sipped her tea with the same deliberation while the restaurant rapidly emptied and its customers returned to work.

At a quarter to three, Kay was standing outside a theatre examining the big, stylized posters of exaggerated poses and grotesque make-ups illustrating moments and characters from the Kabuki plays offered inside. The old Kabuki-za had been burned out during the raids and only the elaborate façade remained, its scarlet-and-gold splendor desolately blackened and peeling. Now the Kabuki companies used this more modest, more dingy substitute for their flamboyant daylong performances.

Hesitantly, Kay went to the box office. The clerk had his back to the window, writing something at a high desk against the far wall of the cubicle. She cleared her throat to catch his attention. He looked over his shoulder with no interest, and then, with slow curiosity showing on his face, asked what he could do for Kay. She made her request with the uncertain over-politeness of a stranger in town, adding hastily that she would, of course, pay for the phone call. He shook his head doubtfully; the telephone was in the back office. He couldn't let anyone through the barrier without a ticket.

Kay assured him that she had, in any case, intended to see the afternoon program; it was well known that no trip to Tokyo could be considered complete without a visit to the great Kabuki theatre. She counted out the money for a ticket in the top balcony and, with a timid smile, pushed the crumpled bills across to him.

He seemed to be making up his mind about something. He glanced around the lobby. There were only a few idlers reading the notices and a couple of women with babies slung on their backs talking in low voices. His gaze moved back to Kay's hopeful face. "It won't take long, your phone call?"

"Only a couple of minutes. It's rather important, otherwise I wouldn't trouble you."

He tore off a flimsy white ticket, handed it to Kay, pulled a wooden shutter down over the box-office window, and reappeared on the other side of the barrier motioning her to follow him.

In the back office, he stood at the doorway while Kay consulted a slip of paper and put through her call. Colonel Peterson sounded busy and, when he heard Kay's voice, oddly weary. "Yeah. Well, the only possibility seems to be an army transport. Scheduled for Thursday afternoon—day after tomorrow. There may be room for a couple of civilians. I'll put you on the manifest."

Only then did Kay realize that she had been holding her breath. "Oh, thank you!" she said, on a gasp. "Thank you very much."

"Look, don't count on it. I can't give you a priority. If there are any SCAP requisitions or any further army personnel needing the space, you'll be bumped. I'm not even sure it will leave as planned. There are often delays—a day, two days."

"I'll take my chances."

"O.K. Well, bring your papers into the office. I'll have them processed and give you a pass for Haneda. It's a restricted area. You'll just have to wait at the airport and see how it goes."

"I'll keep my fingers crossed," Kay said almost gaily.

"Good luck."

"Will tomorrow about four o'clock be all right?"

"I guess so. I'll leave instructions in case I'm tied up." He didn't much want to see the girl again, but in some oblique way, without attempting to clarify his reasons, he felt it a matter of conscience to try to help her.

Buoyantly, Kay swung away from the phone, surprising the box-office clerk with the radiance of her smile. She left him in a flurry of bows and courtesies at the entrance to the checkroom. Unencumbered, at last, by her suitcase, she found her way to the gallery stairs and into the dimly lit auditorium, and took her seat near the back. Far below her was the brilliantly lit rectangle of the Kabuki stage and the *hanamichi*, leading through the audience to the back of the theatre. Along that raised passageway, the actors made their important exits and entrances.

Kay had glanced at the program perfunctorily and realized that the actor on stage in his high, glossy wig and pale make-up, his elaborate kimono and gold-patterned *obi*, was the young and lovely bride Tamate Gozen. Through the measured cadences of the old play, the story of the gallant, misunderstood girl would slowly unfold with all its poetry and pathos to the final sacrifice of her life. Kay was prepared to watch this remote tragedy with a stoic detachment. The merciful unreality of the stage, the period, the formally elegant movements of the actors were precisely the impersonal distraction she needed, and the unlikely story could in no way engage her feelings. Indeed, the inflated emotions, the noble sentiments on stage could, in her present mood, provide an almost humorous counterpoint to her severely practical thoughts. She had never been to the theatre with Beaver and, treating herself somewhat like an invalid with certain sensitive areas which must not be touched, she had deliberately chosen to spend the rest of the day in this alien world of extravagantly make-believe happenings.

As it turned out, she saw virtually nothing of Tamate Gozen's misadventures and even less of the succeeding episodes from different plays. Exhaustion overcame her like a fainting spell and she slept fitfully, her head flopping forward, all afternoon and evening until the resonant wooden clappers heralding the final curtain woke her.

Suddenly alert, she sped downstairs to reclaim her suitcase

and then returned to join the last of the departing audience, moving slowly with them toward the exit until she saw an opportunity to slip unobtrusively into one of the empty theatre boxes. These were constructed like the boxes in an old-fashioned opera house, a small plush-lined anteroom opening, through a curtained archway, into the jutting arc of the seating area. Here she hid until all the spectators and ushers had left. Through the slit of the partly open door of the anteroom, she watched the approach of the cleaning man with his basket and broom. He entered each box in turn, dusting, sweeping, and picking up dropped programs, and when he was busy in the box next to hers, Kay crept silently into the one he had just finished. She listened nervously until she could no longer hear his gentle clatter, and at last prepared herself to spend the night in the spooky darkness of the deserted theatre.

"Good afternoon, Miss García." The starched young man in the Philippine Diplomatic Mission office gave her a cool and slightly cynical look. Kay waited without a word, afraid of how her voice would sound if she spoke, while he checked over the papers on his desk. "I'm sorry that we cannot issue you a passport."

Kay sat down abruptly in the chair across from him. She clutched her handbag to hide her shaking hands and stared at him with wide, despairing eyes.

"You see," he continued, "we went through your file and were not entirely satisfied with the information it contained. There is a record of your commitment to the internment camp, but none of your release from it. Did you escape?"

Kay shook her head.

"We thought not," he agreed complacently. "The Japanese

are very thorough. There would certainly have been a notation to that effect—even if the attempt had been unsuccessful. Some Filipinos tried. Others took the opportunity for release after the Philippine surrender. Still others made their own—ah—*private* deals with camp officials or guards." His tone was conversational, as if this were an ordinary discussion of the Filipino character, but his expression was accusing. "Also, we are somewhat—well, *puzzled* by your failure—or neglect? —to apply for a passport when the representation from the Independent Republic of the Philippines was first established in Tokyo." He paused to give Kay an opportunity to offer some satisfactory explanation, but was met with only a defeated silence. He gave a small shrug and went on, "However, you have the right to repatriation. We have made out a travel document for you, valid for only one journey to Manila."

Kay's bag fell from her lap as she snatched the papers from his desk. "You could have told me right away!" she burst out, caught between relief and anger.

Icily, the young man said, "You must report to the police authorities immediately upon your arrival in Manila. We are informing them accordingly. Meanwhile, we shall pursue our own inquiries here. . . ."

"About me?"

"About your activities during the war."

Kay tucked the papers into her bag and picked up her suitcase. She thought fleetingly of Nobuo and Oba-san. "Good hunting," she said. The young man was rather taken aback by the ironic merriment of her parting smile.

Only when Kay was safely on the plane, after many hours of uncertain waiting in Haneda, did she allow herself to think at all about Beaver—and, even then, more to close the door on the whole calamitous episode than to explore her feelings or assess her loss, which was not, in any case, her way. She could not forget, but did not wish to remember, that the summer had been the only period in her life that had offered her any real joy.

Her homecoming or, more accurately, her escape from Tokyo had not been accomplished without anxieties—even the promise of dangers. A promise that continued to haunt her after her arrival in Manila.

There was a long delay at the Manila airport. The army personnel were cleared first, then came the other priority travelers, and at last the officials turned to an inspection of Kay's papers and suitcase. There was a whispered discussion between them. Someone consulted a telegram. Someone else was dispatched to an inner office and could be seen, through the glass-paneled door, to be making a telephone call. The questions, when they came, were brief but ominous. Only "Where does your family live?"

"I have no family."

And "What will be your address in Manila?"

"I don't know. I'll stay at a hotel, I suppose, until I find a place of my own."

"Which hotel?"

"The Manila Hotel," she replied at random.

Incredulously, "You have a reservation?"

"No."

"Almost certainly, they will not have a room for you. Manila is very crowded."

"Well, have you any other suggestions?"

A worried exchange of glances, some possibilities doubtfully presented. "You could try the Granada, but that, too, is likely to be full. Or the Casa Andalucía ..."

"I'll try both. If neither can take me, they may know where else to send me."

One of the men was writing with great deliberation in capital letters on the back of a printed form. "As soon as you have found a place, you must go, in person, to this address. Take the duplicates of your travel documents with you, and register there. We need to know, as soon as possible, where we can reach you."

"Very well." With a mild cynicism that rather embarrassed the officials, Kay added, "I suppose the police will want to question me."

In fact, she had no intention of being questioned, but her offhand acceptance of the idea seemed to assure the officials that she would carry out their instructions. She picked up her suitcase, thanked them politely for their courtesy, and left them staring after her as she made her way to a taxi.

Throughout the ride to the Granada Hotel, Kay gazed out of the taxi window at the shattered city with a sickening and oppressive sense of recognition. In a way, Tokyo had been better. There so many of the houses, constructed of wood and paper, had, after the incendiary raids, left only charred spaces, quickly cleared, as reminders of their destruction. Here the buildings had been of stone, concrete, and adobe, and their stark skeletons, less easily ignored, continued to make their uncompromising statement on the impersonal catastrophe of bombs and war. Listening absently to the driver's complaints about the massive traffic jams that built up because there was only one remaining bridge across the Pasig to Escolta, the downtown section of Manila, Kay once again turned her attention to severely practical matters and reviewed her program for the day.

At the Granada (which was indeed full), she made no attempt to plead for accommodation, and asked instead for names not of other hotels but of pensions and boarding houses. From the first pension, also full, she got another list of possibilities. Eventually, continuing this procedure and introducing herself by a different name at each address, she found a room, expensive considering its cramped facilities, but offering her at least a temporary obscurity. Here she called herself Miss Kay Gómez, and as soon as she was alone, before she washed or unpacked her suitcase, she tore her travel documents into tiny pieces and threw them away.

PART II

In the House of Strangers

♋Doña Luisa Jiménez de Salablanca sat in her bedroom reading old love letters. Through a lifetime's habit, she sat very straight, without touching the back of the chair. The disciplines of long-dead governesses and the convent schoolrooms nearly sixty years ago had given her the elegant rigidity of spine and the excellence of carriage that were, by themselves, an incontrovertible stamp of another age in another world. It never occurred to her to criticize the sloppiness of the new, postwar generation, because she never saw them except in fleeting glimpses on the streets of Manila when her car was held up for a traffic jam or a change of lights. Then the thin, ravaged face and the brilliant eyes would stare for a moment at a laughing group of girls on a corner. In spite of their tight, flashy clothes and meticulous make-up, she would decide in her mind that they were poor, making the best of a bad living at home, putting on a brave face. When she saw a young couple, arm in arm, loitering toward a soft-drink stall, they faded quickly into some memory of her husband, who had died twenty years before but still occupied so much of her time and thought.

Their deportment with each other had always been impeccable, graceful, well-mannered, and serene. But then, she reminded herself, it is easy to behave well when you are both loved and financially secure. They had always contributed generously to charities and the church—he from a knowledge of what it meant to be poor (or, rather, the strain of being genteelly impoverished, of trying to maintain the standards and company of one's class without the means to support the life and surroundings), she because she felt that proper conduct depended on it, her own and the recipients'. She hoped, indistinctly, that those girls on the street were reached by some part of her charity.

There were silences in her love letters (written fifty-two years before, when she was a girl of eighteen), silences of meaning and of expression. He had never, for instance, written that he loved her, only that he wanted to marry her. Spanish (the language that they had always used in letters and in speech to each other) lends itself to formality—formality with degrees of intimacy. Whenever she reread the letters, she summoned for herself, in an instant, the correct, courteous, and delicately searching nature of their marriage.

In those hot afternoons of October, Doña Luisa seldom slept. When she was younger, she had enjoyed the tranquillity of the siesta hours, the diminishing activity in the house, faintly heard from her room, the slow uncoiling into the light dream-filled sleep of daytime. Now she needed less sleep even at night, waking sometimes at five in the morning, and none at all in the afternoon. Instead, she would change into a white *robe de chambre*, intricately tucked and pleated, with deep lace at the throat—Tomás had once admired just such

a robe, and since then there had always been one exactly like
it in her closet. He had been sharp-eyed and appreciative of
her clothes, remarking even a new ribbon threaded through
a camisole, or a different tracery in the lace of a new glove.
She could not now forget the habit of dressing to please him.
When she had loosened her hair, she would sit at her rose-
wood desk or on the stiff little gilded sofa near the windows.
There the sunlight, double screened by the curly iron grille,
thick with clinging jasmine outside and the wooden jalousies
inside, would fall in striped and mottled designs across her
book—one of the neat leather-bound books from her husband's library, the carefully fashioned lines of Juan de la Cruz
or Lope de Vega, sometimes lives of the saints, occasionally
a novel, more often the biographies that her husband had
once urged on her with the remark "The British have a talent
for this kind of writing. They have learned to come as close
as possible to gossip without reaching vulgarity."

"Gossip?" she had repeated, alarmed. "Vulgarity?"

A fleeting look of impatience showed on his face, but there
was no irritation in his voice. "They will amuse you by their
omissions, the shadow of the private man lurking behind the
public figure." Even now, when she opened *Eminent Victorians,*
she would read the nameplate inside the cover, *"Ex Libris
Tomás de Salablanca,"* and wonder briefly if she had seemed
silly to him all those years ago. Then she would begin to read
the familiar pages.

Frequently—at least once a week—in the moist afternoon
heat and breathless silence of the house, she would reread
the love letters. She counted them all as love letters, beginning with the first formal note in the third person in which
he had requested the honor of calling on her, and ending
with the letter that had reached her on the night before her

wedding, two years later. "My dear betrothed, I shall leave this at your house on my way to dinner with the Morenos, where I shall not speak of you at all, but equally will not hear the trivialities they talk about. . . . This letter, then, must be my presence in your house and in your heart—my shadow on the wall—for this last evening that I shall not be with you. . . ." Of course, there had been many other letters in the course of their married life—love letters, too—but that particular one was always saved to be read last, because it never failed to transform her, in her thoughts, to the thin, inarticulate girl of her youth, saved from plainness only by a pale complexion and the large dreaming eyes of myopia. By the end of the letter, she could always feel at least some echo of that past reassurance, amounting sometimes to triumph, in her marriage.

At five o'clock, Doña Luisa rang for Angelita, the bright-eyed maid who had come to live in the house nine years before, as a child of fourteen from the Visayan sugar estates. Since then, Angelita had lost her country manners and her tendency to giggle, but there had been no cure for the twisted foot and the lumpish, rolling effort of walking that it necessitated. Years before, driving through the Negros estate, Tomás had halted the car at one of the *nipa* huts where Angelita, a baby, was playing in the dust beside the road. The contrast between the small laughing face and the dragging, twisted foot had touched them both, and Tomás had extracted the easy promise from her that the child would always be taken care of and perhaps, one day, suitably married if such a bargain could be arranged for her.

Long after his death, she had remembered this, as she remembered almost everything else about him, and had sent for Angelita to train her for her modest future. Now both her manner and her voice were subdued. Neatly dressed in white glazed cotton, she fetched a rose silk dress for Doña Luisa. She arranged her hair swiftly and expertly, fastened her stays, hooked the high boned collar of white lace around her neck. She held the dress low as her mistress stepped into it, and then fastened the thirty tiny buttons down the back. Finally, clumsily, she sank to the floor to slip the silver buckled shoes onto Doña Luisa's narrow feet—all this without saying a word.

At last, Doña Luisa said, "Thank you, Angelita," and then the young woman smiled, opened the door into the hall for her, and returned to draw back the shutters and tidy the room. When Angelita heard the light measured footsteps retreating down the corridor, she began to sing, very softly to herself, one of the sentimental ballads of the central islands. At the window, she pulled in a spray of jasmine and, with gestures that had become stylized through long repetition, broke off the flowers, held them swaying to her nose, and tucked them in her dress.

The staircase in the Salablanca house was very wide, wooden, uncarpeted, and built on a lovely curve. Years of training enabled Doña Luisa still to walk down the center of the stairs without touching either the banister or the wall. She retained a slight scorn almost unrecognized—or, anyway, very quickly suppressed—of women who fussed, clung to support, or watched their feet with an ungainly hunching of neck and shoulders as they moved down toward the pillared entrance hall. She, as always, glanced critically at the ferns and orchids set against the walls, at the expanse of black-and-white marble floor in a checkerboard design, broken only by the round carved table and its silver tray for calling cards. Then she raised her eyes, allowed her feet to find their precise accustomed position on the steps, and walked to the *sala* for tea as though she were making an entrance at a ball. In fact, there had been balls here in the old days, and she remembered walking down toward the blur of uniforms and gold and ruffled shirts. Her eyesight had improved with age, but even then it had never betrayed her on one point; she always knew where Tomás was standing and went straight to him, head high, confident of the hand that would lead her to the music.

Now her social life was of quite another temper. Drastically reduced to the point of austerity, it consisted almost entirely of occasional calls from old friends. Some evenings, the chauffeur would bring the big, prewar Mercedes to the front door. Marta, the fat, flurried *muchacha*, rushed down the steps in a confusion of gathered skirts and muttered concern. She held the door open to Doña Luisa's more peaceful progress, to the last moment advising both a shawl and a fan, warning against too much or too little breeze from the window. The Mercedes always moved off before she could finish, and Doña Luisa, sitting as erect in her car as she did in her own room, watched the hibiscus and bougainvillaea that banked the turn of the drive, the break in the shrubbery through which she could see a corner of her carefully nurtured rose garden— tiresome to grow in Manila's steamy climate—and then the high white adobe walls cut by severe wrought-iron gates.

This evening, at the corner where the narrow private road met one of the city's wider streets, Ramón, the chauffeur, slowed to a stop as usual. Manila streets were still filled with the hectic, rattling, makeshift traffic that combined legacies of the war days, when there was no gasoline and people traveled in pony-drawn carriages and on bicycles, with the reappearance of a few private cars and the postwar "jeep-

neys"—surplus army jeeps converted into little buses. Along
the roadsides moved slower processions of pushcarts, wheel-
barrows, and pedestrians, and street corners were loud with
the chatter of women selling duck eggs or boiled sweet
potatoes. There was always a few minutes' wait before Ramón was able to find a space in the cross traffic and, sounding
his horn almost continually, could maneuver the Mercedes
through the haphazard bustle to the small, tree-shaded
square where the church of Santa Teresa still stood, untouched by the bombings, incongruously serene.

Doña Luisa had, from her girlhood, worshiped in Santa
Teresa's whenever her family had been in Manila. She walked
up the shallow stone steps, Ramón solicitously at her elbow,
through the carved wooden doors, and into the familiar darkness of the interior. There she knelt in the aisle, crossed
herself, rose with her customary deliberation, and moved
toward the candlelight and faintly smoky fragrance of in-
cense surrounding the altar. Before she settled in the corner
of the pew she always occupied, she knelt in prayer, her
mantilla folding in soft shadows along her face. She then sat
back, her missal in her lap, her fingers busy with her rosary
of pearls, and waited for the service to begin.

In those few moments, Doña Luisa saw that a girl sat in the
pew immediately across the aisle from her. Something about
her appearance teased at Doña Luisa's memory, but she
could think of no occasion when they might have met. The
front of the church was nearly always empty in the evenings.
The sparse congregation which had gathered to make the
novena to Saint Anthony sat mostly in the back pews, their
baskets and bundles beside them, having come directly from
work for this short period of worship before they hurried out
of the door to their scattered homes. Doña Luisa noticed with

approval that the girl wore no make-up, that her straight black hair was modestly and conventionally dressed in a bun high on the back of her head, covered with a muslin scarf, that her plain white suit was obviously much worn but clean and neatly pressed, and behind each observation she worried at the thought that she had seen the girl before.

At the first sound of chanting, Doña Luisa addressed her full being to her devotions. Piety had always been as natural to her as good manners, but since her husband's death she had found in herself a capacity for religious experience that she had not suspected she possessed. It had been like discovering an underground stream, hidden for years beneath a placid stretch of country, that had gushed to the surface from some immense shifting of rock strata deep within the earth. Even this she attributed obscurely to Tomás's protective power, and gratefully accepted almost as a parting gift from him the strength to bear his loss through this new awareness of communion with God. The prayers she said for Tomás's soul, the novenas she offered, her daily attendance at Mass, and her regular visits to Santa Teresa's to make the Stations of the Cross were far from formalities. They were, by now, the occasions when she felt truly alive, the source of spiritual refurbishment from which she drew the courage to take her, with equanimity, through the duties and regime of her days.

When the last words of the Benediction had been said, Doña Luisa rose to leave. She stepped into the aisle to genuflect, to cross herself once more. The girl in the pew across from her didn't move. She was sitting rigidly, almost unnaturally still. As Doña Luisa turned to make her leisured way out of the church, the girl suddenly hid her face in her hands. The slack slumping of the body, the trembling shoulders seemed a clear indication that the girl was crying.

Doña Luisa walked on a few yards, the click of her heels on the stone floor clearly audible in the emptying church, and then paused to consider what she had seen. Very seldom had the mysterious (but obviously distressing) plight of a stranger been brought so sharply to her attention.

Outside Santa Teresa's, the chauffeur stood beside the big gray Mercedes watching for Doña Luisa to appear on the steps. She was usually the last to leave and he had idly watched the others, knowing from experience that he was unlikely to find any pretty girls among the evening worshipers. Early-morning Mass was usually much more satisfactory. He had waited for some time, admiring the high gloss he kept on the car and raising his eyes at intervals to the cavernous doorway, before it occurred to him that Doña Luisa was unusually late. His immediate thought was that she must be taken ill and he leaped up the steps and into the church ready for an emergency. He found her standing halfway along the aisle, her back to the entrance.

She turned at his precipitous approach. "Do not look so worried, Ramón," she said. "I am perfectly well, only concerned about that young woman in the pew there. She appears to be in some kind of trouble."

Ramón flicked a quick look at slender ankles and a trimly modeled figure, and then at the shaking hands covering the girl's face. "She is crying, Doña Luisa," he said, as though he had never seen such a thing before.

"Evidently. Please ask her to come to me." She watched him carefully as he walked the short distance, touched the girl lightly on the shoulder, and muttered something indistinguishable to her. Properly enough, the girl's first expression was a mixture of irritation and astonishment. She replied to

Ramón in a low tone but sharply and, Doña Luisa guessed, arrogantly. Ramón burst into further whispered speech, pointing to the stiff old figure still standing in the aisle. The girl said nothing. Ramón began again, a longer exposition. At last, the girl shrugged and stood up. Doña Luisa found herself pleased both by her evident reluctance and by the straight Victorian character of the girl's walk as she approached.

"You will forgive my intrusion, I hope," Doña Luisa began. "A privilege, or so I excuse myself, of age."

"It is very kind of you to be concerned. I didn't mean to make my troubles public—that's why—"

"That's why you are in church and not at home."

"I often come here, to—settle things, or anyway to think about things—"

Doña Luisa saw that the girl had not, after all, been crying. She took the unemotional voice and expression for a deeper kind of despair. "I understand now the reason why I thought I knew you. Probably I have seen you here before."

"Possibly. Fewer interruptions here from—well, fewer interruptions. I often come."

"But you are distressed about something—"

"Please—it's very kind of you—but I'm not sick, or unhappy, I mean about—"

"About matters of the heart?"

"No. Only matters of money."

"That is much simpler," Doña Luisa said, moving down the church and including the girl in her progress as if it were the most natural demand of etiquette. "Matters of money can always be arranged, and in that I can perhaps help. Please, if you are not expected elsewhere, get into my car. We will drive together and talk—"

"Oh, no—and why should you worry yourself about a stranger?"

"My friends need no worry, and it is only strangers that one can help in so straightforward a way."

"You're too generous. People must—"

"Not generous. Probably it would be more correct to say that I am selfish. I have found that it is truly better to give than to receive, but, I am afraid, in a more mundane way than the Gospel intended us to understand. In giving I was showered with rewards. It must be selfish, then, to seek such satisfactions."

Still the girl hesitated, looked helplessly at Ramón, a tidy white wedge of a figure in his gold-buttoned uniform, holding the car door open in a correct stance, his face alive with curiosity. "But," she said, daunted at last, "but—I could be just anyone."

Doña Luisa laughed with a sudden girlish gaiety. " 'Anyone' is the person we seek," she said. She climbed into the car, patted the seat beside her, and, as the girl followed, added, "My husband taught me that. He was 'just anyone' when he courted me. He ended by being the only person in my life."

"Won't he be angry?" The girl arranged herself in her corner, feet together, knees covered.

"*Wouldn't* he have been?" Doña Luisa corrected. "He is dead. No, he wouldn't. He was always pleased to see either generosity or impulse in me. It is the only form of adventure left, he used to tell me."

"I'm not much of an adventure," the girl said, returning sullenly to her own trobles.

"You can't tell," Doña Luisa said, and then led them into an exchange of names. She frowned at the girl's response.

"Kay?" she said. "That is not a name. And what of your family?"

"Catalina," the girl amended quickly. "I am used to being Kay at my work. My family name is Gómez—we come from Mindanao, where we had pineapple plantations—"

"Gómez. There is a family Gómez near us—sugar—in Negros—"

"Related. But we don't speak since my family, *and* our poor pineapples, were ruined in the war." She paused and added bitterly, "Money, you see."

"I see. But they could have helped you—"

"Not the Gómez family. Not even my own bit of it. My mother was too filled with mourning for my two brothers— both killed. A daughter was no comfort to her, only someone to see safely married to get off her hands. I wanted to be an artist—I couldn't bring myself to marry, just like that, I mean, just not to be a liability."

"I understand. If one is brave about nothing else, one must be brave about that. I, too, married against my mother's wishes."

"But you—" the girl began, and then tact or second thoughts kept her from continuing.

"But I, you were going to say, could afford to. I didn't think so at the time. It was the most courageous act of my life. Money imposes penalties—not the least of them is that the penalties seem so trivial to the poor. No, quite simply I was in love, you see, as well as rich. You, on the other hand, appear to be neither."

"I hadn't intended to ask for sympathy."

"And I didn't expect to give it. In words, that is. I wanted only to help—does that seem impertinent to you? I know it can seem an insult—"

"Oh, *no!*" the girl said. "How *could* I have made you feel that!" Her emphasis and her spurt of warmth changed the whole tone of the conversation. "The fact is, I'm not even suffering splendidly for—you know—my art. No starving in garrets, no desperate choices between a loaf of bread or a new canvas, no—well, no romantic poverty, in short. I work in a dress shop in Escolta, Madame Rosa's, where the pay is adequate—enough to eat and share a room, that is—but the hours are long. Even if I had the space, by the time I get home the light for painting is gone."

"What sort of painting interests you?"

"A special kind," Kay said. "Even when I was a little girl at the convent. Before I knew such painting had a recognized name. The sisters were first puzzled, and then disapproving. I couldn't help it."

Doña Luisa recognized the intensity in Kay's voice, but entirely misunderstood her words. "My husband was very tolerant of modern painting," she assured Kay. "Before it was fashionable, I mean, so don't be afraid that you will shock me. I am used to stretching my mind beyond its comprehension." She said this rather grandly, as though some criticism had been implied.

"He sounds wonderful," Kay remarked.

"Yes," Doña Luisa replied soberly, "wonder is exactly what he brought to my life." Thinking of Tomás, she decided he would have approved of Kay, her manner, her rather sedate Spanish. (Like Doña Luisa herself, he had detested slang, but for a different reason. He loved the grace and cadence of the language; she felt that slangy talk was merely a mark of poor breeding.) Most of all, he would have liked Kay's determined independence. He knew the toll that straitened means could take of one's dignity. "Tell me," she said, "if you are willing, a little more of what brought you to this—to the moment I witnessed in Santa Teresa's, I mean."

Ramón took his usual route, following, as much as possible, the wide beautiful arc of Manila Bay, taking advantage of the rebuilt stretches of Dewey Boulevard, avoiding the ruined palaces and churches of Intramuros, the old walls enclosing now only graceful façades backed by rubble, blinded houses around a fine plaza, squatters' huts, goats, pigs, barefoot children scrambling over crumbling masonry. But today the old lady was too immersed in conversation to look out across the muddy green water of the Bay to the brown and green islands beyond the harbor, to the misty crocodile outline of Corregidor and the bracketing peninsulas of Cavite and Bataan. Ramón stared ahead himself, trying hard to listen to the low-pitched talk behind him. As it turned out, he heard nothing clearly until they all returned to the Salablanca house. There he held the car door open for Doña Luisa. The girl stepped out first and offered her hand to the old lady, who nodded politely but made no use of it. "Very well, then, Catalina," she said in a friendly way. "I will see you here tomorrow. Come at one o'clock. Luncheon is always at two. We can talk before."

"Yes, Doña Luisa, tomorrow."

"Ramón will drive you home." She had one foot on the steps when the girl broke in, "No—no, thank you. It would require too many explanations—a car like this. I live in a poor quarter."

Doña Luisa turned, with a suddenly vulnerable look on her face. "Forgive me, my dear. How thoughtless of me—of course, please, return as you wish."

Ramón, however, had the brief excitement of announcing the news to Marta, Angelita, and the other servants. Marta looked at him with scorn. "Publish it in the papers," she said. "Had you forgotten tomorrow is Sunday? Of course there will be a guest for luncheon—Señora Moreno, as usual."

Smiling straight into Angelita's eyes, Ramón hadn't bothered to turn to Marta as he described the encounter with Kay and the invitation overheard on the front steps. He was pleased with their incredulous response—a *guest* after all these years, a *real* guest (not counting, of course, the regular visits of Señora Moreno, of the priest, of the secretaries of various charities)—a penetration of outside life into this shuttered house. But later that night, lying in Angelita's arms, he could give no answer to her sleepy questions "But *who* is she?" and "Why? Just because she was crying? Everybody cries."

"I don't," Ramón said lightly, "not when I'm with you," to which Angelita answered vaguely, "*She* doesn't either. She is only sad all the time," and then, as Ramón got up and dressed hurriedly and worriedly because he would be missed, she added, "I shall be the one to cry, in the end."

Even the next day, when Kay arrived promptly at the appointed time, the puzzles about her and her place in the house remained unsolved. She and Doña Luisa talked privately for most of an hour. Later, they were joined by the other guest, old Mrs. Moreno. Marta served luncheon in the big, cool dining room, eavesdropped unobtrusively, but learned virtually nothing. Mrs. Moreno, who was entertained at the house at least a couple of times a week, was the obstacle. Her lively drumming of conversation filled the slow afternoon with news of engagements, marriages, births among her own and other people's children and grandchildren, of recent parties (with detailed descriptions of the food served —"the kind of house," she remarked of one, "where they serve the cheese *after* the fruit"), of visiting relatives, or visits to haciendas, of clothes, of heat, of the changing society of Manila. She was a plump, smiling woman, with fat little hands moving constantly. Her gush of talk displayed great good humor and occasionally an unexpected grasp of the nature and motives of the people around her.

Kay was almost entirely silent. Doña Luisa made an occasional inquiry about someone or something with an expression that hoped to hear only that all was well. At three, she rose from the table, smiled at Kay, said goodbye to her guests, and followed her usual regime of retiring to her room for the siesta hours. Small cups of sweet black coffee were served to the others in the green-and-gold *sala*.

Facing Mrs. Moreno warily across the coffee table, Kay prepared herself for a much more exacting inquisition than Doña Luisa's unworldly questioning. It had taken her considerable time, careful reconnoitering, and, of course, that measure of good luck without which no plan succeeds to make her way into this house. She was determined not to lose this first foothold to the knowing, if cheerful, mind behind the clouding talk of Mrs. Moreno. She must acquit herself honorably in the exchange and, if possible, make a friend— or at least an ally.

Mrs. Moreno began her devious inquiries with the most disarmingly social remarks. "I am so pleased that Luisa invited you. I take it as a good sign that she has allowed a new interest to come into her life."

"But surely she must have many interests."

"Her charities? No, those are duties more than interests."

"Perhaps she simply sees me as part of them."

"Luisa owes you no duty," Mrs. Moreno said, with a wide, merry smile to cover the harshness of her words. "Such excellent coffee! And isn't this charming china? It was given her as a wedding present—the de Luzes? No, I can't remember now. My memory is entirely deserting me!"

Kay frowned and said awkwardly, "I only meant that Doña Luisa seems so generous she probably extends her help to anyone who needs it."

"And you need her help?"

"Well, not exactly—"

"But perhaps you would rather not talk about it. I hope you'll forgive me. You see, you are what I might call something of an *event* in this house." She added, "I am very fond of Luisa, you know," and Kay was quite aware that the comment was not irrelevant. It was equally clear that Mrs. Moreno expected her to explain her presence.

"Doña Luisa and I met in church and she very kindly invited me to come here today."

Quite unsatisfied with this bald statement, Mrs. Moreno gave a little laugh of protest. "But so kind of *you* to give up your time so freely! It's a consideration one no longer expects from the young."

"The alternative would have been a sandwich in a snack bar —not much to give up."

"Ah, there are the compensations of youth and liberty with the sandwich, a better relish—excuse me for sounding fanciful—than the cook's delicious sauces. However, quite selfishly, may I hope that I will see you here often?"

Kay decided that nothing less than directness and a full unvarnished story would make a favorable impression on Mrs. Moreno. Accordingly, she set her coffee cup down with care, fixed her candid gaze on the shrewd, round face opposite her, and said, "I'll be coming every Sunday. Doña Luisa has been good enough to offer me a room where I can work at my painting. I daresay it's ridiculously ambitious, but I hope to be an artist, and at home—that is, the boarding-house room that I share with another girl—there is neither the space nor the light for painting."

"And you expect to become an artist working only one day a week?" Mrs. Moreno seemed gently amused.

"Idiotic, isn't it?" Kay's voice was cold. "However, I have no alternative. The rest of my days are spent, quite sordidly, in earning a living."

"How admirable! Believe me, there are few things that I respect as much as independence in our modern girls. When I look back on it, our youth provided us with such a *limited* life. We were equipped for really nothing more than mar-riage and motherhood. Oh, I know I must sound ungrateful for our privileges—I don't mean to be—indeed, I'm not. For, after all, every girl ultimately wants to marry and have chil-dren. But for those—like you—who have brains and talent beyond the simple needs of domesticity—which is, to be frank, a regrettably narrow world—I'm sure a career must seem a necessity for—for *self-fulfillment*! And to have the courage to pursue it! Truly, I admire you!"

Kay couldn't help laughing and received, in exchange, a sly, appreciative look from her companion. "I must assure you, Mrs. Moreno, my work is in no sense a career. Like you, I have no training. But the sisters in the convent in Zam-boanga did teach me embroidery and sewing. And now," she added unemphatically, "I'm employed in a dress shop."

"A seamstress?" asked Mrs. Moreno, startled.

"A seamstress is exactly what I am, though Madame Rosa—the owner—prefers to call me a 'fashion consultant,' be-cause I can sketch a few designs for customers who aren't quite certain what they want. She feels that having a fashion consultant gives her establishment a bit of class. But you're right in thinking I wanted independence."

"Your family must be very proud of you. Imagine taking on the difficulties of such a life in a city like Manila! And all for the sake of the ideal of independence! Without a doubt, they are filled with approval and respect for such a brave spirit."

"Not at all," Kay said, and then answered Mrs. Moreno's real question. "I left home against their wishes—or so they maintain. Actually, I think they were quite pleased to get rid of me. Don't look so shocked—they are not heartless people. Uncaring, perhaps, but not intentionally cruel. You see, my mother was widowed when I was a baby. Ever since I can remember, we have lived with my uncle and his family. My father was the younger brother, and while he was alive he and my uncle managed our pineapple plantations together. After his death, we became not exactly poor relations—they were very good to us, perhaps reluctantly so, but still honorable about giving my brothers and me a proper education—but we were always made aware of our dependent position in the household. I'm afraid I would seem very petty and touchy to you if I were to describe all the small humiliations—the clothes, altered and shortened, handed down to me by my cousins; the visits to Dansalan on which we were not invited because of the extra expense—none of them important by themselves, only galling, but taken all together over the years . . . Anyway, I made up my mind when I was very young to get away as soon as I could. My brothers and I plotted it together. They promised to look after me, and as soon as they got jobs of their own, they saved every penny to send me to college in America, where I would, at last, be free. That was the year of Pearl Harbor—"

"And you couldn't go?" Mrs. Moreno interrupted. "What a disappointment!"

Kay stared out into the garden as if she were scanning some distant horizon beyond the flame trees. Continuously following Mrs. Moreno's lead, Kay said, "Yes. I stayed on in Zamboanga. My brothers joined the army."

"But after the war? Couldn't they—"

Kay shook her head.

"Oh, I can guess," Mrs. Moreno exclaimed, in a voice that knew the fickle ways of the world. "It happens so often! They got married and suddenly found that there was, after all, no place for you in their homes."

"They were both killed in the war."

Mrs. Moreno looked suddenly very old and very tired.

"I have always been deeply patriotic," she said. "My husband was a great friend of Aguinaldo. He always believed and worked for our independence. I'm afraid I was too feminine —perhaps 'frivolous' is the more accurate, though less flattering, word—to be of any practical help to him. However, I sympathized with all my heart. Perhaps it is fortunate that he did not live to see our humiliation at the hands of the Japanese. Yet he would have been proud—*so* proud—of our young men—like your brothers—who fought so gallantly. But when the price of such ideals is extracted from our very hearts—as it was for you—patriotism becomes too harsh a taskmaster. How you must hate—as I do—those who killed your brothers! And—let us be honest—those among our own people who collaborated with them in their villainy!"

There was a silence and then Kay continued, without any plea for condolence in her tone. "However, I did manage to get the independence I'd set my heart on. I hadn't expected it would be quite like this—in fact, I hadn't really known what

I did expect when I came to Manila. The freedom of a big city, certainly, and all the golden chances for a life of variety and interest. That sort of thing, yes, and most of all *people*. I don't, of course, mean just crowds. I thought, in an imprecise way, of being surrounded by stimulating individuals who were all *doing* something. I hadn't formulated exactly what I fancied they'd be doing. I'm sure I sound very foolish to you."

Mrs. Moreno was listening to Kay with an intent, judicial air.

Kay thought that she must somehow have managed to overcome the first, most obvious barrier of Mrs. Moreno's suspicion. Feeling on slightly firmer ground, she went on, "I had very little money when I arrived. I found it was even less than it seemed—I hadn't allowed for the high cost of living in Manila and—oh, well, there were so many things I hadn't taken into account. I hadn't ever been on my own before, so you can imagine how ill-equipped I was to cope with the simplest things—a place to stay, a job, my next meal—anything. I was entirely untutored in the ways of a big city." She smiled at Mrs. Moreno. "I'm afraid there isn't any dramatic finale to this story. You learn quickly, when you have to, that the city imposes its own terms. I went to the usual employment agencies and took the first job that was offered me. Now all my giddy imaginings have shrunk to a routine of days in Madame Rosa's steamy little establishment, and evenings when I try to work—that is, to do what I consider my 'real' work. It is also my only pleasure."

"You mean, I suppose, your painting."

"Sketching, to be exact. I take my sketch pad to a café or to any sort of oasis I can find—the garden of the Manila Hotel, a bomb site in Intramuros, often to the Santa Teresa church steps." Indeed, it had been in that peaceful square that she had first seen the big gray Mercedes and the imposing figure of its occupant. On subsequent occasions, she had learned from the verger, in response to her casual inquiries, of Doña Luisa's great wealth, great piety, and great generosity. "I couldn't very well carry about all the paraphernalia of canvases and easels and paints to such places. That is why Doña Luisa's kind offer means so much to me." Kay said all this with the utmost simplicity, knowing that Mrs. Moreno's encouraging nods and small sympathetic exclamations were no gauge of her response.

"So young and so unafraid! I would have been quite daunted by the mere idea of making my way alone in Manila! But then I'm sure you must have friends—family contacts, or those you have found for yourself?"

"Friends?" Kay repeated, giving the word an almost archaic flavor. "No. No friends. Not that the girls at Madame Rosa's are forbidding. On the contrary, we talk incessantly about clothes, new hairdos, their boyfriends."

"I see what you mean."

"As for my family, you would think them hopelessly provincial, I'm afraid."

"My dear child—" Mrs. Moreno fluttered her hands in protest.

"And you would be right. They have no contacts in Manila."

There was silence for a moment; then Kay said, in a voice that was both troubled and determinedly honest, "I know what you must be thinking, and I know that, quite rightly, you want to protect your friend and must regard me with some suspicion. What I *don't* know is how to convince you that I am not here to take advantage. After talking to Doña Luisa, I had even thought—perhaps impertinently—that I might be able to do something for her in return."

Mrs. Moreno gave her a close look. Clearly the girl was astute. As to her good faith—well, possibly, on occasion, it was wise to take a risk, thought Mrs. Moreno, who liked excitements. "She has needed solace of some sort and found none. Old friends—it is unfortunate but true—are of little use except to pass the time. There was the church, naturally, but even the church, I'm much afraid, can only console you about your own death, not the loss of other people. She was nearly mad for a while after her husband died."

"From her description, he seems to have been a marvelous person," Kay said with enthusiasm, as much because she felt she had passed some unstated test as from any real appreciation of the dead man.

"Remarkable," Mrs. Moreno commented blandly. "But they had no children—that's really the trouble. There was nothing left for her when Tomás went, except to tend her private shrine. That, perhaps, is where you can help. She prayed and prayed for children."

"Be a daughter to her, do you mean?" Kay asked, with a touch of irony.

Mrs. Moreno smiled appreciatively. "I suppose that *is* what I mean—"

"It may not, however, be what she wants of *me*—or what I'm capable of—"

"We must leave that to time and temperament," Mrs. Moreno said, almost as a conspiracy. "And now I must be going." She rose and smoothed her skirt with her padded hands. "Can I drop you anywhere?"

Kay accepted the ride with alacrity, feeling that it would be a good thing for Mrs. Moreno to see where she lived, to be able to carry away with her an impression of very modest but respectable surroundings to lend confidence to her picture of Kay. All the way, while Mrs. Moreno produced further little freshets of talk about the inconveniences and disorganization of postwar Manila, Kay re-enacted their earlier conversation in her mind and was moderately satisfied.

In the weeks that followed, it was an easy shift for Kay (listening intently and gauging each mood, each confidence to determine her own behavior as both receptive and independent), particularly with Mrs. Moreno as an ally, to become absorbed with virtually no fuss into the Salablanca household. On Sundays, she came to the house in the morning, scattered her equipment on an upstairs veranda, and, interrupted only for meals, painted away until the light changed to the useless gold of evening. Soon these occasions became proper weekends when she arrived on Saturday afternoons, stayed for dinner and the night, and could begin her work early the next day.

One Sunday, at luncheon, with Mrs. Moreno smiling and nodding approval, Doña Luisa made her suggestion—her thoughtful proposal which she claimed was prompted by self-interest—and Kay, with becoming reluctance, accepted it. Arriving the next day with an American fiber suitcase and a straw basket filled with her things, she was shown to the room that Angelita had prepared. Partly from caution, partly because she was determined that this should be a permanent change in her life, she had left no address either at Madame Rosa's or with the girl whose room she had shared. She intended now to take her duties seriously, to establish that tricky balance (as she described it to herself) between paid companion, guest, and relative of sorts—at least someone with rights.

Afterward, when she was, as usual, alone with Mrs. Moreno for coffee in the *sala*, she said with gratitude, "I'm sure this must be your doing—"

"My dear child! Luisa would have thought of it anyway. Perhaps I hastened the plan a little and that is all to the good. Neither Luisa nor I have many more years. And what about your youth? That will not last forever, either!"

"Oh, *youth*—"

"No, no! Do not take on that air of easy scorn simply because youth does not yet seem of consequence to you. We cannot waste this precious—and oh, so perishable!—asset in toiling away at Madame Rosa's."

Touched by Mrs. Moreno's "we," Kay said, "Well, I shall do my best to put it to Doña Luisa's service," and meant it.

"I haven't a doubt that you will—and, believe me, it will give me great pleasure, too, to see you established here. I had one anxiety—I always think it best to express such feelings openly—I worried that your position here might carry distasteful, or even abrasive, reminders of your life at home. I wanted to assure you—"

"Mrs. Moreno," Kay interrupted with remorse in her voice, "how *could* you be concerned about that? It's all my fault! Truly, I never intended to seem so pitiable. But nothing could be more different from my home than this house and the atmosphere and people it contains." As a matter of fact, though Kay had more or less anticipated some kind of offer from Doña Luisa, she hadn't dared to hope that it would be so all-embracing. Neither had she expected Mrs. Moreno's sensitivity to the hazards in this change which, clearly, she had engineered. She added, in all sincerity, "Mrs. Moreno, I'm not used to such consideration. I don't know what to say."

"Say nothing, my dear, say nothing! That will make a very pleasant contrast to my volubility! Let me give you a few hints that may be of service to you. . . ."

When she had settled in, Kay conscientiously learned and accustomed herself to the steady tempo of life in the Salablanca house. Like Doña Luisa, she breakfasted in her room, and met the old lady only at ten o'clock for a ritual tour of the garden. By then, Doña Luisa had already been to early Mass, had sipped her chocolate in her room while she gave orders to the cook and to Marta for the day, had changed into one of the pale gray or blue linen dresses that she wore for the mornings, and had stood for a few moments on the conservatory steps under her parasol surveying the garden as a whole before she made her more detailed inspection. Together they examined the clumps of little white orchids, with woody stems, attached at shoulder level to the boles of palm trees; admired the *cadenas de amor*, a tendrilly pale green vine, with bright pink bell-like flowers, tumbling over the low hedges; inhaled the fragrance from the patches of *sampaguita* that grew hidden and shy like lilies of the valley. The gardener followed respectfully behind them, listening to Doña Luisa's loving descriptions of the character and ways of different flowers (for Kay), interspersed with instructions about pruning, cutting, or transplanting (for him). Later they separated, Doña Luisa to sit at her desk in the library, answering letters and appeals from charities, going over the estate accounts sent to her weekly by her manager in Negros, remembering to acknowledge birthdays, saints' days, and anniversaries, refusing invitations; Kay to return to the veranda outside her room, her canvases, her paints, and her schemes. Like partners in a slow minuet, they met again (for luncheon), parted again (for the siesta hours), met again (for *me-*

rienda and a drive in the Mercedes and sometimes for church), parted again (to change for dinner), met again (for the late-evening meal and conversation afterward), parted again (for bed and their separate, incommunicable dreams).

Sometimes Doña Luisa would suggest that Kay break the routine—telephone a friend, go to a film. "Isn't this too quiet for you?" she asked. "An old woman and her empty house?"

"No," Kay said, smiling at her in the lamplight of the drawing room. "No, I prefer it here. I have no friends—not the girls at Madame Rosa's anyway." Privately, she assured herself that there was time enough.

"You see, I have had enough of wandering through the streets of Manila, of going to movies alone because I didn't wish to return to my room. This house—and you in it—have a great air of contentment."

"It is an air that Tomás left. I am glad to share it." And once again Doña Luisa would slip into reminiscences of her husband. "Once," she said, "oh—years ago, before you were born—I had to leave him to go to Switzerland with my mother. She was very ill, and it was a long slow cure. Tomás had, of course, long since taken over the management of the estates in Negros. He loved the place—so did I in those days—and he stayed behind to take his usual vigorous part in estate affairs. Oh, yes, he had great acumen for such things, for all his sensibility to art. A month went by, six weeks, two months—I received no letter from him. I was first worried, then angry, then afraid that he had found a life without me. At last, a letter came. It contained nothing but a poem he had written for me."

Doña Luisa closed her eyes and recited softly,

"How shall I write across
These continents and seas

Of other lives
In other centuries?

Should I wish you here?
Should I attempt to set
Shows in the tropics?
Give a weapon to regret?

This unconnected time
Moves slyly, while I frame
Unanswered questions,
Listen for your name.

North and South dissolve,
Journeys in love's day
Have only one direction,
Can only lead away."

"This unconnected time," Doña Luisa repeated, her eyes
filled with tears. "It was such a simple explanation, really,
although my mother never understood it—continued to feel,
until her death, that Tomás had been remiss."

Kay, unembarrassed, asked, "Your mother never could
accept your marriage?"

"She neither accepted nor disrupted it. She retired from
it." Retired, Doña Luisa recalled, thankful to leave behind a
situation that was too much for her. From the beginning, she
had repeated helplessly, "If only your father were alive, he
would know what to do." The girl Luisa had repeated equally
often and with great decision, "But *I know* what to do," and,
in fact, she had known from the first time that she had met
him. She had gone with her mother to pay a formal call on
the Morenos after their marriage and had found Tomás sitting in the *sala*, among the ladies and the teacups, laughing
at some remark. All the later arguments that pounded away
interminably at the facts that he had no money, no position,

no future—a good family, yes, but impoverished beyond reclaim and relying only on wits and charm to get along—all
this was useless against Luisa's conviction. To a remark
which lost its edge with repetition—"He is an adventurer,
can't you see?"—she would only reply inflexibly, "I know him
and I know he loves me," until her mother, despairing and
in tears, would say, "Talk to Father Joachim about it—that is
all I can think of—perhaps he can help. . . ."

Other fragments of their story and their life Kay heard
from Mrs. Moreno in their afternoon talks, which had, by
now, become habitual landmarks of the week, satisfactory to
both. "Oh, their first party—she had no idea, had never given
a party before. Of course, Tomás came to me and between
us we did it all, though their staff was bigger then, like
everybody's—but even the flowers! And you know she's good
at flowers. Poor Luisa! She was terrified, really white with fear
(and none of us wore cosmetics in those days), walking
blindly down the stairs to face, from her expression, a firing
squad. Tomás was magnificent with her, guiding her constantly, enlisting one's help—mine, at least—simply with a
smile, a look. I suppose, in a way, he *must* have loved her."
Mrs. Moreno shrugged, somehow indicating both generosity
and skepticism.

Kay stared at her. "He was very good-looking, I take it?"

Mrs. Moreno looked amused. "Not at all. A shortish man,
and his features were too bold for his build. Luckily, he was
fair of skin, and he kept his hair." She added distantly, "He
had a charming singing voice."

Kay heard more about this later from Doña Luisa, about
the short hot evenings of the Visayans when they drove in
their carriage through the estate, past the cottages where the
men had returned from the sugar fields and the girls curtsied

to the carriage as it passed. She heard, too, about the hours of the sapphire nights when they sat on their deep porch surrounded by friends from neighboring haciendas ten and twenty miles away, and by relatives and visitors who came to stay for six months at a time. And the women in their muslin dresses with the starched, ballooning organdy sleeves, pale as moths in the shadows and moonlight, and the men in thin embroidered shirts and narrow linen trousers, cigars glowing fitfully between laughter and talk, and the lilting of the girls as they sang love songs against the sweet complaining of guitars, and through it all the voice of Tomás singing with half-ironic intensity of fickle women, deserted suitors, and the sadness of love, his voice in whispered conversation and the touch of his hand in the dark—Kay was told it all in the city evenings of the lonely green-and-gold drawing room.

"And you never go back there any more?" she asked, at last.

"Not any more," Doña Luisa replied abruptly. "It isn't the same any more," and she rose, as though offended, to go to bed.

Another day Mrs. Moreno, in turn, contributed an explanation of this uncharacteristic sharpness. "Luisa's right, of course; it isn't the same—nothing is—but that isn't the reason why she doesn't go back. No. Oh, it was terrible . . . terrible. I wept with her myself. But should one weep for twenty years? I've told her—yes, often!—that she diseases herself. Surely even the greatest tragedy must fade, *should* fade? But she is beyond reach. He died there, you see, suddenly, without her. . . ."

"Oh, poor thing . . . poor thing," Kay said, hardly interrupting Mrs. Moreno.

"Yes. We all felt that, couldn't help feeling it, though she

was not so very popular, Luisa, too cold. Still, it was so unexpected, and to her—well, to everybody—so inexplicable."

"Why inexplicable? After all, people die and we—"

"He didn't die, like that; he was killed. Stabbed. An old-
fashioned kind of crime, I thought then, like vengeance,
though it seemed to everyone pointless . . . pointless, and, as
it turned out, perfect. They never found either the man who
did it or the dagger, and worst of all she wasn't even there,
so he died in the arms of another woman—"

"But there must have been a *reason*," Kay insisted, the
whole arched attitude of her body rejecting this melodrama.
"Robbery? Madness? *Some*thing—and this woman in whose
arms—"

"Oh, she was just a woman. That is, Luisa—and all of
us—could take her as just a woman. He died there by mistake.
We never knew why he was driving through the estate at that
hour of the night. One supposes that someone must have
stopped him on the road—his car was still there, hardly a
hundred yards from the nearest cottage. The same someone
evidently stabbed him and ran away. Not robbery—his
money and the gold ring he always wore were still on him.
She wears it now, on a chain around her neck. He dragged
himself to the cottage—really dragged; the path was black
with blood, or so they said. The woman and her husband who
lived there—sugar workers, naturally—could think only of
trying to help him." She opened her hands with a delicate air
of distaste. "Too late. And by the time they brought word to
the house, it was morning. Too late for everything. The
woman—Angelita's mother, as a matter of fact—must be
considered merely an accident, but to Luisa a heartbreak—
Tomás to die with another woman's hand on his forehead."

"No wonder."

"Yes, no wonder. She shocked a lot of people at that time because she wouldn't wear black. We, the rest of his friends, were the ones to mourn him publicly."

In Kay's memory, Doña Luisa's voice said, "I never wear black. Tomás didn't like it. He said that all my life I had been surrounded by black skirts—so many black skirts, governesses, religious instructors, my widowed mother, and her old friends. 'We must get rid of all these black skirts,' he said. 'They don't suit you or our life together.' So we did."

"She was still trying to please him," Kay told Mrs. Moreno. "And I think she was right. That loyalty took precedence over public convention—after all, he *did* love her, and he made her happy. She told me once he filled her life with wonder."

Mrs. Moreno, choosing her words with care, said, "Yes. He made her happy. One cannot ask for more than that." She sounded rather weary as she added, "Her money couldn't have been better spent."

Kay had been living with Doña Luisa for several months when she decided to make a place, a real place, for herself in the household—gradually and with hesitation—on a different kind of footing.

The moment seemed to have arrived when she could consider herself more relation than companion, someone who shared the intimate life of the household, knew family secrets, possessed a family loyalty. Tomás had brought to the life of Doña Luisa a knowledge of gaiety, a kind of exuberance. She might conceivably restore some of that lost vitality. Later, possibly, she could persuade Doña Luisa to go out, and, protected by the most imposing of chaperons, she could enter other great houses of Manila, those fortresses of the inaccessible families from whom she hoped to choose a husband. She had no doubt that she could provide for one of them (as perhaps Tomás had done) an equitable exchange of worldliness, charm, and a dutiful respect in return for security. She did not consider happiness. In a certain sense, she wasn't selfish.

It was a brief conversation with Doña Luisa that brought Kay to her suggestion. The old lady had been looking through a large portfolio of Kay's early sketches of the bombed sections of Manila. It did not occur to her that the pictures were clever rather than profound. She found in the quick, sure strokes of brush and ink that the city scenes lost none of their continually shifting activity, unfamiliar to her, and even in black and white kept a feeling of heat and intense color. She was especially touched by the barefoot children with enormous eyes and skinny legs playing or begging in Intramuros, climbing over the fluted, fallen columns, crouching forlorn on shattered steps in front of those beautiful shrapnel-chipped façades. The deceptively simple studies of women selling eggs and fruit on the pavements moved her as did the harsh and exact drawings of the slum alleys, the groups of dangerous young men, the saucy girls all paint and brave print dresses stepping from the filthy doorways. All of them indicated to her a depth of compassion in Kay, a bitter indictment of human misery from war and the predatory nature of city life. She remarked, with humility and almost inaudibly, "You have been given a tragic vision."

"How noble that sounds! No, these"—Kay flicked her fingers at the sketches—"are only what I saw of the city around me before I came to live here."

Doña Luisa said soberly, "I am afraid that your present surroundings may offer you another kind of desolation. I wish this were not so."

Kay paused a long time before she said, with a question in her voice, that perhaps—just perhaps—it might be pleasant to have a musicale some evening when the terrace, so lovely, and the piano, so seldom played, might be put to use and pleasure. A guitarist, perhaps, and a few people to enjoy the occasion. "It seems such a waste that only the two of us have the glory of these evenings. Am I imposing? Is silence what you prefer?"

With her big myopic eyes, Doña Luisa looked at Kay with a kind of incredulity. "Oh, that is just the sort of thing Tomás would have suggested! Without him, my imagination seems to have disintegrated. Yes, of course! While the flowers are in full splendor!" Instantly, she began to think of a list of guests. The Morenos, of course, both the old lady and her sons and daughters-in-law. Would their children be too young? Yes, we'd better omit the grandchildren. And then they might have some friends that they'd like to bring to such a party. "Tomás always said that there should be a mixture of ages. 'The old bore each other,'" she quoted mistily, "'and the young are so limited in their range of talk and feeling. Together they find much to enjoy in the contrasts.' Tomás knew about such things."

"He never bored anyone?"

"Never!"

Ever since Kay had arrived in the house, she had taken particular pains to get on well with the servants. She would make a point of complimenting the cook on an especially tasty meal, on the lightness of a soufflé, the subtlety of a sauce. To Marta, who was perhaps the most wary of this new arrival, she gave clear indications that she would in no way infringe upon Marta's position as more housekeeper than maid; and she never interfered with Marta's domination over the little *muchacha* who was her assistant.

With Angelita, Kay had a special subterranean understanding. From her veranda, she had often seen Angelita keep her secret rendezvous with Ramón in the garden, and watched her deep in conversation or responding to Ramón's impudent banter with gales of flirtatious giggles though her eyes were brimming with love. The first time Angelita had caught sight of Kay, she had been alarmed. But Kay had smiled and waved so pleasantly and so casually that Angelita, quite correctly, saw no reason to fear that Doña Luisa might hear of her affair. She occasionally came to Kay for advice about her clothes and entirely trusted her judgment about whether or not a certain style or color was becoming. Whenever they met on the verandas or stairs, they always exchanged a few words, and Kay soon learned that Angelita's moods, troubled or gay, depended on whether Ramón had been kind and affectionate or indifferent to her.

Even the *lavandera*, who seldom saw Kay, found her unexacting about how her clothes were washed and ironed—a welcome contrast to Marta's tyranny about the household linen and Doña Luisa's laundry. The boy whose sole job was to polish the floors with half a coconut husk and a heavy cloth fell into the habit of taking an inordinately long time over the upstairs veranda where he could watch Kay painting. One day, delighted and flattered, he posed for a sketch, and, when Kay formally presented it to him, rushed away to show it off to the other servants.

All of them were exhilarated by the preparations and fuss for Kay's musicale. Quantities of flowers, an elaborate menu, the best china and silver, the rearrangement of the *sala* furniture for the guitarist—the excitement and novelty of the occasion infected them all. They were quite as triumphant as Kay when the musicale turned out to be a great success.

At Kay's request, Mrs. Moreno had enthusiastically undertaken to supply the guest list. This had, of course, included her younger brother and his wife, her two sons and their wives. Around this central core of family members, she had cannily invited two friends of her sons', both bachelors. After all, she argued to herself, with Luisa's unassailable status to provide a background, there was no reason why Kay shouldn't move in the right social circles, and if it should happen that some young man . . . well, certainly Luisa could be counted on for a suitable dowry and—who knew?—perhaps even more.

Doña Luisa dressed, in her phrase, "correctly for the occasion" in a full-skirted long dress of beige satin, set off by dark topazes which her husband had given her because, he had said, they were the color of her eyes, and how amusingly surrealistic to wear "your eyes around your neck and on your earlobes, don't you think so?"

Mrs. Moreno, less magnificent but equally formal, arrived with her son and daughter-in-law. As the rest of the party joined them, she kept up a running commentary on social evenings as they used to be. The days in Iloilo when distinguished families gave dances that were really and truly Grand Balls—Grand Gestures, anyway—times of lavishness when the dancing would open with the *rigodon de honor*, a quadrille which established the dignity of the occasion. Later, one danced the *lanceros*, a measured Spanish dance popular with the aristocracy of the last century. The children were allowed to watch for a while and were then herded off to bed by starched and scolding nurses.

"Oh, but now, Luisa," she said to Doña Luisa, in a voice verging on doom, "where will we ever see those evenings again?"

"Alas, never. The old life of the haciendas is gone."

"Ah, think of the old days!" Mrs. Moreno said, ready for an exchange of complaints.

"Why?" Doña Luisa asked sharply, thinking, The old days would have been nothing without Tomás.

"Why, indeed?" agreed Mrs. Moreno, thinking, It is only Tomás that made the old days worth recalling.

However, with her chatter and her anecdotes, conversation flowed quite smoothly before dinner. Kay, balancing delicately between her roles as part daughter of the house, part guest, was unobtrusively careful to pay particular attention to the wives. Their conversation was not really so different from that of the girls at Madame Rosa's—clothes and hair styles and the doings of their friends. Children and servants were the only additional topics.

With the young bachelors, Kay was a warmly appreciative listener. Both had been in the army, and the one who took her in to dinner had fought on Corregidor. He gave her a detailed account of the campaign, finding her soft-eyed interest wonderfully stimulating. He seemed impervious to the inappropriateness of his grim story told amid the candlelight and flowers, the gleaming silver and the elaborate sequence of dishes. Contrasting in her mind the young man's description of his war experiences with her own pinched life of hiding and compromise in Japan, Kay was taken unawares by his sudden change of tone. "But why am I telling you all this? You were, perhaps, in Manila yourself through it all?"

"No, I was with my family in Zamboanga. Of course, we read about Corregidor."

"Ah, then you must have come in for the American bombings and landings—more destructive, I'm told, than the Japanese occupation."

Kay nodded. "Sometimes it was hard to remember they were rescuing us."

"But we *must* remember that they did," the young man said loyally. "General MacArthur promised he would return, and he did!"

"Oh, yes!" Kay agreed quickly. "We must never cease being grateful for that." She steered him then into less disturbing talk and set herself to entertain him without seeming in any way eager or flirtatious, for he was the one she had decided to concentrate on.

The other bachelor was less articulate but openly admiring of Kay's appearance—cool in light silk the color of lemon ice—though, as she learned, he was already engaged to be married. However, he danced with her repeatedly after dinner. On the terrace, half lit by the *sala* lamps, the young couples swayed together to the pianist's popular tunes, returning indoors, fanning themselves and smiling, for long intervals of the spidery intricacies of the guitarist's playing. The guests seemed, quite plainly, to be enjoying the evening. It was nearly one o'clock when they left.

Kay, alone in her room, was too excited to undress and go to bed at once. She sat by her open window watching the big stupid moths bumping against the lamp, and planning. With this first triumph behind her, she thought about expanding life in the old house in other ways. She would suggest different kinds of parties. She might take Doña Luisa to one or two art shows and similar outings. They might, for a change of scene, dine in that formidable stronghold of Manila society, the Spanish Club, which Kay had only heard about but never entered. And, of course, she must manage an occasion quite soon to meet the unattached young bachelor (at Mrs. Moreno's house?) and refresh his memory of her. Kay, looking contentedly down the vista of the months to come, felt with relief that she had, at last, found a future for herself.

The crisis about Angelita came steaming up through the house from the servants' quarters like a smell of cooking. It started with distant sounds of weeping, argument, persuasion, and then came flooding up the stairs on a note of voluble misery. In the bedroom, where Doña Luisa had breakfasted but had not yet been helped to dress by Angelita, it exploded into hysterics and finally a mulish obstinacy. Kay, standing on the veranda outside the bedrooms, could hear only the subtle sternness of Doña Luisa's words through the shuttered doors, but Angelita's frenzied crying rattled shamelessly through the corridors of the old impervious house: "I love him—I don't care—I want to stay—I *love* him!"

Kay, walking timidly in, found Angelita on her knees, covering Doña Luisa's hand with kisses, and saying, "I beg you —oh, I *beg* you—" Doña Luisa, standing straight as ever, glanced across at the half-open door, and before Kay could formulate her offer to "do something," she had commanded, "Catalina, will you please take Angelita back to her room? I will dress myself this morning."

Angelita had been too distracted between misery and fright to say anything more than "Please ask her—you can ask her, please, for me—" all the way to the kitchen, where Marta took her into a compassionate embrace. So it was not until Kay was walking through the garden with Doña Luisa later that morning that she heard the story.

"I'm afraid," Doña Luisa said austerely, "her predicament is more unfortunate than remarkable," and in the baldest possible words explained that Angelita was pregnant. "I would not have expected it from Ramón, who has a pleasant and respectful wife. His behavior cannot be excused. However, it is clear that Angelita must go, though in her very natural distress she seems unable to understand that.

We must wait until she is calmer."

Kay made no answer to that "we," and the morning proceeded in its usual form with only a sense of uneasiness from the servants' quarters and a furtive scurrying about the housework. Mrs. Moreno came to luncheon, and Marta, grimly serving the food and wine, did not even bother to eavesdrop, knowing that nothing of interest could be said in the dining room. Later, she listened to the talk over coffee while Doña Luisa took her siesta, and heard what she wished to know. Kay would have recounted the affair quite briefly, but Mrs. Moreno insisted on details, punctuated the talk with worried questions, and seemed distracted in a most uncharacteristic way.

The afternoon hours grew dense with the thickening atmosphere created by Mrs. Moreno's insistent repetition in varying forms of the barbed question "Well, what *can* be done about Angelita?" "Especially," Kay said, "when all she asks is to stay with Ramón no matter what."

"That is impossible! No, no, quite impossible! But it is Ramón who must be dismissed."

"And his wife? His children? That's what Doña Luisa says, you see—why should the entirely innocent suffer?"

"They suffer in any case. And why, for that matter, Angelita?"

"It's a tricky problem in morality—"

"Morality?" cried Mrs. Moreno in rising distress. "I'm talking about kindness, not punishment."

"But kindness to which of them?"

"Angelita, of course, Angelita!" Her hands flashed and fluttered like hummingbirds. "There can be no choice about that!"

"I'm afraid it's been made. She'll have to go—"

"Go? Go where?" She seemed quite disproportionately

heated. "Oh, listen—listen. I don't know what to do . . . what to say—"

"Nothing, I should think, unless you want to argue with her, and there seems no point in that. She sees no room for opinion in this decision."

"That is what I mean! Shall I tell her she *must* make room? That it might be a boy? That the name might continue?"

"I don't think I—"

"Haven't you wondered—or guessed? There was no mystery about Tomás's death, except to Luisa. The woman in the cottage—"

Kay said, "Oh—" on a long breath.

"—Angelita's mother, that is. During that long absence of Luisa's in Switzerland, we all had suspicions. But so, evidently, did he."

"The husband? The stranger on the road at night. I see." After a short, wretched silence, she said, "Vengeance, after all."

"Jealousy, rather. And anger. Perhaps they combine to make up vengeance—I scarcely know. I told you it had too fierce, too—too *historical* an air for my understanding. But you do see, don't you, why Angelita must stay and Luisa protect her? Tomás's child—"

"Tomás's child," Kay repeated numbly. She sat immobile in her chair, a trapped and hopeless expression on her face more suited to something hunted. With a kind of dreary impartiality, she surveyed the situation and saw her bright future slipping away. Self-pity does not become me, she thought, and I must start from that. "You must tell her," she said flatly to Mrs. Moreno, sounding like a schoolmistress.

"But it will break her heart!"

"Rubbish!" said Kay angrily. "His death did that." She

added, "As if some paltry infidelity could cancel out the happiness he gave her!"

"I think he loved her—Angelita's mother, I mean." And wistfully Mrs. Moreno thought, I know he did. It broke *my* heart.

"You needn't tell her that. We can be certain she won't ask." She frowned. "He must have been a splendid actor."

"Don't judge him! Don't make him seem so *commonplace*, a casual deceiver! You forget that he was very kind."

"In any case," Kay said, her affection for Doña Luisa bitterly taking precedence over her own concerns, "she must be told."

"And what about *you*—"

"I do not plan to oust Angelita."

"All the same—"

Mrs. Moreno broke off abruptly because both of them heard the steady, unmistakable footsteps of Doña Luisa on the stairway. Absorbed in questions, arguments, explanations, neither had noticed the afternoon sliding toward the early evening. "What shall I *say*?" Mrs. Moreno whispered, tense and urgent.

"Just tell her," Kay said, in a normal voice.

A moment, and then Doña Luisa entered. "Good afternoon. What a pleasant surprise that you have decided to stay for our *merienda*. Catalina must have entertained you well."

Mrs. Moreno, flustered and trembling, said, "I don't know where the time went. . . . I'm sorry . . . I'm so sorry—"

"Sorry?" Doña Luisa advanced without hurry to her usual place on the sofa. "My dear friend, why are you sorry? You have always been welcome in my house at any hour. How can I ever forget that it was in yours that I first met Tomás."

"Oh, Tomás!" Mrs. Moreno said, springing up in agitation from her chair. She sounded on the edge of tears. "We were talking—we were just talking about Angelita—*really*, I'm sorry—"

Doña Luisa smiled. "I know you like to talk; you talk easily. When we were girls, I used to be afraid of silences and admired you for your ready conversation. I found it a protection, too."

"But about Angelita—"

"Personally, I never listen to gossip. Tomás thought it vulgar. However, I am well aware that you take a great interest in the events of other people's lives. And surely, between old friends, it is unnecessary to apologize for gossiping about Angelita."

"Luisa, you must listen to me! I wasn't just gossiping about Angelita. I was wondering—I still don't know—how to tell you—what to do—"

"But I have already made up my mind about what to do. She must be sent back to Negros, of course."

"Oh, Luisa, Luisa!" cried Mrs. Moreno, somewhere between bewilderment and pleading. "Angelita is Tomás's daughter! Don't you understand? That's why he asked you to look after her—oh, my dear Luisa!—she is carrying his grandchild—please believe me, I wish it were not so! But I *had* to—" She broke down in uncontrollable sobbing and ran to the terrace doors.

Doña Luisa waited until she had quieted, and then said bleakly, "Please come and sit down. Marta will be bringing tea in a minute. Unless, of course, you would prefer coffee? We used to be told, when I was young, that coffee was bad for the complexion, but probably there is no truth in that."

"I have always drunk a lot of coffee," Mrs. Moreno said meekly.

"And have always had an excellent complexion. It proves,

I suppose, that one believes almost anything when one is young."

"Which does not," Mrs. Moreno reminded her with kindness, "remove the joy of either."

"Either?"

"Either youth or one's beliefs. And the joy they brought, I mean."

Doña Luisa nodded in a faraway manner. That was the first day in the memory of the household that she excused herself from dinner and retired early to her bedroom instead.

As Kay had known, it was only a question of time, and for all her useless wishing, she was hardly surprised when, some days later, Doña Luisa, with the most apologetic courtesy, dismissed her. An air of exhausted gentleness enveloped her as she said that of course no move would be made until suitable arrangements for Kay were properly settled. But to Kay this was a sentence (really in the judicial sense) and came with the unfairness of defeat.

Hopelessly, she tried not so much to argue—there was no arguing with gallantry, she felt—as to present a figure. The frame was less persuasive this time, and the calculation that had informed the pathos of the pew in Santa Teresa was now tempered with a true respect for dignity, also with fondness. Clasping her hands tightly on her knees and sitting very straight, she said, "I would like to— I mean, may I stay here with you?" She was determined not to make theatre out of this. "I could be a help to you—instruct Angelita—we get on well together—"

"Dear child—"

"I know I have no right to ask, after all the kindness you have shown me—kindness I have no way of repaying—"

"We do not speak in such terms, Catalina. 'Rights' and 'repayment.' I made no loans to you—"

"Gifts, then—"

"Or gifts. I told you when we first met that I am a selfish old woman. I needed the sense of life you gave this house. After so many years."

"And now it will be provided in a different way," Kay said, as a statement.

"But not in this house. No. Angelita will, of necessity, be elevated in station." (Of course, Kay thought. Too embarrassing for everyone concerned to remain here.) Doña Luisa continued, with complete simplicity, "I have decided to close this house. After so many years. I shall return to the Negros estate with Angelita. Together we will wait for the baby. And learn to love each other."

Kay stared at her hands. The opponents were too formidable. The daughter of Tomás holding the hostage, Tomás's grandchild, would receive from Doña Luisa the greatest acknowledgment she could offer (and one that he had surely merited) of her happiness with him.

"However," Doña Luisa said, "it is possible that you, too, may come to Negros. I shall be writing to the Gómez family, the ones with a plantation near mine—you remember you told me you were related?" She did not catch the sudden look of alarm in Kay's eyes and continued her placid explanation with all the careful consideration in the world. "I knew, my dear, that you would be too—if I may be excused an old-fashioned thought—too proud to ask their help yourself."

Breathless, as if she had been running, Kay protested ineffectually against this disaster. "Oh, no—oh, no—"

"Do not upset yourself, Catalina. It is their duty as relatives to take you in. They will surely see that. The alternative would be to write to your mother, but, knowing how you feel about life with her, I think this will prove much more satisfactory. My husband always told me that real strength lay in being pliable, like a bamboo, bending with pressures that would break more rigid branches, but always returning to one's true course of growth. He was right, of course. You cannot return to some fly-by-night existence on your own in Manila.''

"But I want to stay on in Manila—"

Doña Luisa did not respond to the plea in Kay's voice; possibly she did not hear it. She turned at the door, a stiff, small-waisted woman, beyond fashion or elegance, yet saved by those beautiful large eyes filled with a bewildered innocence. "I am certain this will prove to be for the best," she said, and left Kay to her confusion and racing thoughts.

Mrs. Moreno lived in three ground-floor rooms of an airy house, large but unpretentious. It was surrounded by rather haphazard lawns, often littered with children's toys, tricycles, slides, a rubber wading pool, shadowed by some magnificent old acacia trees. The major part of the house was occupied by her son, his wife, and their five children, whose high-pitched voices and entourage of nurses, tutors, visiting relatives, filled the rooms with sound and movement restless as the sea, lapping over steps, in and out of the rooms, flooding into the garden, trickling off at night into an indistinct murmuring from the nursery quarters.

Kay, punctual as usual, was greeted with smiles and the undisguised curiosity that this urgent occasion demanded. After the rapid courtesies of do come in, please sit down, something to drink?—tea? coffee?—Mrs. Moreno said, "Or perhaps you would prefer something a little stronger? You sounded so troubled on the telephone."

Kay arranged her white skirt over her knees, asked for a glass of water, and, while the maid went to fetch it, apologized for disturbing Mrs. Moreno's morning.

"Is Luisa ill? Has the—"

"No, no. Nothing like that. I would have told you at once."

"I suppose she is wondering what to do now. She must be under great strain—you see, she always left decisions, even tiny ones about the color of a scarf or what kind of soup for dinner, to Tomás."

"But she doesn't seem confused by her new situation. She acts almost as though it offered her a view of an unexpected landscape."

"She always was more courageous than the rest of us." For a moment, far away from her bustling and expansive manner, she looked reflective, even sad, wondering how much she and Luisa—or, indeed, any of them—knew about each other in those far-off days and nights, how much they knew about love.

Her thoughts washed about like the waves of sound in the house, half present in the *sala,* half dreaming under the shade trees in the garden long ago, but she returned quickly to her sharp-eyed flutter when Kay blurted out, "I told a lie and I don't know how to set it right. You see, I can't hurt her now, and I'm sure I will and I don't know what to do—please help me—"

"Slowly, my dear, slowly," Mrs. Moreno answered to Kay's incoherence. "What are you trying to tell me? How can I help you? *Can* I help you?"

"I don't know. You were my only chance. I have nobody else to ask."

"Luisa is very fond of you. She has helped you before and would again."

"That's just it, just why she can't help me in this—"

"And I can? Really, Catalina."

"Well, perhaps you can't or won't. Anyway, I thought I could ask you. She is leaving Manila—"

"Taking Angelita to Negros. Yes, naturally she would do that—the only sensible thing."

"And I am to leave her."

"And is *that* what you're so worried about?" She laughed, partly out of disappointment, partly from relief. "Luisa would never leave you stranded. She will be certain that your arrangements are all in order before she leaves. You can count on her good heart and her sense of propriety."

"Perhaps we all count on them too much! You see, it is precisely those arrangements that are going to cause trouble."

"One must learn to be grateful for lesser—"

"Mercies? Yes, that is what I hope for, a small mercy. She is going to write to the Gómez family about me."

Mrs. Moreno frowned. "Gómez? Which Gómez?"

"From Negros, friends and neighbors of hers."

"Oh, yes, yes, friends from long ago. But why write to Juan and Carlotta? Why about you?"

On a deep breath, clumsy as a schoolgirl confessing to the infringement of a rule, yet keeping Mrs. Moreno's lack of gullibility in mind, Kay said, "There is no excuse for it. She thinks I am related to the Gómez family. That's what I told her when we first met. I didn't think that the matter would ever come up, or that she would remember."

In a harsh but puzzled voice, Mrs. Moreno said, "Of course she would remember. Family always meant a lot to Luisa."

"So I learned. She told me that, as relatives, they would naturally take care of me." With every evidence of honesty and remorse, she added, "But they aren't my relatives, and soon she will know that."

Mrs. Moreno, looking at her without much sympathy, remarked, "Oh, it is easy to understand. I assume you needed a background she would recognize. Luisa demanded at least that much reassurance about you. I was the one to give it to her." Coldly, she asked, "Did you, perhaps, lie to me as well?"

Kay answered her without hostility. "No . . . no, there was no reason to tell you anything but the truth. But she—well, she half suggested that I might be related to the Gómez family she knew, and I simply let her think I was. After all, a stray pickup—"

"—with no recognizable connections would hardly have found herself so comfortably installed in Luisa's house. You'll have to explain your deception to her as best you can."

"I cannot do that. She has already had to accept one betrayal—and such a terrible one. Even though mine is trivial in comparison, still I think she is fond of me, and to hear that I, too—"

"—have hidden things from her, have been less than entirely honorable. I see. I suppose you are afraid she will hold it against you, will not continue to help you. But you, of all people, should know that Luisa is not vindictive, can be counted on for—"

"For her blind generosity?" Kay made no attempt to disguise her scorn. "No, Mrs. Moreno. That is not my reason. Quite simply, I do not want to hurt her any further with my story. She has lived through too many stories in the last few days."

"I see." Mrs. Moreno, drifting back in memory, counting stories off in her head, listed Tomás and herself first, and smiled. Then, seeing him as a kind of spider spinning out the web of his own romantic life composed of wit and drama, added Tomás and Luisa. Such disparate giving and getting, affection and money and longings—oh, he had such longings! Then Angelita and her mother and Tomás. Had that woman loved him as well? Flattered, charmed, bought? Per-

haps warm and accepting, possibly just honest and unde-
manding? "Come to think of it, the father, too," she muttered, scarcely aware that she was speaking. That shadowed
assassin, the righteously jealous murderer, had any of it led
to justice? Or begun in love? There were too many secrets
for her taste. And what about Angelita? Her story and her
child, Tomás's grandchild? Stories breeding yet more stories. Even Ramón had stories, with his wife, with Angelita,
with Luisa, who had employed him, protected him, unknow-
ingly introduced him to a mistress, and unhesitatingly com-
mandeered his child. All tangled enough in love and ethics
to suit even the awkward problems that this girl raised, this
girl with so elusive a background, sitting so still, a graceful
white figure against the deep red silk of the chair.

Kay waited for Mrs. Moreno to say something more, but
the silence seemed to stretch interminably, and at last Kay
decided to break it herself. "Perhaps you are right, and I
should just tell her. Perhaps it is only self-importance that
makes me think she might care one way or the other that I
allowed her to accept a lie in what will certainly appear—even
to her—as an attempt to make use of her 'blind generosity.'
As for my own future, I am quite prepared to manage on my
own in Manila. I can't say I look forward to the prospect of
returning to Madame Rosa's or some similar establishment.
Still, it's more appealing than the thought of going home,
which, I expect, is what Doña Luisa will suggest."

"It is also what I might suggest," Mrs. Moreno said coolly.
"You are older now, and surely beyond the pinpricks and
humiliations of your childhood. And I see no reason why you
could not, if you insist on some form of independence, find
a job—there must be work of *some* kind—in Zamboanga."

"That is quite impossible." Kay said, with a lack of emphasis quite out of keeping with her words. "Nothing could

induce me to go back and face my mother's hatred."

Mrs. Moreno looked at her with both astonishment and distaste. "*Hatred,* Catalina? Come, now—"

"Yes, I know it sounds melodramatic. But still it is really the only accurate word. Of course, by her own feverish logic, she had reason to hate me. Because I was still alive, you see, and she couldn't forgive me that."

Mrs. Moreno, sensing that some teasing mystery about the girl was about to be explained, watched her intently, but Kay's unrevealing gaze was fixed on the dappled shadows outside the window and her voice remained evenly paced. "It started when she got the telegram telling her that my brother, her younger son, had been killed. Naturally, she was distraught with grief—we both were. Later, when the news about my older brother came, she slipped completely out of reach, far beyond any sort of consolation—if there is any sort of consolation for such senseless tragedy. She tore her clothes and threw away her rosary, and kept muttering, 'Dead, all dead,' as though she and I were dead, too. She wouldn't let me come anywhere near her. She just sat in the *sala* in her torn clothes, her fingernails broken, her hair uncombed, rocking back and forth, repeating, 'Dead, all dead,' like some terrible litany.

"I called our priest to come and see her, but she wouldn't speak to him—didn't offer him cake and wine, in the usual way, didn't even look at him. Only when he told her that she must accept God's will did she move from her chair—so suddenly, and with a look of such blazing outrage, that I thought she was going to attack him. But she didn't. She just laughed at him. At least, I suppose it was a laugh, a dreadful, parched sound. And it didn't stop.

"I think he was frightened—I know I was. Anyway, he blessed her and left immediately. Perhaps he had other calls to make. There were so many bereaved at that time. When I saw him to the door, he told me to stay with her, that she needed me more than ever now.

"He was wrong, of course. I saw that the minute I returned to the *sala*. Her first words to me were 'Why have you come back?'

"I said, 'Father Antonio told me to stay with you.'

"I have never seen an expression of such fathomless hatred. *'You?'* she said, 'Who are you?'

"Oh, she wasn't out of her mind," Kay added, although Mrs. Moreno had made no such interruption.

Kay had been choosing her words and her tone carefully, but now she ended her account on a note of unaffected sadness and loss. "She couldn't bear the sight of me—do you understand? I was a continual reminder that her other children, her beloved sons, were dead, when it might have been me, when it could have been my life, not theirs. And, almost as bad, I had a right to share her grief. She couldn't allow me that. She became very jealous of her sorrow—as if it were a lover."

Mrs. Moreno, emotional, kind-hearted, easily touched for all her canniness, asked, "But you stayed on, in spite of everything?"

"Where was there to go? The war wasn't over. There were still the bombings that were wrecking far more than just our lives and our pineapple plantations."

"Yes," Mrs. Moreno agreed. "A whole world died with the war." While Kay had been talking, Mrs. Moreno began to see a new shape to the story of the past months, a different view of the relationship between Luisa and this calm, bereft girl. She remembered, in her first conversation with Kay, flippantly throwing out the suggestion that she might "be a daughter" to the old lady, and Kay's tremulous reply, "It may not be what she wants of *me*—or what I'm capable of—" She now thought that it might have been instead what Kay wanted —wanted more than anything, more than the comfort or security or possibilities of Luisa's home, and had now so unjustly lost. "Didn't your mother's attitude ever change?" she asked. "After the first shock, I mean—people are hardly responsible for their behavior when they receive such terrible news—but with time and—"

Kay shook her head. "No. I had hoped for that, too. Certainly, in unimportant ways, her attitude became less extreme. She took to wearing formal mourning, and eventually went about her household duties with some semblance of composure. But she never looked at or spoke to me if she could help it, as if we were uncongenial strangers staying, by chance, in the same hotel. I, too, tried to avoid her as much as possible. I knew only that I had to leave as soon as I could manage it. I started to give drawing lessons to some children —the sisters at the convent where I studied helped me to find pupils—and I saved all the money I earned to be able to get away. It took me four years."

Mrs. Moreno, really moved now by Kay's sparse and stoic account, said gently, "It is all in the past, my dear, and should remain so."

"Yes. That's what I've wanted, why I've never spoken of it. But I suppose I'll have to tell Doña Luisa if she asks why I can't go home, why I'm prepared to be on my own and start all over again in Manila."

"Oh, no, no!" Mrs. Moreno pleaded in great agitation. "No, no—it would all be quite beyond Luisa's comprehension—she only understands how people *ought* to behave, not how they *do*—she would be immeasurably distressed—and she already has too much to contend with—"

"Then what shall I do?"

In any case, Mrs. Moreno could never resist a predicament, and Kay's predicament engaged both her affectionate nature and her pleasure in dallying in other people's lives. "For the moment," she said, with a sunshiny beam of a smile, "you will do nothing. I will concern myself, make no mistake—already I have an idea—we will see. In my girlhood, at moments of discontent, we used to be advised, 'Count your blessings,/Name them one by one,/And it will surprise you,/What the Lord has done!" She fluttered her hands, making a joke of the old schoolroom jingle recited by governesses, nurses, nuns.

"Blessings?" Kay said stonily, staring into the moist breathless garden beyond the trellised windows.

Mrs. Moreno rustled to her side, shaking her arm to command her attention. "I will speak to Luisa, persuade her not to write to the Gómezes. If she knows that I have undertaken to look after you—that perhaps you want to attend art school here—something of the sort—she will readily agree. Come, we will make an adventure of this—we will embark on it together!"

Quite properly, in Mrs. Moreno's opinion, Kay covered her face with her hands, sobbing silently. To all Mrs. Moreno's patting of shoulders, soothing noises interspersed with encouraging phrases about everything will be all right, the strain must have been intolerable, yes, go ahead and cry, you'll feel better now, Kay said only, "I can count one blessing—I have a good friend."

"Here, take my handkerchief," said Mrs. Moreno, and handed Kay a beautifully embroidered square of batiste.

PART III

The Wide Mosquito Net

◩The International Club had
two distinct atmospheres and characters, the daytime one of
women and athletics, of youngsters playing tennis on the
pinkish courts near the sea wall on the edge of Manila Bay,
of mothers with small children at the shallow end of the
swimming pool, which was divided from the lawns and flower
beds by a long loggia covered with jasmine and enclosing an
air of impossible sweetness. At lunchtime, the terrace would
fill up with the less determinedly sporty types who were at the
Club largely to while away an idle afternoon. The little tables
set against the banks of scarlet and yellow cannas were soon
the focus for slow informal lunches consisting of long cold
drinks, followed by thin-making salads and fruit. The cheerful wave and smiling acknowledgment of acquaintances, the
uniform appearance of bright, expensive sports clothes, the
chatter about last night's party, of weekend plans, of home
news, of local gossip, the afternoon card games—all were
equally a part of the Club until six o'clock.

The evening brought with it a change of aspect and a shift

in the cast of characters that made the Club their *mise en scène*. It was considered a necessary courtesy by the Club committee to offer, regardless of nationality, temporary membership to officers of the various armed forces who were on leave, or on brief assignments, in Manila. This privilege was gratefully and extensively used, but in each case only for a day or two. The temporary members found the Club surroundings pleasant but dull. Too frequently, they ended up buying each other drinks in the bar, and then drifting off to see if they could find something more lively, some gaiety more appropriate for a short leave than the sedate atmosphere the Club could provide.

Originally, it had been Mrs. Moreno's suggestion that Kay work at the International Club. As a respected member of the Administrative Committee, which she had been ever since the Club was founded soon after the war, Mrs. Moreno felt certain that she could propose, with success, her new protégée for some kind of position there. And besides, she told Kay, "I think the surroundings would be pleasant for you—better than being a governess or returning to a seamstress's workroom." Even as she said it, she was struck by how bleak Kay's prospects seemed.

Only the week before, she and Kay had talked to Doña Luisa all one evening. Together they had explained Kay's wish to remain in Manila, where she could take courses in the art school. Mrs. Moreno had, as well, extended the offer of protective watchfulness, and supplied more practical help in the form of a room in a very genteel boardinghouse run by her former housekeeper, who spent her time in church work and met her expenses by taking in paying guests. She had noted with approval Kay's efforts to spare Doña Luisa any anxiety on her behalf through all the crowded bustle of closing the old house, so that Doña Luisa could devote her undivided concern to Angelita, to the return to Negros, and to the reshaping of the hacienda life, so pleasurably and so painfully remembered.

The next step was, of course, to find Kay a job. However, in the end it was Kay herself who, after a few meals at the International Club listening thoughtfully to Mrs. Moreno's accounts of Club activities, formulated a plan. Sitting on the terrace in the gilded light of early evening and watching the bar filling up with uniforms, or catching sight of an occasional lonely stroller in the gardens, Kay said, "What the Club needs is a Hospitality Committee. And what the Hospitality Committee will need is a paid executive secretary. Me, in short. Let me explain."

Recently, the women had been urged to take a more active part in the functions of the Club, instead of passively remaining the acquiescent members they automatically became when their husbands joined the Club. So far, they had scarcely ventured beyond mah-jongg tournaments and an occasional Club dance for a special holiday night—New Year's Eve, for instance, or Independence Day—when the ladies would make the posters and plan the decorations in a series of rather ill-organized but quite entertaining conferences to decide wording, motifs, colors. A Hospitality Committee, Kay asserted, would not only provide an extension of their Club activities, but provide it with virtually no effort on their part. "People love feeling responsible—don't you find? —as long as they are not required to do any work."

To Mrs. Moreno's question "But what is this Hospitality Committee supposed to do?" Kay replied, "You must call a meeting of the ladies and tell them that the Club is ignoring a very important part of its purpose. After all"—she gestured in the direction of the bar and gardens—"these continual visitors are guests of our country, guests for only a short time, admittedly, but people who will be returning to their own countries and will describe their stay here. Surely, we all want them to carry away happy memories. We are famous for our hospitality, so it is essential that our friendly, informal social life should, in a true Filipino manner, be shared with others.

"Impress on the ladies that some of these guests are from good families, well-connected; some are well-informed, some are well-known. Many of them are, quite simply, nice young men eager to learn a little about our life. The Club already offers these visitors—don't call them transients because, you must explain, all of you hope that they will always feel that something of their lives and thoughts remain in the Philippines—well, the Club offers these welcome visitors temporary membership, but doesn't follow this up. Now the time has come to give more meaning to this gesture. Tell them all of that to begin with. It will appeal to their sentimentality and their patriotism."

Mrs. Moreno was listening with fascination and already imagined herself addressing the Club ladies in warmly confidential tones. "But I must have some concrete proposals to put to them. Something that they will find entertaining and not too strenuous."

"Absolutely," Kay agreed. "When you come down to it, most of the fellows only want a good time without having to spend a lot of their precious leave getting acquainted or finding a girl who isn't a bar pickup to go out with."

Looking rather startled, Mrs. Moreno said, "I know nothing of 'bar pickups,' as you call them. I trust that you are equally unfamiliar with the demimonde?"

"Entirely," Kay said, laughing.

In reply to some note of unexpressed experience in Kay's voice, Mrs. Moreno said haughtily, "You are not suggesting that we supply them with women, are you?"

"Dear Mrs. Moreno! It is the evenings, not the nights, that present a problem. I expect they can manage for themselves whatever shady arrangements are to their taste for later on.

"No, I'm suggesting three or four evenings a week of informal Club dances, and besides that some well-chaperoned afternoon occasions. You'll see, you'll get an especially enthusiastic response from the mothers of débutante daughters."

Mrs. Moreno saw the attractions of the scheme at once. It was both safe and useful. Such a series of entertainments would most certainly provide the girls with delightful additions to a year of innocent preening and pleasure before the more sober joys of marriage. Mrs. Moreno was sure that the ladies would recall, as she herself did, how short a time it had seemed, how brief a spreading of damp butterfly wings, how heady the excursion into admiration and society, how soon the babies began arriving. And then, naturally, there was no recapturing that careless season.

When, a few days later, Mrs. Moreno outlined the whole idea to the Club ladies, the final, decisive factor that made the Hospitality Committee a reality was the introduction of Kay. "We all understand," Mrs. Moreno said, "the organization and planning of such a Committee needs a very great deal of time, and of continuing work. I feel it would be most unfair to impose on our members to perform this community service unaided, although I am sure there would be many volunteers."

She didn't raise her eyes to the apprehensive looks from

her audience. "All of us will have to approve the programs for each month, will make suggestions and offer comments or criticism—already this will require serious and responsible thought. But I am sure you will all agree that we will need a paid executive secretary to run the Committee, one who can be relied on to treat her duties with proper care, who can be at the Club every evening to watch over the arrangements we approve, who can deal with unexpected problems. She must be—please forgive this apparent snobbishness—she must be of our class.

"This is really only a practical consideration, because hers will be rather delicate work, combining efficiency with good taste, a knowledge of a certain background with a familiarity with our ways." (Mrs. Moreno was remembering Kay's flat remark, "People don't mind too much whom they come across in their work, but they like to take their pleasures with their own kind.")

The sort of candidate that Mrs. Moreno had described seemed to the ladies impossibly difficult to find. A girl of good family would probably feel that holding a regular job was beneath her, and would almost certainly be inexperienced as well. A married woman would have her own ménage to attend to and couldn't recklessly sacrifice her own social life, and her family's demands on her time and presence. An ordinary working girl wouldn't know the subtler forms of etiquette and the nuances of social distance, would be instantly out of place in situations that required of her a watchful blending of ease and decorum. So it came as no surprise that the Committee members accepted the nomination of Kay with relief.

Well-mannered, modest, eminently presentable, Kay won their support at once on her deportment alone. Mrs. Moreno guaranteed her respectability, hovering over her like a guardian angel. Added to this, Kay gave the impression of being competent, commonsensical, and eager to work.

Afterward, over a cup of tea in the red *sala*, Mrs. Moreno told her that the ladies had accepted her as an unlooked-for gift, more delightful for being so improbably what they wanted and so neatly timed. Like successful collaborators, they smiled at each other, enumerating fringe benefits as they occurred to either one of them.

"So I can have most of the day when the light is good for painting—"

"If you look on the evenings as amusement rather than work—"

"Of course, a ready-made social life—"

"—with very nice people. At least the Filipinos will be of good family. Who knows? You might meet someone—"

"You're incorrigible! Whom could I meet? A lonely soldier? A good bridge partner?"

"Not necessarily a *bridge* partner," Mrs. Moreno said naughtily.

"No." Kay was making a statement of fact. "Not among the Filipinos, at least. With no established background or family, I could only be considered a *mestiza* by them. Adequately educated, perhaps, and not too clumsy in manner, but certainly not the sort of person to be eagerly welcomed as a daughter of the house."

Mrs. Moreno, experienced in the ways and thinking of the kind of people whom she had known since childhood, was compelled to accept the unembittered realism of Kay's remarks, though she hoped for romance. Troubled by the thought that one cannot measure one's deserts, the satisfactions or the pains, or their just proportions, she said, "Surely there can be exceptions," and didn't listen when Kay replied, "I doubt it." Very formally, Kay added, "I don't know how to thank you for all your help," with a curious valedictory note in her voice.

Mrs. Moreno, half hearing it but unable to account for it, was thinking, There are satisfactions in this for me, too. As there must have been for Luisa. To have youth and a kind of excitement enter our lives . . . which of us, in the end, is the benefactor?

The Club ladies, already delighted with Kay, chattering about her as they would about a new acquisition, happily added an element of mystery and sorrow to their gossip. With the outlines vague, the content fluid enough to allow for stretches of indignation, imagination, and some contradictions, Kay's story took on a rough and rather trite design. She was generally accepted to be a war orphan from the southern islands. Knowing Doña Luisa's charitable nature, no one seemed to find it too bizarre that she should have given Kay a home. Somehow it came to be assumed that she had intended, after a while, to adopt Kay. Everybody knew of Doña Luisa's personal disappointment, amounting to humiliation, at being unable to give her husband the only gift he would really have cherished, and Kay fitted easily into the picture of a rich old woman's wish to resolve, too late, a helpless inadequacy. So even warmer sympathy went out to Kay at her loss of so enviable a future, at her reticence about any princely expectations, and her continuing affection for Doña Luisa.

Consequently, the Club members were, on the whole, cordial, and whatever wariness they might have felt about the possibility of Kay's presuming on an artificial social equality was soon dispelled. They encountered no awkwardness in

Kay, who was clever at judging social frontiers and who had marked as out of bounds the eligible young Filipino men who came to play tennis on the weekends, or sometimes accompanied their families to a Club dance before seeking more unconstrained company in the cabarets. Instead, she concentrated on spending time and effort on the visitors and temporary members, who were, she declared, her special charge. They were introduced to girls at dances, to tennis, bridge, or golf companions at other occasions. They were invited to picnics, amateur theatricals, and cocktail parties. Everyone seemed cheerfully surprised by the facility and the variety of the entertainments.

Mrs. Moreno, watching Kay's success with affectionate pleasure for the girl and listening to appreciative comments from the members and the visitors, couldn't resist the self-congratulation of someone who has picked a winner, and waited for some fresh excitement. Poor child, she thought. Good judgment seems to have brought her to some kind of temporary plateau in her life at last.

She said to Kay, one day, "Sometimes I wish you were not quite so conscientious—that you would look out for—what shall I call it?—for other chances."

"I shall," Kay said, understanding her perfectly.

Kay had been working at the International Club for nearly three months when she met Jeremy Wilson. She had by then grown quite accustomed to the flow of arrivals and departures in not quite the rhythm of the tides, yet always unexpectedly different and mostly, in principle, the same. The needs of these transient men were easy to guess and usually fairly simple to fill. Almost every evening, she arranged suitable introductions for them and appropriate entertainment, found a sympathetic audience for homesick laments, a light-hearted companion for merrier occasions. Wilder or more overtly sexual encounters were not within her realm.

She had, that evening, already seen to it that the married men who had come in were pleasantly engaged in conversation with one or another Filipino family group, that the bridge enthusiasts had found a fourth. The younger men, flushed after a day of golf or returning from an excursion in the country, shiny and trim in their tropical uniforms, danced with the girls from those nice families. They flirted with them, smiling at the light teasing this elicited, walked with them in the dark jasmine arbor, moving soundlessly, like ghosts in their pale clothes dappled with shadows, stopping for most innocent kisses in all that heady sweetness, whispering, ". . . Oh, my dear—" ". . . So lovely, lovely—" and hearing, "I must go in now . . ." meaning, "Make me stay," all lost in the more emphatic whispering of the sea. Such girls retained their respectable romance, were respectably taken back to their waiting parents, and with respectable affection took their places in an intangible memory book of enchanting girls known briefly on short leaves, too close to the conventional image to leave a deeper impression.

Jeremy Wilson had arrived in Manila that afternoon only to find that even in the unfamiliar surroundings of the Air Force Officers' Mess, even after a shower, a change of clothes, and quantities of hot tea (which he doggedly described to himself as English, as opposed to Chinese, tea), he still couldn't release himself from Shanghai, an atmosphere of feverish uncertainty and staleness. He had looked again, with more attention, at the card that the Filipino corporal at the desk had given him. He thought that the International Club, where, he read, he was invited to be a complimentary member, might be worth a visit. He knew nobody in Manila; indeed, that had been one of his chief reasons for coming—that and the offer from one of his colleagues of a free ride on a military transport, part of the same unspoken arrangement of mutual courtesy between fliers that allowed him to stay at the Mess.

He wanted to use his leave to enjoy what he thought of as a short stretch of sanity, among strangers, before he returned to Shanghai and had to decide whether or not he would sign on for another tour of duty with the Civil Air Transport. He felt that such a commitment might be advantageous, even necessary, for his particular plans for his future, but the idea of another year in China left him immeasurably depressed and weary. He had long ago stopped calling this malaise "homesickness." "Home" belonged to a distant period of his life, in feeling, if not in time, a matter almost of fantasy now, but a fantasy tenaciously clung to as an antidote to the realities of war, first in Europe and now in China. Home and, of course, Margaret—whom he thought of in a private silence, perpetually sunlit against the sweet summer meadows, like a photograph without dimension, change, or possibly life—comforted him by her remembered innocence for the painful design of his days.

When he walked into the International Club, Jeremy Wilson was hoping, quite simply, to find a girl, preferably pretty, preferably accommodating—someone to share holiday activities, which he hadn't really defined in his mind, in and around Manila. He knew that he didn't want to spend his leave drinking with fellow fliers, searching with them, in the foolish camaraderie of liquor, for some kind of excitement or release in the tawdry nighttime life of the city. He settled himself at the Club bar where he could hear the dance music, and gazed with approval across the softly lit terrace at the beguiling femininity of the girls, and the eager, vulnerable young men so bravely decked out for love and war in white and tan and gold.

However, it was Kay who caught his special interest, partly because he admired her looks and her grace of movement, partly because her quaintly decorous demeanor provided so unexpected a contrast to the fluttering girlishness of the dancers. Most of all, she did not seem to be guarded by shrewd-eyed, warmly welcoming chaperons. In fact, he thought, she might have been deftly stage-managing a children's party for all her deferential cordiality to new arrivals and regular members.

Kay was looking thoughtfully at the couples on the dance floor when he came up behind her and remarked, "Charming sight, wouldn't you say? All organdie and gardenias and clear-eyed youth—"

She turned to him, smiling, "Yes, quite charming."

"And I was wondering why it should make you look so concerned?"

Puzzled by his air of impartial inquiry, which didn't at all match his light tone, Kay replied, "Not really concerned, just mindful of my duties. I'm a sort of hostess for the Club's Hospitality Committee, and I'm supposed to watch and see that things are going smoothly."

"Yes, you were pointed out to me by the bartender. Katarina Gómez."

"Catalina. Old Wong can never get his 'l's and his 'r's straight."

"Katarina suits you better. Or Kate. Not, let me quickly add, because you look shrewish, but Kate has a nice direct and competent sound."

"And that suits me?"

"I think so. I've been watching you putting on a most polished social performance. I, incidentally, am Jeremy Wilson, and anyone who abbreviates that to 'Jerry' does so at unspeakable peril."

"Oh really?" Kay asked. "Why?"

"Well, just a wartime hangover. We used to call the Germans 'Jerries.' "

"I don't know much about the German war."

In a rush of embarrassment, he thought, Of course not. Why should she? They had their own troubles here.

He was a fair-haired, nice-looking young man, easy of movement and speech, but with a half-hidden sobriety under his casual manner. His accent made it plain that he was English. For some reason, he seemed out of place in the International Club, but since Kay couldn't imagine what sort of milieu really suited him, she offered him her usual formula. "May I help you in any way? Perhaps you would like to meet some of these people? Or there is a card room, if you would prefer that?"

"I tell you what." He sounded as if he were giving the choice a most judicial consideration. "Suppose you have a drink with me while I look the field over. Can't just plunge into these major decisions so recklessly."

Kay smiled. "Very sensible. Let's sit over there," indicating a table on the edge of the dance floor near the terrace, "an excellent vantage point for your reconnoitering." As they seated themselves, she said, "Shall I ask Old Wong to make you his special drink? We call it the International Understanding."

"What goes into it?"

"Well, I'm not sure. Different kinds of rum and some

Cointreau, I think, and bits of fruit."

"Very appropriately named," he said. "International Understanding. It sounds sweet and impossible. No, I'll stick to whiskey. And you?"

She paused doubtfully. "Things seem to have got off to a fairly good start. I think I'd like a Coca-Cola, please."

"I say, that *is* daring of you," he said solemnly.

"It's just that I—"

"—have to be mindful of your duties. Don't apologize. Just try to think of me as a problem case that requires your professional attention for a while. That way you won't feel guilty of negligence. And anyway," he added, gesturing at the dancers, "you seem to have made those others happy enough. And later, when parting is such sweet sorrow, I haven't a doubt that they will look into each other's eyes and think, 'It might have been.' "

Kay listened to him with amusement, the light pleasant voice and the serious face. "You mustn't mock them," she said. "It's not a bad arrangement for a two- or three-week leave. Too expensive or too short to go home, too long to be without some attractive little adventure. For the girls, it's fun to get dressed up, go dancing, be admired, safe from embarrassing entanglements."

"On both sides," he said severely. "Don't forget 'the girl back home.' "

"Some of them do, but clearly you aren't among them." She narrowed her eyes at him, considering this moment's revelation. "Let's see, now. She is a blue-eyed blonde and she lives on the Downs."

"Blue eyes, but put in, as they say, with a sooty finger. Which means only that she has dark lashes and hair. And she lives, as I do, in Somerset." Briefly, in the moist Manila night, he thought of Margaret—and, for that matter, of Somerset— as some area of unreality in his mind, as one might remember a pleasant but irrelevant dream.

"That's too bad," Kay said. "I've always liked the sound of 'the Downs,' like swan's-down, but green. Is Swansea on the Downs? It would make a lovely address—Swansea, the Downs, England."

"Swansea," he said instructively, "is a simply hideous port town in Wales, best known for its soot and vile language—"

"How disappointing!"

"However, even if we can't give you Downs in Somerset, we can, if you like that sort of thing, offer you a fine selection of thatched roofs and cottage gardens and villages with names like Lesser-Wetting-in-the-Ditch, or Lower-Wenching-in-Cognito, or even," he added, his gaze following a young Navy officer who was leading his smiling partner from the dance floor to the dim garden beyond, "or even Little-Necking-in-the-Arbor."

Kay laughed her sudden, released laugh. It made Jeremy wonder idly why she carried an air of such expert restraint and containment of what might be a joyous nature. Kay said, "With all that *and* your blue-eyed girl at home, what brings you to Manila?"

"Oh, the splendor of the tropical sunsets, the pounding of the surf," he recited rapidly, "the beauty of the island girls, adventure, romance, the thrill of distant tom-toms—"

"You're traveling just for pleasure?"

Suddenly sobered, he paused and then said, "I suppose that's exactly what I'm doing. Isn't it odd? It never occurred to me that this is the first time I've ever traveled for pleasure. My lot do most of their traveling on orders."

"Army?"

"No. I'm a flier, which, to put it in the mildest possible way, fills me with despair. RAF during the war, and now, when I'm unfashionably horrified by planes, with no Young Lochinvar left in my nature, I fly for the Civil Air Transport in China. I'm in Manila, to answer your question, for that familiar leave —something over two weeks—and already dreading the thought of returning to Shanghai and those damn planes."

"I'm told that planes—or, rather, flying itself—has a pretty powerful fascination."

He shook his head. He had never, he remembered, been taken by the Saint-Exupéry mystique. And only briefly (long enough to regret it) by what he called the Raffle-Baffle—all the much-publicized esprit de corps, morale, the devil-may-care, understated courage, the RAF manner. The Raffle-Baffle. Designed, in the end, to make killing look like sport. With a sour air of distaste, he said, "Not to me." He had found it impossible in the RAF to lose himself sufficiently in the means to ignore the ends of all his flying. Not a sport, just plain killing and destruction.

"Then why do you stay with it?"

"For the money," he said, unwilling to be explicit about the real reason for his being in China, hardly admissible to himself, never to a stranger. "I was never trained for anything except flying; there wasn't time. The Yanks are very generous, and I save as much as I can." He turned to her with his earlier good humor, "You can guess the rest, can't you?"

"Back to Somerset? Back to the prewar life?"

"Ah, you sound skeptical. You're wrong, you know. The prewar life may have packed up, but some things haven't."

"What, for instance?"

He said, as much to reassure himself as to convince her,

"The seasons, for instance. I've always wanted to be a farmer. To watch the seasons from, so to speak, a professional point of view. Don't you miss the seasons? Or is that only an English sentimentality? The—do laugh—the first blush of spring, March winds, April showers, and so on? Summer and bluebells in the woods, and the first damn cuckoo? No—how could you—you've never known the seasons here in Manila, have you? I don't suppose they exist in that way. And have you ever wondered what snow would be like?"

Kay said flatly, "I know what snow is like."

Noticing her suddenly withdrawn expression, he added, "And don't much like it, apparently."

"The associations were rather disagreeable." With hardly a break and with a return to her former tone of impersonal and courteous inquiry, Kay asked, "How are you planning to spend your leave, now that you have all the tropical delights you mention to choose from?"

"Well, I was rather hoping that you would help me with that decision. I only know that for this brief period I want to forget Shanghai and the Chinese civil war ever existed."

"Shanghai is where you work?"

"Where I'm based. The Civil Air Transport, among whose valiant ranks I am proud to be numbered, delivers supplies to the Nationalist Chinese forces at the front—when we can find them. They're a nomadic lot, and so we have to behave like sort of aerial Bopeeps. Between missions we live in Shanghai in billets known, with predictable wit, as the CAT house. You can see that it isn't the most enviable of lives."

He didn't describe the aspect of Shanghai that troubled him most, the floods of wretched, ragged refugees that crammed the city, neither did he mention that he had to remind himself from time to time—driving to the airport, going out of an evening to a foreigners' party—that Shanghai, to him a place of unspeakable despair, was to them a city of hope, however temporary, a possibility of escape. "Anyway, doctor," he continued cheerily, "What do you recommend for a severe case of jaundiced viewpoint?"

Kay smiled. "Total contrast," she said promptly. "Flying, however great the distance you cover, seems like a very sedentary occupation. Do you like to swim? The pool here is quite nice. You could come tomorrow morning, and then stay on for lunch. We are rather proud of the buffet we serve on Saturdays—all typically Filipino food and a delicious sort of purplish ice cream made from a vegetable called *ubi*. Of course, most people take a siesta in the afternoons, but if you want to sightsee, I could tell you where to go. And then our Saturday night dances are rather gala affairs—you know, with competitions and prizes and formal clothes, though that isn't necessary for visitors."

"You're doing beautifully," he said. "Keep going."

"Well, you won't have much of a chance to 'watch the seasons,' even from an amateur point of view, but a number of our members have haciendas not too far out from Manila, and I'm sure they'd be delighted to take you out for the day. You'd see something of the countryside, get a glimpse of our kind of village life—"

"The natives are friendly? Well, that will certainly make a change from Shanghai. You will, I do hope, be doing all these very enticing things with me? You look surprised. Am I being too abrupt?"

"No—no. I'm not often— I mean, people usually accept my position for exactly what it is—a Club employee."

"You don't, then, put yourself in a class with those 'attractive little adventures' you promised me?"

Kay said slowly, as if she were considering the matter for the first time, "I don't. I've found that my adventures are apt to become bigger than I had bargained for. And they usually go astray."

In the hearty voice one uses to an invalid, Jeremy said, "Well, we'll see if we can't remedy that. Surely you don't have to be at the Club all day every day?"

"Only tomorrow, because it's Saturday. Sunday and Monday are my days off, and then I'm supposed to be here all the other evenings."

"Otherwise you are free?" he asked, meaning, Is there a man in your life?

Understanding him perfectly, Kay replied, "Yes, I am free, except that I have art classes some mornings."

"*Art* classes? Do you give them or go to them? You see, I put no limits to your accomplishments."

Kay smiled acknowledgment of the casual compliment. "I only go to them. There was a time when I wanted to be an artist—thought I could be. I now know that the best I can attain is a kind of insignificant competence. But still I like to keep my private record of humanity." She said this with a certain caution, as if she were revealing some suspect eccentricity. "Some people take photographs to capture their experience of living."

"And some people," Jeremy said lightly, thinking of himself, "try to forget about it as fast as possible."

With great gravity, Kay remarked, "That is exceedingly foolish, since it is the only thing you have."

"What is?"

"Your experience of living."

Taken a little off guard, and interested by the authority of her tone, Jeremy found something gallant in her unruffled social competence and wondered again what experiences she was so stoically refusing to dismiss. It had been a long time since he had wanted to know about another person. Margaret, in her beautiful simplicity, known from childhood, held no secrets for him, and the people he had known in all the wartime years had been important to him only as they functioned well or badly in the performance of his work, by its nature a cooperative venture. "I expect you're right," he said. "Anyway, it's cowardly not to recognize things as they happen."

"Oh, I'm a terrible coward," she said, with such apologetic eagerness that he couldn't help laughing. "The war proved that to me."

Suddenly remembering the shattered streets and houses of the dark city beyond the secure frivolity of the Club, he asked, "Where were you during that glorious chapter of our history? Manila?"

Kay thought for a long moment and then said, "No."

Later, when it was after midnight and the band was playing something suitably sentimental, Jeremy watched Kay, and Kay watched some of the older Club members coming from the air-conditioned card room, noting the pause by the dance floor, the brief envious glances at the dreaming, dancing couples, girls with closed eyes humming softly into their partners' ears. She caught Jeremy's eye and said rather hesitantly, "You didn't get very far with your reconnoitering. Are you sure you wouldn't like to get to know some of these people? Two weeks can be an awfully long time."

"It can indeed. But then, I'm rather looking forward to spending the time growing old gracefully with you."

Kay laughed and said, with a rush of gaiety, "All right. I'll look forward to it, too." She rose. "Till tomorrow, then."

People were leaving, gathering for a few moments on the steps where the spilling of light from the Club and the headlights of the cars on the driveway caught the banks of flowers in a theatrical radiance. "Good night ... good night ..." "Can we give you a ride?" "Such fun ... thank you so much ..." "Good night ... good night."

Kay walked back through the empty Club as the last lights in the public rooms were being turned off. She slipped behind the bar, through the service door, and into the steamy pantry behind it, where glasses were being washed, metal grilles pulled across storage shelves, cupboards locked, and where Old Wong was slowly taking off his white bartender's jacket to hang it up in his locker. He looked frail in his shirt sleeves, although his tidiness and economy of movement remained unchanged. Fatigue only made him more deliberate. He smiled his wrinkled smile of great gentleness at Kay's approach, and remarked, "You spend long time with that man. English man."

"He seemed rather nice."

"He army man?"

"No. A civilian. He's a flier. He told me he was with the Civil Air Transport in China."

"He stay here long time?"

"Something over two weeks, he said. I was thinking he might be willing to take a letter back to your son, since you don't trust the mails."

He looked at Kay gratefully. "Maybe can do."

"I'll ask him. Wong, you look awfully tired. Are you feeling all right?"

"Yes, yes. Old Wong O.K."

"Just worried about your family?"

"Always worried like that."

Old Wong had grown very fond of Kay during the months she had worked in the Club. Almost every evening, they had their early dinner together, sometimes joined by a few of the waiters, an arrangement Kay far preferred to the suggestion of the Club Secretary (who felt that eating with the servants would be beneath Kay's dignity) of a lonely meal served on a tray in the office.

At first, Wong had been courteous and helpful, showing Kay the behind-the-scenes mechanics of the Club's functioning; later, in reply to Kay's unemphatic inquiries (he always looked so anxious), he told her about his son and daughter-in-law and his grandchildren, who were all in Shanghai. He was much respected by the waiters and busboys, over whom he exerted a quiet authority, while between him and Kay there existed a kind of mutual protectiveness. She saved up small items of Club scandal that came her way to divert him from his private woes. He, in turn, warned her off the heavy drinkers whom, from long experience, he recognized on sight, and alerted her to those who were too single-mindedly on the make. "He no-good man," Old Wong would say flatly, and Kay would write off whoever it was as what she labeled "a no-concern-of-mine."

That night, she looked at his troubled face and said, with as much confidence as she could manage, "Listen, there has to be a way of getting them out of China. Just don't upset yourself so much."

"No letter now four months."

"You think their letters are intercepted?"

"Maybe they frightened. What you think, Missee Kay, this fly-man maybe take money in letter?"

"For your son?" she asked, startled.

Old Wong nodded. "For get out Shanghai. For come Manila."

"But, Wong, I've only just met him—I don't know. Perhaps things aren't as bad as you think in China. I could ask him that much."

He shrugged resignedly. "Communists win Shanghai—no mistake. They win. You wait-see."

Kay could think of no reassurance for that. Old Wong's son worked in some minor capacity in one of the Kuomintang government offices. A Communist victory would, without question, be a disaster for him and his family. "Even if he'd do it—and I have no way of knowing whether he would—the real point is, could we trust him?"

"Old Wong trust Missee Kay," he replied simply.

"Well, at least get some rest tonight. I really came to ask you if you wanted a ride back to your place. I'm going to take a taxi anyway."

Kay stood on the edge of the swimming pool with one sandal on and one off, shaking the water from her foot. "It doesn't either look or feel refreshing," she remarked.

Jeremy gazed up at her in the bemused indolence of sun and water, his wet hair slicked across his forehead, his eyes very blue in the morning glare. "I've been giving it some thought," he said. "About the temperature and consistency of turtle soup, I decided."

"Well, then, if you are ready to come out, we could walk down to the sea and look for the sleeping goddess."

"Any particular goddess?"

"Particular, of course," Kay said with dignity. "I wouldn't ask you to search for just any old goddess that happened to be lying around. You can find the shape of her body in the hills that edge the Bay, or so I was once told. When she wakes, she will bring the Golden Age to the Philippines and there will be peace forever."

"Then we can be fairly sure of not waking her."

"I've never even been able to see her outline. But perhaps you'll have better luck."

Jeremy splashed out of the pool and vanished, dripping, into the changing room. In a few minutes, he reappeared looking almost aggressively clean in a white shirt and drill trousers, his hair still holding the stiff furrows of a comb. "Come on," he said, full of energy. "Let's see if we can make that lazy goddess of yours come out of hiding." But, standing at the sea wall, they could only identify disconnected features here and there—a breast, a sweep of green and purple hair spread out along the shore, the curve of a hip. "Not at all what I'd call a properly composed figure," Kay said.

"True," Jeremy agreed, his eye caught by a huge rusting shell of a wrecked ship rearing desolately out of the water ahead of them. "Of course, it may never have occurred to her that she might get caught up in the war herself and be dismembered. Asking for trouble, really. Such an obvious target, sleeping away, caring not a fig for the consequences."

Kay nodded. "And along Manila Bay, of all places."

They watched a Filipino fishing boat with its square sail and double outrigger, brightly painted and crammed with people, sliding between the shafts and plates of half-submerged wreckage. "The Japanese were very thorough, weren't they?" Jeremy said, and, after a moment, added, "But then, so were we."

"We?" Kay asked, struck by the uncontrollable bitterness of his inflection.

"In the RAF, I mean," Jeremy said, speaking from his

recurring waking nightmare of bombing missions.

Kay, watching his expression, said, "I never thought about what the men in the bombers might feel."

"Why should you? I suppose you were always, so to speak, on the receiving end."

"Well, yes." Her voice held no emotional overtones of any kind, certainly neither anger nor self-pity.

"And compared with that," he elaborated for her, "the guilts and furies of the fellow in the plane must seem inconsequential."

Kay was rubbing her finger thoughtfully on the sea wall, apparently absorbed by the thin crust of salt it displaced. "I don't know," she said slowly. "I think it's just that in a war you simply aren't permitted to consider the other side as people, too. Unless, of course, something stronger forces you to it."

Jeremy glanced at her unrevealing profile sharply and with interest. "Such as what?"

"Well, I suppose I only mean the things that happen to you —the crucial things."

"Your 'experience of living'?"

She turned and smiled at him. "Yours apparently did."

"Mine?" And then, without really wondering why he was telling her this, Jeremy found himself saying, "You see, I was brought up a Quaker, and that sort of early indoctrination dies very hard—well, any sort does, I know—but, anyhow," with a deliberate attempt at flippancy, "my heart wasn't altogether in the job of killing people." Embarrassment or something of the kind kept him from telling her that some inchoate part of his reasoning in taking the CAT job was that it used his flying expertise to save rather than take lives. Shy of grandiloquence, he hadn't formulated this even to himself either as the expiation of a guilt or as the settling of some sort of debt he owed to people—any people. Instead, he said with apparent irrelevance, "In the CAT, we fly mostly medical supplies to what the journalists call 'the front.' I won't tell you what we call it. And we leave the killing to the poor sods in the Flying Tigers and other such outfits." Then, grateful for Kay's silence as an assurance that she was not going to lead him on to any treacherous areas of feeling, he went on, more impersonally and with more confidence, "Of course, it's even worse for them, in a way. They're knocking off their own people, ruining their own country. And confusing, when you think that such a short time ago they were brothers-in-arms with the gallant Communists fighting the despicable Japanese, who are now their gallant supporters against the despicable Communists."

" 'Yesterday's enemies, today's friends,' the Japanese say."

"Do they? For some reason, that sounds much more noble than "Yesterday's friends, today's enemies."

"Though, in the end, it hardly matters who is responsible. The death and destruction are the facts that can't be changed." She gestured toward the unseen ruins of the city behind the pleasant whitewashed, pink-roofed buildings of the Club. "Half of that was the result of American bombing." She turned back to stare across the choppy water of Manila Bay. "And out there, on Corregidor, where my brother died, Americans were killed along with our soldiers by the Japanese shells." Abruptly, she changed her rather somber tone and said, "But I was forgetting, you didn't want to think about the war at all, did you? At least during your leave."

"Silly thing to say. One can hardly help thinking about it all the time." His strange, agonized compound of dire affection for the world and contempt for its workings was reawakened by Kay's words. He remembered how in the most stormy, changeable weather, especially when the mass of his plane's intricate machinery was, with a miracle of accurate performance, carrying him through the turbulent air, he would, with furious cussedness, contrast the grand orderliness of nature with the chaotic functioning of men. It was at those times that Margaret's schoolgirlish letters—full of village gossip, never mentioning the war except indirectly through the account of some funny incident involving one of the evacuees, or an absurdity of rationing regulations—seemed most precious to him. A promise that ordinary English country life would always continue had a greater reality than the murderous routine of his Air Force existence. Even later, when he knew this was untrue, he was touched by her hero worship and couldn't tell her that all the things she most admired—the ribbons on his uniform, the citations, the dangers faced so casually—filled him with an overpowering sense of defeat. To this girl beside him, who mentioned personal tragedies so neutrally, he felt that no explanations would be necessary, because they were already understood.

Kay was saying, "We'd better go and get Old Wong to mix you something soothing to drink."

"And you, I suppose, have to return to the care and feeding of your charges? All right. But do spare a thought or two for the war-weary flier who sits alone with his beer, unheeding of the gaiety around him."

"I can't see any reason why the charming foreign flier should sit alone."

"That's precisely what I was hinting toward. You'll join me as soon as you can?"

They strolled across the lawns to the small crowd that was already gathering on the terrace. There Kay glanced quickly around at the members and guests to see where she might be needed. Jeremy watched her brief professional survey unobtrusively, hoping that she wouldn't spot some self-conscious young newcomer to whom she must extend the smiling introduction with its invitation to sit down, talk, have a drink, look around the Club. He was relieved to hear her say only, "I must just go and have a word with Old Wong," and accepted, without comment and with some amusement, the neat way she handed him over to a lively Filipino group to be entertained while she was gone. "I'll order your beer for you and have it sent to the table," she said, and made her way, stopping here and there to exchange greetings, toward the bar.

Old Wong was busy, in his unhurried way, mixing drinks for waiters to carry out to the terrace and for the few dedicated drinkers, alone or in pairs, at the bar. To his questioning look, Kay replied, "I'll come and talk to you when the rush is over."

He nodded, and then drew her attention to an American soldier perched uneasily on a stool at the other end of the bar, looking wistfully through the open glass doors to the swelling activity and noise outside. "That man come in just now. He ask me drink with him."

"He looks easy enough. At a loose end, like so many of them," Kay said after a moment's consideration. "But he'll probably want to talk, and that will take a little time. I'd better check the buffet arrangements first." And, what with one thing and another, it was not until nearly an hour later that she returned to the terrace to discover Jeremy, his meal half eaten, listening to the high-pitched, heavily accented conversation of Mrs. Torres, who evidently found him very acceptable company. An attractive, diminutive woman, she looked much too young to be the mother of the pretty girl beside her, who laughed frequently at nothing much and interrupted occasionally with comments and questions—"That was the night the Villareals came for dinner?" or, "I was still at school then. . . ." They were dressed in almost identical pastel sundresses and chiffon scarves, with flimsy sandals of thin leather thongs, like spiders, on their feet. Their accessories were expensively simple, a gold chain bracelet on a wrist, a Paris necklace of sea shells made to look like primitive folk art, a coarse straw peasant basket cunningly lined with silk and fitted with a gold compact and lipstick. Both had hair clipped short and elaborately disheveled, both turned smiling lacquered faces up to Kay as she approached. "Miss Gómez! Please be seated! Octavio—a chair for Miss Gómez!"

Plump, silent, acquiescent Mr. Torres pulled over a chair from the next table and benignly returned to serious concentration on his lunch. Jeremy, who had stood up politely, looked ostentatiously at his watch, and began a sentence, "Isn't it about time that—"

But Mrs. Torres broke in, "Miss Gómez! We are trying to persuade Mr. Wilson to join us on a picnic tomorrow. Just a few friends and—"

"I'm afraid I—"

Kay said reassuringly to Jeremy, "But that sounds like exactly the kind of thing you might enjoy."

"You see?" Mrs. Torres continued with animation. "We have hired a motor launch—and do not worry about permission! Though it is still a military area, my husband is a friend of the commanding officer. He says it is beautiful—no question, beautiful! And the view from the lighthouse at the very top of the hill! In every direction! Out to sea, across to Cavite, Bataan, the Bay! The jungle has all grown back by now. You know, at the time of the surrender there was no green anywhere—the whole island had been burned black by the shelling. Of course, my husband wouldn't allow Nena and me to stay in Manila during the war, but he says that Corregidor at that time looked like a giant stick of charcoal floating on the water. Can you imagine?" She smiled winningly at Jeremy, who didn't meet her eyes.

The daughter said, "You should really see it—it's so historical!"

Kay said something about having to make sure that everything was in order for the afternoon's bridge tournament, and excused herself, leaving Mrs. Torres to explain yet more enticing details of the proposed picnic to Jeremy.

It was some minutes later that she heard the door to the card room open and close, and Jeremy's voice calling, "Kate? Kate—"

"New pads, sharpened pencils, clean ashtrays—" Kay counted them off on her fingers.

"Kate, she's just a thoughtless woman and couldn't realize —well, anyway, I'm sorry," he finished lamely.

"What are you sorry about? It's not—"

"What I meant was . . ." He paused. Not unusually, he was apt to gauge another person's feelings by the intensity of his own. "I meant about Corregidor," he said, in a gentle voice.

"Oh, Corregidor." Kay sat down abruptly at one of the card tables.

She stared out at the garden drained of color in the fierce early-afternoon sun, the deep foreshortened shadows under the trees, and the heat haze over the water beyond. As Jeremy seated himself tentatively across the table from her, she said, "We used to call it the Rock. It was our Gibraltar, you see,

impregnable. In the end, it was more like our Singapore."
She spoke deliberately, a distant image in her mind of Doña
Luisa's candle-lit dining table and the talkative young bachelor of whom she had hoped so much. With her fingers, she
sketched on the green baize table top the thunderous peninsulas of Bataan and Cavite, closing in like parentheses on the
slender little island. "We had no air cover. The Japanese
could fly as low as they liked and bomb where they wished.
It wasn't protected against an attack from Bataan. Everything
was designed to meet an attack from the sea. From the sea,
Corregidor was made of iron.

"It was the water-storage tanks that finished it. Great, con-
spicuous concrete towers. Horribly easy targets. It was when
the tanks were shattered that our people accepted the end.
There is no fresh water on Corregidor. They were told to
save rain water, but, of course, April is the dry season. The
typhoons don't begin until July. And it was *hot*. They used to
sleep beside their dugouts. They could hear the sound of the
shells leaving Bataan—it is so near. They would wake and
know that they had only enough seconds to roll into the
dugout. But at least they got a little sleep in April. There was
a calendar scratched into the rock face behind the big gun
emplacement. April, 1942. And May, ending suddenly on the
sixth.

"That first week in May, the shelling went on day and night.
In the last three days, there wasn't even ten minutes' break.
Shall I tell you how my brother died? He overslept." She
paused, because, so Jeremy thought, she was afraid of a
tremor in her voice. After a moment, she added, "Isn't it
ridiculous? Like a suburban bank clerk. He didn't hear the
alarm." She sat very still, her hands gripped together on the
table. She seemed to have nothing more to say.

"Go on talking, if you want to," Jeremy said urgently. "Cry, behave badly, make an ass of yourself—anything. They say it exorcises ghosts."

"I don't believe them," Kay replied. "Some ghosts cannot be exorcised." Jeremy heard her words with the sickening sense that somehow she was pronouncing his own doom as well. "Tell me," she continued in a different tone, one of dispassionate interest, "what makes them write their names in all sorts of odd places? Carved into concrete blocks, etched on gun barrels, scrawled on barrack walls? 'Staff Sergeant J. C. Fernández was here.' Mike Cularde, Ane Larmiato, names and names and names. Why do they want to leave such a pointless record?"

"Some sort of an affirmation that they were alive, however briefly, I suppose. Though I doubt that they reasoned it out like that." Jeremy spoke slowly, thinking that his own ghosts were all nameless and perhaps he should consider himself lucky.

In the silence, broken only by the low breathy humming of the air conditioners, he saw Kay's eye caught by some movement beyond the terrace doors, and with a rush of feeling, which he scarcely identified as compassion, watched her expression change to one of polite helpfulness, the familiar welcoming smile, the rather reserved cordiality. "Oh, damn," she said, almost inaudibly. "Here come the first of the tournament players. They're early. I suppose they just want to cool off for a while before they begin."

"Don't you ever get any time for yourself?" Jeremy whispered angrily.

"Tomorrow," she promised. "Tomorrow we'll do something nice by ourselves." She rose to greet the little cluster of people strolling across the room toward them, making good-natured exclamations partly to her and partly among themselves. "But so *hot* outside!" "What a relief! ...." "We can have our coffee here. ...." A flutter of fans. "My husband lives for his bridge—it's like a drug. ...." "No—no, I don't play—I haven't the brains! I'm just going to watch. ...." "Miss Gómez, can we order our coffee—or something cold —in here?"

"Yes, of course, I'll see to it at once. Have you met Mr. Wilson? He is with us for only two weeks." They turned bright, friendly faces to Jeremy, immediately eager to ask him, with genuine interest, about his impressions of Manila, the Philippines, the people, the life. "I don't know if Mr. Wilson plays bridge," Kay forestalled them.

"No, I'm afraid I don't."

"What a pity! But we will gladly teach you—"

"Thank you, but—"

"Or you can sit with us and watch. Really, it is very interesting!"

"Well, I—"

"Where are you coming from, Mr. Wilson?"

Kay slipped away in the middle of the questions and hospitable suggestions while Jeremy set about extricating himself as firmly, though courteously, as possible, which took a somewhat longer time.

In the bar, now virtually deserted, Kay asked Old Wong to send a waiter to take the orders from the people in the card room; then she climbed onto one of the high stools, propped her elbows on the polished teak in front of her, and held her face, frowning slightly, in her hands.

"What you think, Missee Kay?"

"I don't know enough yet, Wong. But I'm fairly sure of a

couple of things. He's very kind, and I think he really *wants* to help people—particularly if they've suffered in the war—any war."

"Then he help Old Wong family?"

"That's what I'm not sure of."

"But he work for Kuomintang, same like Old Wong son?"

"Not quite. The CAT is apparently a sort of international outfit, mostly American, that just supplies the Kuomintang forces with nonmilitary things, like medicines. At least, that's the way it sounded."

"But they not help Communists."

"True. It's not because of politics that I'm uncertain of his willingness. It's just that I think he may be a rather law-abiding person, and I was wondering whether there were restrictions about taking pesos into China."

"Pesos no good Shanghai, Missee Kay." Old Wong sounded almost shocked at Kay's innocence. "Must take dollar, American."

"And you can change pesos into American dollars?"

"Can do. Plenty black money in Manila."

"I see. But I suppose he'd have to declare whatever dollars he brought with him?"

Old Wong nodded unhappily. "Must tell bring so-much dollar American. After, must change for Chinese dollar at bank or government money-changer. That way lose plenty money."

"So what we'd really be asking him to do is to smuggle in the money without declaring it. Then there would be no record at the airport or anywhere else and he could simply give it to your son. Who would then buy the plane tickets to Manila for himself and his family. In whatever way is most convenient."

"Also need squeeze money, passport, visa. Old Wong send enough. Never mind."

"I'm not worried about that," Kay assured him. "I know you'd send enough if it meant printing it yourself. What I don't know is whether he'll take it—without declaring it, that is—if it's against the rules."

"Why you tell him, Missee Kay?"

"You mean just ask him to take a letter—or, rather, a small package—without telling him what's inside?"

"Letter," he said with certainty. "Old Wong get big bill dollar. Not many bill."

"Well, a letter, then. And say that you're worried about your family, that you haven't heard from them for a long time, that you don't trust the mails, that you want to get news to them—and from them." Kay listed the points, emphasizing each one with a tap of her knuckles on the bar.

"That much very true."

"I know. But how thorough are the airport people? What if they question him and he says he's carrying a letter? No reason why he shouldn't, if he thinks that's all it is. What if they open it? Confiscate the money, get him into trouble?" Seeing Old Wong's helpless expression, she added kindly, "I'm only trying to decide whether it would be better to tell him the whole thing and ask him to hide the letter—smuggle it, that is—and hope he'll be prepared to do it. Or to *not* tell him and trust to luck."

"You good lady, Missee Kay. You find out."

"I'll try. Look, tomorrow's my day off, and I want to take him on a trip somewhere in the country—he loves the country—and it will give me a chance to be alone with him. Have you any suggestions?"

"Pagsanjan Falls," Old Wong said without hesitation. "Tourist all like Pagsanjan."

"But we'd need a car—"

"Old Wong fix. Never mind. Old Wong fix. Give you also sandwich lunch you take along."

Kay touched his arm lightly across the bar. "Get your siesta while you can. It's going to be a heavy evening. Saturday. And the special dance." She slid off the stool, arched her back as if she had been cramped. "I'm going to rest, too. I'll be in the Secretary's office, but don't tell anybody. They can manage the bridge for themselves. Everything is arranged; they know who they're partnering. All they have to do is start playing."

In the office, Kay went straight to the telephone on the desk. After a few moments, when she heard Mrs. Moreno's voice, she said, "This is Catalina. I hope I'm not disturbing you in your siesta?"

"Not at all, my dear child. We have only just finished our lunch. How pleased I am to hear your voice! You must have had a very busy week?"

"Well, yes, and—"

"And I hope you are not telephoning to say that you wish to cancel our usual lunch tomorrow. Ever since Luisa's departure, I have come to look forward with special pleasure to our Sundays together."

"So have I. I did, in fact, call to cancel our lunch, but also to ask you if I might come and see you in the evening—about half past six or seven? And may I bring a young man to call?"

Mrs. Moreno made no attempt to conceal her excitement. "Of course you may bring your young man! I should expect to meet any young man that you like. Tell me about him. Who is he? Did you meet him at the Club? Has he—"

"Slowly, slowly," Kay begged, laughing. "He's not 'my'

young man in that sense. But I like him, and want you to meet him," and proceeded to answer Mrs. Moreno's questions, stated and unstated. English. A flier. Here on leave. Respectable country family, as far as she could gather. Wants to see something more of Manila life and its surroundings than just the Club, the night spots, the ordinary—you know—"*sights*."

"There are not many of our extraordinary 'sights' left," Mrs. Moreno said, irony in her voice. "Do you count me among them?"

"Well, to be frank, yes. You are somebody— Doña Luisa was, too—that the casual and transient visitor is not likely to meet. A kind of Manila life—a deeply *Filipino* life—that isn't open to most foreigners however long their stay here. But that isn't why I want to bring him."

Mrs. Moreno, complimented, and assuming more than Kay had actually said, continued effusively, "Dear child, you need not explain your reasons. Just bring the young man when you wish. I shall be very interested to meet him—you know that any, well, *event* in your life concerns me."

"I don't think he'll turn out to be an 'event'—"

"You never know! You never know! You remember, I told you that—"

"I remember. We'll see."

"Indeed, we'll see. At least, I will look forward to seeing you both tomorrow." Mrs. Moreno paused, and then asked unexpectedly, "Catalina, are you happy?"

"Happy?" Kay repeated as if she had never heard the word before. "I don't know. I'm not *un*happy." She went on quickly, "They're very nice to me at the Club, everybody's very friendly, the work isn't difficult—I really have no complaints—"

"That isn't what I meant. No—no, don't trouble to answer. I will see for myself tomorrow."

"Until tomorrow, then. I'm sorry about lunch. I'm taking Jeremy out to Pagsanjan Falls. Old Wong is arranging everything."

"Very good! Very, very good, if Old Wong makes the arrangements. Pagsanjan is beautiful, also cool. Yes, that will be a very suitable outing."

"I thought he might enjoy—"

"He will! He will! Pagsanjan is a place for—enjoyment!" Mrs. Moreno had almost said, "for lovers." "What else are you planning for his enjoyment?" she asked, accepting, with her usual realism, that any young man on leave in a strange city is likely to find, disconcertingly, that he has long stretches of idle time on his hands, and will feel disproportionately grateful—even dependent—on whoever happens to fill them for him agreeably.

"Apart from our call on you?"

"What a very charming way to phrase it! No, I meant apart from Pagsanjan."

Kay hesitated a moment, and then said tentatively, "As you know, I am not required to be at the Club on Mondays. I had thought that—if you approve, of course—I might take Jeremy to dinner at the Spanish Club."

That rich, rigid, conservative institution was, as Mrs. Moreno well knew, another stronghold of the established Manila society which transients seldom penetrated. She realized, without rancor, that there was indeed another reason for the visit Kay had proposed. Without Mrs. Moreno's sponsorship, Kay, who was not a member of the Spanish Club, could not take her young man there. However, it seemed to Mrs. Moreno rather touching that Kay should want her approval, and very sensible of her to provide herself with a background of such unimpeachable respectability. "Yes," she replied obliquely, "it is evident that your Jeremy is not just anyone."

"Doña Luisa once told me that 'just anyone' could be the person that we seek."

Startled, Mrs. Moreno thought, Another Tomás? Impossible. "That was true for her," she said, with a note of warning, "but—"

"But her circumstances were very different? I know they were. That is why—"

"Naturally that is why." She was satisfied that they understood each other so well, and would not admit to a faint disappointment in the girl's unromantic common sense. Very affectionately, she said, "Catalina, you know I am your friend."

"If I could not count on that, I don't know what would become of me." Her words sounded desperate although her voice did not, but all the same, Mrs. Moreno spent much of the afternoon in detailed and practical consideration of Kay's future.

Jeremy Wilson ran up the steps of the International Club early that evening, and walked through to the bar, where he saw Kay standing very straight with her hands behind her, like an old-fashioned pupil reciting her lesson. She looked cool and rather beautiful in a precise way, her hair coiled high on her head, her long dress, of the very palest green, exposing the delicate modeling of tanned shoulders and neck. No jewelry. Gold sandals. She had been on his mind all afternoon, even when, unable to find her after his escape from the card room, he had returned to the Air Force Officers' Mess and had written a letter to Margaret, inconsequential, fond, and of suitably reassuring length. Now he watched Kay appreciatively for a moment, wondering what she was saying so intently to the bartender, and then crossed the almost empty room to stand beside her.

"What absolutely enthralling conversation am I interrupting?" He placed his hand on her bare shoulder.

"We were talking about you."

"About *me?*" He accepted her smile and saw no deviousness in her wide, ingenuous eyes. "Surely there must be more amusing subjects—the prevention of rose blight with chemical sprays, for instance, or whether the price of Nicaragua copper is likely to rise, or how many tons of goat and mohair are imported annually by Portugal— What," he interrupted himself, as though the point were of great moment, "what do you suppose a 'mo' is? Other than being hairy, I mean."

Laughing, Kay said, "I have no idea. However, I don't expect that we shall meet any on our picnic tomorrow."

"You are coming to the picnic?" Jeremy asked warily.

Kay looked away. "Not *the* picnic. *A* picnic. Old Wong is arranging an excursion for us to Pagsanjan Falls. I told him I'd promised you at least a glimpse of the countryside, and Pagsanjan is particularly lovely."

"That's uncommonly kind of you," Jeremy said to the old man.

"No trouble. If Missee Kay want. Some drink, sir?"

"Yes, why not? It must be sundown by now."

"Whiskey-soda, no ice."

"What a good memory!" Jeremy turned to gaze at Kay while she followed Old Wong's neat movements mixing the Scotch-and-soda and setting a glass of ice water beside it on the bar top.

As he moved away to the other end of the bar, Kay said, "We were also talking about Shanghai—or, rather, I was asking Old Wong questions about it. I was interested, you see, because that's where you're stationed." Jeremy found the simplicity of this remark unexpectedly affecting. "His family is in Shanghai and he worries about them incessantly."

"And I suppose he wants to join them in his declining years. Even after all this time, I still can't make sense of the Chinese and their attitude to the family. Respect them out of all reason, but keep up the most rigid barriers against affection. Live anywhere in the world, but never leave home. It's beyond me."

"Is your attitude so different?" Kay asked. "What about Somerset and that fiancée of yours?"

"True," he answered quickly, in a self-deprecating tone. "How inconsistent one is! Margaret is not, however, my fiancée. We have one of those very British agreements in which no one is irrevocably committed, in words, to anything. Nevertheless, a kind of decent behavior is expected all round. In a vague sort of way. All the same," he added unemphatically, "even if it weren't for Margaret, I do—just like Old Wong— want to go home."

"*Un*like Old Wong, as it happens. He doesn't want to return to China. His family feeling is quite as strong as you imagine, and he does indeed want to join them—but not in Shanghai. He wants to get them here to—well—to safety, or—"

"—or a better life, or at least some kind of hope for some kind of bearable future." Jeremy frowned at his drink. "Poor bastards," he said, in a low tired voice, thinking of the colonies of refugees spreading like an uncontrollable fungus on the Shanghai streets.

"Why do you say that?" Kay asked anxiously. "Is it really impossible to escape from Shanghai?"

"Not impossible. If, of course, his family has connections—"

"I'm afraid not."

"—or a lot of gold—American dollars, that is, with a known and reliable value as distinct from Chinese dollars, which are almost literally worth the paper they are printed on. It's rather a heady feeling, though inconvenient, to pay a million dollars for a packet of cigarettes."

"I don't think the money would be too much of a problem," Kay pursued. "You see, Old Wong is a very frugal man, and he must have saved or invested practically everything he's earned for years—all for his family, naturally."

"Naturally. But unfortunately he's saved the money *here*, where it can't do them much good."

"And there isn't *any* way of getting it to them?"

"Legal way?"

"Well—"

"The *il*legal ways would require some very fancy footwork, and I daresay he has scruples about that. If he hadn't, you wouldn't be so concerned about him—wouldn't need to be. Sordidly enough, just about anything can be fixed in China with the right amount of bribery to the right people." He considered the sound of his words for a moment, and then said, rather fastidiously, "How slipshod the English language is! What I meant was, the suitable amount of bribery to the appropriate people. 'Right' is quite the wrong word."

Kay didn't appear to have heard his last remarks. "Are scruples so important?" she asked. "When it's a question of survival?"

Jeremy, who had, so far, listened to her questions with

indulgence for what he took to be both her good intentions and her naïveté, now looked at her with surprise. "You don't admit any—let's call them *conditions* for survival?"

"Oh, *conditions,*" she said. *"Principles,"* as though they were some tiresome interruption. "How can they matter if you are not, first of all, alive? That's all. Just alive."

"And in staying alive, as in love and war, all's fair?"

"Well, it is—isn't it? The first love, and the ultimate war—survival?" She turned to smile at him guardedly, but her voice was conversational as she added, "In any case, nothing's fair in anything I know of, and certainly it's most unfair of me to burden you with Old Wong's problems. I like him, you know, and wish I knew a way to help him. He has been so very good to me."

"Understandably," Jeremy said, with a return to his cheerful gallantry. It was the change in her tone, the deliberate dismissing of her brief, somber comments, that convinced him the world had given her a grimmer education than even the fragment of her story she had told him that morning had indicated. *"Less* understandably," he continued, "he is being very good to me, too. Tell me about tomorrow's jaunt to the Falls—what's their name?"

The Club was beginning to fill up, at first a trickle of servicemen who inevitably made their way directly to the bar, some young, shy, silently pleading for company, others more assured, who, in Jeremy's words, "obviously knew the form," had a few days of experience behind them in Manila, or had made contacts, or were keeping appointments. Later, members and their guests, parties who were dining at the Club, began to arrive. Kay, attending to her role as director of a kind of performance, made introductions, watched groupings, unobtrusively rescuing people from boredom or embarrassment, stopping to talk to acquaintances, eliciting help and cooperation from Club habitués. After dinner, when the dance band began with a flourish of drums, more parties appeared, the girls in full-skirted dance dresses, some of the older ladies in *patadiongs*, with starched, ballooning gauze sleeves, the men in tropical dinner jackets or in the thin, loose, exquisitely embroidered shirts called *barong Tagalog*, all apparently in high spirits, buying raffle tickets amid much laughter, merrily circling the dance floor in swirls of lace and chiffon and perfume.

The evening started, at last, to take on a momentum of its own, separating the people in the Club into the dancers, the card players, the drinkers, and the talkers. The terrace, lit now only by the small table lamps under palm-leaf shades and the diffuse glow from the bar, held a few clusters of people talking quietly. Out in the garden, there was an occasional flare of a match or the bright arc of a cigarette being thrown away, and beyond that a glimpse of starlight on the Bay.

Kay, with a sigh, sat down next to Jeremy. "There," she said. "At least for the time being."

"May I offer you a stiff Coca-Cola to revive you?"

"I ought to persuade you to dance or something. It doesn't look right your sitting here all by yourself."

"I'm more than content, secure in the knowledge that eventually you would return to hearth and home."

"I'd love a Coke. And I'm glad you don't want to dance. And I can't tell you what a relief it is not to have to compliment you on your new hair style, or to warn you without actually telling you that the pretty girl over there is engaged to be married so you'd better be discreet."

Jeremy laughed. "How on earth do you remember it all—

the names and which girl is wearing a new dress, and which young man needs to be clued in to what?"

"I have to. It's how I earn my living."

"You ought to marry a diplomat."

"And do the same thing for a living? What a future to wish on me!"

"What sort of future do you see for yourself?"

"Something much more modest." She suddenly sounded uncertain.

"I have trouble imagining you in a rose-covered cottage," Jeremy said, thinking that, in fact, he had trouble imagining her anywhere at all—or, rather, that wherever she was, even the Club, she would always seem to be somehow removed from her surroundings.

"You have no idea," Kay said. "I'd settle for the cottage even without the roses."

"As long as it contained Mr. Right?" Jeremy suggested, hoping to make her laugh.

But Kay shook her head. "As long as—" and then she appeared to change her mind about how to proceed, smiled brightly, and said, "As long as it didn't have a mortgage."

The rest of the passage of the evening was punctuated, for Jeremy, with Kay's intermittent presence at his table. Meeting and parting, meeting and talking, he found himself thinking that they were like some sort of conspirators, observing the formalities in public but sharing a private knowledge that was beyond the grasp of the company that surrounded them. He did not try to formulate the unspoken understanding that he felt they shared, was satisfied that she was easy and responsive to talk to but under her amiable manner hid, as he did, a whole region of experience that would be forever foreign to the laughing, dancing Club girls.

Or, for that matter, to Margaret.

Late that night, they strolled in the moist and murmurous garden and Jeremy took her hand, feeling the small pliable bones fold together as if her hand were collapsing inside his. He thought it was like holding a bird, soft and unexpectedly tiny. They stood for a while in silence watching the shadows walk across the lighted doorways, the moving frieze of dancers, and peered into the air-conditioned card room through the tall French windows. In eerie silence, each table of players offered its absurd pantomime. Isolated groups, lit by green-shaded lamps, inaudibly recited practiced lines and speeches, shook back jangling tangles of jeweled charm bracelets without a sound as they dealt the cards. The watchers in the garden followed the movements, noticed the dedicated expressions, as if they were seeing some incomprehensible foreign ritual for the first time.

"Will you become one of those someday, Kate?"

"I don't play card games."

"That's not what I meant."

"I know you didn't. I was trying to evade your question."

"Whatever for?" Jeremy, who had spoken only out of a vague curiosity, making some attempt to give substance to Kay's setting, her past or her future, was now provoked into genuine interest in her answer.

"Well, the truth is a bit complicated. And embarrassing. And I didn't want you feeling—you know—*sorry* for me."

Annoyed with himself for having unwittingly touched on some area of her reserve, he quickly apologized. "I'm a clumsy ass—I really hadn't intended to pry."

"No, no—oh, heavens, now I've made you feel guilty! The fact is, quite simply, those people wouldn't have me—not in their families, that is."

"What cheek!" Jeremy said indignantly.

He could hear the smile in her voice as she said, "Try to think of me as they do. A sort of war orphan. Someone to be kind to, perhaps, but—"

Shocked, Jeremy began, "Your *entire family*—"

"The war did that to a lot of people," Kay interrupted, without inflection. "However, as *they* see it—and you can't really blame them for guarding their own interests—with no money and only a vanished background, I'm not in any way an ideal match for one of their sons. Especially"—she nodded in the direction of the dancers—"when there are all those delightful girls to pick from."

Jeremy gripped her hand more tightly, lacing his fingers through hers. "It's a funny world," he said, meaning, of course, exactly the reverse.

Squeals of excited amusement and brief fanfares from the band announced the distribution of the raffle prizes—marvelously inappropriate, which elicited yet more laughter and conviviality. A bottle of French perfume for a burly Marine captain. A magnificent doll, dressed in meticulously exact native Filipino clothes, for an elderly gentleman. A box of Manila cigars for one of the girls. And so on.

Jeremy led Kay away from the merriment of exchanging prizes, the joking comments called out from party to party across the dance floor, into the jasmine arbor, where he put his arms around her, remarking, "Don't, for Christsake, ask what Margaret would think of this."

"Nothing could be further from my mind," Kay said, and kissed him on the mouth. A few kisses later, they walked, swinging clasped hands, down to the sea wall because, Kay told him, it was the only way of explaining her disarranged hair.

"Will anyone believe that?" he asked, smiling at her sedate attitude.

"Of course not. But they will pretend to. One must allow other people to keep up appearances, you know, to be able to keep up one's own."

"I have no complaint about your appearance," he said, and then asked if he might take her home after the Club festivities were over. The shadowy figure beside him seemed as insubstantial as mist, but the cool voice was clear enough as Kay accepted his request with pleasure, and Jeremy felt a sudden unforeseen rush of elation at the expected answer.

He stood attentively behind Kay as she saw the last of the guests and members off from the front steps, and listened to her unflurried exchange of meaningless formalities, feeling again that they were the only two adults at a children's gathering. When, at last, they climbed into the back seat of a rickety taxi, it seemed to him that they shared a separate territory, like an island, both surrounded by another element and isolated from it. Seeing the darkened houses beyond the window as a blurred drift of gray and black, splashed here and there by pools of lamplight, and conscious of the cooler air of the small hours, sticky with salt, blowing in from the sea across his forehead, Jeremy felt as if he were on some unexplained journey. The curling fingers in his seemed the only reality in a mysterious sense of no time, no place, no language for speech—or necessity for it. Had the driver said, "Your destiny?" No, of course not. "Your destination?" and Kay had explained the tangle of back roads that led to the Residencia Flora.

She sighed and leaned back, and Jeremy said "Tired?" and pulled her over to rest her head on his shoulder, and was quiet the rest of the way. It seemed a relatively short ride through the empty streets, but Kay was almost asleep when she stumbled out of the taxi into Jeremy's arms. He held her close to his side, his mouth on her temple, kissing her gently while they waited outside the gate, arched over with vines. The old night watchman shuffled out while they could still hear the rusty clanging of the bell vibrate into silence.

"I'm sorry I can't invite you in," Kay said. "My landlady would be horrified by a visitor at this hour."

If Jeremy was disappointed, it didn't show in his voice. "Sleep well," he said. "Sleep late." He waited while the night watchman looked up and Kay followed his bobbing flashlight along the short path through a humid, overgrown garden, until he heard the closing of the front door, loud in the quiet night.

Jeremy was to remember, long after, the excursion to Pagsanjan as a sort of enchanted time, so far removed from both China and England in atmosphere and event that it held the special magic of a daydream, the sense of wonder of an accidental discovery. His experience of Asia had been limited to a few rainy days in Hong Kong, and then China proper, where, for all his brief missions to cities and towns in the interior, he felt familiar (though very much an outsider) only with Shanghai. Consequently, the most ordinary—indeed, inescapable—elements in the life and landscape of the tropics seemed to him exciting, novel, and vividly pleasing to the eye. The profligate extravagance of color—emerald rice paddies, unnamed flowers in profusion, flame trees set against the shiny green of banana plantations—seemed to him too foreign to invite either contrasts or reminders of the muted northern landscape that made up his only knowledge of "the country."

At one of the *barrios*, a haphazard cluster of palm-thatched huts around a marketplace, Kay insisted that they should stop to buy fruit, but Jeremy went straight to a stall that was virtually obliterated by massed ranks of flower garlands, frangipani, hibiscus, thick little daisies with crisp, papery petals in brilliant purples and magentas. "Can you beat it?" he exclaimed in amused delight, "Daisy chains!"

For Kay, of course, his words conjured up no image of the limp, fragile strings of those most modest of English wild flowers, or of conventional English children laboriously linking them, stem through stem, in distant summer fields. "Why do you laugh?" she asked. "Do the colors seem too garish?"

"On the contrary, that's just what's so splendid about them!"

And, infected by the casually intemperate use of flowers all around him (they would surely, in this heat, without water, wilt in an hour or two at most), he bought half a dozen garlands for Kay, feeling that it was an almost improperly reckless act. The look of Kay, smiling in confusion, and the encouraging comments and laughter of the villagers and vendors added to his pleasure in this small, uncharacteristic display of an insouciance he didn't know he possessed. At another stall, he ate chunks of papaya with lime juice squeezed over them, without a thought to the cleanliness of the man's knife or whatever dust might be embedded in the little tray of woven palm fronds on which the fruit was served. Kay bought other varieties, as well, to take with them—*rambutan, santol*, mango—all strange to him, and consequently infusing even that ordinary transaction with mystery.

She even persuaded him to try one of the *baluts* that the children were peddling, explaining that it was a Luzon delicacy, a duck egg that is kept until the duckling inside is almost ready to be hatched, at which point it is boiled and eaten warm. "Feathers, bones, beak, everything?" Jeremy asked uneasily.

"Except the shell."

"It sounds vile."

"But tastes surprisingly good. You'll see."

"This is a far, far braver thing I do . . ." Jeremy said, and swallowed the *balut* in one gulp in the correct fashion, to the applause and approval of the children and the small crowd enthusiastically joining in the mild diversion their presence in the market occasioned, Kay, too, was laughing at Jeremy's expression of comic heriosm. "It's not at all bad," he said with astonishment.

"I told you—"

"And you don't even notice the feathers and things."

"Naturally not. They're much too soft. It's only the idea that seems bizarre."

The Chinese driver deputed by Old Wong to take care of them carried their purchases back to the jeep. He spoke virtually no English but was apparently quite fluent in Tagalog, and had been talking in a worried way with a couple of men from the *barrio*. He seemed eager to hurry on, and Jeremy, who was enjoying the unforced pace of the day and the unaccustomed sense of infinite leisure, asked what the rush was all about. Kay's questioning of the driver elicited the nervous assertion that they had to return to the city before nightfall. Huk, he explained flatly, assuming that no further comment was needed.

"What on earth is, or are, the Huk?"

"They're the Communists, rather active in the countryside, particularly in the north."

"Oh, Lord," Jeremy said drearily. "I didn't know you have your Communists, too."

"Like yours, they were very useful—very much admired—as part of the underground guerrilla movement during the Japanese occupation. A considerable embarrassment to the government now."

"Yesterday's friends . . . ," Jeremy said with exasperation.

That was their only mention, in the course of their outing, of the muddled disorders and distresses of their times. From the moment they arrived at the point where they left the jeep, Jeremy was totally absorbed in the immediate exhilaration of their activities and the wildly exotic setting. The driver bargained with the boatmen—short, dark, sinewy men who maneuvered their narrow canoes with an admirable offhand skill upstream, through the gorges, between boulders, around sudden eddies, and across glassy shallows to the main fall. Jeremy felt there was something almost wicked, in a charming way, about the abundance of orchids growing unnurtured from the seams in the rocks or trailing like hovering butterflies from the giant tree ferns on the banks. The Falls themselves, cascading tempestuously down a dark green chasm, ended in a milky restless pool, treacherous to look at and startlingly cold to swim in.

They scrambled out onto the rocky bank, gasping and breathless as if they had closely escaped some minor peril, with the unaccountable high spirits that such moments engender. Kay stretched out in the sun, wet hair clinging to her shoulders, and said impulsively, "I haven't felt so carefree for ages! What a genius Old Wong is!"

Jeremy looked at her with some curiosity. "What do you usually do for enjoyment?"

"I don't think much about enjoyment. What about you?"

"Exercise," he answered promptly. "I have the English-man's unshakable belief in both the virtue and the pleasure of meaningless physical activity."

They drank beer which had been cooling in the pool while they swam, and with great appetite ate the lavish lunch Old Wong had provided, finishing with the fruit Kay had bought, which Jeremy found perfumed and incredibly sweet. Afterward, with a long mock groan, he announced, "I must go for what we call a 'brisk walk' to reassure my digestion. My insides must be so surprised at this mad deluge of strange food."

Kay warned, "This sun is stronger than it feels down here in the canyon."

"I know," he answered. "Mad dogs and Englishmen ... I've always thought that a dreadful slander of mad dogs," and he got up, stretched, and set off happily over the slippery rocks to where the path into the steamy jungle began.

Kay watched him leave thoughtfully, noticing the easy way his body adjusted its weight and balance to the uneven surfaces. She distributed the remains of the lunch and the fruit to the villagers who had sat about, shaded by their woven palm-leaf hats, regarding the picnic with friendly interest. At last, she lay down again, one arm across her eyes, and began to think very methodically about the sequence of the next few days.

For Jeremy, the most memorable part of the outing was the return trip, when their boatmen took them on a tempestuous ride skimming down the rapids, dodging great boulders set in the ferment of water and foam. The sight of Kay, hair streaming, face taut with excitement, slender figure cutting through the rainbows caught fleetingly in bursts of spray, and his own feeling of well-being, of being intensely alive, combined to fill him with a sort of undirected gratitude. Only later, on the long jeep ride back to the city, did he repeat in his mind Kay's abrupt, remembered remark of the day before, ". . . first of all, alive. That's all. Just alive," and marveled that the same word could hold such extremes of meaning.

Kay broke a long easy silence to tell him about their call on Mrs. Moreno just as Jeremy started to ask her where he could take her to dine that night. They both laughed, and together said, "You first," which provoked them to even further amusement. Still caught in that moment of silly gaiety, Jeremy was instantly interested in Mrs. Moreno and wanted to know all about her. But Kay said only that he would see for himself; that, apart from Old Wong, Mrs. Moreno was her only friend; that she represented a kind of world he might never otherwise come across in the Philippines. "I thought that she—and her surroundings—might give depth to your picture of Manila."

Jeremy thought that Mrs. Moreno might give depth to his picture of Kay, but didn't say so. Instead, he asked her if she would mind waiting at the Air Force Officers' Mess while he changed. "Not more than ten minutes, I promise you. I do want to look presentable for your Mrs. Moreno."

They went from there to the Residencia Flora, where Kay ushered him into the musty little parlor with its fringed table-cloths, religious prints on the walls, and massed potted plants in the windows. To his request to see some of her paintings, she replied, "Well, all right," doubtfully. "I hope you're not too critical."

"Not a chance," he assured her cheerfully. "I grew up, you see, in the kind of house where a lot of fruit with a dead pheasant in the foreground, meticulously painted—you could recognize every feather—was considered suitable art for the dining room. The drawing room had water colors done on a tour of Brittany by my aunt. I expect your things are much more sophisticated."

But when Kay brought out her portfolio of sketches and a few rather conventional portraits, he was impressed more by their simplicity than by any expected sophistication. She left him looking at the city scenes, which had so touched Doña Luisa, while she went to dress. Jeremy found in the candor of the sketches no blurring with romantic charm, and was struck by the contrast they presented to the assured and impervious prosperity of the Club life—the only setting in which, so far, he had had the opportunity to place her. He now began to consider Kay a stark realist, compelled by circumstances to see the landscape around her without illusion. He thought that her composure must be a very hard-won attribute, and admired her as much for her vulnerability as for the protective disguise of her social manner. With a surge of warmth, with Shanghai in his mind, he thought, We are very much alike. The idea settled in him with the weight of a conviction, and he didn't realize until much later how wrong it was.

With less attention, he leaned the portraits up against the wall. One of Doña Luisa, whose dreaming eyes stared mistily out from her narrow face with an air of expectancy. She could have been listening for a footstep or the sound of a familiar voice. Ramón looked dark and appropriately scandalous; Angelita shy and hopeful. He wondered whether they were members of Kay's lost family. Friends, perhaps? Art school models?

When Kay returned, he was looking at a painting of an old woman dressed in peasant clothes, shapeless and familiar and beyond period or place. She, or someone just like her, had always sat, her head covered, her hands busy, a basket beside her, just outside the doorway of a hut, in a pose of infinite weariness. Yet the bare feet so solidly placed on the ground, the determined mouth, and the undeluded eyes suggested a sort of stamina beyond physical health or optimism. She was a figure from some timeless order of life, not accusing, not forgiving, just implacably surviving.

"That," Kay remarked, "can be counted as a self-portrait."

Ready to laugh, Jeremy turned toward her, saw that she seemed entirely serious, and felt that he had learned a lot about her in a very few seconds. They set off, with no further comments about Kay's pictures, on the next episode of their day.

Mrs. Moreno, in her setting of crimson damask and little ornaments, aroused his attention as Kay had promised. The kind of woman he had not, in his short stay, met or expected to meet in Manila. She welcomed them, noting behind her little cascades of talk, her offers of sherry from prewar stocks, that Kay looked very precise and level-browed next to Jeremy's rather pleasant unruly blond-and-red coloring. He caught her canny glance and realized that he was being presented for approval. Guilelessly, he supposed that with no family to watch over her choice of companions, Mrs. Moreno had become a valued arbiter and guardian for Kay.

If it was at all important to her, he thought, rather touched by her transparent arrangement, he would naturally do his best to get in Mrs. Moreno's good graces. He accepted the sherry with the remark that he hadn't been offered good sherry since . . . well, ages ago. Unbidden, the image came to his mind of the shabby, chintzy, comfortable country living room in Margaret's house. Her father, who called him "My boy" and wished he were young enough to fight in this war, too. The faded mother, with her bird's nest of hair, her warm smile, her Ladies' Guild activities. And, of course, Margaret herself, almost painfully young and without artifice, wrinkling her nose at the taste of her first sip of sherry. From outside the open windows, the early twilight and the autumn smell of the orchards. A wood fire in the fireplace.

He quickly brought his thoughts back to Mrs. Moreno and her lightly disguised curiosity, and began to talk about his very surface impressions of Manila, of a city littered with street names and memorials of great figures from the history of the Philippines. "It makes me feel so ignorant," he remarked.

"This is no surprise," Mrs. Moreno joined in joyfully. "So many times I have observed this same ignorance. Really, it is our fault; we have no history books, and so people say, 'Philippine history is nothing—three hundred years in a monastery and fifty years in Hollywood! Why trouble to read about such a history?' "

Privately, Jeremy thought it a rather good description of the modern Manila he had seen, only through taxi windows: the young men in flashy rayon shirts, trying to look American, and the black-clothed figures of religious processions in penitence and mourning, defying the tropical sun.

Mrs. Moreno was saying, "My husband was a great friend of Aguinaldo—do you know who he is?"

"Well, his name is everywhere—a historical figure of some kind—"

"You see? He is the savior of our country. Nothing less. Our admired hero who led us first against the Spanish, then against the Americans! To you he is a street sign!" She smiled disarmingly. "I mean no criticism. I am sure you wish to learn—unlike most. It is a strange reversal, is it not? For so long, we in Asia had to learn about you. Now you must learn about us! It is painful, perhaps?"

"Sometimes," Jeremy admitted.

"Catalina!" Mrs. Moreno said, in exaggerated reproach. "How have you allowed this?"

"No, no," Jeremy protested. "I was thinking about China."

"Ah, China." Mrs. Moreno nodded, and smoothly led him into talking about his work, with practiced conversational dexterity avoiding any semblance of overt inquiries into his "prospects."

For his part, Jeremy, intent on entertaining her, gave only the most cursory outline of his duties as a civilian pilot in Shanghai. He concentrated, instead, on recounting amusing or surprising aspects of Chinese life as he had happened on them.

There they sat, and, glancing occasionally at Kay, the change of shadows on her face in the softening light, Jeremy talked without constraint. He told them about a Chinese crew member of his whose mother consulted the family astrologer every day, convinced of the wicked spirits waiting for vengeance on the men who, in her phrase, "flew through the air," disturbing their proper realm. Before every flight, she would visit the man who was skilled in the reading of ancient prophetic bones, who would, with full ritual, throw the bones on the floor, judging by the design of their falling and the meaning of the scratched ideographs inscribed in the yellow surfaces the possibilities the future held. "Her son, a first-rate radioman, and a very unsuperstitious type, 'flies through the air' regardless of dire predictions, but always carries a jade talisman given him by his mother for protection."

"Why does 'flying through the air' sound so much more

hazardous than just 'flying'?" Mrs. Moreno wondered aloud.

"I don't know, but it does. Perhaps the chastening thought that we are relying only on air, entrusting our lives, machinery, everything to the most unstable of elements."

"I can well see that it looks like magic to the mother," Mrs. Moreno said. "And your friend is quite right to respect her wishes."

With pleasant, inconsequential exchanges of this sort, the conversation moved along at a brisk pace while Mrs. Moreno, shrewd and talkative but also receptive and observant, placed Jeremy, as was her habit, in an appropriate social niche. (Her private summing-up was: Very English, by which she meant decent middle-class, well-mannered, reliable, without glamour.) She thought that Kay's taste would have run to something more unusual but was relieved that the girl showed rather conservative good sense. With a certain inward amusement, she considered how cautious the young seemed to have become. In the days when she had loved Tomás de Salablanca, they had been far more reckless, and excitement had shivered like lightning between them.

That remembered experience was still vividly in her mind when the young people got up to leave. Kay, who had taken very little part in the talk that evening, content to let her studied and casual meeting take its own course, now tipped her head inquiringly at Mrs. Moreno, who, benevolently aware of the question, replied in her own way: "Well, Mr. Wilson, you have given me much pleasure coming here this evening. Catalina tells me that she would like to take you to dine at the Spanish Club tomorrow night. If you will allow me, I shall perform the necessary introductions for you, and you will, of course, be my guests, though I shall not accompany you. The food still is excellent; you may, however, find the atmosphere a little staid." To her and Tomás, the dull old Spanish Club would only have been interesting as the *mise en scène* of a subterranean comedy, laced with dialogue rich and risky with illicit innuendo, enacted under the innocent chaperonage of their elders. Still, and she mentally shrugged, these two would make a very handsome couple at their uninspiringly proper rendezvous. (No one had ever called Tomás handsome.)

Taken a little unawares by the thought that planning and discussion about him had secretly taken place between the two women, Jeremy said, "Kate hadn't mentioned it to me . . ." and immediately realized the reason both for the meeting and for her reticence. Pleased with the idea that he had made an acceptable impression, he turned to Kay and said, with unaffected warmth, "How quite extraordinarily generous you are being to a total stranger whom you'll probably never see again."

He didn't notice Mrs. Moreno's twinkling glance at Kay as she said, "The more reason we should try to make your holiday pleasurable. Where are you thinking of dining tonight?"

"The Bodega Sevilla," Kay said promptly, "where we can listen to their really inspired guitar player."

"Very good! Very good!" Mrs. Moreno cried. "The perfect contrast to the Spanish Club—informal, badly lit, even bohemian! Every holiday should be full of diversity and surprises—do you not agree, Mr. Wilson?"

In the days that followed, Kay skipped her art classes altogether. With Mrs. Moreno's knowing encouragement, she devoted all the time she could spare from the Club to seeing that Jeremy was entertained and amused, but most of all, occupied. Jeremy, still carrying, with more assurance now, the unfamiliar holiday mood he had first felt on their excursion to Pagsanjan, was captivated by this period of undiluted and unworried enjoyment. He could not remember any comparable time in his life, and felt that he was discovering unknown and surprising faculties in himself. It reminded him, oddly, of when he had, one childhood summer holiday, learned how to swim. A sudden feeling of mastery, ease, and freedom in a new dimension—a sense of triumph almost.

The somber red-plush-and-mahogany atmosphere of the Spanish Club had delighted him with its uncontemporary grandeur. Watching jai-alai games, he and Kay, with no expertise to guide them in their knowledge of form, had placed their own wild bets along with the serious, canny spectators around them, choosing their players because of an attractive name or the design of an insignia on a shirt. Somehow this haphazard gambling gave their small winnings the added pleasure of an undeserved windfall, and they spent the money at once in the restaurant that opened off the glass-enclosed gallery above the jai-alai court, ordering champagne and toasting their winners with an enthusiasm quite out of proportion to either the skill of the players or the rather inferior quality of the wine.

Often, during the day, Mrs. Moreno lent them her car for short drives to lunch at a country inn, or for sightseeing in town, where, although there was no escaping the evidences of war, neither of them mentioned the extent, the incoherence, or any personal response to the devastation that stretched behind the graceful souvenirs of Spanish colonialism. Mrs. Moreno always hospitably suggested a cup of coffee before they left or an apéritif when they returned, and found no reason to revise her original assessment of Jeremy.

Evenings when Kay had to be on duty at the Club, Jeremy good-humoredly accompanied her, and Old Wong made sure that a particularly good dinner was served to them, in private, in the Secretary's office. He refused to accede to Kay's appeal to continue her practice of eating in the kitchen, and shook his head at her suggestion that Jeremy might enjoy joining them. "Better you do like Old Wong say," he said, and put an end to any further argument by adding, with a note of almost tremulous pleading which Kay had never heard in his voice before, "Please, Missee Kay. You do this for Old Wong."

Whenever it was possible for Kay to leave the International Club early, and even, however briefly, after one of the late dances, she and Jeremy returned to the Bodega Sevilla, finding in its public privacy precisely the right setting for conversation or for silence. In a way, it contained that mixture of intimacy and distance that Jeremy felt existed so subtly and pleasurably between him and Kay. A small, dim room with wooden tables along its walls. An unobtrusive bar. A swing door at the back leading into the kitchen, from which issued a faint smell of garlic and heating olive oil.

It was in the guitar-filled twilight of the Bodega, late on Sunday night, a week after Kay had first brought Jeremy there, that the most extraordinary conversation of his life occurred. He had watched her fidgeting with her glass and the sodden paper napkin for some time, and, puzzled by this uncharacteristic display of ediness, at last asked her if something was troubling her.

"I'm trying to get up the courage to ask you a favor," she replied.

"Yes," he said with immense gravity. "I can see that requires any amount of courage. There's simply no knowing how I might react to being asked a favor."

"It's rather a serious favor."

"I'm braced."

"Will you marry me?"

There was a long pause while Jeremy Wilson sipped his Fundador, attempted to collect his wits, and finally said, "Did I hear you correctly? Did you propose to me?"

"I made a proposal to you, which is different."

"How is it different?"

"I mean: Just marry me. Nothing more."

"Nothing more than what?"

"Than the papers signed, the legal formalities completed."

" 'In name alone'? You must be joking."

"It would be a poor joke. I told you I was being serious."

"Just possibly it has escaped your attention, but you should know that there is—"

"—'the girl back home'—"

"—Margaret—"

"Margaret. No, she has not escaped my attention. Nor has your commitment, however unspoken, to her."

"Well, yes." He was quiet for a considerable time before he said, "Well, if you want to be serious, I'm expecting to marry Margaret when I get home. She's a real person. I get letters from her." For a moment, he was not entirely sure if she was, actually, a real person. He knew he got letters from her.

"Margaret need never know."

Incredulously, Jeremy began, "She need never—"

"—*know* is what I said."

"That's what I thought I heard."

"Because it would have nothing to do with what you feel about Margaret."

Jeremy shook his head in perplexity. "Kate, for Christsake, *what* are you talking about?"

"About marriage, not love. And about getting me out of the Philippines. That's really what I'm talking about."

With mild sarcasm, Jeremy said, "People travel all the time nowadays. It's become an international hobby. I'll tell you how it works—it's not insuperably complicated once you get the hang of it. You go down to the airlines office—"

"Jeremy, *please,*" Kay interrupted. "I can't just travel like that. And if you'll listen for a moment, I'll tell you why."

Arrested by her desperate earnestness, he shifted uncomfortably in his chair and waited silently for her to continue.

"Do you remember asking me once whether I was in Manila during the war?"

"You said you weren't. I assumed you must have been with your family and that you didn't wish to speak about that particular tragedy."

"Now I'll tell you where I really was. I was in Japan. I was a student there, in Tokyo."

Jeremy stared at her as if he were seeing, for the first time, face to face, some dreaded figure from a dream. Kay saw the change in his expression and sounded impatient as she continued, "You are thinking, of course, about internment camps and what, in your English way, you would evasively call, 'all that.' Well, yes, there were internment camps and 'all that.' But I was going to tell you something that it's less easy to be sympathetic about. I was bailed out—isn't that the phrase that fliers use?—by a Japanese family. I spent the war there, protected by them. Do you see why I can't just go down to the airlines office, on a whim, like a tourist? I'm considered a collaborator."

Reluctantly, Jeremy found something very courageous in

her hostile manner and uncompromising words, even though she was saying, "When I was repatriated, I was too cowardly to face police investigations and what would follow. I destroyed my travel documents. I changed my name—Kate Gómez isn't a real person, she doesn't exist. Or, rather, she exists but is not Kate Gómez. It is somebody else that is wanted by the police, though eventually it will be Kate Gómez who is caught by them. A matter of time. The hatred for the Japanese is very strong here, as you must have noticed."

"I have noticed. And virtually anywhere in Manila I can see why."

"Yes, but I am asking you to see something more difficult. I was sheltered by them—the Japanese, I mean. In a way, I was on their side—do admit it, as senselessly as the others they killed, they were also killed—the difference, to me, was that they protected me. With that history, do you think I could even apply for a *passport?*"

"They killed your brother," Jeremy said, as though some statement of known fact could somehow bring this dialogue to a level of acceptable reality. He hadn't expected Kay to laugh.

"It makes a neat problem, doesn't it? One is saved, one is killed. You know, I first heard about Corregidor in Japan as a victory, with accounts of the grateful Filipinos welcoming the Japanese as liberators from colonial rule. It was only after I came back to Manila that I was told about it as a defeat, by a friend of my brother's who had fought with him. Can you tell me the moral of that story?" Suddenly grave, without waiting for his answer, she said, "I don't think I could stand any more reprisals. All I know is that I must leave the Philippines and can't, unless I have a legitimate way."

"And I'm to be the way?"

"It sounds insulting," she said without apology, "but, yes, I had hoped so, had hoped to go to China with you."

"As my wife." Caught in a situation that was altogether too muddied for indignation, Jeremy said, "To begin at the beginning—though I'm not sure where the beginning is, certainly not here, in the Bodega Sevilla—let me tell you right off that although I find you most unusual company, I am not in love with you."

Kay took a deep breath, and said in the reasonable tone of voice one uses to someone who doesn't, in spite of earnest effort, quite understand one's language, "Of course you aren't. In fact, that's the whole point. Don't you see that if you were in love with me, I couldn't ask this of you?"

"How true," he said, with a last halfhearted attempt to make a joke of it all. "You can really only ask a chance acquaintance to marry you."

"It's a smaller request," Kay remarked, unsmiling, "than if I were asking you to love me. I know it seems like an unconventional arrangement."

"You have a real gift for understatement. But—"

"But then it would also be a very brief arrangement. As soon as we got to China, we'd apply for a divorce—"

"And then, just like that, you quit? And I'll once again be that enviable creature, the bachelor Jeremy Wilson, without a care in the world, with a girl back home, with a good if slightly hazardous job? Right? A job that will eventually earn him enough money to take him back to England, to Somerset and—let's not forget—to Margaret?" As he spoke, he conjured up in his mind the sunlit picture of Margaret, the image he had carried with him through the war. It seemed curiously insubstantial in the presence of this other girl with the dark desperate eyes, the smooth hair, the deceptive composure.

She was saying, "I can only give you my promise for my part of all that."

"Is a divorce so easy? Or so private?"

"I don't see why not, since we'd both be in agreement." Seeing his appalled expression, Kay continued, with more urgency, "What does it amount to anyway? We sign a couple of papers at the Consulate here, we leave Manila on the same plane—oh, listen, for heaven's sake, I'll pay my way, I've saved the money—we arrive in Shanghai—"

"As a married couple."

"About whom nobody, except perhaps the airport officials, need to know even that much—"

"Margaret would have to know. I couldn't not tell her."

"If you feel you must, by all means tell her."

"That I'm saving a girl from a fate worse than death?" he asked, smiling.

Very soberly, she answered, "There is no fate worse than death. Tell her you are keeping a girl alive. It is the truth."

" 'Just be alive'?" He quoted her remembered words with all their meanings in his mind.

"It's the biggest favor anyone could possibly ask."

"I must say, in comparison, whatever other favors I've been asked seem hopelessly lacking in imagination." Jeremy called for another drink, remarked that the room was hot, the guitarist excellent, and thought, Well, why not? People had done it in Germany; British and Americans had made such marriages just to get girls out of some intolerable situations. "I don't know that there's much to be said for 'being alive' in Shanghai," he said at last.

"Oh, don't worry about that—I'm not expecting to be your responsibility there. I'll manage. I always have. I'm used to working. And from Shanghai the ex-Mrs. Wilson can go anywhere—anywhere in the whole world—" Suddenly aware of an unexpressed change in his attitude, a relinquishing of his defensive flippancy, she asked, "You'll do it?" on a note of breathless hope that Jeremy found both pitiful and shaming.

"I seem to have agreed without at all intending to," he said with difficulty.

"You're not drunk?" she asked anxiously.

"Not even slightly," he answered, and indeed he seemed not only controlled but abstracted, as though his attention were focused on some private debate.

There was, of course, no recapturing the light atmosphere of casual holiday entertainment, and later, when Jeremy said good night to Kay at the vine-covered gate of the Residencia Flora, he did not kiss her.

In the morning, Kay called on Mrs. Moreno. She waited for none of the fussy formalities, but said at once, "I wanted to tell you that I'm engaged to be married."

Mrs. Moreno, drawing the loose lace of her morning dishabille closer around herself, said, "Dear child, I'm not surprised." She thought, How little is left of romance, intrigue, the factors of life that make for interest.

"To Jeremy Wilson."

"Yes, of course. Who else could it be?"

"I just thought you should be the first to know."

"I already knew when you brought him here. He is very appropriate—very—I don't know. Quite the right one for you."

"I think so."

"Catalina, love is a very private matter—I know from experience—and I am so happy that you have found that special world." She didn't believe a word of what she said.

Kay rattled on about how, in any case, the "season" was ending; how, by now, it would be easier, or perhaps unnecessary, to fill her place in the International Club (the staff was trained, especially Old Wong); how, in any case, there would be less work and the regular Club Secretary could handle it. But Mrs. Moreno wasn't listening. She was wondering why she was obscurely disappointed when she should be pleased that Kay was—as she had planned and hoped—at last "settled in life." Something was missing. Perhaps wonder? Or excitement? Intuition and Kay's manner told her that this girl didn't love the quite ordinary young man of the past week. But then neither had she, Mrs. Moreno, loved her husband when their marriage—properly arranged between families in the customary way, with heavily chaperoned parties and the occasional few minutes alone in the conservatory, with everyone noting the time and guessing whether it was a kiss or a mere holding of hands—had taken place fifty years before.

Ah, but there had been Tomás. He was the one that had made Luisa's marriage so extraordinary. But, more than that, he had changed the texture of Mrs. Moreno's own marriage. Well, no point in thinking about Tomás. He was another, yet another story.

"You seem displeased," Kay said. "I had thought you liked Jeremy."

"Oh, I did! I do!" Mrs. Moreno fluttered on in her usual manner, her rings glittering and her eyes bright. "And I am very happy for you! I will give you a present! No, don't even try to guess—I have already decided in my mind! It would spoil the pleasure for me if, by chance—an unexpected, no, a *miraculous* chance—you should happen to be right!"

"But you needn't do anything. Unless you'd be kind enough to be a witness—"

"Ca-ta-lina," Mrs. Moreno insisted, somehow made guilty by her thoughts. "Leave it all to me. I am very, very happy for you!" Meanwhile she was thinking, How sad, how very sad, that now she will become a country English housewife. Is this our fate as women? And only because we bear children? What will happen to her spirit?

What she said was "And now you will begin on a great adventure! Marriage is, as you must know, an adventure."

"I never thought of it quite like that. Though Doña Luisa did."

"But you must! Enter it with a high heart—even nervousness, if you prefer the word. But never forget that learning to know—I mean *really learning to know*—another person is the biggest adventure in the world."

"Doña Luisa said—anyway, regarded her marriage in those terms."

"And what you are really saying is, she never learned to know Tomás?"

"Well, yes."

"She had the adventure, and so will you. The rest will depend on your perspicacity. Luisa, much as I am devoted to her, had none. She simply, very simply, loved Tomás."

"And never understood him?"

"Understanding is another matter altogether."

Kay sat silent for quite a long time. Eventually she recited, in a considering kind of voice, "Love, adventure, perspicacity, understanding. Of those, I think I have only one."

Mrs. Moreno, cautiously and wisely, did not ask which one. She said only, "Don't listen to the rambling of an old woman. I'll help you with all the arrangements, now that there *are* concrete arrangements. It will be my pleasure. I am so delighted that you are happy" (meaning, Now that you have made a respectable contract). She kissed Kay formally, on both cheeks. "Tonight I will take you both to dinner."

That evening, although Monday was a holiday for Kay, she went to the International Club. Her explanation to Jeremy was, in part, the truth—that she must give her formal resignation to the Club Secretary and, even more important, say goodbye to the staff. She refused Jeremy's offer to accompany her. "I hope you're not worrying that I might tell them we are to be married."

"No. No, I'm not. Not really. What will your reason be—for leaving, that is?"

"That I have been offered a better job."

Jeremy smiled. "I suppose that's one way of looking at it."

Imitating his tone, Kay said, "After all, the work will be light, the future prospects are good—"

"—the pay is rotten."

"Well, for an honorary job, what else would you expect?"

"Perhaps there will be other compensations. Travel. And you'll avoid meeting such interesting people. The police, for instance."

"I can't ask for more," Kay agreed. "Mrs. Moreno has invited us to dinner. She is the only one that must know our plans. In spite of all her chatter, you can count on her discretion."

"I bet I can," he said, vaguely apprehensive of these obscure maneuverings.

"She thinks we are in love," Kay added, without expression.

Monday nights were, in any case, very subdued at the Club, although the card room still attracted a moderate quota of enthusiasts. Old Wong had no hesitation about leaving the bar in charge of one of the more experienced waiters while he obeyed Kay's summons. The lights in most of the public rooms were on, but the ballroom was in darkness, and it was outside in the garden, on one of the stone benches, that Kay and Old Wong sat talking blindly to each other.

He had heard the farewells in the Clubhouse, the announcement of a new and better job about which she was not yet permitted to be more explicit. Without preamble, assuming correctly that there was no reason for secrecy with him, he asked, "Where you go, Missee Kay?"

"I'm going to Shanghai, Wong. I don't think I shall be returning to the Philippines."

There was so long a silence that the rustling of the evening garden, the faint erratic clamor of the insects, the Bay, took on an authority that made it seem as though Kay had not spoken at all. "Shanghai," she repeated more loudly. "I'm not coming back again."

Old Wong still appeared not to understand. He stared at the pale, motionless figure beside him, a lighter shadow in the obscurity around them. "Shanghai," he repeated, an unknown place, an invented word. "Shanghai."

"I've been talking to Mr. Wilson," Kay went on, with exaggerated clarity. "In fact, I've had all week to talk to him. I know—I now *know* that he is not the kind of person we can ask to break regulations, certainly not to smuggle money in to give to your son. But there's another thing I've learned about him. He's not at all stupid, and he'd be most suspicious of just any letter we asked him to take to Shanghai. He's very well aware of how much corruption there is in the city, that many people are trying to escape—trying *anything* to escape. And although he sympathizes very much with them, he would never take part in the corruption." Kay drew a deep breath.

"So I'm going to Shanghai, and I will personally—well, run your errand."

He could hear the smile in her voice and she could hear the tears in his as he said, "Missee Kay, you do this—you do all this for—"

"For you, Wong? No. I'm thinking of my own future. Mr. Wilson tells me there are many good jobs to be found in Shanghai working for the Americans. He has promised to help me, and—"

"Communist," the old man said almost inaudibly, sad to be putting an end to all Kay's bright planning for both of them.

"When they take over, you mean?" Almost gaily, she assured him, "I expect I'll be in America by then. I've always wanted to go—what Filipino hasn't? Shanghai is only a starting place, but one that can be useful to both you and me."

Unsure, but wanting to be convinced, Old Wong said, "Who take care Missee Kay? This fly-man—"

"—has *promised* to take care of me in Shanghai. And I believe him. You should, too. You know I am quite good at —at—"

The old man needed no elaboration of this aspect of Kay. "Missee Kay say he take care, will do."

"And you also know that I'll see that the money reaches your son. Can you get it together by the end of the week?"

"Can do. Easy can do," he replied eagerly.

Now it was Kay who was silent a long time, sitting close to the old man on the bench in the perfumed garden, incongruously, like lovers, with half the Clubhouse in darkness and only the fitful moonlight to confirm the appearance of an illicit rendezvous of quite another nature. At last, she whispered, "I'm afraid there's one other problem, Wong. A rather awkward obstacle." In an embarrassed rush of words, avoiding Old Wong's worried, wrinkled regard, she said, "I can't . . . I mean, I haven't got enough money to pay for my own ticket—I don't know what—" His light, restraining touch on her arm halted her, and after a moment she responded to his reassurance. "You see, there will be no indebtedness between us," she said as she might have said goodbye.

The rest of the week was, for Kay and Jeremy, a dizzying sequence of appointments, interviews, formalities, papers to be signed, regulations met. Dashing about in Mrs. Moreno's car, Jeremy lightly dismissed the thought that he was behaving like a lunatic by telling himself that in a lunatic world it was perhaps the only sane way to behave. He was lulled, too, by Mrs. Moreno's enthusiastic chaperonage and cooperation, which gave the whole performance a contradictory air of conventional respectability. Kay, in contrast, was quiet, practical, considerate, and so entirely matter-of-fact that he could almost believe that she was engaged in nothing more emotionally entangling than the arrangements for a business trip. He wasn't sure whether he was relieved or disappointed.

When, at last, after the brief ceremony at the Consulate, Mrs. Moreno disclosed the nature of her wedding present, Kay and Jeremy could not bring themselves to look at each other, and listened to her laughing, affectionate explanations with the uneasy politeness of a shared deceit.

She had provided a honeymoon—only the weekend, admittedly—but still a honeymoon. Plane tickets to Baguio in the misty green hills, the bridal suite reserved in the luxurious Palace Hotel, flowers on every table, buckets of champagne on ice, a light and delicious supper, and instructions to the staff that on no account, even by a telephone call, were the newlyweds to be disturbed.

But that Friday night, the food and wine untouched, their small suitcases still unopened, Kay and Jeremy sat there, the whole room between them, silent and furtively aware of the dominating presence of the double bed, which ritually carried the name of "the matrimonial."

Jeremy was the first to speak. "Tell me, Mrs. Wilson," he said conversationally, "as a matter of more than academic interest, have you ever been in love?"

Kay gazed at her hands clasped on her knees, and after a while replied, "Yes. Once. With an economist. In Japan."

"With a *what* ? A Japanese economist?"

"American. Quite a lot older than me."

Jeremy took a deep breath. "How extraordinary," he remarked, as though Kay had told him a recondite and passably interesting scientific fact. "What happened?"

"Well, nothing came of it, obviously."

"I meant, what went wrong? Something must have ended it?"

"He decided he didn't want to marry me."

"That's all?"

"Isn't that enough? It's why I left Japan and came back here."

"But things don't end like that." Jeremy sounded disconcerted, rejecting this flat account. "I mean, he must have— I mean, didn't he—"

"Love me? Yes. For a while. Then he found he didn't. Did we have an affair? Yes. For a while. Then that, too, ended."

But, hearing no finality in her voice, Jeremy asked, "Are you still in love with him?"

"Oh, no," she said. "Not at all." She might have been replying to some polite inquiry about whether she felt chilly and would like the window closed. "Anyway, it seems like a long time ago now, and—"

"—and that was in another country, and besides the econo-mist is dead?"

"What makes you say he's dead?" Kay demanded, in sud-den alarm.

"Oh, my poor Kate!" Jeremy said, disarmed by her in-voluntary admission. After a moment, he stretched out his hand to her. "Come here," he said very gently. "Come over here to me."

Kay walked across the big, pinkish room to stand before him in her familiar prim pose, hands behind her back, an attitude strangely suggesting both obedience and rebellion. A rigid little figure in the inviting opulence and rosy lamp-light of the bridal suite. At last, as if it took some effort, she put her hand, knotted in a small tight fist, on his extended palm. He closed his fingers around it and found that they covered it almost completely from sight. It took no strength to pull her down into his lap, and even then he hardly felt her weight. He kissed her very deeply and for a long time, until she pulled her mouth away, gasping.

She started to say something, her voice barely under con-trol, but Jeremy interrupted. "Hush," he said. "Just stay quiet."

The silence stretched and stretched until Jeremy felt her body curve and soften against him. Then, somewhat indis-tinctly, he said, "After all, we're married, aren't we?"

Kay woke to the watery blue light of the early Baguio morn-ing, slid carefully out of Jeremy's arms, and stood for a mo-ment by the bed looking down at his shadowed face, secret in sleep. She moved across the room to her suitcase, still unopened, on the luggage rack. The small metallic explosion of the lock as she unfastened it startled her, and in that unguarded moment she answered Jeremy's sleepy questions, "What are you doing? ... Why are you up? ..."

" 'I get up and search,' " she said almost inaudibly, at last admitting to her mind the memory of other weekends restless with the sound of the Chiba surf.

"Search? Whatever for? At this hour ..."

"A dressing gown." Silently, she completed the *haiku*: I get up and search,/I lie down and reach across./How wide the mosquito netting seems.

Jeremy's voice, amused and confident, was saying, "You won't need a dressing gown. Here ..."

She returned slowly to the bed, half hearing, plagued by the *haiku* written long, long ago. By a courtesan? The only one she ever wrote. Her lover died? Anyway, he left her. And that was all she could say. "I get up and search. ..."

Kay lay down and reached across the wide bed, aware of his enveloping warmth before she touched him, before he said, "Ye-ess," on a drawn-out note of content.

Some time later, when Jeremy drifted back into sleep and whatever fragmentary dreams he encountered of war or happiness, she remained awake and thought about Margaret.

PART IV

Beauty, Reason, Virtue

◢§"Well, here it is. The city of your dreams," Jeremy said, a world of depression in his voice. "You're out of Manila and in Shanghai. Or, to put it more accurately, if less originally, out of the frying pan into the fire."

Kay looked around the airport, the haphazard muddle of temporary shelters, Quonset huts, raw concrete buildings, vast ugly hangars roofed with corrugated iron—all clouded with dust and deceptively somnolent in the late-summer afternoon. "It's beautiful," she said.

A CAT jeep had been sent to meet them—or, rather, to meet Jeremy—but the Chinese driver, wearing ill-matching items of castoff army uniforms, stripped of insignia, showed neither surprise nor curiosity at Kay's presence. She, however, gave him a radiant smile, including him in an undirected surge of relief, gratitude, and soaring spirits.

She hadn't really expected much trouble at the airport, guessing (correctly, as it turned out) that Jeremy's CAT credentials would see them smoothly through most of the formalities. Like the other pilots and crew members, he was known to the airport personnel, and one of them had even asked Jeremy if he had enjoyed his leave. He had glanced at Kay, and then replied gravely, "Unusually interesting."

Even the Currency Control desk, which she had approached with justifiable nervousness, presented, in the end, no complications. The bored official who flipped through Kay's new British passport and Jeremy's shabby one seemed not at all concerned that Jeremy declared only something less than fifty dollars in his possession. He dutifully stamped the figure on the final page of Jeremy's passport, gave him a form that he would have to present on leaving the country to show that this small amount, at least, had been exchanged at the legal rate, and didn't ask Kay any questions at all. Clearly, he knew the perfectly legitimate system under which CAT pilots received their salary, and apparently assumed that Kay, as a dependent, would benefit by the same arrangements.

Kay, superstitious about small things, had worn her lucky white suit, a silly outfit for traveling, but worth the absurdity for the self-assurance it gave her. She had, as well, taken more practical measures and had been quite willing to declare the two hundred dollars in traveler's checks that she carried undisguised in her handbag. The fact that this sum had not been registered in her passport gave her the heady feeling of having received an unexpected bonus, and even the drive into Shanghai didn't temper the optimism so unfamiliar to her nature. In any case, the bomb damage, compared with Tokyo or Manila, seemed almost inconsequential. She saw no great stretches of the city flattened to rubble with only a factory chimney here and there, no odd concrete buildings left standing freakishly like tombstones in an untended cemetery. Only later did she discover that Shanghai knew a different kind of war.

At the CAT house, Jeremy watched, frowning, while the bags were unloaded, told the driver that he would be needing the jeep again in an hour or so, nodded absently in acknowledgment of the driver's sketchy salute, and, picking up a couple of flight bags, strode through the doorway. "Just a moment," he said over his shoulder to Kay. "I'll send someone out for the heavy things." He seemed quite unapproachable behind a barrier of guarded efficiency, and Kay, unwilling to relinquish her mood and unable to share it, nodded peaceably in assent.

Soon she followed the porter into the lobby, where Jeremy was standing at the reception desk writing something in a brisk, impatient way, asking a question of the Chinese clerk, picking up a small pile of accumulated mail, and shoving it in his pocket without looking at it. Watching him, she thought it probably contained letters from home, from Margaret. He turned to see her standing beside the porter and the luggage, and walked toward her, still abstracted and rather grim. "Bloody climate" was all he said, and picked out his own suitcase.

He was already moving toward the elevator when Kay, suddenly uncertain, seeing him resuming what she thought of as his "real" life, said, "I suppose I should thank you now. And say goodbye."

Jeremy swung round abruptly to face her. Unsmiling, he said, "Don't be such an ass, Kate," and distractedly, "It's just this filthy city. . . ."

"This beautiful filthy city."

"If you insist. Anyway, we've got to find you a room somewhere in this beautiful filthy city. But first I'd better stow my gear and get a shower and change."

And read Margaret's letters in privacy, Kay added to herself.

"Will you mind waiting here? I won't be long."

"I shall love waiting here. In Shanghai."

"Some people have the most perverted tastes."

While she was sitting in the lobby, Kay watched the traffic in and out of the bar, men arm in arm with slender Chinese girls, or with foreign girls of indeterminate nationality who had more make-up and more gaiety but less style. Some of the men were in uniform, some in tropical civilian clothes, all of them seemed to carry a transient air—not like that of tourists, but simply of people passing though a city, any city, on their way to a permanent destination.

A young American came up to her as she sat so tidily quiet in her corner, and said, with utter guilelessness, "Anything I can do to help you, ma'am?"

"Thank you, no. I'm waiting for my—my husband." Her hesitation was not deliberate, only the result of the novelty of the words, but she was interested in his response, a very skeptical "Oh? Well, yeah. O.K."

It occurred to her that by simply allowing people their assumptions, she could perhaps save Jeremy many of the social embarrassments and explanations that their somewhat unorthodox marriage would certainly engender. If, that is, Jeremy expected to be seen socially with her at all.

The young man seemed reluctant to leave, and the vague possibility that Kay had half formulated in her mind was suddenly confirmed by the comically astonished expression on his face when he saw Jeremy, blond and suntanned, in stiffly clean clothes, leaving the elevator and heading directly and obviously for their corner.

"*Jeremy Wilson!*" he said softly to himself, and when

Jeremy came closer, added casually, his face alive with curiosity, "Hi, there, you look great. Good leave?"

"Fine, thank you."

"You didn't get to go home?"

"Not enough time."

The young man flicked a quick disingenuous look at Kay. "Too bad," he said. "Still and all, you didn't stick around this dump, did you?"

"No, Manila."

"Well, that's just—"

Kay's unhurried interruption was just this side of a snub. "Would you mind taking me to my hotel? I find I'm rather tired." Her words were addressed to Jeremy but intended for the consideration of this inquisitive stranger.

"Excuse me, Mrs.—uh—Wilson. I'll bet you *are* tired after your long trip. From Manila?" It wasn't really a question. "Didn't mean to hold you up."

If he had expected to ruffle Kay's composure or catch a guilty exchange of glances between her and Jeremy, he was disappointed. Her voice held only faint amusement as she said, "I'm sure you didn't, Mr.— I don't believe I caught your name?"

"Jarvis. John Jarvis. Just plain Johnny to friends."

"Mr. Jarvis. I thought it most courteous of you to wish to help me, even though, as you see, it's unnecessary."

"My pleasure, ma'am. Yes, I do see you're well taken care of." He nodded goodbye to her, touched Jeremy lightly on the shoulder, said "See you around," and walked off to disappear into the bar.

"He's a terrible gossip, is our friendly Johnny," Jeremy remarked, still watching the swing doors of the bar.

"Mm. Isn't it lucky that people have such scandalous

minds? It's all going to be much easier than I feared."

"Yes?" Jeremy seemed puzzled by her comfortable manner.

"Yes. He tried to pick me up while you were upstairs. I told him I was waiting for my husband. The nice thing is that he didn't believe me—not that I was waiting, I mean, but that you were my husband."

"*Now* I see," Jeremy said, laughing uneasily.

"I expect he thought, Well, if *that's* what she wants to call him . . ."

"And took it for granted that ours was the usual stopgap liaison?"

"In a way, he's right. It's rather convenient to have a factual truth accepted as a lie—even though the lie is really the truth in the end. Anyhow, I see no reason to disabuse him."

"Won't you mind?"

"Being taken for your temporary mistress? Why ever should I? Surely you're not worrying about my *reputation?*"

"Which is, in fact, blameless."

"But for our purposes needn't appear to be."

Only a short while later, Jeremy returned from the telephone after talking to "a very useful type I know" at the Palace Hotel. "He can give you a room for a week. Key money, of course. Twenty dollars gold, which isn't bad considering the demand these days. He'll probably renew it for another week for another twenty. Anyway, it will give us time to look around a bit."

"I seem to live exclusively in palaces these days. Do you think it will give me ideas above my station?"

"Certainly not. Exactly the right setting for a mistress—however bogus."

The CAT jeep took them to the hotel, and though Kay noticed that Jeremy dismissed it for the rest of the evening, she didn't remark on it or allow herself to think of what changes or confirmation Shanghai might bring in her equivocal life with Jeremy. She signed the register at the reception desk while Jeremy went off to make his separate transaction with his "very useful type."

Only after she was installed in her room, her luggage neatly arranged, after the room boy had been tipped, asked to send up two Scotch-and-sodas, no ice, and had left—only then did Jeremy relinquish his constrained manner and smile at her properly for the first time. "Mission accomplished," he said, and took her in his arms.

"Oh, *yes*," she replied, kissed him, and added, "We've got to talk about money."

"Fascinating subject. What is your opinion of money?"

"I meant—"

He held her in a long and searching kiss. "Well, *I* think money is the root of all evil, but then my judgment is often considered eccentric."

"Oh, Jeremy," she whispered, wrapped tightly against him, her voice submerged, "you're—"

"Impossible. I know. No powers of concentration. It's a dreadful failing. . . ."

". . . impossibly . . . kind . . ."

"Kind?"

She felt his amusement shiver through her body, and, quickly alert, felt his hand moving strongly down the line of her back, smoothing her jacket against her. Almost rudely, she stepped back, out of his embrace. "The room boy will be coming back in a moment."

"But only for a moment."

She picked up her handbag from the desk and hurried into

the bathroom. She stayed there rather a long time. First she turned on both the taps above the tub. Then, as the cascades of water covered all sounds from the next room, she took off her jacket and held it up before her, gazing thoughtfully at the lining. Then, with a hairpin, she delicately unpicked the stitches along the lower edge and extracted four flat, muslin-wrapped packets of Old Wong's money that had been sewn in between the lining and the outer fabric of the jacket. She tucked them safely in her bag, and at last undressed to take a leisurely bath.

When she returned to the bedroom, her hair pinned up on top of her head, the large bath towel wrapped around her like a sarong, Jeremy was lying on one of the twin beds, propped up on all the pillows, replacing the telephone beside his half-empty glass on the bedside table. "Had to report in," he said. "Resume duty tomorrow."

"So soon?"

His hand was stretched out toward her. "Can't be helped."

Moving in response to his hand, she thought fleetingly, How curious it is, no endearments. In fact, no words, really. "I suppose not," she said.

"Sufficient unto the day"—he caught the edge of the towel and gave it a quick, downward tug—"are the pleasures thereof."

Kay asked the taxi to wait outside the big, tightly slatted gates set in a stucco wall that told nothing. The district looked run-down, but more prosperous, for all its squalor, than some of the slums she had passed on her way. Poverty and difficult conditions of living had not, for many years, shocked her, but she found something intensely disturbing in the haunted, fearful atmosphere of Shanghai. As the taxi had wound its way through streets jammed with pedicabs, rickshaws, bicycles, and pedestrians, the driver had kept his finger on the horn almost incessantly. Glancing into the seething human confusion and dirt of the side alleys, Kay explained to herself the prevailing air of instability and fright in this way: If someone were to disappear into one of those by-lanes, nobody would miss them. It was the most terrifying thought she could imagine.

In that neighborhood, Kay would, in any case, have attracted attention. Clearly a foreigner from her clothes—a cotton shirtwaist dress, high heels, a large bag slung over one shoulder—her appearance still left some doubt about her nationality. For her part, the inescapable inquisitiveness of Asia was too much an accepted area of her life to warrant any discomfiture. She hardly noticed the small crowd of children and idlers who collected around her to stare, absorbed, not friendly, not unfriendly. The man on the corner selling dumplings halted his trade with the usual passers-by and yelled to the taxi-driver. She didn't understand what he said, but the answer was clear enough. "Palace Hotel," and some explanation followed.

They all watched with dedicated interest the insignificant little drama that she provided to enliven the morning. To her determined knocking, an old man, bald, stooped, and tremulous, made a tremendous performance of rattling chains, slipping back the wooden bar across the gates, and opening them only a small way to stand there gazing at her silently. Behind him she could see a narrow slice of what appeared to be a dirty courtyard, with little mounds of garbage here and there. A couple of dogs started barking on a shrill plaintive note she had never heard before.

Speaking very slowly and clearly in English, she said, "My

name is Mrs. Wilson. I have come to see Mr. Wong."

The old man obviously understood not a word, and remained there, sad and suspicious, shaking his head. A lively chatter had started up among the watchers, and the taxi-driver came over to join them, Kay showed him the letter from Old Wong on which he had written his son's name in both English and Chinese. "Please explain," she said, "that I want to see this man."

A long exchange followed, with comments being passed back to people on the edge of the crowd who couldn't hear properly. There seemed to be much discussion, many questions, several suggestions. At last, the taxi-driver said, "Not here. Wong go office."

"His wife. Is she here?"

Another elaborate debate; the crowd had swelled and the relay of information and comment took longer, but at last, with a nod of long-delayed understanding, the old concierge motioned Kay in, leaving her just enough room to step over the threshold of the gate and sidle through the narrow opening. She waited while he fumbled with chains and bars through the business of locking up behind her. Then she followed him, without a glance at the messy courtyard, across to another door, up two flights of stairs to the Wong apartment.

There the old man knocked and shouted. A woman's voice answered. There were further high-pitched questions and replies before the door was unlocked and opened. Wong's wife seemed both astonished at Kay's appearance and utterly bewildered by the concierge's declaration that this immaculate foreigner wished to call on her. However, in a flurry of confusion, invitation, courtesy, and curiosity, she ushered Kay in and closed and locked the door in the concierge's face.

It was a small, stuffy room filled with shoddy, impersonal furniture, and an unappetizing view of the courtyard through partly shuttered windows. Wong's wife made some remark to Kay, and then scurried off as though she needed something to hide behind. Reluctantly, Kay sat on a wooden chair and gazed about her more openly. The whole place bore the unmistakable stamp of a pinched, uncertain life. Nothing looked as if it actually belonged to a family, had been chosen for pleasure, comfort, or pride. It could all be abandoned at a moment's notice without regret or even memory.

However, in the immediate situation, Kay thought that it held one sort of reassurance. A woman who lived like this, a woman who was so hesitant to unlock her door even to the known voice of the concierge, who left it open for the bare minimum of time to admit a caller, was unlikely to gossip to neighbors about the nature of Kay's errand.

Kay wondered idly, out of habit, what sort of story the woman would concoct—or, rather, what sort of explanation she herself might give of such a visit. "A friend"—no, not a friend; better to say, "An acquaintance of my father-in-law's . . . He works in a club in the Philippines. . . . How did they—? I don't know how. I didn't like to ask her. . . . I suppose she must have been a member of the club. . . . She brought news of the old man. You know, we haven't heard from him for many months. . . . A letter. Yes, he is well. He asks after the health of the children. . . . My husband will have to call on her formally, to thank her. . . . At the Palace Hotel. . . ." Well, something along those lines.

Kay extracted from her bag a pencil and a sheet of Palace Hotel writing paper. "MRS. KATHERINE WILSON," she printed in block capitals. "ROOM 307. PLEASE ASK YOUR HUSBAND TO CALL ON ME AS SOON AS POSSIBLE. TELEPHONE FIRST." Unfortunate, but necessary to prolong the contact. She had badly misjudged the length of time it took to get about in Shanghai, had hoped to catch Old Wong's son before he left for work that morning. While she trusted the wife's discretion about her visit, she thought it wiser to deliver the money itself directly and solely to the husband. Kay, mindful as ever about bargains and debts, even unspoken or unacknowledged, felt that Old Wong's confidence and generosity deserved at least that much care from her.

The harried little woman shuffled back in her straw slippers, set out teapot and cups, poured and smiled and poured again. Kay smiled back, resigned to the prospect of polite tea-drinking, to be conducted, in this case, either silently or with incomprehensible exchanges of Chinese and English. "I've brought this for you to read," she said, and handed over Old Wong's letter, gesturing to the wife to open it.

As she read, the young woman's face first relaxed into comprehension, and then, almost farcically, tensed into timorous incredulity. She burst into agitated speech, but, as Kay kept shaking her head, finally calmed down, still continuing to grip the letter as if it might disintegrate at any second.

In the ensuing silence, Kay sipped her tea, nodded or smiled from time to time, but her hostess seemed close to tears, unable to take her eyes off the letter, her cup untouched. At last, Kay rose to go and gave her the message printed on the Palace Hotel paper, assuming that the woman would have sense enough to get it translated. At once, she began a stream of timid but voluble remarks which Kay took to be the usual sentiments and proper invitations. However, Kay bowed politely, in a totally inappropriate Japanese manner, and left the woman alone with her wonderment and hopes.

Returning to the taxi, she asked the driver to take her to the British Consulate. During the ride, she sat back to watch the passing city, at last coming to some realization of its massive tragedy and the tormented life it contained, the ranks of beggars everywhere, the women clutching babies crouching hopeless and idle against any wall space, small family groups huddled around a single bowl of some kind of food, dipping their chopsticks rapidly in and out.

Along the Bund, the wide road edging the Whangpoo river, in shocking contrast stood the great prosperous bastions of the old foreign life in Shanghai—the solid blocks of insurance and shipping companies, Dutch, Scandinavian, British, American, the marble-fronted Messageries Maritimes, the vast pillared façade of the Hong Kong and Shanghai Bank, the domed Cathay Hotel. Here the busy river traffic moved fairly freely, accentuating the stationary hulks of a couple of American warships anchored in midstream, the fussy, shrill tugs, the barges, the freighters, the graceful junks with their translucent square sails.

But the taxi took her on past creeks and inlets useless for navigation, where the sampans were moored with hardly an inch between them, and large families, impossibly crowded, lived somehow on them, cooking on the tiny afterdeck on charcoal braziers, scooping water from the filthy sluggish little canals, marketing from the narrow rowboats that slithered with extraordinary dexterity between them, sleeping in a huddled mass under the flimsy awnings—lucky to have any place at all to live. All around her, stronger than the traffic fumes, was the smell of overcrowded humanity. Every now and again, this hot, musty air was spiced with the fleeting delicious fragrance of cooking.

At last, they entered the cloistered, peaceful gardens within the walled enclosure of the British Consulate. There, in a terrible miasma of unreality, Kay fulfilled the required formalities of registering her presence in Shanghai, dealing briefly and efficiently with some anonymous secretary. He noted down her name, her passport number, her "home" address (c/o Jeremy Wilson). He thanked her and added, "Please inform us promptly of any change of address. We want to be able to reach you immediately when dependents and civilians are required to go home."

"When," Kay noticed. Not "if."

"Yes, of course," she said. "In fact, I have to start looking for a place. I can't stay in the hotel very long."

"Tall order these days," he replied, and showed no signs of offering help or suggestions.

Kay returned to the hotel, sweaty and stale from her morning's excursions, asked the desk clerk to pay the taxi for her and put the amount on her bill, and went up to her room. There, in the impersonal, unexpectant atmosphere, peeling off her damp clothes, Kay found herself overcome by an exhaustion that had nothing to do with physical fatigue. She lay, apathetic on the apathetic bed, all yesterday's exuberance evaporated, checking off items on a mental list she had compiled the night before.

One item was accomplished, one half accomplished, and there remained the following: money, an apartment or room, a job, a divorce. Dismissing self-pity, she could not account for the sudden tears that constricted her throat, and could only repeat to herself, "It's beginning again. It's beginning all over again," which somehow expressed the diffusion of her thoughts. Unbidden, the memory of Mrs. Moreno saying, in quite another context, both more profound and less

complicated, "And now you will begin on a great adventure!"
And of yet another occasion, when she had told Jeremy that
she distrusted her own adventures.

Kay had never been given to self-analysis, to questioning
her motives or assessing any but the most superficial, practical reasons for her actions, but somewhere along the way she
had come to draw an inexplicit, undefined distinction between two aspects of her experience of living: situations and
people. The first she found treacherous, and sometimes ex-
plosive. In the second, she had learned to have more confidence. With people, she found room to maneuver, or
manipulate, anyway she expected to be able to establish an
orderly exchange—if one were willing to pay for their assist-
ance in whatever currency, emotional or literal, that they
valued.

She never thought about her feelings, and if they forced
themselves upon her attention (as only once in her life they
had), she suppressed them—or, rather, buried them in that
accumulation of useless debris that occupies some part of
everybody's mind. She was, therefore, quite unprepared for
the tumultuous effect of David Marius's entry into her life
later that evening.

Toward the end of the long afternoon of not exactly
thought, still less of action, the telephone rang, and Kay
answered it vaguely expecting to hear Jeremy's voice.

"Mrs.—uh—Wilson? This is Johnny Jarvis. Remember
me?"

"Good afternoon, Mr. Jarvis. Yes, I remember you. How
did you know where I was staying?"

"Oh, word gets around." He paused. "Tell you the truth,
I heard old Jeremy telephoning."

"I see. Well, what can I do for you?"

"Now, the nicest thing you could do for me is let me take you to dinner tonight."

"That's very kind of you. But I'm not sure—"

"Don't tell me that you're waiting for your—uh—husband, Mrs. Wilson. I happen to know he's out on a mission and isn't due back until tomorrow evening."

"That's more than I know. Or—so Jeremy tells me—am supposed to know. Are you sure?"

"Sure I'm sure. Ground staff. Useful to have friends with an inside line, isn't it?" He hesitated. "I hope."

"I'm not sure what to say."

"Well, now, suppose you just say yes. That way we save a lot of argument, and I'm sure you don't care for arguments."

"I don't."

"You see? I'm a fantastic mind reader."

Kay laughed. "You see? So am I."

"Why, Mrs. Wilson"—his voice was full of reproach—"I don't know what you think I'm trying to pull. All I aim to do is show you a good time and see that you aren't, uh, lonely. I thought we'd have dinner—in a restaurant, of course."

"Of course."

"And then, maybe, stop by the dance at the French Club."

Instantly alert, Kay asked, "What is the French Club? A night club or a proper club?"

"A very proper club, I'd say."

"I mean, does it have members, secretaries, that sort of thing?"

"Certainly. Don't worry, it's a very exclusive place. Very respectable."

"I'm sure it is. And, thank you, I'd be delighted to dine with you tonight. In a restaurant. And go to the French Club, Mr. Jarvis."

"Johnny."

"Johnny."

"That's great! I'll come fetch you at seven-thirty, Mrs.—uh
—Wilson."

"Katherine."

"Kathy."

In the French Club, the music had paused for an interval.
The long lovely dance room was filled with people returning
to their tables between the fluted pillars along each side. The
tall glass doors at the end were wide open to the terrace and
the windless warmth of the late-summer night outside. Driving up to the Club, Kay had heard the sound of the dance
music spilling over the garden into the pest-infested squatters' huts built on the sidewalks up against the enclosing
walls, washing all that densely, desperately packed humanity
with an incredible mist of gilded gaiety.

In the entrance hall, among the groups arriving or leaving
or just standing about between dances, Johnny led Kay past
the whispering fans, the white tropical dinner jackets, the
nervous foreign laughter, and the restless eyes and chatter to
a door on one side marked "BUREAU." It was locked.

"Well," Johnny said, "there are four possibilities. One, the
Secretary is busy. Most unlikely. Two, he's in there by himself, stewed to the gills. Could be. Or, he's in there with a girl.
Somebody else's girl, that is. Also quite possible. Or—you'll
never believe this one—he could have finished his work and
gone home."

Kay laughed as expected. "But who organizes and runs
dances like this?"

"No one that I know of. I guess they put up a notice on a
board somewhere. Anyway, word gets around, people come

along. There isn't much to do in Shanghai in the evening, you know. Chinese dance halls, of course, with the taxi-dancers. They're good—the dancers, I mean. But that's all they do. Dance. You buy your ticket, you pick your partner, she follows like you'd been dancing together for years, and then 'Good*bye*, Charlie.' "

"I suppose they don't speak English."

Johnny shook his head. Then he said, "O.K., I tried. *Now* will you tell me what's so great about this Secretary guy that you have to see him before I can even get us a drink?"

"I want him to give me a job."

"A *job*? Doing what, for Christsake?"

"A sort of social and entertainment secretary, arranging functions of this kind." She nodded toward the activity resuming in the dance room, the musicians gliding into the introductory bars, the singer pouring the words, like cream, over the dancers "You are . . . the promised breath of spring-time." Kay continued, in a neutral voice, "It's work I've done before—I'm quite good at it. That's how I met Jeremy, when I was hostessing a dance in a club in Manila. But perhaps they don't need it here. People don't come to Shanghai to spend a leave—"

"Not unless they have rocks in their heads—both of them." Kay looked so dejected that he added, "Look, if you're worried about your social life, with Jeremy away so much, forget it. I'll take care of it. I promise—it will be a pleasure."

"I'm not worried about my life. I'm worried about my living. I need a job."

Johnny's smile had a knowing edge to its kindly concern. "What, no dependent's allowance? Poor Kathy."

"I prefer to be independent."

"Yes, indeed. But, for now, let's dance and get a drink. Or, if you'd rather, we could get a drink and dance. See how easy I am?"

"May I do just one thing first?"

"Ladies' room on the right—"

"No, no. I want to leave my name and a note for the Secretary. I could come and talk to him tomorrow—there may just possibly be something."

"We'll leave a message with one of the boys—"

"But he may not remember—"

"Look, the Secretary sure as hell isn't so busy you need an *appointment*—"

"But it seems more businesslike if—"

It was after this trivial exchange—when Johnny had summoned one of the club attendants and was saying to him loudly and clearly, "Mrs. Jeremy Wilson. Will you remember that? *Mrs. Jeremy Wilson.* Tell the Secretary . . ."—that a big man, curiously light on his feet for his size, detached himself from a group of guests near them in the lobby. He had been idly watching and half listening to their mild wrangle, clearly uninterested in the eager conversation of his companions. Now, without a word of apology to them, he walked over to address himself directly to Johnny. "Please forgive an unjustifiable intrusion. Are you Jeremy Wilson?"

Johnny looked up astonished. "No, I'm—"

"But *you*"—his full attention was turned on Kay—"are *Mrs.* Wilson?"

"Yes."

"May I introduce myself? I'm David Marius."

Johnny's voice was excited as he answered, "I'm happy to know you, Mr. Marius. I'm—"

"I wanted to meet your husband," David Marius continued, speaking to Kay as if he hadn't heard Johnny's interruption.

"He's away on a mission."

David Marius frowned slightly. "That's right. He has the Peking run, hasn't he." It wasn't a question.

"I'm not supposed to know."

Suddenly David Marius smiled, a broad smile of piratical charm, though his eyes remained cautious. "Excellent," he remarked, as if Kay had performed some minor but clever conjuring trick. "You're new to Shanghai. I'd better give you my card." From the inside pocket of his dinner jacket, he produced a small white rectangle, engraved with his name and an address on Hungjao Road, in English on one side, Chinese on the other.

Kay stood staring numbly at the card, not daring yet to raise her glance again to the dark, irregular, somehow hazardous face of this stranger. Johnny took advantage of the brief silence to say, "My name is Johnny Jarvis, sir," and extended his hand.

David Marius gripped it perfunctorily, said, "How do you do?" His eyes were still on Kay, and his voice faintly impatient. "It's a business matter. I'll call on you when your husband returns, if I may." (But this wasn't a question either—or even a request.) "Where are you staying?"

"The Palace Hotel. But he doesn't—" Kay broke off, unaccountably unwilling to complete the sentence "doesn't live there with me."

"He doesn't what?" the stranger persisted.

"He doesn't let me know when he'll be back. It's against the security regulations."

"Of course, of course. However, I expect we'll be able—"

"He'll be back tomorrow evening, sir," Johnny put in helpfully.

David Marius said gently, "I know." He might have been speaking to a child.

Undaunted, or unaware, Johnny blundered on. "Would you care to join us for a drink, sir? Kathy and I were just—"

"Thank you, no. I was about to leave when I overheard you talking to the Club boy. I must say goodbye to my hosts, and I will wish both of you good night now." He gave them a slight bow—something between a bow and a nod, really—that carried the air of a formal leave-taking for all its casualness.

Johnny said, "Another time, maybe?"

Kay said nothing at all while David Marius turned and walked away from them with his light, secret gait. She watched his back, powerful, expensively tailored, perfectly correct, bending toward the ladies as he made his parting remarks, shaking hands with the men with a politeness that bordered on insolence.

Entirely at ease himself, he seemed to communicate among them some indefinable uneasiness, leaving them overanxious to talk, to laugh, to urge each other to the dance floor or the bar.

Johnny was saying, "What do you suppose *he* wants with old Jeremy?"

"Something dishonest would be my guess."

"Everything's dishonest in Shanghai."

"Who *is* he, anyway? Your Mr. Marius?" Kay asked irritably.

"I couldn't rightly tell you. Everyone knows the name. Old China Hand. In business of some kind—several kinds. Very,

very rich, but nobody asks how he got that way. He swings a lot of weight around here."

"American? He doesn't look or behave like one."

"We're the great melting pot, didn't you know? It takes all kinds to make an American."

Kay was thinking about his manner of speaking, for behind the absolutely confident English there was the echo of some other language, too faint to be an accent. Marius. The name could be anything. "Well, I don't like him," she said with unnecessary emphasis, and then, tempering her tone to indifference, "Jeremy won't like him, either."

"You'll keep in good with him if you're smart."

"It's not *me* he wants to see."

"That's the basic difference between him and me." Johnny took her arm. "Come on, drink time." Both, for different reasons, had forgotten the message for the Club Secretary.

But as they crossed the lobby, Kay took tiny, fastidious steps in her high heels, slowing Johnny down long enough to watch David Marius climb into a huge, ostentatious American car. The back seat was empty, but he sat in front, next to the uniformed Chinese chauffeur, and immediately began to give him lengthy, rapid instructions that were inaudible to her; the chauffeur nodded and nodded, interrupted a couple of times, nodded again, and at last, still listening, started the car down the driveway.

"He speaks Chinese," Kay said, as if this were yet another exasperation.

"How do you know?"

"You can tell by the way they were talking *that* wasn't pidgin."

"Live here long enough, I guess, and you're bound to pick it up. Me? I got another three months, and then Stateside, praise the Lord. Beats me why anybody'd want to *stay* here."

"Perhaps he likes China."

Johnny laughed with exaggerated incredulity. "Yeah. Or perhaps he makes plenty, plenty lettuce here."

"Lettuce?"

"Shekels, money, D-O, dough."

"Yes. I expect that's more likely."

They didn't speak of David Marius again the rest of the evening, but some uncomfortable residue of their fleeting encounter remained in Kay's mind, mocking her automatic responses to Johnny's childishly flirtatious attentions. Bedeviled by conflicting feelings of boredom and anticipation, she performed, almost without thinking, a routine that was by now too familiar to her to require much effort—pleasing and entertaining a man without showing a trace of contempt.

Late that night, driving back to the hotel, Johnny held Kay's hand in the back of the taxi. Slightly drunk and sentimental, he said, "Tell me something, Kathy. Are you in love with Jeremy?"

"What impossible questions people ask," Kay replied pleasantly. "Am I in love with him? Is he in love with me? What difference does it make? And to whom?"

Johnny seemed foggily reassured. "Well, that's all right then," he said, and tried to kiss her.

Kay was surprised by the vehemence with which she pushed him away. So, apparently, was Johnny. "Loo-ok! What gives—?" he began.

"Nothing. Nothing at all beyond my company for the evening." She paused, then added wearily, "It hardly seems worth all the trouble and expense, does it?"

"You're just 'not that sort of girl'?" He wavered between injury and sarcasm.

"I don't know what sort of girl I am." Kay's tone was level, but some note of fright or sorrow hidden in her words brought a kind of uncomprehending apology from Johnny.

"I guess I shouldn't have rushed you," he said. "I mean, our first date and all— I mean, maybe you feel that one of old Jeremy's friends—"

"I don't feel anything."

Johnny shifted his position, leaning away from Kay's still figure. "I won't tell Jeremy. I swear I won't."

"There's nothing to tell."

"Even that I took you out or—"

In the darkness, he heard the spurt of laughter in her voice. "You won't need to. I'll tell him myself."

"What's that supposed to mean?" Johnny sounded somewhat apprehensive.

"Only that dozens of people saw us together, so I'd rather he heard it from me."

"You *are* in love with him." Earnestly, Johnny continued, "Listen, Kathy, he's not going to marry you, you know. He *has* a girl in—"

"Margaret, in Somerset. They're more or less engaged."

"He *told* you about her?"

"Oh, yes."

"And you don't—I mean, you didn't—"

"Mind? Expect to displace her? No. I don't, and I didn't."

Johnny sat in confused silence for a moment, shaking his head. At last, he asked tentatively, for once uncertain of his ground, "Do I get to see you again?"

"If you wish to." The taxi was pulling up outside the hotel. "There'll still be nothing to tell Jeremy, so perhaps you won't wish to." Kay got out quickly, closing the door before Johnny could follow her. "You'd better keep the cab," she said through the open window. "You may not find another at this time of night."

Johnny watched the slight figure in its pale silk dance dress cross the sidewalk, turn at the hotel entrance, and wave a shadowy, smiling good night. He shrugged his shoulders and muttered, "What the hell . . ."

Kay's first indistinct thought on waking the next morning was, Something—something disturbing happened last night. Still half asleep, she ran through the unremarkable events of dinner with Johnny, and came fully awake only when she recalled the lobby of the French Club. Yes, David Marius. Unwilling—indeed unable to determine why he so forcefully suggested dangerous territory to her, Kay, by habit, turned her mind to practical matters. However, when the telephone rang, her hand shook as she picked up the receiver.

Old Wong's son, speaking stilted but adequate English, thanked her for delivering his father's letter, and asked if he could come to the hotel that evening at six. Kay made a note of the appointment. She decided that she would finish dressing quickly and leave the hotel at once, as much to avoid any further telephone calls as to get on with the business of organizing her life in Shanghai. The sight of her shaking hand had filled her, even alone in her room, with an angry embarrassment to which she was quite unaccustomed.

She went first to the French Club, not with any high expectations of getting a job immediately, more because the Secretary might have some suggestions for her—might, at least, put up a notice on the Club bulletin board, and she had to begin somewhere. Certainly he would know the names of other clubs in or out of the old International Settlement, and in the course of his work must have come across consular officers or foreign businessmen—anyone who might need a receptionist or a personal assistant to screen visitors, perform minor diverse duties, make arrangements, appointments, reservations, that sort of thing. What she hadn't expected was to find a jovial, middle-aged Frenchman who laughed amiably at her careful explanations and requests, as he might at an appealing feminine whim, and invited her to join him for a cup of coffee to alleviate the boredom of the morning.

At this time of day, the Club was virtually empty, and the terrace to which he led her, dotted with wicker tables and chairs, contained only two other occupants at the far end, talking intently over the teapot and cups cooling unnoticed between them. The Secretary was saying, "I assure you, madame, I admire your spirit, but why waste your time on such menial jobs as you describe? You tell me you do not know typing or the shorthand. You do not speak Chinese. The old days are gone, unhappily, when one would employ a charming young lady in an office simply for her delightful appearance."

Kay scarcely heard his well-meant gallantry, for at the distant corner of the terrace she had caught sight of the unmistakable back of David Marius, covered, this time, with improbably white starched linen. He was sitting half turned in his chair, long legs stretched out, crossed at the ankles, immaculate white shoes. His elbows were on the table, and he drew one thumb slowly along the line of his jaw again and again as he gazed out across the lawns and listened to his companion, an elderly Chinese man in a conventional, light gray, Western business suit.

Coffee was served, the Secretary was still talking, and Kay brought her attention back to him with an effort. "You should take up a hobby, madame, to occupy your time. Let your husband take care of the jobs and the money—that is the purpose of husbands, is it not so? My wife, while she was here, learned Chinese cooking—we shall have a most exotic kitchen when I return to France. She had, besides, the care that the children should maintain their French. The little one was so devoted to her *amah* that she spoke better Chinese than French—and even French with a Chinese accent, imagine!"

"When did you send them back?"

"It has been six months. It was time for the boy to go to a proper school. I, too, shall be leaving soon. All this"—he moved his hand in a regretful arc from the building to the gardens—"cannot last long. Ah, in the old days there was much of the world and much life here. Sport. The hunt. Riding on horses. Boating parties. The grand picnics we made to temples nearby! But now? Now those of us who are left have not the courage to venture outside the city for fear of bandits. Everybody tries now to leave China."

"Except me."

"Except you, Madame. But you are recently married, and your husband is away from you on his duties too much. Believe me, I understand your difficulty, and I repeat, find yourself a hobby to pass the time."

"I have a hobby—at least, that's all it is now. I used to think it would be my life. I'm a painter."

"But that is very good!" he assured her enthusiastically. "Very good! You will, without doubt, find many interesting subjects here for your painting!"

"I expect I will. But for an actual job—a paying job, that is—you have no suggestions?"

"Unfortunately." He shrugged with an expression of discouragement. "I will, most gladly, do as you ask and put a notice on our board. Apart from that, if you ask at the Press Club, it is possible that some foreign journalist can offer something. It would be of short duration—many pass through Shanghai, a few days, two weeks. The permanent representatives of the press have already their assistants— usually Chinese, naturally."

Across the terrace, David Marius was signing a chit and handing it to a waiter. Kay rose abruptly. "You've been very kind," she said. "I'm afraid I've taken up a lot of your time."

"Not at all, not at all—"

"I'll try the Press Club, and thank you again." She shook hands with him and left him standing by the table a little discomposed by her unceremonious departure.

Kay was poised on the top step of the flight leading down to the driveway, staring thoughtfully at the two cars parked at one side, when the voice she had been trying to summon up in her memory broke the morning quiet with a conventional greeting. "Good morning to you, Mrs. Wilson. Pleasant surprise."

Kay turned with deliberation. Her manner was unruffled, but her eyes when, warily, she raised them to his, were wide with surprise, desperation, or timidity. "Good morning, Mr. Marius."

"If you are hoping for a taxi, this is a foolish place to wait."

"There seemed to be plenty last night."

"Of course. The dance. They can be pretty certain of fares on dance nights."

"Perhaps the Secretary could phone for one?"

"Not nowadays, not in Shanghai." He seemed distantly amused about something. The white, reckless smile and the watchful eyes caught her unprepared, as they had the evening before. "If you'll wait a moment, I'll drop you where you're going."

"Just to a taxi—"

"Whichever," he said carelessly, and turned to make some remark to his Chinese companion. The elderly man had already signaled for his car. David Marius walked down the steps with him, helped him in, added another comment or two through the window, and watched the car drive away before he beckoned his own chauffeur.

Kay remained where she had been standing, feeling oddly invisible, so totally had she been ignored during those few moments. Everything about him is too big, she thought, his build, his car, the massive head on those thick shoulders, his air of utter assurance. Seeing him for the first time in full sunlight, she noted, in a disconnected way, other points about him. His skin is coarse. His hair is beginning to go gray. It is because his eyes are so deep-set that his expression appears more penetrating than his mind, in all probability, is. He must be vain to be so meticulously barbered, manicured, dressed. His voice is modulated in such a way that although he appears to be talking normally, nobody but the people directly addressed can hear what he says. I suppose he could shout if he wanted to, but I can't imagine what would make him want to, what would make him angry.

"Won't you get in?" He was standing beside the open door of the car, and Kay ran down the steps like a guilty schoolgirl. She climbed in with more dignity, avoiding any contact with him, and settled herself in the back seat, staring straight ahead, aware of every movement beside her, and finally the slam of the car door. "Well, where to?"

"I was going to the Press Club, but if we pass an empty taxi—"

"Broadway Mansions," he ordered the chauffeur without waiting for her to finish. There was a brief silence before he said conversationally, "Do you make a habit of cruising from club to club all day? Or is this just a passing idiosyncrasy?"

"I'm job-hunting," Kay said, refusing to be made fun of. "I hope the Press Club isn't too far out of your way, because I can always—"

"It's not where I'm going, if that's what you mean. That would be one coincidence too many."

"How many is too many?"

"One coincidence—overhearing your name last night—is merely a coincidence. Two coincidences—finding you here, taxi-less, this morning—is still only an equivocal signal. But if your destination were the same—well, that would be too many. That would be uncomfortably like a portent."

"Are you afraid of portents?" Kay asked, interested.

"Any sensible person respects them. You don't believe in the unseen forces that people dismiss as luck?"

"As it happens, I do. But I always thought it silly of me. Like wanting to pacify the devils of the air."

"What do you know of the devils of the air?" he asked sharply.

Until now, Kay thought, he had been obliquely laughing at her. Had he perhaps seen her on the terrace? Been entertained by her transparent little maneuver to reach the Club steps ahead of him? Now he sounded serious. Seriously, she replied, "Only what my husband has told me—or, rather, what his Chinese radio operator told *him*—that the devils of the air threaten the fliers who invade their domain. He always wears a jade charm to protect him. The radio operator, that is, not Jeremy."

"Yes," he said slowly, "jade—some kinds of jade have, for

centuries, been believed to have magical properties. Yes, the right kind of jade would protect one from devils. All sorts of devils. Jeremy, I take it, finds the whole performance ridiculous?"

"He doesn't believe in magic."

"And you do?"

"Well . . . anyway, I'm frightened of it." That, Kay thought (since she couldn't find a name for whatever it was that flickered intangibly between them), must be it. Some kind of magic. For the first time in her life, she was afraid of a person.

David Marius seemed to have lost interest in the subject. "What sort of job are you looking for?"

"Anything, really. Anything that will pay enough to live on for a while."

"For a very short while. The end of the year, I'd say, although you may be asked to leave before then."

"So everyone tells me. Meanwhile, however . . ."

"Yes. Meanwhile. And you expect to find something at the Press Club?"

"I hope to, though the Secretary at the French Club wasn't very encouraging." She began to describe her qualifications, which seemed all the more fragile for the complete silence with which they were received in that absurdly opulent car crawling through the steamy, turbulent streets. "It's not much to offer, is it?" she finished, attempting an unconcerned laugh. She turned her head to find him staring at her.

"No," he said, "it's not. I can't imagine who would hire you or for what."

She felt yesterday's unshed tears fill her eyes, and quickly turned away to watch the blurred crowds beyond the window.

"You say you are an artist. What sort of painting do you do?"

She waited, swallowing painfully, until her voice was under control. *"Sumi-e,"* she answered with some arrogance. "I don't suppose you've heard of it. I had a Japanese instructor—"

"I've heard of it. It seems an unusual speciality for a girl. Usually, only men—"

"I know. Zen monks mostly—"

"And your instructor was a monk?"

Like a phantom, Nobuo's gaunt figure took shape in her mind, the thin, expert hands, the eyes closed in concentration. "No. No, he wasn't. He'd studied— Well, I can't imagine that this interests you."

The car had slowed to a stop in front of what looked like an office building, separated by the road from one of the boat-jammed, fetid canals. "You'll find the Press Club on the fourth and fifth floors. The office is on the fourth floor, across from the bar and dining room."

"You come here often?"

"Almost never."

"You don't enjoy the company of journalists? You prefer the people at the French Club?" Kay knew that she was senselessly and perhaps irritatingly prolonging this conversation. Something about the overpowering press of blue- and black-dressed figures on the road, the sidewalks, the boats, the bodies pushed up against the car, the faces peering aimlessly in the windows, filled her with a terrible sense of futility combined with a stubborn unwillingness to abandon the small island of immunity within the car, to force her way— even those few yards—to the entrance.

David Marius was replying to her with impersonal politeness. "In fact, I don't enjoy the company of either. I find the French Club useful on weekday mornings when I want to talk to someone without interruptions. And, of course, for a certain kind of business entertaining— Are you feeling unwell?"

Kay had slumped back in the seat, her head resting on the white drill that covered the leather. "It's only the heat . . . Just a few moments . . ."

He considered the clean lines of her profile, the soft dark sweep of lashes, the narrow tendons of the delicate neck, the heavy knot of hair flattened against her head. "It's the people," he said, "not the heat."

"Yes . . ."

"It takes a little getting used to."

Kay opened her eyes, reached for her handbag on the seat between them, and straightened her back.

"Take your time." He was still watching her. "Would you prefer to go back to your hotel?"

"No—no, thank you. I might as well try the Press Club now that I'm here. . . . I'm not usually so feeble."

He helped her out of the car and across the sidewalk, a courteous hand on her arm, an indifferent presence at her side. In the building, he asked, "Will you be all right now?"

"I'm sure I will. Do forgive me for—for troubling you."

"No trouble." As he was leaving, he said, "I'll call on your husband this evening, about seven. He should be back by then. Unless, of course, you have other plans."

"None that I know of."

"Then perhaps you will give me the pleasure of dining with me?"

"Wouldn't you rather see Jeremy alone—if you want to discuss business?"

He seemed to be suppressing a smile. "I think it improbable that he will wish to leave you to a solitary evening. Our business transactions will find their own occasion in due course, don't worry." He gave her his slight, ironic bow. "Until tonight, then."

She turned away toward the elevator, and eventually found the undistinguished rooms of the Press Club, restless with the subdued clatter of typewriters from behind closed doors along the corridor. A dull, utilitarian atmosphere, very far removed from either the morning serenity or the evening grace of the French Club. It was only then that it occurred to her that David Marius, unlike the others, had not mentioned a dependent's allowance or wondered why she needed a job.

Kay spent part of the afternoon composing two letters. She had thought at first that she would give the letter for Old Wong to his son, to be delivered in person, and later decided that it would be wiser to enclose it in a letter to Mrs. Moreno. She didn't know how long it might take for a Chinese family to make travel arrangements, or whether they would be searched, all papers and documents examined, and she wanted to set the old man's mind at rest as soon as possible —at least that her end of the bargain had been completed. She was fairly sure that mail from a foreigner to a foreigner, both with such respectable addresses, would not be tampered with.

The letter to Mrs. Moreno ran:

My very dear Mrs. Moreno,
   This is my first opportunity to write to you at leisure and to assure you of our safe arrival, our good health, and our happiness. You know too well (and I can never forget) how much you contributed to make my present contentment and security possible, so I will not embarrass you with repeated thanks, but will try

to prove my gratitude in the way that I think would most please you—by making this "adventure," as you once called it, a success. That is, by honoring Jeremy's true love, and by giving him no cause to regret our sudden marriage.

We are at the moment comfortably, though modestly, installed at a hotel, but hope to find an apartment soon. However, conditions in Shanghai are exceedingly tense and unsettled, and I am continually reminded that all "dependents" (among whom I am now numbered) may be repatriated in the near future. For me—and this is a very strange prospect—it would mean "returning" to England, a country I have never seen! But, unlike many of the wives of foreigners who have already deserted their husbands (usually, to be fair, at their husbands' insistence), I am determined to stay in Shanghai as long as possible.

Jeremy resumed his duties the morning after we arrived, but is due back again this evening. I do not yet know how many days he is permitted to spend in Shanghai between flights—or, indeed, of what duration the flights are likely to be. But, as the wife of a pilot, I suppose I must accustom myself to this sort of uncertainty, and am attempting to find some suitable way of using my time while he is away. I may even return to my painting in earnest when I have more space than a hotel room.

In this short time I have, naturally, not accumulated a great deal of news to relay to you, and this letter is largely to set your mind at rest about my welfare, and to tell you that I will remain forever

Your grateful and affectionate
Catalina.

P.S. Would you be kind enough to send the enclosed note over to the bartender at the International Club? I discover, to my dismay, that even after working there with him for so long, I never found out his full name. He had asked me to get in touch with his family and find out if they were well—he has never seen his grandchildren. I felt that after all his kindness to me at the Club this was the smallest return I could make, and spent yesterday morning on that errand.

Kay read the letter through critically and decided that it was phrased with enough formality to please Mrs. Moreno, and enough spontaneity to carry conviction. In fact, except for the words "our happiness," at the beginning, she was satisfied that she had told no lies, had complacently used true facts (and omissions) to give an entirely false impression.

(Mrs. Moreno, reading the letter a few days later, believed not a word of it, but in her heart she at last said goodbye to Kay, and wondered dimly—even a little enviously—what her next step, her next "adventure," would be. She did, of course, ask her chauffeur to deliver the enclosure to Old Wong at the Club.)

The letter to Old Wong read:

My dear friend,
When you receive this letter, you will know that the small commission you entrusted to me in Shanghai has been fulfilled, and I am happy to be able to tell you that your family is well. They expect to be moving from their present apartment to a new address in the near future. Meanwhile, they send you their affectionate respects, and wish you a long life that your grandchildren may have the honor of seeing you.

I send you my greetings and my hopes that you will soon find relief from your worries.

With warm regards,
(Missee) Kay

Safe enough, Kay thought, even if he has to have it read to him by someone else.

She sealed both letters in a Palace Hotel envelope, and crossed out the name and the return address, replacing them with "c/o The British Consulate, Shanghai," but she didn't take it down to the desk to have it mailed until after the visit of Old Wong's son. The telephone rang promptly at six o'clock, and Kay asked the reception clerk to send the gentleman up to her room, adding, in passing, that he had come at her request to pick up some papers.

He was a well-mannered young man, with thick, oiled hair and a brisk, busy air, far removed—more than a generation, it seemed—from his father's gentle, self-effacing ways. Their business was quickly completed. Kay handed over the packages of currency, keeping aside the thinnest one, which Old Wong had, with agonized hope and generosity, insisted that she keep for herself, to pay her immediate expenses until she found a job.

"You'd better count it," Kay said, wanting to cut short the expected expressions of gratitude and other formalities.

The young man complied, flicking through the notes with rapid dexterity. "It is correct," he said. "I thank you."

"How long do you think it will be before you can leave Shanghai? Your father is very anxious."

"With this," he held up the packages, "not very long. One month, maybe three weeks. Tomorrow I will buy passports—"

"*Buy* your passports?"

He tapped the packages with his fingernail. "Squeeze money," he said, as if that explained everything. "Then we wait only until tickets are available."

"I see." Even Kay, who had never underestimated the power of money, was somewhat taken aback.

"You are a very kind lady, Mrs. Wilson," he said abruptly.

Kay, answering the question he was really asking—Why have you done this for us? Taken these risks? Smuggled illicit dollars?—said, "Your father was very good to me. He helped me a great deal when I needed him most."

"Again I thank you."

"Please don't mention it." They shook hands, two smiling and intimate strangers. The whole encounter lasted not

more than ten minutes, but as Kay closed the door behind
him, she felt that it marked some decisive moment in her life,
the breaking of her last link with—even the death of—
Catalina Gómez. She moved her shoulders and arms, rear-
ranged her body inside her clothes—she might have been
trying on a new dress—and then went into the bathroom to
put on her make-up with extra attention for the evening.

At seven, when she heard David Marius's voice on the
telephone, she replied nervously, "Jeremy isn't back yet, Mr.
Marius. Perhaps you'd rather—"

"Never mind," he said easily. "I expect he'll be along
soon."

"Well, I don't know—"

"His plane has landed all right. Don't fret. Suppose you
join me downstairs for a drink? I'll leave word at the desk to
tell him where we are when he comes in."

"Yes. Thank you. Yes, if you're sure—"

"I'm quite sure."

She couldn't decide whether his voice sounded merely
bored, or whether it held an undertone of impatience at the
uncharacteristic, breathless flutteriness of her broken sentences.

She deliberately did not look at herself again in the mirror,
picked up her bag and room key, and found a certain satisfaction in slamming the door. In the lobby she saw him at once,
standing monumentally at the desk, his presence seeming to
push everything else—the clerk, the furniture, the other people—into insignificance. He didn't walk to meet her but,
when she reached him, said mildly, "Good evening. Is something the matter? You look as if you were about to face a
firing squad."

She smiled with an effort. "Just worried about Jeremy."

"Unwarranted—in this instance, at least." He led her to the combined bar-restaurant, seated her at a table, talking in sympathetic terms about the chronic anxieties of fliers' wives, and ordered drinks. Kay looked around the room, heavily paneled in wood, solid, dull, respectable—curiously out of keeping with the raffish, just-before-the-deluge atmosphere of the city. The tables, except for those alongside the bar, were set for dinner with white damask, weighty silver, and glass, some of them already occupied. The center of the room was cleared to form a dance floor, and a platform at the far end, intended for the orchestra, at the moment held only music stands and a set of drums emblazoned with the words "ROY'S BOYS." The room was filling up fairly fast, mostly with foreigners in and out of uniform, and girls of much the sort that Kay had seen at the CAT house, and a very few parties of Chinese.

In answer to Kay's comprehensive scrutiny, David Marius said, "There's dancing later, as you might expect. This and the Cathay are about the only Western-style places left. But we won't dine here. The food is atrocious, and the din, once the band starts, insupportable."

"Who are the girls?" Kay asked. "Not wives, certainly."

"No, not wives, if you mean the foreign girls. They're the stateless ones. Refugees originally—or their parents were— the jetsam of many nations, mostly White Russians. Hating China, unable to return to their own countries, always thinking of themselves as sort of in transit."

"But what do they *do*?" Kay asked with helpless intensity.

"Odd jobs to keep themselves alive. And they dog the consulates, pleading for visas to go to another country—any other country. And they hound the billets and hotels where foreigners stay, hoping that someone will take a fancy to them, help them, marry them, anyway get them out of China. One of the minor tragedies of Shanghai." He was not looking at Kay when he added, "It's not an unfamiliar story to you, is it?"

Again it was not a question, and Kay could have passed it by with some generality about the frustration of one sort or another that seemed to hang like a miasma over the city, pretending to agree that it was a familiar sight and story to anyone in Shanghai. Instead, she said, "No. It's a story I know quite well. I didn't, however, know it would appear so obvious to"— she compelled his attention— "to a stranger."

"A rather experienced stranger. But even so, I do assure you, it is far from obvious."

"Johnny Jarvis, the man I was with when we met, assumes that I am not married to Jeremy, and hopes to take advantage of that assumption. The Secretary at the French Club assumes that I'm a bored housewife, and suggests a hobby. Why do you assume—"

"I don't assume anything," he interrupted coolly. "When I want to know, I take the trouble to find out. Ill-informed guesses are of no interest to me. One of my people did a little simple checking at the British Consulate this morning—just the registration of your passport and the date and place of its issue. I myself looked through the book at the reception desk here, and saw that your room is reserved in your name alone. Gossip—which, if you don't already know, you will soon find out, is as much a part of the Shanghai air as dust and the smell of cooking—gossip at CAT headquarters informs me that Jeremy has a fiancée in England. And, finally, you tell me you are looking for a paying job—what's more, a paying job of a sort that you cannot hope to find in Shanghai—instead of relying on your husband's, your *legal* husband's, support. It doesn't take much wit, does it, to realize that yours was a marriage of convenience? And hastily contracted, since you hadn't even looked ·into the difficulties of earning a living here at this particular time. You must have been under considerable pressure of some sort to leave Manila quickly—and to acquire a new nationality."

Kay kept her eyes averted, sipped her Coca-Cola, and said unsteadily, "I wouldn't have thought it worth your time to find out so much about me."

"I was finding out about Jeremy."

"I see." Her voice was without inflection. "A business matter. Routine." Feeling she had foolishly exposed herself, she then remained silent and watched the "stateless ones," recognizing at once the sleazy evening dresses copied, by some local tailor, from pictures in magazines. Under the thin veneer of confidence, the bright lipstick, the curled hair, the spurious gaiety, she caught the telltale signals of despair, the avid hold on a man's arm, the eagerness to please in the manner, the pleading eyes, and she thought not, How calculating they are, but, How brave! and in her heart she wished them luck, and knew that few of them would get it.

"You know," David Marius said, apparently not at all disconcerted by her abstracted silence, "you might be wise to accept a dependent's allowance for the time being—"

"I have no intention of being any further burden on Jeremy."

"An admirable sentiment, however misplaced." He was smiling. "It's no burden on Jeremy. All the CAT personnel are entitled to it from the moment they get married."

"But it would mean telling the authorities, or whoever handles salaries and things, that he *was* married."

For the first time, David Marius seemed astonished. "And you had really hoped to keep it a secret? *Jeremy* told you to keep it a secret?"

"Well, not exactly—"

"I should think not. He certainly knows that he has to report it to his commanding officer. The rest follows automatically—the raise in pay and so on."

Kay said obstinately, "I don't want to take money from him as well as everything else."

"You could, of course, repay him when you find a job, if that would ease your rather mystifying conscience. Whatever your future plans, you—"

"I plan to get a divorce as soon as possible."

David Marius was laughing openly now. "To free him for the one he loves?"

"Is that funny?" Kay asked angrily.

"Yes." He continued to chuckle massively. "But charming, too. What sort of literature do you read?"

"I don't read much."

"Really?" Then he remarked with obscure and wondering satisfaction, "An original. It makes a pleasant change." Catching Kay's grave, enclosed expression, he said, "That was a compliment."

"Thank you. Though I'm not sure what you're complimenting me on. Not reading?"

"No. Well, yes, in a way."

"A negative sort of accomplishment," Kay said austerely, and turned to the bellboy who was hovering at her shoulder to summon her to the telphone.

She took the call at the front desk, blocking one ear with her finger to deaden the swelling volume of noise in the lobby as more people were arriving. "Jeremy?"

"Yes, can you hear me? Where are you? It sounds awfully rowdy."

"In the lobby."

"Where?"

"In the lobby."

"Oh. Well—have you had dinner?"

"No—"

"That's good. I'll come and pick you up as soon as I get a shower and change. I hope you aren't starving. I couldn't get to a phone earlier—"

"Jeremy, we're dining out—"

"You're dining out, did you say?" The stunned disappointment in his voice, tinny and far away, sang like a mosquito in Kay's ear.

"We're both dining out—"

"Yes, certainly!" Relief flooded through the receiver. "Wherever you want—"

"—with David Marius."

"Where? Well, never mind. We'll decide when I get there."

"I said, with— Oh, Jeremy, I can't explain over this horrible phone. Just hurry up and come."

"What?"

"Hurry!"

"I will. I've kept the jeep, so I won't be more than half an hour. All right?"

David Marius rose when Kay re-entered the restaurant, and held her chair for her. "I'm sorry, but he got delayed," she said, formal and hostile. "He'll be here in half an hour. There was so much noise that I couldn't explain that you had, so very kindly, invited us to dinner."

"It's of no importance. If, when he arrives, he is too tired

—or anything—we can easily postpone it."

Kay listened for irony or insinuation in his tone, but found neither. "Yes," she said. "Or cancel it entirely. Then you could arrange a more suitable time for your business discussions with him."

"If you prefer."

Kay turned to him suddenly, appealingly, unable to read the expression in the shadowed eyes under the heavy brow. "Do forgive me— I don't know why I'm being so rude to you—"

"Don't you?"

"It isn't the way I normally conduct myself— It's just that I feel," she continued wildly, unable to prevent herself, "I can't help feeling that you present some threat—some danger to—to Jeremy."

"To Jeremy. Well, calm yourself. I only wish to offer him an opportunity to make some money in return for a favor he could do me. There is nothing to keep him from refusing should he find the transaction not to his taste."

"But why Jeremy?"

"Because he's a pilot. And trustworthy—yes, another piece of routine business checking."

"You want him to *fly* something or somewhere for you?"

"Suppose we leave the details for the time being?"

"Yes, of course. I'm sorry—it's no concern of mine, I realize." She looked straight into his eyes, in spite of their obscurity, at last able to smile without constraint, as though some unforeseen good fortune had brought them, shaken but uninjured, through a storm together. "You know," she said, "Jeremy has a dream—I'm telling you because it is not the sort of information that your business checking is likely to uncover. And it may be of—well, of use to you." She noticed that David Marius was listening with undisguised interest. "Jeremy's dream is to have a farm—*buy* a farm—in Somerset. That is why he took this CAT job. The pay is good, *and* it's in dollars, and he is working to save as much as he can toward the realization of his dream."

"He wants to be a *farmer?*" David Marius asked, with soft amazement.

"He told me once that he wanted to watch the seasons— from a professional point of view. Oh, I know it sounds absurd, but then most people's dreams are absurd. His—like his engagement to his English girl, his Margaret—is based, I imagine, on some kind of yearning for life as it was before the war—a dream that would wipe out everything that has happened in between. It is no less compelling for being unrealistic."

"You are telling me, I gather, that the money would definitely be an attraction for him?"

"More important, I'm telling you that he's the kind of person that has a dream."

"I see. Thank you." His voice was lightly satiric again. "You advise me to frame my proposal to him accordingly."

"It's not advice. It's a warning."

He looked at her severe expression and said soberly, "I shall take it as such."

Jeremy saw Kay before she noticed him, and it struck him forcibly, a matter for sudden wonder, that she was beautiful. She was sitting motionless, decorous as always, hands clasped in her lap, back straight, listening attentively to the man who shared her table. Jeremy thought, with some annoyance, that one could hardly expect that she would sit alone in public without *somebody* trying to pick her up. After all, in a manner of speaking, he had done the same thing himself when they first met. He hurried to the table, and Kay gave him a guarded smile of welcome.

Before either of them could speak, David Marius got up and introduced himself. Jeremy raised his eyebrows at the name, but gave no other indication of surprise. They shook hands, sat down, and David Marius went quickly and effortlessly through the performance of asking what Jeremy would drink, of ordering a whiskey-and-soda, and of extending his invitation to dinner afterward.

"Well, that's very kind of you," Jeremy said, clearly unable to find a graceful way of refusing. "Kate said she'd like to go out tonight."

"Excellent. Your wife had given me a qualified acceptance earlier—subject, of course, to your approval and to how tired you might be."

Kay said quickly, "I tried to tell you on the telephone, but—"

"Yes. I could hardly hear you."

"Mr. Marius said he wanted to talk to you about a business matter, and I didn't know—"

"That can wait until tomorrow. Shall we say ten-thirty at the French Club? Or would you rather I picked you up at your billet?"

He seemed to take it so much for granted that Jeremy would meet him that, almost hypnotized, Jeremy said, "The French Club will be fine."

"In that case, we can happily keep this a social occasion. I hope you both enjoy Chinese food? There's a restaurant that I like particularly—Northern food. I suppose you didn't have an opportunity to get a proper Peking meal on this flight?"

"Unfortunately, no. We got there very late—there were some other stops to make first."

"No chance to look around the city at all?"

"Hardly. There's always so much paperwork to be done with these deliveries. Copies to UNRRA, copies to the government authorities, copies to the local C.O., copies to the medics—it's endless. But, driving out to the airport this morning, I did get a glimpse of the place. And the walls of the Forbidden City. Most imposing. Next time, perhaps."

"I hope so, for your sake. You haven't very long."

Jeremy nodded. "They're all over the Northern Hills already, even the Summer Palace is cut off, and in the city just about every wall was plastered with slogans. And banners across the streets. But it looked like just students marching and shouting."

"Never underestimate the students."

"You may be right. A matter of weeks—according to the local gossip, of course."

"And then it will be inaccessible for any of us."

Something about David Marius's attitude, or an arresting note of sadness in his quite ordinary remark, made Kay ask, "Do you know Peking well?" and it was no longer a small-talk question.

"Exceedingly well. I was at school there," he replied unexpectedly. "I suppose it is the only place in all the world that I'll really miss."

"School?"

"And college. My family lived here, you see. Here and in Peking. When the time came for me to be sent 'home' to school like the children of most of the other expatriate families, I, in my cussed way, made such a drama about being forced to leave that my parents—from exhaustion as much as anything else, I daresay—allowed me to remain. They didn't really understand my reasons—not extraordinary in parents, of course. It was no use saying I 'liked' China. They, in their own way, liked it, too—or, rather, their kind of life in China. But that didn't seem to them a reasonable reason. China was where you made money and the best of a good life until it was time to go 'home.' Luckily, they never had to perform all the emotional acrobatics that recent years have required of us. ... The argument that did at last reach them was that I couldn't bear to leave my pony. I'd broken him and trained him myself. That was something they *did* understand. It tells you just about all you need to know about the old life in China, doesn't it?" He seemed amused by his own fragment of reminiscence, not allowing them to take it seriously.

"Were you there during the war, then?" Jeremy asked.

"Which war?"

The question was quite noncommittal, but Jeremy's answer was very flustered. "I meant, of course—"

"The European war. Of course. I'm sorry. China has been at war of one sort or another for nearly twenty years, so one's apt to get a bit confused. Yes, I was in Peking for part of the Japanese occupation, and then later in Chungking."

"With General Stilwell?"

"It was an entertaining situation," David Marius remarked smoothly. "Stilwell was fighting Chiang Kai-shek, Chiang was fighting the Communists, the Communists were fighting the Japanese, and the Japanese were fighting, primarily, the Americans. It's an appalling city, Chungking. Have you ever had the misfortune to fly missions there? The only great thing about it is the Yangtze, a magnificent river, especially its gorges—but they, of course, are much further east. One gets no idea of its splendor here in Shanghai, at its messy, boggy mouth."

Jeremy thought, The fellow must have been in Intelligence. Can't talk about his war service.

Kay thought, He lived under a Japanese occupation and I lived under an American one. We *lived* ... And we know. ...

Leaving no opportunity for further questioning, David Marius resumed his usual impersonal manner and suggested politely that if everyone had had enough to drink they might all go on to dinner. He steered the conversation into pleasant and less treacherous channels, and turned out to be, for the rest of the evening, a cordial and entertaining host.

He took them to a part of Shanghai that Kay did not recognize from any of her crisscrossing of the city, a broad lively street flashing with neon signs, in Chinese, above restaurants, shops, cinemas, with crowded sidewalks dotted with food stalls, or benches displaying trinkets, toys, combs, porcelain, toothpaste, cigarettes in a funny, haphazard mixture, each lit by the eerie green of gas lamps. Leading away from it on either side were the black, anonymous alleys. When the car stopped at a red lacquer door, flamboyantly decorated with gold dragons with curling tongues and tails, he gave some brief instructions to his chauffeur before he escorted Kay and Jeremy into the restaurant and to a superb meal served in a long succession of courses.

It was after dinner—among the exclamations of how good the food had been, how shamefully everyone had overeaten, and how, no, they didn't at all mind walking the short distance to where the car was parked, in fact, *needed* the exercise —that it happened.

David Marius had, apparently, told his chauffeur to park the car in the alley behind the restaurant, get his own dinner, and go home; he would drive back himself. The three of them strolled to the corner and turned in to the engulfing darkness of the first alley. They could see the gleam of reflected light from the chrome of the car parked on the other side of the cobbled lane. There were no proper sidewalks, only a narrow ridge that ran between the wall and the gutter, along which they had to walk single file. Kay was the first to step off the ridge to cross to the car, but some invisible obstruction caught at her foot. She stumbled and fell to her knees on the filthy cobbles, hearing as she fell a soft explosion as of a half-inflated balloon, and then an almost inaudible hiss as the indescribably sickening smell of rot and corruption began to rise from the gutter.

David Marius and Jeremy were beside her in an instant, helping her to her feet. Only then did she turn to look at what had tripped her. "Oh, my God . . ." she whispered, "Oh, my *God* . . ."

The body of a child lay in the gutter, its swollen belly, ripped by Kay's high heel, flattening slowly as it released its gaseous burden of human decay, sinking to the level of the rest of the emaciated frame and the other garbage that choked the gutter.

Kay began to run crazily up the center of the alley, turning her ankle in her ridiculous shoes, stumbling on, away from the car, toward the glittering street. David Marius, with his light, rapid stride, appeared not to be hurrying at all, but caught her with an arm around her waist before she reached the corner. She stopped suddenly, feeling his hold, bent over the spotless white sleeve, and vomited on the ground. He stood in silence, without shifting his arm, bending a little to give with her body. When at last she straightened, he picked her up in one easy movement, as if she were a sleepy child, and carried her to the car. Eyes closed tight, she pressed her face against his shoulder, smearing it with lipstick and the thin, bitter saliva of her uncontrollable retching. Jeremy followed them anxiously saying, "Are you all right? Kate, are you *all right?"* a frightful tenderness in his voice.

David Marius set her down gently, steadying her with one hand while he extracted the car keys from his pocket and unlockèd the door. "Better let her sit next to the window," he said to Jeremy. "Do you mind getting in the other side?"

"Ought we to just *leave* it there?" Jeremy asked shakily. "Shouldn't we *do* something? Call someone?"

"What or who would you suggest?" David Marius sounded both tired and grim. "No. It will probably be picked up to-morrow, early—with the others—when the wagons come round."

They drove in silence for a while, Jeremy wedged in be-tween the other two in the middle of the front seat. He took Kay's hand, giving it, from time to time, a small comforting pressure.

"I'm afraid I've ruined your jacket," Kay said, in a tight unnatural voice.

"It's easily cleaned."

"How long—how long do you think it had been there?"

"Since sometime this morning, I would guess. Everything rots very quickly in this weather."

"And all day people have walked past—"

"They live on the streets," David Marius said. "Where else are they to die?"

"It—he didn't belong to anyone—"

Neither of the men answered the hopeless desolation in her voice, but Kay seemed unable to stop. "It isn't that I haven't seen dead bodies before—I mean, after air raids—and things. . . ." She was trying to talk in a rational tone, but her voice kept rising. "But they *mattered* . . . somebody—everybody *cared* . . . people spent hours and hours digging through the ruins of houses—bombed or burned houses . . .

even when they knew there couldn't be any survivors—just on the chance, the freakish *chance*, that *one* might have . . . And even the dead bodies . . . oh, God—they were respected . . . somebody *mourned* . . . they weren't just—rubbish—" She broke off on a queer, abrasive note. After a moment, she said, "I sound hysterical, don't I? I'm not really."

"It's the shock." Jeremy said. "Try to put it out of your mind, Kate. It can't make any difference to the dead that nobody—"

"I'm not talking about the dead!" she answered shrilly. "I'm talking about the *living*. . . ."

David Marius pulled up outside the Palace Hotel, and walked around the car to open the door for Kay, but she was already on the sidewalk, with Jeremy beside her saying, "I'll come up with you. I'll—"

"No, no. Please don't. I'd rather you didn't—"

"But you shouldn't be alone—"

"I *want* to be. Please, I want to—to take a shower, to—just to go to bed."

Frowning and doubtful, he said, "If you're sure you'll be all right—"

"Really, I'm sure."

"Will you go straight to bed? Take an aspirin or something, and go to bed."

Suddenly, Kay laughed. "Yes, I'll do that. I'll take an aspirin." She turned to David Marius standing in attentive silence. "Thank you for dinner, Mr. Marius."

He gave her his quick, wicked grin, and fugitive bow. "My pleasure, Mrs. Wilson."

Kay spent a restless morning waiting for Jeremy. He had called her just before he left for the French Club to ask if she was all right. She had replied that she was fully recovered. "It was just, as you said, the shock." Her voice had sounded quite normal, and he reflected that her knowledge of death was far more intimate than his for all the blazing towns, villages, factories he had left behind him in his wartime European flights, or even the impersonal fury of aerial dogfights. His knowledge, he admitted bitterly, had been from the "clean" dealing out of death, lacking the stench of mortality.

Kay did a number of small, insignificant things like washing her hair, sewing a loose button securely on a jacket, smoothing the edges of her fingernails with an emery board. She had dropped her high-heeled sandals into the wastebasket the night before, as soon as she had entered her room. Now she held up the dress that she had worn the previous night and examined the stains on the skirt. She telephoned down to the desk to ask about dry cleaners. She fidgeted about with one thing and another, and all the time she thought about David Marius—thought, that is, not in any coherent sense. It was more as though he had taken up residence in some intransigent part of her mind, and remained there, an invisible, observant presence in everything she did, an unwanted guest refusing to leave, violating her privacy, making her annoyingly conscious of every movement or gesture. And laughing at her.

Jeremy knocked on the door at about twelve-thirty, and Kay said, "Come in," with a gasp, as if she had been holding her breath. He stood in the doorway and looked at her anxiously, and then, with his own sigh of relief, said, "Well, you *look* all right. In fact, you look terrific. What have you been doing?"

"I washed my hair," she answered, and as he crossed the room to kiss her, instinctively, without meaning to, she quickly said, "Don't!" and, forcing a smile, added, "It will all come down. It's not quite dry yet."

"Never let it be said of me that I caused your hair to fall down," Jeremy said. "Is it dry enough to come downstairs and have a drink? As pants the hart for cooling streams, so pants this particular fly-man for a glass—a tankard—a gallon of cold beer."

"By all means," Kay said. "I've been wanting to get out of this room all morning."

"Well, here's your chance. Mind you, I don't offer this privilege to just any pretty girl I see who happens to be bored in her hotel room."

Laughing, Kay walked with him to the elevator. "You seem in remarkably good spirits. Was Mr. Marius's business proposal so attractive?"

"That isn't what's so attractive. No. To be perfectly frank, Mr. Marius, even with the most enthralling proposals, doesn't hold a candle—I'm speaking quite objectively, you understand—to present company. He doesn't for instance, have long, semidry hair which may come down any moment at the lightest touch."

"Do be serious," Kay said, still laughing. "What *did* Mr. Marius want of you?"

"I'll tell you downstairs, when the beer has sobered me up a bit. At the moment, I'm rather intoxicated on tea and the thought that we haven't one single bloody thing to do for the rest of the day."

Kay, rightly interpreting this to mean that he wanted to make love to her, asked, "Do you have to fly again tonight?"

"Early tomorrow morning. Dawn's crack, in fact."

The bar smelled dank and, with its somber, polished wood and heavy brass fittings darkened to twilight against the heat outside, seemed like a doomed ship, the passengers, having given up all hope, fatalistically drinking gin-and-tonic and waiting for the end. All men, they sat in pairs at the tables, in tropical suits or bush jackets, talking—Kay supposed—business, or stood singly at the bar, sweating, lifting their glasses listlessly. They all turned to give Kay's slight figure a brief or long-drawn-out scrutiny, depending on whether they were seated facing her or not. Jeremy, involuntarily, gripped her elbow and took her to a table behind a fat, paneled pillar.

Kay, unwilling to show any further eagerness, waited patiently while drinks were ordered and Jeremy took his first long gulp of beer. "There," he said. He smiled and then looked troubled. "He's a very peculiar type, that David Marius."

"He suggested a very peculiar transaction, do you mean?"

"That, too. But I can't make him out at all— I don't know where he stands on anything. It's like trying to get a good firm grip on an eel to get a straight answer out of him. He *can't* be pro-Communist, living the way he does—and besides he appears to be matey as the devil with the appropriate officials in the Nanking government. He says, however, that politics has nothing to do with it, that—in his words—'history will make fools of us all in any case.' So why not just be humane—*humane*—especially since I'd get *paid* for it? 'It's a great mistake,' he said, 'to think one cannot serve both God and Mammon.' But I think he was joking in that odd half-serious way that he has."

Kay could, almost too easily, picture the sudden ironic smile.

"He wanted me to fly a shipment of penicillin to the Reds."

"Has he got a *plane* of his own as well?" Kay asked, amazed.

"No. That's why he needs a CAT pilot. He wanted me to do

it on a regular run. In Peking. Of course I said no."

Kay sat in silence for a few moments, bewildered and vaguely disappointed by what she had heard. A scheme of such transparent impracticality, such outlandish ingenuousness, *couldn't* have come from the experienced, calculating mind that she attributed to David Marius. "I can't believe it," she said, feeling her words inadequate.

"You would if you'd been in China a bit longer. Any sort of corruption is possible here—not just possible, a matter of course, an expected way to behave, a way of life."

"So people keep telling me. But I meant I couldn't believe that Mr. Marius would suggest such an obviously impossible plan. He must know that it's UNRRA material that you transport, that the medical supplies all have to be checked—only last night you were talking about the paperwork, and copies of everything to this one and that one—"

"That's just it. 'This one and that one' can all be bought."

"I don't understand you," Kay said, shaking her head, although she was beginning to see a faint outline.

"The way it works is this," Jeremy said, as though his words had a nasty taste. "UNRRA ships the supplies to Shanghai, where they are delivered to the representatives of the Nanking government. These are the people who, in turn, assign the various supplies—food, medical aid, whatever—to their ultimate destination. These are also the people who can be bought."

"So the whole project would be with government connivance?"

"That's what he indicated—rather delicately—not connivance, exactly. More a question of turning a blind eye. He assured me that all the papers would be in order; they would simply be made out to a different place of delivery in Peking."

"Then why did he have to ask you at all? Wouldn't you just have taken the supplies wherever you were told?"

"Not under those conditions. You see, I *know* where and to whom deliveries are made in Peking, and since, ultimately, I am responsible for seeing that they get into the right hands, I would certainly question such unorthodox orders—in fact, I'd have to report the whole thing to my C.O., who would, in turn, report it to UNRRA. And if I didn't but somebody else *did*, I'd have to take the blame and the consequences. It's for that silence, and that risk, that our Mr. Marius is willing to pay me ten thousand dollars.

"*Ten* th—"

"Deposited in a bank in Hong Kong. He's thought of everything."

"I still don't understand," Kay persisted. "Why would the government officials want to allow the sale of penicillin to their enemies?"

"Oh, my sweet innocent Kate! For money, what else? For money." He resumed his rather sour fastidious tone of voice. "The UNRRA supplies are a gift. But since they consist of valuable, not to say crucial, items passionately needed in this country, the temptation to sell them rather than *give* them is pretty irresistible."

"But their *own* soldiers—"

"—often do the same thing. I've known too many cases when the army officers in the field—or at the front, if you prefer—sell off a good part of the supplies they receive to be shocked by that."

"To the Communists?"

"Sometimes. Often to civilians—anyone who can afford to pay." He shrugged resignedly. "But there's nothing I can do about that. It's out of my hands by then."

Kay was thinking hard. "What sort of currency would they pay in, I wonder?" she asked casually.

"I asked him the same thing. He said dollars—gold, of course, though they aren't quite as flush with American dollars as the Nationalists. And jade."

"*Jade?*"

"That's what he said. It's very valuable if you know the market."

"Which I'm sure he does."

"I daresay. However, that's enough about David Marius and his devious plots. We can find pleasanter subjects of conversation." He smiled, hoping to restore them to their earlier gaiety. "I say, I say, I say! Have you heard the one about the bishop and the chorus girl?"

Kay, however, in her methodical way, had been putting the scheme in order, step by step: 1. The UNRRA supplies arrive. 2. They are delivered to the correct government agency. 3. David Marius buys a shipment of penicillin from the official in charge—at not too high a price, Kay guessed, because the official's alternative would be to hand it over to the CAT people for no payment at all. Also, considering the confidence that David Marius seemed to enjoy among the Kuomintang officials, his guarantee of secrecy would probably keep the price low. (She wondered briefly how the official would explain the absence of a shipment to *his* superiors, or even the UNRRA people, and then decided that it was probably something very simple—just a rubber stamp saying, "DAMAGED IN TRANSIT," or an explanation to that effect—and in any case it didn't matter.) 4. David Marius gets a CAT pilot, Jeremy (or someone else), to fly the shipment to Peking and have it delivered to his contact there. 5. Clearly, it is sold at a big enough profit to allow him to pay Jeremy (or someone else) ten thousand dollars in Hong Kong.

Or someone else.

"Jeremy," Kay said, interrupting the story he was telling, "why don't you do it?"

"Do what?" The cheerfulness drained out of his voice.

"Accept David Marius's offer."

"Are you serious?"

"Oh, yes. Yes, perfectly serious. Are you so dedicatedly anti-Communist that you don't want them to have medical supplies that obviously they desperately need?"

"It's not that exactly—"

"I mean, does it matter to you *which* lives are saved? That child in the gutter last night—if you could have fed him, kept him alive somehow, would you have asked what his or his parents' politics were?"

"Kate, that's different—it's an unfair question you're asking."

"It *isn't!* Why shouldn't you? They're all Chinese, aren't they? More important, they're all *people*. And, as you once told me in Manila, 'yesterday's friends.' "

Shaken by Kay's earnestness, remembering the upheavals and absurdities she had experienced under the twin banners of politics and loyalty, he understood and admired what he took to be her larger concern for humanity, something more ennobling (not that he would have used that word) than the stingy spirit that concerns itself only with the welfare of its own. Harshly determined not to mince words, however self-lacerating, he said, "Kate, don't forget that I'm a mercenary—one of the few creatures on earth whose loyalty is absolutely clear-cut. The only loyalty expected of a mercenary is to who pays him."

"Ostensibly, you are working for the Nationalists, and if

they *themselves* blackmarket surplus UNRRA supplies—"

"Ostensibly. In fact, as we all know, the Americans pay me. I can't—pious as it may sound—violate that trust."

"And the people for whom they're doing this—employing you, sending help, whatever—*they* can? It's a strange point of honor."

Feeling defenseless and troubled, Jeremy asked, "Do you *want* me to do it, Kate?"

She sounded unaccountably angry and impatient when she replied. "I want you to have your *dream*. Your damn *farm* in Somerset. Your *Mar*garet. The seasons, and the bluebells and that idiot *cuckoo*—" She broke off, and Jeremy noticed that there were tears in her eyes. "I'm a fool, you see," she continued almost in a whisper. "I like happy endings."

Inexpressibly moved, he said, "A very sweet fool."

She looked away. "Let's talk about something else. You're right. This is a horrid subject for conversation. But it's all your fault," she added resentfully. "You shouldn't have such —such *ridiculous* dreams."

"Let's talk about lunch, instead. Shall we just have something to eat here?"

Kay nodded absently, and said she hadn't much appetite anyway. Afterward, with no prompting from Jeremy, she led the way to the elevator up to the third floor, and along the corridor to her door.

Early that evening, lying in bed with Jeremy in the shadowed hotel room, Kay broke a long bemused silence to ask, "What time is it?"

"Does it matter?" Jeremy said, through cloudy, drifting thoughts.

"No, not particularly."

Stretching lazily for his watch, he said, "Almost five-thirty. Are you—have you an engagement?"

"Not tonight. I expect I will have tomorrow, though. I expect your friend Johnny Jarvis will telephone me in the morning."

"Has he been bothering you?"

"He took me out to dinner while you were away, and tried to kiss me in the taxi coming back. He promised not to tell you, and warned me most sincerely that you would never marry me."

Jeremy laughed, a little uneasily. "Disillusioned, refusing any longer to occupy the 'back street' of my life, you flung yourself at his mercy—"

"Certainly not," Kay said primly. "Anyway, mercy was the furthest thing from his thoughts. He was, of course, rather drunk."

"He'd be the same sober." After a pause, Jeremy said, "I suppose you get a bit lonely here, Kate?"

"I manage to keep myself busy—job-hunting, mostly. I'm afraid it's going to take somewhat longer than I had hoped."

Another pause. Then Jeremy said slowly, "You know, I am entitled to—"

"—a dependent's allowance for your wife. Yes, I know. I don't want to accept it—to take even more from you. I'll find a job sooner or later, I expect."

"Oh, Kate—Kate—" He rolled over and buried his face in her neck. She couldn't hear what he said, could only feel his lips moving against her skin.

Kay answered the telephone on the first ring. She had put down the receiver only a few minutes before, and was still standing at the table, absorbed in her thoughts, frowning at her open evening bag and the neat lettering on the card beside it.

"Good morning. David Marius here. I got a message that you wished to speak to me?"

"I'm afraid I only had your home number.... They reached you very quickly—"

"Yes?"

"I mean—" Kay tightened her grip on the telephone, and forced her words into an orderly cadence. "I wanted to make an appointment to see you." When he made no reply, she added, "It's a business matter," rather sharply.

"I see." (Did he sound amused?) "Just a moment." (Consulting an engagement pad?) "I could come to your hotel early this afternoon, say, half past two or a quarter to three? Or perhaps you sleep in the afternoons?"

"Not as a rule. However, I'd prefer not to meet you in a public place. I'm remembering what you said about gossip in Shanghai, and I'd rather Jeremy didn't hear that I'd been seen with you."

"Indeed?" (No question about the amusement in his voice now.)

"May I come to your office?"

"I have no office."

"Your home, then?"

A silence. "Very well. I don't see why not. Come for tea, if you like. I'll show you some rather fine jade." He laughed a brief interior chuckle, as at some private joke. "I'll even show you some charms against the devils of the air. My car will call for you at four."

"I can easily take a taxi. I have your address."

"The house is rather a long way out. Taxi-drivers aren't always willing to come this far unless they're paid for the drive back as well."

"Oh. I didn't know. . . . It's very kind of you. I'll be ready at four."

When Johnny called, not long after, saying repentantly, "Kathy? Am I forgiven? Can't blame a guy for trying," she told him that their whole evening together was forgotten (as, in fact, it virtually was), but that unfortunately she couldn't go out with him that night. He said, in a hurt voice, "You're trying to brush me off, aren't you? Kathy, I promise—" But when she interrupted to explain that she had been invited to see a private collection of jade amulets, the excuse seemed to him so unlikely that he half believed it, and suggested, "Tomorrow, maybe? Jeremy won't be back until the day after. I'll call you in the morning, O.K.?"

The drive out to David Marius's house took almost an hour, mostly spent maneuvering through the chaotic tangle of rickshaws, pedicabs, pushcarts, pedestrians, and the traffic of regular cars, both rattlingly old and moderately new. Hungjao Road itself, when they finally reached it, turned out to be a very long, relatively quiet residential street, with walls on both sides. Occasionally, through a wrought-iron or an open gate, Kay caught a glimpse of gardens and lawns or a substantial-looking house, set well back from the road. Otherwise, only the tops of the trees showed over the high, forbidding walls. At last, the driver stopped before a tall, solid gate and sounded his horn several times. An answering shout came from the other side, and a man in the inevitable black shiny cotton clothes and rope-soled slippers swung the gate open.

The car drove directly into a stone-paved courtyard and stopped in front of a couple of shallow steps leading onto the deep veranda of what appeared to be quite a small house, Chinese in style, and rather somber in color. Black lacquer pillars supported the curving tiled roof. The front door, too, was black lacquer, and the walls on each side of it dove gray. Once inside, however, Kay realized that this was only one of many pavilions, some enclosed, some with only one wall, some with three, all opening, in an elegantly stylized maze, onto more courtyards, small gardens, terraces, some embellished with stone carvings, some with flowering shrubs, some with lily ponds.

The room into which Kay was ushered she took to be David Marius's office only because he was seated at a long polished table strewn with papers. The rest of the room bore no resemblance to an office at all. Cabinets containing porcelain and jade were set against one wall. Comfortable chairs, a low sofa, a coffee table with some Chinese books lying on it, and a group of T'ang figures occupied the other side of the room. The double doors behind David Marius stood wide open, but the view into the garden beyond was obscured by a large flat wooden screen, carved with a profusion of peonies. Over the doors, in a plain black lacquer frame, were three Chinese characters, executed with an incredibly bold and flowing skill in black ink on rice paper that age had turned a very light caramel in color.

David Marius had stood up when she entered, and made some ordinary expression of greeting, but, seeing her gaze fixed on the calligraphy above his head, he said, "Yes, it's splendid, isn't it?" without turning.

"I can make out 'Beauty,'" Kay said, still staring, "but not the other two."

In some surprise, he told her, "'Reason' and 'Virtue.' They're all the poetic symbols for jade."

"Jade? How can a stone be reasonable? Or, for that matter, virtuous?"

"Like reason, jade cannot be destroyed. And then, like the purity of virtue, it cannot be soiled. At least, that's what the Chinese immortals thought. We moderns could probably give them plenty of evidence to the contrary about either reason or virtue. But they weren't concerned with facts, only with the truth. How," he continued with a lift of curiosity, "do you happen to read the characters?"

"At one time, I—I had a Japanese art instructor. I told you, I believe."

"So you did. So . . . you . . . did." He seemed to be considering the words with care. With a brisk change of tone and manner, he said, "Well let's have some tea, shall we? And then you can tell me, as conspiratorially as you wish, what brings you here."

Kay had worked out in her mind, before this interview, what she wanted to say to David Marius. It was to be a dry, perhaps cynical transaction which, she thought, might astonish him but would appeal to him with greater force than any attempts at subtlety or indirection. It didn't evolve in quite the way that she had hoped.

"You know," she began, pushing aside her teacup, "Jeremy told me all about the deal you wanted to make with him."

"I thought perhaps he might."

"Did you?" She couldn't easily read his expression because his back was to the light, further obscuring his already dark face. "Then why didn't you ask him in front of me, at dinner that night?"

She caught the rapid flash of his smile as he said, "Because the thought didn't occur to me until after dinner—until that rather unfortunate incident after dinner."

"I'm not sure that I understand what you mean, but I suppose that doesn't matter."

"No, it doesn't. You were about to suggest to me a deal of your own devising?"

"In a way. But first I wanted to ask you one or two questions, if you don't mind?"

David Marius stood up impatiently, and Kay suddenly found herself looking up at him in a pose uncomfortably like a supplicant. He strode away from her, returning to his table, apparently in search of papers or documents of some kind. As he moved, he said casually, as if he were dismissing unnecessary, minor preliminaries, "Let's see, now. You hope to find out how badly I want Jeremy to fulfill my commission. If, for whatever reason, the matter turns out to seem urgent or important to me, you, I expect, will offer to persuade him to make the flight. For a price."

Kay sat absolutely still, caught somewhere between frustration, embarrassment, and fury. At last, she said, "Are you afraid that I couldn't?"

"I haven't a doubt that you could. However, it's really not worth your effort—if, that is, it would be an effort. There are other pilots, I'm sure, with fewer scruples than Jeremy. Of course, that is apt to make them less trustworthy than Jeremy would have been, but I'll have to take my chances and provide my safeguards—"

"Oh," Kay cried, "why did you let me come here? If you knew all that and were going to refuse, why didn't you just—"

"Say so on the telephone? I was interested in what price you would ask. That's why."

"Idle curiosity?" Kay inquired, her voice corrosive with scorn.

"Curiosity, certainly. But don't judge me—or yourself—too harshly." His tone softened. "I also thought your artist's eye might enjoy looking at some of these things"—he waved a hand vaguely in the direction of the cabinets—"and that it would be pleasing for me to show them to you. I won't have them much longer." He paused, selected the paper that he wanted, picked up a pencil, and returned to the chair near Kay. "Tell me," he said, "what price *did* you have in mind?"

"I don't know how much it would cost in money," she said slowly. "I was going to ask your help in getting a divorce."

"That's all?"

"Is it so easy? I don't know any lawyers, nor do I have the money to pay them. I don't even know whether a divorce in Shanghai would be valid in England."

"I expect that can be arranged." He placed the paper on the coffee table, and Kay saw then that it was a blank sheet. He leaned forward from his chair, his profile suddenly close to Kay, and wrote a name, "Mason," and a telephone number on the paper. "Here," he said, sitting back and handing it to her, "get in touch with him tomorrow. I'll phone him about your problem in the morning."

"But you said—I mean, I can't—"

"Don't let it bother you. He owes me a favor anyway. China runs on a system of mutual indebtedness, you know."

"I don't like to feel indebted."

"To me? Or in general?"

"In general."

"What nonsense!" he said pleasantly. "We all live with debts we can't square."

The idea was a strange one to Kay, and she didn't believe it. She wondered instead what form of repayment he might eventually ask, and felt peculiarly impoverished, sitting there staring at the paper beside the T'ang statuettes.

"Those are fakes," he said, ending, by his tone of voice, a business discussion that had never really begun. "The real ones were sold long ago. They're quite decorative as imitations go, but I shan't mind abandoning them."

"Abandoning—?"

"When I leave China."

"You're going to abandon all this?" Kay's glance swept the room, uncertain where to focus, settling eventually on David Marius himself.

"The place—the house, the property? Unfortunately, yes."

"Can't you sell it? It must be worth a lot—"

"Used to be. Nobody would be foolish enough to buy it now. I've given it to some Chinese friends who may be able to come to some sort of arrangement with the Communists. Anyway, they have no wish to leave their country—nor, for that matter, have I."

"It must be a disagreeable feeling," Kay said thoughtfully. "I have never been sorry to leave a place. But then I have never had possessions of this sort that I might regret."

"You mistake my meaning. It is not the possessions that I shall regret. I have already said my grateful farewells to them. It's China. And, even more, the people. Have you never had those, either? Childhood friends? People you would be sorry to lose?"

His words had been lightly inquiring, conversational, but Kay was unprepared for the flooding memories they engendered. Her reply was very precise, as if he had asked her a scientific question which required the greatest accuracy. "I had friends when I was a child. I lost touch with them during the war. I was—"

"No need to continue." His interruption was unexpectedly gentle. "This isn't a courtroom."

"Courtroom?" Kay gripped her hands tightly together to keep them from shaking, and saw simultaneously that David Marius had noticed the involuntary clenching of laced fingers.

"All kinds of things happen in wartime, many of them inexplicable afterward."

"Oh, I can explain—" Kay began eagerly.

"You don't owe me any explanations. In any case, what does it matter now?" His voice became almost clinical as he went on, and Kay found this remote recital, infused with no emotion, blame, or praise, or even interest, oddly comforting, as though someone had diagnosed a chronic illness and in the process offered an unlooked-for cure. "You must have known the Japanese pretty well—a collaborator in the Philippines, perhaps? How else would you have studied *sumi-e?* How else could you have learned even a few characters or an appreciation of calligraphy? Why else would you have needed to change your nationality with a marriage of convenience? But none of it is of the smallest importance any longer."

Gradually, Kay relaxed against the back of the sofa. "You know," she said, "from the first I thought you dangerous—"

"I remember. 'A threat to Jeremy,' you said, though I knew that was not what you meant."

"No, I didn't mean Jeremy." Suddenly tipping her head back, she laughed without restraint for the first time in a very long time. "How stupid you must have thought me!"

David Marius looked at the long and lovely line of her throat, the moving sculpture of chin and mouth. "Not stupid," he said. "Just frightened." He got up and offered her his hand. "Come. Jade is the best antidote I know for needless worries and fears."

Kay rose with laughter still in her eyes, and allowed herself to be led to the cabinets across the room. He talked easily, as to a familiar fellow collector, while he unlocked the glass doors. "I'll show you first my most recent and most valuable acquisition. It may be of particular interest—or, anyway,

some ironic amusement—to you. It arrived the day before
yesterday from Peking, on Jeremy's plane." He handed her
a gleaming, milky-white, translucent disk, exquisitely carved
with a design of flowers and birds. She felt its slight weight
in her palm, and David Marius watched with approval as her
fingers instinctively caressed the smooth and intricate relief
of the surface. "To answer the question you haven't asked,"
he said good-humoredly, "no, Jeremy didn't bring it himself.
Henry Wu, his radio operator, has been working for me for
some time."

"The devils of the air?"

"The same one. He wears any cheap bazaar soapstone
charm on the outward trip, and a piece of real jade, delivered
to him by, let us say, a mutual friend, on the return journey.
Most people can't tell the difference, but, in any case, he's
never searched. Jeremy and his crew have a remarkable reputation. In fact, it was Henry who suggested him to me for the
more extensive operation I had proposed."

Burning with shame, Kay recalled the high-handed naïveté
with which she had asked for this interview—and, worse, to
offer a shoddy little bargain for which David Marius had no
use. Kay looked down at the delicate medallion in her hand
and said in a low voice, as though it were an apology, "I never
knew jade could be white."

"The most precious kind—that particular piece was carved
in the eighteenth century, the greatest period, when the Imperial ateliers of Peking were the most famous in the world.
There are some other colors over here—" He was smiling
not at Kay but at the perfect ornaments clustered in groups
or isolated on individual stands. She placed the medallion
carefully back on its satin cushion, and turned to stare at the
huge figure beside her picking up each small object with the

tenderness of a lover. Pale green, blue-green, the softly brilliant jewel green, the marbled fusions of different greens, yellow, red, white—he set the little figures, the flowers, the medallions, the miniature animals, out in the light for Kay to admire.

"Beautiful, beautiful," she kept repeating. "Oh, how beautiful!" He seemed scarcely to hear her, absorbed in his own delight. But she was noticing, too, the shadows gathering in the corners of the room and thinking that soon she would have to leave and there would be no further reason to see David Marius again. Her voice held all her own sense of loss when she said, "What will become of all these extraordinary things when you go?"

"Oh, I won't abandon these, though I'll sell them all eventually. They—and the bulk of the collection that has already been sent to await me in Hong Kong—are, so to speak, my fire insurance. Unlike the houses and the land, they're portable. I suppose that there's a moral of some sort to be drawn from the fact that what started as a private extravagance—an indulgence, in fact—turns out, in the end, to be my most practical asset."

"Because—quite apart from their loveliness—they're all very valuable?"

"Almost priceless—to people who understand jade, that is. Years ago, when as a child I first became infatuated with it—and it is an infatuation stronger than any other passion and quite as unreasonable—I used to go at dawn to the jade market outside Hatamen Gate in Peking to watch the dealers and learn to distinguish quality. I once copied out a passage from Confucius about jade that became my personal book of rules. It ended, as I remember, 'It shows a pure spirit among the hills and streams, and in the whole world there is no one who does not value it." Sadly enough, that's not strictly true, but the people who *do* value it treasure it above gold and diamonds."

To Kay—listening more to his voice than his words, a fragmentary picture caught in her mind of untrammeled childhood, of freedom and ease beyond her imagining—one name, mentioned in passing, imprinted itself with the clarity of a warning sign. Hong Kong. He would be leaving for Hong Kong.

David Marius was telling her that she should not look at too much jade all at once; it dulled one's appreciation. Ideally, she should hold just one piece for hours, if necessary, to familiarize herself with its feel, to examine it as it gradually revealed its full beauty, to strike it lightly and listen for its resonance, " 'a pure, far-reaching sound, vibrating long but stopping abruptly, like music.' That's Confucius, too."

A servant came into the room to light the lamps, and was followed almost immediately by a Chinese woman of such startling elegance that it took Kay a deliberate effort to keep from staring like an ill-bred child and to return her bow of greeting with some degree of composure. She was dressed in blue figured silk, and Kay noticed that while there was nothing truly memorable about her features, the flawless skin, the confidence of carriage, and the way she held her head gave the impression of great beauty. In age, she could have been anywhere from thirty to forty—or even a little younger or older.

The woman said something to David Marius in Chinese, to which he replied, and then broke off to say, "Ching-li is an old friend. She knows who you are, but there doesn't seem much point in introducing you formally as she doesn't speak English." He returned immediately to his conversation with her.

Kay, standing still by the cabinet, fixed her gaze on the piece of jade in her hand, noticing how lamplight changed the opaque lustre of its surface. She recalled a moment on the French Club steps—David Marius turning to his elderly Chinese companion, exchanging a few remarks, helping him into a car—and confirmed an earlier observation in this present encounter. David Marius had a trick of concentrating so completely on the person he was talking to that anyone else present immediately felt deserted. She wondered remotely what it would be like to be able to walk into David Marius's house unannounced, with the careless assurance of long familiarity, to command his attention without excuse or explanation.

She became aware that David Marius had asked her a question, and must have been waiting some time for her answer. "I'm sorry," she said. "I wasn't listening."

"Would you like to stay and dine with us?"

With us. "Oh, no," Kay said hastily. "No, no. I've stayed much too long already. I really must get back. Anyway, I have an appointment for dinner."

David Marius made no protestations of regret, merely offered to drive her back.

As the car left the gates and turned on to Hungjao Road, Kay, without really intending to, asked, "Does she live—I mean, is she staying with you?"

"Yes."

In the neutral silence which followed, Kay watched the big competent hands on the wheel and then glanced furtively at the unrevealing face. She said, "I'm afraid that sounded most impertinent. I only meant, is Shanghai her home?"

"Peking." His voice showed no trace of discomfiture. "Her father was one of my professors, a scholar and a poet. He tried to persuade me to join him in Kunming when the University moved there and thousands of students walked across China, carrying what they could of the books from the great library on their backs. At the time I thought I had more urgent work to do. I was wrong as it turned out. In any case, I never saw him again."

"He never returned to Peking?"

"He died in Peking. In prison. Under torture."

And now Ching-li lives with you. From compassion? Shared affection for her father? Realistically, Kay rejected both possibilities. "What had he done?"

"According to the secret police, he was arrested for harboring 'anti-Nationalist thoughts'."

"What on earth does that mean?"

"In his case it meant sympathizing with the students' protests about the atrocities of the Kuomintang regime."

"How frightful," Kay said, matching David Marius's prosaic tone. "I've lost count of the pointless frightful things that happen, even just the ones I know about." After a moment she added, "I don't suppose Ching-li will ever want to go back to Peking. I don't suppose that it's the one place in all the world that she will miss."

Maneuvering expertly through the Shanghai streets, David Marius made no response to Kay's speculations about Ching-li. He said abruptly, "You haven't really a dinner appointment, have you?"

"No, I haven't. I didn't want to—"

"In that case, unless you still have objections to being seen with me in public, I'll take you out to dine."

"But aren't you expected home?"

"Not necessarily. It is, after all, my home, and I return or don't as I see fit. I'll telephone from the restaurant to set your mind, and my cook's, at rest. I would, in any case, have had to come in to see a couple of people after dinner."

"More business meetings?"

"Of a less agreeable sort than ours," he said, deliberately uninformative. "In my line of work, appointments seldom come in office hours—or in offices."

"What," Kay pursued, "*is* your line of work?"

"At the moment," he replied with easy evasiveness, "I suppose it could be described as 'liquidating one's assets.' It involves some curious varieties of bargains, and long and often astonishing chains of barters and exchanges." He told her a little story that had been going the rounds in Shanghai, about an American newcomer who had exchanged a couple of army shirts for a case of sardines, but found, when he opened the battered cans, that in the course of innumerable similar transactions, the contents had gone bad. Indignantly, he returned the case to the shopkeeper and was met with surprised apologies. "But you didn't tell me you wanted to *eat* the sardines."

Still talking lightly and unspecifically, he stopped the car in front of a restaurant.

Winter came early and suddenly to Shanghai that year, with an impact as unarguable as the news of a death in the family. It seemed as if one week any casual conversation was laced with complaints about the stickiness of the heat, and the next a silence as sharp as the cold itself entered everybody's life.

The look of the city changed, too. Dark winds swept up the river and along the streets, blowing paper and the lighter rubbish into grimy drifts of refuse against walls, buildings, curbs. People began to appear in padded gowns or trousers and tunics, with felt shoes, instead of the flapping cottons and straw slippers of summer. Hands were tucked into

sleeves for warmth, and the crowds on the roads walked
hunched and hurrying, heads bowed before the wind. And
the city was even more densely jammed with new waves of
refugees in rags, with bandaged feet, eyes streaming, shud-
dering hopelessly in doorways, trapped between the famine
of their home villages far inland and the bitter, ungiving
prospect of a scratched living in Shanghai. It was too cold for
panic. All that the city allowed now was despair.

Kay had no winter clothes. Her heaviest coat was a silk
evening wrap, and the wardrobe that she had gradually accumulated in Manila, pretty and cool, suitable for the tropics,
for life in Doña Luisa's house or her work at the International
Club—the crisp cottons, the floating dance dresses, the
flimsy high-heeled sandals—contained not even a pair of
stockings. She spent a little of her dwindling money on a coat
of cheap fabric, lined with thin quilted cotton. No amount of
clever tucking and shaping, of tricks learned long ago at
Madame Rosa's, could make it look anything better than
ungainly, and Kay, knowing it gave a bad impression to look
needy (unused, in any case, to feeling dowdy), nevertheless
went doggedly on with her excursions from consulate to
consulate, from club to club, even to foreign billets, searching in vain for a job. She traveled now by pedicab instead of
taxi. It was much cheaper, naturally, but each errand took a
great deal longer, and the slow trips gave to the daily tragedy
of the city streets an immediacy that was quite out of proportion to the insulation offered by an ordinary pane of glass in
a taxi window. There was time, sitting behind the bent, pedal-
ing figure of the driver, to absorb, however numbly, the tiny
individual dramas of this blind beggar, that homeless,
scrawny child, another woman doubled over under the
weight of some enormous package she carried on her back,

those coolies pushing and pulling a loaded wooden cart too heavy for a draft horse, gasping out a monotonous chant of some sort to keep the rhythm. And the seething, muted life in the narrow anonymous alleys.

She occasionally gave a carefully edited account of some of her activities to Jeremy, forestalling any worried questions by describing her journeys on foot or by pedicab as essential aspects of the absorbing business of learning about a new city, the best way, really, to get a close look and a feeling for its day-to-day life. Jeremy found her attitude admirably in character, typical of her refusal to put a sentimental gloss on realities. Remembering her sketches of the Manila slums, he thought, poverty and squalor, even on this scale, naturally don't appall her, are already an accepted part of her "experience of living." He asked only, "Don't you get cold?"

"Not particularly," she replied and, flicking her fingers at her coat, added, "this ugly thing is only a temporary measure until I find a good tailor. No point in wasting money on something fancier when all the readymade clothes are so unbecoming."

Kay had given up any thought of finding a cheap apartment or a room; she realized now that it had been a laughable hope. Jeremy's "very useful type" at the Palace Hotel had come to a safe and profitable agreement with her, permitting her to stay on in her room as long as she continued to pay week by week, and in American dollars.

In the evenings, she sometimes dined with Johnny, insisting that they eat in the Palace Hotel restaurant, because, she said, she wasn't accustomed to this climate, it was too cold for her to go out. Actually, of course, she was ashamed to be seen in her only coat. She listened with every semblance of attention and sympathy to his endless homesick stories of his

Stateside life, assured him that he would be the first person she would inform when she stopped being "Jeremy's girl." On those occasions, she also ate the only full meal of her day. When Jeremy was in town, it was understood that she spent the time with him.

The only event that brought her, even indirectly, into contact with David Marius was her telephone call to Mr. Mason. Somewhat to her surprise, the voice that answered was quite clearly Chinese, though the English was fluent with a slight American accent. He seemed quite alarmed by Kay's request for an appointment. "I think it inadvisable," he said hastily. "Such matters are much better handled through intermediaries."

"But Mr. Mari—"

"Our mutual friend has already given me the relevant details of your predicament."

"Oh." Kay hesitated. "I just thought that a lawyer would—"

"I'm not a lawyer, Mrs. Wilson. Our mutual friend sometimes calls me an 'organizer.'" He sounded amused by the description. "I will 'organize' the procuring of the necessary papers and affidavits."

"And the judgment?" Kay asked incredulously.

"They would be of little use without the judgment. Later on, some of the documents will need your signature—and that of your husband."

"Will the papers be *forged?*" Kay demanded recklessly.

"No, no. Most surely not!" Mr. Mason replied, mildly shocked by the suggestion. "Everything will be genuine. It will take some days and some—"

"Squeeze money?"

"Probably. But—"

"How much is that likely to be?" Kay tried to keep her voice steady.

"—But our friend said you should not be troubled with such incidentals."

"You mean, Mr. Mari—our friend said he'd—"

"He said you should not be troubled. I will contact you if there is anything further for you to do."

Kay's next telephone call was to David Marius, who was not at home, and when he returned her call the next day, he seemed highly entertained by her bewilderment. Kay asked him, "But who *is* Mr. Mason? He sounded Chinese."

"Very possibly because he is Chinese. Mason is an anglicization of 'Ma-sun.' He's an old acquaintance of mine from my Chungking days."

"I don't understand it— He doesn't want to see me, doesn't need any information—"

"As a matter of fact, he *has* seen you. One morning at the French Club, when he and I were having a cup of tea. He drew my attention to your presence across the terrace. . . ."

Kay said, "Oh." She remembered the neat elderly man who had seemed absorbed in his conversation with David Marius —remembered much more than that, and, hot with embarrassment, tried to keep the memory out of her voice. "But shouldn't I consult a lawyer, discuss what grounds—"

"There's only one certain—"

"Adultery?"

"Of course," he said.

"Won't that need witnesses and—and people?"

"Yes, it will."

"And consequently a lot of squeeze money?"

"Not in this case."

"But a lot of people will have to know about it."

"Not in this case. Your secret," he added darkly, "is safe with me—and, of course, Mason. Never fear."

Kay couldn't bring herself to take the whole thing as some kind of frivolous escapade. She asked, "It will be legal, won't it? Valid and—?"

"As it happens, it will." The good humor evaporated from his voice. "And would it really matter if it weren't? You only want to assure Jeremy that he's free. You wouldn't sue him for bigamy if he married his English girl, would you?"

"Oh, no—never!"

"Well, in any case, the question won't arise."

With an effort, Kay said, "I don't know why you are doing all this for me, but I would like—"

"It relieves the tedium of my days," he told her. "There aren't many funny things happening in Shanghai at the moment."

"And I'm one of them?"

"Don't be offended. I meant it as a compliment."

"You pay some very unusual compliments," Kay said with restraint. "I had intended to—"

"For God's sake, don't *thank* me," he interrupted.

"Very well, I won't!" Kay snapped, and hung up.

One evening, Jeremy telephoned as usual after a mission, from the CAT house, and Kay noticed a puzzling tone of urgency in his voice. "Is something the matter?" she asked. "You sound so— Was it a bad flight? If you're very tired, I wouldn't at all mind—"

"No, no. I want to talk to you. But not on the telephone. I'll be along as soon as I've cleaned up."

Kay languidly finished dressing and, waiting for him, thought that she would have far preferred to spend the evening alone. She attributed her unaccustomed lassitude to the fatigue and disappointment of her long days, and remembered, in passing, the exhilaration verging on triumph that had attended her arrival in Shanghai. Her life since had distorted the stretch of time to make those recollections seem like the distant past.

When Jeremy arrived Kay went automatically into his embrace, but he released her quickly. He moved nervously about the room, as though he had never seen it before or was searching for something. He stopped, at last, near the telephone table, still with an air that combined excitement and apprehension, and Kay asked if he wanted to order a drink. "Not yet. No. I want to phone David Marius first."

Kay sat down on the straight chair at the desk and waited rigidly for him to continue. "Kate, I've come to a decision— At least, I think I have. I don't know." He gave her a rather tense smile. "You can see it's rather an indecisive decision, but then I'm nothing if not resolute. I'm going to do it. Yes, I'm almost sure I'll do it."

Kay didn't need to ask what "it" was. She said, instead, "What made you decide?"

"I was thinking about what you said at lunch that day, for one thing. And then there was something that Henry Wu told me—you don't know him, he's that crew member I told you about, my radioman. We had a delivery to make at—well, never mind the name, it's a small place on our way to Peking. It's colder up there. It was snowing. The airstrip is rather a long way out, and Henry and I were driving into town. There's just a country road—unsurfaced, of course— winding through the fields, and we passed a line of men walking along, barefoot in the snow, roped together, with armed guards in Nationalist uniforms. I took them for Communist prisoners, but Henry said, no, they were new recruits to the Nationalist army." He glanced at Kay's intent face and continued, straining to keep his voice even. "The procedure

is eminently straightforward. It seems a group of recruiting
officers go into a village—any village—and simply round up
all the able-bodied men at gunpoint. They rope them together and take away their shoes to make it harder for them
to desert—a good many manage it anyway, but still . . . However, if a man is absolutely crucial to his family—the only son
left, for instance, to run the farm and do the work in the fields
—they can buy him out of army service. The going rate,
Henry says, for a recruit is forty dollars." Anger and disgust
were in the words, but not in Jeremy's eyes, which looked
wounded and defeated. "It's expensive," he said. "I don't
know whether I'm explaining this properly— Do you see what
I mean, Kate? Do you see that it was the thought of a family
sitting down to calculate how far ahead they could afford to
mortgage their crops or land or whatever to buy their son
back that somehow did it?"

"Oh, yes," Kay replied. "Oh, yes. Certainly," as if he had
asked a small favor that was easily granted.

"Yes. I thought you would—*knew* you would, actually."
Some of the tension seemed to leave him, but she could still
see the shadows of sleeplessness and interior turmoil on his
face.

"I have David Marius's number. You'd better phone him
at his house." She took the card from her handbag and gave
it to Jeremy. "If he wants to see you this evening," she added
consideringly, "it had better be alone. The less he thinks I
know about it all, the safer it will be."

Kay listened to Jeremy's end of the telephone conversation. "May I speak to Mr. Marius? . . . Jeremy Wilson . . .
Yes." A pause. "Yes. . . . Very well, thank you. . . . Did you?"
(with some surprise) . . . "As a matter of fact, I am. . . . Well,
I wanted to talk to you about it. . . . Two nights and a day.

That is, I leave again day after tomorrow morning. . . . Yes, I think I could. Dinner?" He turned to Kay, eyebrows raised in inquiry, and put his hand over the mouthpiece. She whispered, "No, but you go."

"All right," he continued into the telephone. "Where would you like to meet? . . . Yes, fine. . . . Well, that's very kind of you" (glancing again at Kay), "but she's not feeling very well this evening. . . . I will. . . . Oh, yes, I'm sure she will. . . . Until seven-thirty, then. . . . Right. Goodbye."

So Kay did, after all, have the evening to herself. Bored and restless, she tried to keep her mind off both David Marius and Jeremy and what they might be saying to each other. She went to bed early, and although she slept, she was troubled by confused dreams of which she remembered little except that she must hurry, hurry to a forgotten rendezvous.

Jeremy told her, of course, about his conversation with David Marius the next day. It was a remarkably brief and undramatic narrative, but of considerable interest to Kay. Apparently, David Marius had foreseen—guessed? hoped? Jeremy wasn't sure which—that Jeremy would change his mind and accept what had seemed to him until recently an impossible shady collaboration. Kay, however, was certain that David Marius's preparations would have been made in any case for whichever pilot he had found to undertake the commission. She thought that Jeremy's reputation for trustworthiness must indeed be impressive for him to be so readily accepted as a replacement so late in the proceedings. The consignment had already been earmarked by a fictitious "Department of Special Operations," which had officially made the correct requests. The papers for the delivery were ready, as were the orders to the Peking authorities. "He even gave me the rubber stamps and an ink pad for the receipts,"

Jeremy said. "And I still don't know what this is all about."

"You know the only important thing—that the wounded or the sick will get the penicillin. Does it matter why David Marius is arranging it?"

"Or why I'm doing it?"

"I know why you're doing it."

"You're wrong. I want the money—"

"Jeremy," Kay pleaded, "Stop punishing yourself. The past can't be canceled out—"

"—or atoned for. There was an awful saying in my childhood. 'A guilty conscience needs no accusing.' What they never told you was that a guilty conscience has no expiation, either. And now I'm like all the others. I don't care. I just want to get out. Do you understand me, Kate? I simply *don't care.*"

"I understand that you want to get out. And I know that you will care to the end of your days. But that can't be helped. The crimes and the punishments are all on too grotesque a scale for me to grasp. All you can do is live as best you can for as long as you can."

"My island of sanity," Jeremy said. "Kate, am I doing the right thing?"

"I have no idea," she replied.

Kay spent most of the next two days with David Marius. He had called up originally to reassure her about Jeremy's departure, to tell her that the briefing had been uneventful, there had been no awkward questions, no unexpected delays. Her colorless remark "So there's nothing to do now except wait, is there?" seemed to trouble him.

"Is that what you're going to do? Just wait in your hotel room?"

"Oh, no," she said hastily, rejecting that pathetic little picture of herself. "I'll—I might go out—"

"Still job-hunting?"

"I'm rather discouraged about that—just for the moment,
that is. Something will work out in the end, I expect."

"Yes. I see. Well, then, let us hope that everything contin-
ues to go according to plan."

Jeremy's flight? And he assumed that Jeremy would share
the money with her? "You're quite wrong!" she said urgently.

"About what?" There was nothing beyond faint curiosity
in his voice.

"I mean, I don't think my plans are quite what you expect."

"Very possibly. However, the next twenty-four hours are
going to be fraught with a certain amount of tension for you,
I imagine. It doesn't seem like a good idea to spend them
alone in your room."

"Twenty-four hours? Will he be back tomorrow morning?"

"Evening. But I shall have news one way or the other by
lunchtime tomorrow."

"And you'll phone me as soon as you hear?"

"Yes. Yes, immediately." He seemed to be thinking about
something else. "Would you, perhaps, like a change of
scene?" he asked unexpectedly. "It sometimes serves as a
distraction. You could spend the day here, if you wanted,
doing—well, whatever you feel like doing. I have a number
of things to attend to, I'm afraid, but the house is at your
disposal."

"Oh, I'd love to!" Kay said with unguarded pleasure. "May
I bring my sketch pad? I promise I won't be in your way—"

"Or I in yours. By all means, sketch away to your heart's
content."

"Have you any ink?"

"Yes." He was smiling. "Brushes, too, if you want."

"I have my own brushes."

"Excellent. I have an appointment in town this morning. I'll pick you up after that."

Whatever his appointment was, it seemed, when he fetched Kay, to have left him in an abstracted, edgy mood. He turned the car on the Bund, and then suddenly stopped it at the edge of a narrow park that ran along the river—hardly a park, really; mostly pavement dotted with infrequent patches of rusty green and the tracery of a row of bare trees against the gray chill of the Whangpoo. "Do you mind if we walk for a few minutes?" He gave no explanations.

"Not at all." She reached for the handle of the door.

He looked at her cheap and shapeless coat and her bare legs for the first time, frowning. "You won't be cold?"

"Not if we keep walking."

In silence, they crossed down to the riverbank and followed the railing for a while. The park was fairly crowded with dark padded figures moving aimlessly about. A group of Chinese men in Nationalist uniforms were doing exercises in time to shrill commands. Some children were watching them. The stone benches at intervals along the railing were empty, too cold to be inviting. David Marius was looking at none of this; his head was turned away from Kay, gazing past the fragile sails of the junks, the smoky fuss of the tugs, at the misty, jagged line of the further bank. "I can remember the time," he said abruptly, "when there was a sign at the entrance to this park saying that Chinese and dogs were not permitted." He still didn't turn to face Kay, but added after a moment, "The Japanese made their own gesture when they took the city in '37. Every foreigner—every white foreigner, that is—was forced to bow when he passed here. Ludicrous, isn't it?"

"Which?"

"Both." He paused briefly at the railing and pointed across the river to an obscure, ugly huddle of factory buildings and tall chimneys. "My grandfather built his first enterprise there. A cotton mill. He came here at the turn of the century to make his fortune. The 'golden days' when foreigners from all over actually *owned* a piece of China."

"And did he make his fortune?"

"Yes. And my father increased it—real estate, here and in Peking. And more mills. And interests in oil refineries. And now it's almost all gone."

"Is that what's bothering you?" Kay asked, keeping her tone neutral.

But he turned and smiled down at her, returning to his usual careless manner. "Do I appear bothered? No, it was a dirty business from the beginning. I'm glad to be rid of it."

"I meant the fortune, not the business."

"Considerably reduced, but nothing to complain about. The cotton mills were easy—there was a wave of optimism after the Japanese surrender when a lot of people thought the Nationalist government was solidly established and were willing to buy industrial properties here, certain that the future would justify their investment."

"But you didn't share that optimism?"

"No. You see, I'd worked with them in Chungking. I had also been to Communist headquarters in Yenan—a wild frontier region on the edge of the Gobi Desert. It had been bombed virtually out of existence." He added, as if it explained everything—the Communist resurgence, the plight of China, his own feelings, "Most of the people were living in caves burrowed into the hillsides." He gripped her arm and swung her back toward the car. "You must be freezing," he said, dismissing his disjointed reminiscences and whatever regrets or successes they held. "Let's find something

hot and nourishing to eat. Have you become thinner since I
last saw you?"

In a small restaurant, he ordered soup and dumplings, and
something spicy with rice, and watched Kay speculatively
through the meal. Uncomfortable under his attentive gaze,
Kay said, "I got the papers from Mr. Mason a couple of days
ago."

"Everything in order?"

"Well, it all looked very impressive and official, with seals
and stamps and everything. It was very nice of you," she said
awkwardly, unequal to looking directly at him, "to—arrange
it all. I should have phoned you at once to thank you, and I
don't know why I didn't." Catching his eye, she added, "Well,
yes. I do know why I didn't. I was too embarrassed. Anyway,
please accept my thanks now for all your trouble."

"No trouble at all," he said.

"Where did you find— Who were the witnesses?"

"Two of my servants."

"Did you—"

"No, I didn't have to explain anything to them. And they
can't read English."

"I expect it seems silly, but I'm rather relieved that nobody
but us knows about this."

"For Jeremy's sake? Or rather, for Jeremy's girl's sake?
What's her name?"

Kay listened for irony in his voice but found none. "Margaret," she said. "No. For my own sake. I haven't told Jeremy
about it yet."

"Oh?" he said, and then, in a different tone, "I see," as if
he understood much more than her words.

He seemed entirely content to leave the subject on that
equivocal note, but Kay, unreasonably, felt that she ought to

correct some false impression and plunged into explanations. "At first I wasn't sure that it would work, and I didn't want to get his hopes up," she said. "And then, when Mr. Mason sent me the completed papers for signature Jeremy was away on a mission. And then when he returned he was so agitated about—about wanting to talk to you, about having changed his mind, about— Well, it just didn't seem like the right moment."

"So it's to be a glorious homecoming surprise?"

Kay shook her head anxiously. "You mustn't talk like that! You mustn't take his return for granted! I'm superstitious."

All that afternoon, Kay moved from pavilion to pavilion in David Marius's house, sketching a view of a courtyard here, an interior there, making a series of quick, graceful records of the tranquil maze of interconnected buildings. Several people called on him in the course of the day, all Chinese, some brisk and preoccupied, carrying briefcases, others, judging from the voices of their arrivals and departures, more chatty and informal. But though she was aware of an atmosphere of busy meetings and discussions, she heard nothing of the interviews or transactions that took place in his study.

He joined her once to see that she had everything she needed, and ordered a servant to bring tea and a charcoal brazier to place beside her to warm her hands. He looked at her sketches approvingly, raising his eyebrows in some surprise, but made no comment beyond "I hope you will let me keep one or two of these. They'll make agreeable souvenirs for when I begin to forget what China used to be like."

"You may keep them all. These are only exercises. Anyway, you'll never forget what China was like. It will always be your reality."

Later, when the thin wintry light was fading into evening, David Marius found her sitting in a doorway, sketching the bleak, geometric lines of the stone garden with the lily pond, seen between the lacquered pillars of the veranda. "Come and have a drink, now. You've done enough exercises for one day."

She looked up at him, smiling, hair disheveled, all trace of make-up gone, and then followed his glance down to her inky fingers. "Yes," she said. "I feel much better, but I expect I look a mess."

"In fact," he said, in a thoughtful, critical tone, "You look rather lovely. However, the servant will show you where to wash and tidy up if you want."

In the study, the lights were on and a tray of drinks was set out on the low table in front of the sofa. David Marius poured a Coca-Cola for Kay and a whiskey for himself. He raised his glass in a slight parody of a toast. "I suppose we should drink to the success of the mission, or good luck to Jeremy or some such suitable sentiment."

Kay sipped her drink and asked, "Did he seem very nervous this morning?"

"I wasn't at the briefing. Henry Wu phoned me from the airport. Why? Was he worried about the danger last night" —he corrected himself tactfully—"or whenever you last saw him?"

"Last night," Kay said blandly. "No, not about the danger. I should think that the danger was the only thing that consoled him a bit about the whole enterprise. In some odd way, there would have had to be a risk to himself in it before he could bring himself to undertake it at all."

"Oh? You know that about him, do you?"

"That the morality of things concerns him?"

"If that is morality—a sort of celestial umpire chalking up

merits and demerits, scoring fouls and goals, and watching to see if you're playing the game according to the rules."

"You have no such umpire," Kay said.

"Nor you."

Kay thought a moment. "Well, it's difficult, isn't it, if you aren't sure what the game is, and don't know the rules?"

"Quite a dilemma," David Marius said. "Still, let's hope that Jeremy wins his silver trophy or whatever it is he's playing for."

"He's playing for his life—his *real* life. Yes, I hope he gets it. Will he have reached Peking yet?"

"Oh, yes. I got word a little while ago—" Seeing the surprise on her face, he explained, "By telephone. There's a government line to Peking that is always open—"

"A *government* line?"

"Remember," he said reasonably, "some of their people are almost as anxious as you or I—or Jeremy—that this project doesn't run into trouble. They'll also be the ones who let me know tomorrow whether the delivery has been satisfactorily accomplished."

Kay nodded. "Jeremy won't be able to sleep tonight. He'll have an absolutely terrible night."

After dinner, drinking tea in the lamplit quiet of David Marius's dining room, Kay, sounding unintentionally forlorn, said, "I wish I didn't have to go back to the hotel. Somehow I can't face that room at the moment. It's astounding that such an ordinary room should have taken on such an indelible character in my mind."

"Indelible and nasty?"

"Indelible and sort of flat. Lifeless. I know exactly how my dressing-gown is hanging . . . and the slippers neatly beside the bed . . ."

"You can stay here, if you want," he offered easily. "The

guestroom is free now that Ching-li has gone."

She looked at him across the table, a sudden vivid look. "Can I—can I really?"

His voice was unconcerned, his face shadowed and expressionless. "I don't see why not," he said. "Do you prefer tea or coffee in the morning?"

The next day, after a long morning of suspense, the telephone call from Peking came through. David Marius opened a bottle of champagne for them to drink with lunch by way of celebration.

Jeremy returned from Peking and came straight to the Palace Hotel from the airport. Rumpled, dirty, his tan shirt stained with sweat under the fleece-lined flying jacket, he entered Kay's room bringing with him an atmosphere of hysterical and exhausted elation. He sat down heavily on the bed and, after a moment, stretched out, lying with his face in the pillows. Indistinctly, his words reached Kay. "I'm not going to talk about it. I've decided I'm not even going to think about it. It's over."

Kay knew, of course, that it wasn't, but she said, "Yes, it's over. And you're free."

"It was so incredibly simple. You can't imagine—there's something really sinister in how smoothly an illegal mission runs when the regular ones are usually such a bloody mess of red tape and confusion and nobody there at the right time and— I suppose it's just that everyone is getting his cut, so it's worth their while to be efficient. Sordid, isn't it? Just for money."

"If that's the most sordid thing you ever have to do for money," Kay said sharply, "you'll be exceedingly lucky."

Jeremy sat up quickly. "Yes," he said, in a sober voice.

"Yes, you're right. We're free. And that's more important than my own tiresome form of self-indulgence."

"Your conscience?"

"My priggish, genteel, supercilious, sickening old maid of a conscience. High time somebody roped the old girl." He laughed painfully. "However, if it's all the same to you, I'd rather not see David Marius again."

"There's no reason why you should. He knows it all went according to plan."

"I thought he might want to—you know, celebrate with one of those memorable Chinese dinners of his."

"We'll put him off. You have something else to celebrate —with a double Scotch immediately, if you like." She turned to the desk to pick up some papers. "All they need is your signature."

"Kate, what on—"

"The divorce agreement. It's perfectly valid, even though all the evidence is false—but then it is in most divorces anyway." She handed Jeremy the papers and continued, in her clear, matter-of-fact voice, "It seems that the only quick and absolutely certain grounds are adultery. So you'll be divorcing me for having been unfaithful to you, and that way the question of alimony doesn't arise. Of course, that part of the testimony is forged."

"Who forged it?"

Kay heard the change in his tone, but paid it no attention. "Not exactly forged—the signatures of the witnesses and so on are genuine. What I meant was that all of us will be perjuring ourselves, but that was understood from the beginning, wasn't it?"

"Who are you supposed to have been unfaithful with? Hasn't there got to be a corespondent?"

"Well, yes. David Marius."

"Good God!"

"It seemed logical," Kay hurried on. "I scarcely know anyone in Shanghai—and he was the only person who knew that we *were* actually married—and he hasn't any family or anyone who might be embarrassed—and he'd given me the name of the lawyer in the first place— Oh, Jeremy, I had to do *something*! I'd promised you—"

"Kate—Kate, I'm not blaming you. It's my fault. I should have told you, but I thought you knew—must have known. And you poor sweet, you've been doing all this on your own. Come here." He dropped the papers on the floor and patted the bed beside him. She walked forward, but didn't sit down. She waited in front of him, dreading his next words, knowing what he was going to say, hoping that by some miracle he wouldn't. She crossed her fingers behind her back for luck.

"I'm not going to sign them, you know," Jeremy said quietly.

"But we agreed—"

"I don't want to divorce you. Surely that's been plain to you for some time?"

"No!" Kay said in a storm of rejection. "No, no it hasn't!"

"Not even—"

"Not even in bed! You're in love with Margaret—you *have* to be in love with Margaret! That's what all this was about, wasn't it? You wanted the money for Margaret and that farm in Somerset. You told me from the beginning—"

"It was true in the beginning—"

"It's still true. And now you've got the money, and now you can get on with it—with that idiotic dream of yours—"

"Kate, will you listen to me a minute—"

"Not if you're going to tell me you don't want to go back to England now."

"I do want to go back—"

"And buy the farm?"

"And buy the farm. For us. For *us*, Kate, Don't you see?"

"I *don't* see—"

"It's not a dream, and it's not so idiotic—"

"Margaret," Kay said harshly, and then quoted, in a caustic imitation of Jeremy's voice, " 'She's a real person. I get letters from her.' "

"Please," Jeremy pleaded. "It sounds rotten. It *is* rotten. She was the dream if you want to call it that—a necessary one at the time that I needed it. In fact, I thought it reality, and the rest a dream—"

"And now you've woken up. And in the clear light of day you think that I—that *I* of all people—could live an English country life—with blue-eyed Margaret as a neighbor and, for pity's sake, *watch the seasons?*"

"You told me once that you'd settle for a cottage, even without the roses."

"Oh, Jeremy," Kay cried, turning away. "Stop it! Stop it!"

To her inflexible back and the tiny, clenched fists, he said, "I'm trying to tell you that I love you, that I want you to—"

"And what about me? What am I supposed—"

"Kate, you've had your mind so fixed on Margaret and that this is an 'arrangement' that you wouldn't let yourself feel what I know you feel—"

"You don't know what I feel—"

"I do. There are times," he said gently, "when you admit the truth—perhaps without realizing it. There are times when nobody can fake—"

"Oh, God!" Kay swung around furiously. "How little you know about—about me!"

Jeremy stood up and placed his hands lightly on her shoulders, but she still stared sullenly at her feet. "Kate, why are

we quarreling? All I want is for us to be happy, quietly . . .
somewhere . . . together. It needn't be Somerset. I'm not
quite the fool you seem to think, though I admit I haven't
given you much reason to believe that. We've both seen altogether too much— Oh, hell, I don't know why I didn't
explain all this sooner—"

"Because it isn't true."

"Yes, it is. It is. Though it may take you a little time to
accept it. I've said it was my fault—I was so preoccupied with
my own little selfish—"

Kay twisted away from his hands. "Selfish! Faults! Guilts!
Conscience!" Her voice rose shrilly. "Your damn celestial
umpire!"

"My *what?*"

"Never mind," she said, suddenly limp and uncaring. "I
don't know what we're quarreling about either—if that's what
we're doing. Much better to just be sensible and sign the
papers." She began to pick them up and, crouching on the
floor, added, "I made a bargain with you and I'm keeping it.
Nothing more than that. In any case, I couldn't fit into your
life. Not in England—not anywhere."

Jeremy watched her, smiling with relief. "If *that's* all that's
bothering you—"

"It isn't. But I can't talk about the rest. All you need to
know is that I can't—and don't want to—stay married to
you." Despairingly, she said, "Oh, *why* can't it all be straightforward—as it was to start out with, and we could all keep our
self-respect—"

"Everything changes," Jeremy answered, "and you and I
with it. I know why you're troubled—"

"No, no, you—"

"—and I know why you want the divorce. But can't you see

that it's my responsibility to explain things to her. You have nothing to—"

"Reproach myself with?"

"Yes. You hadn't *planned*—"

"No, I hadn't."

"Neither had I. However, it's happened. You'll get used to the idea soon. Here"—he held out his hand—"let me throw those papers away. As soon as you allow yourself to start—"

"Jeremy—"

"My darling, you'll see I'm right—"

Kay recoiled from his words, from his look. "Oh, Jeremy," she whispered, "you must sign. You see—you won't be perjuring yourself."

In the silence that followed, Kay walked stiffly to the desk, set the papers on it, and stacked them meticulously, edge to edge, exactly even. She placed a pen beside them. She heard Jeremy say, "David Marius," in a dead voice; then she looked at him with big, honest eyes, her small figure electric with hostility, "Of course David Marius," she said. "What did you think I'd been doing all those evenings when you were away flying missions? Sitting here forlornly nibbling on sandwiches?"

"I thought you didn't like him."

"What difference does that make?" she said bitterly. "What you thought—"

"You were lonely," he begged. "You went out with him. I do un—"

"I went to bed with him." Her tone was ruthlessly candid. "Because I wanted to. I spent last night at his house. We waited together for the news from Peking. We had champagne with lunch to celebrate."

"Kate, you're making this up. You want to—"

"Have I ever lied to you?" She saw Jeremy begin to shake his head, and continued quickly, "Well, yes, I have—in bed. But that was only by way of saying thank you." She laughed and, watching Jeremy's haggard, stricken face, added almost tenderly, "I was—*am*—very grateful, you know."

Like a sleepwalker, Jeremy moved past her to the desk and picked up the pen.

Responding to Kay's instructions, the taxi-driver sounded his horn outside the tall gates and heard the answering yell from behind the wall. He drove into the small courtyard of David Marius's house, where Kay climbed out and paid him for the ride and for his return journey. The servant who had opened the gate smiled at her in recognition and, unsurprised by what seemed to Kay one of the most daring gestures of her life, obeyed her little pantomime of request by unloading her suitcases. She waited there beside them while he closed the gates behind the departing taxi, and then followed him into the entrance pavilion.

Rigid with a chill that had nothing to do with the icy wind outside, Kay stood staring at the carpet, deliberately counting the faded gold flowers against the silky background of its design. The large, sudden shadow in the doorway, the faint sound of the familiar, rapid, almost stealthy walk made her, reluctantly, look up.

"What on earth," said David Marius, "are you doing here?"

"I've come to stay," she answered jauntily, shivering.

"*Stay?* With *me?*"

"Naturally. It's your house, after all. And you have a spare room."

There was an unsmiling silence before David Marius asked mildly, "Did it cross your mind that I might not be able— might not want—to have you here?"

"No," she said, lying. "It didn't. If that is the case," she added with great seriousness, "I really don't know what to do next."

"Burnt your bridges?"

"Oh, yes." She frowned as if the question were too obvious to require more than a word of acknowledgment.

"Touching little fool, aren't you?" he said absently. "You'd better at least come in and sit down." He turned and led the way into his study.

There Kay huddled in a corner of the sofa while David Marius, moving restlessly about, his big presence filling the room, ordered tea, seemed for a few moments to give intense concentration to various objects in the room, walked to the door to shout something in Chinese to the retreating servant, came back and waited irritably until the tea was served. "I thought," he said at last, "that you would have started on your plans by now."

"I haven't any plans."

"Plans to get out of China, damn it! Plans to go back to England with Jeremy. Plans to—"

"I'm no longer included in Jeremy's plans. Surely you know that—you arranged the divorce papers that he signed."

"He *signed?* He couldn't have—he's too plainly besotted with you—it's why he flew the mission—he *couldn't*—"

"He did, though."

"What did you tell him? You must have told him something."

"I had to. I honestly didn't want to. But I *had* to—he wouldn't have signed unless I—"

"All right, all right. Well, what bit of housemaid's literature did you produce?"

"I'm afraid you may be angry."

"I'm angry *now*."

"Then I can't make it any worse, can I?"

"I wouldn't put it past you."

Kay took a deep breath and said, in a rush, "I told him that it wasn't perjury. That it was all true, that I *had* committed adultery, and that you really were the—well, the corespondent."

"Good God! And he believed you?"

"People always believe what they're afraid of."

David Marius sat down heavily in the chair at his desk. For a moment he said nothing, and then he began to laugh. He put his head in his hands and he laughed and laughed, unable to stop, unable to speak coherently. "To think," he gasped, the heavy table shaking under his elbows as in a slight earthquake, "to think . . . that I was convinced . . . that your whole divorce gambit . . ."

Lightheartedly, Kay finished his remarks for him. "Was just a way of getting Jeremy to see that he wanted to stay married to me after all? Certainly not. It was most embarrassing." Her clear, precise, rather disapproving tone sent David Marius into fresh spasms of laughter. "In any case, he only *thinks* he's in love with me at the moment, because I'm *here*, and we're in China, and everything else seems so remote."

"I expect . . . I expect there are other reasons. . . ."

"Oh, *those*. Well, any girl can provide those reasons for him."

"You are—you really *are*—"

"An original?"

"That's not what I was going to say, but let that pass."

"So I may stay, after all?"

David Marius nodded. "For a while."

"For as long as you like," Kay said. A little anxiously she added, "I'd better tell you another thing before you have my luggage moved in. I've run out of all the money I had." And, with quick appeal, "But I haven't left any debts."

For some reason, this started David Marius laughing again. He shook his head from side to side in vast helpless amusement. "Your luggage has already been put in your room," he said when, at last, he could form the words.

On New Year's Eve, 1948, Kay sat curled in her usual corner of the sofa in the study of David Marius's house in Shanghai. She was warmly wrapped in a sable coat a little too long for her, and her feet were encased in impractical Chinese embroidered satin slippers. She had twisted her hair into a sleek formal coil on top of her head, which, since she was wearing no make-up, gave her a look of slightly comical childishness.

She glanced idly around the room, at the cabinets on the far side now emptied of their jade, the marks on the walls where pictures had hung, the long table at last tidy and clear of papers. In the previous six weeks, the whole house had gradually acquired a bereft, enclosed air, like an invalid retreating behind his eyes from pain, into some private area of reserve.

Eventually, she looked up at David Marius standing by the table in the subdued lamplight, his enormous shadow stretching across the floor. She raised the pale gold of her glass and remarked, "This is the fourth time in my life that I've ever had champagne. And the first time I've liked the taste. Could it be the effect of the sables?"

"Quite possibly," David Marius replied. "They've been known to change a woman's character, why not her palate? I think you'd better have it shortened."

"Oh, no," Kay said firmly and, kicking off her slippers, tucked her bare feet up under the edge of the fur. "One can't possibly have too many sables."

"An irrefutable argument."

"Wasn't it a very extravagant exchange?"

"Not really. You needed a winter coat." His voice was eminently prosaic, though he was smiling down at her from his dark height. To her clear peal of laughter, he added, "And we have the use of the car until we leave. We couldn't have taken it out of China anyway. Sables—"

"—are *portable*," they finished the sentence together, in the tone one uses for a familiar, much-quoted joke.

David Marius studied his watch for a minute, then said, "It's midnight. Happy New Year."

Kay sipped her champagne in response and asked, "Do you suppose it will be? 1949. Happy, I mean?"

"Is anybody happy—once they are no longer children?"

"Certainly," Kay said with conviction. "I'm happier now than I've ever been. But then I had rather a gray childhood —an orphan, and brought up mostly in convents. My aunt and uncle were quite nice to me, but not much interested— understandably. They had children of their own." She shook her head. "But I can't remember being *happy*." Holding up her glass, she said, "May I have some more champagne?"

He filled it, placed the bottle on the coffee table, sat down in a chair, and stretched his legs out lazily. "As it happens, you can have champagne every day until we leave. My stock should just about last."

"Oh? Have you decided the date?"

"Next week. You don't, of course, read the papers."

"Well," Kay said, as if it were only common sense, "I know you'll tell me anything important, so there doesn't seem much point, does there?"

David Marius laughed. "All right. The only thing you need to know is that the big Communist offensive at Hsüchow has been successful—"

"Hsüchow?"

"It's a vitally important railway junction between Tientsin and the Yangtze. And now the really definitive attack on Peking and Tientsin has begun. There isn't any doubt about its outcome."

"And all the time up to now you've been stubbornly hoping about Peking? Is this why you've finally fixed a date for leaving?"

"Good Lord, no!"

Kay, knowing he meant yes, said, "I find it very comforting that you can be as irrational as anyone else. Where will we be going? Not that it matters particularly . . ."

"Hong Kong, at least for a while, to—so to speak—reorganize finances."

"And then?"

"I haven't given it much thought. America, perhaps?"

"America," Kay repeated with wonder. "America. How strange it seems. A long time ago, when I first left the Philippines, I was on my way to America. It seemed possible then. My father had left me a little money, and I was going to spend it on going to college there."

"What happened?"

"I got stuck in Japan. Because of Pearl Harbor. I haven't told you that part of my story, have I?"

About the Author

Santha Rama Rau was born in Madras, India, the daughter of the Indian diplomat, Benegal Rama Rau. Her childhood was spent in the various countries in which her father was stationed, and in 1941 she came to America to attend Wellesley College. During her vacations, she wrote for the Office of War Information, and shortly after her graduation, her first book, *Home to India,* a Harper "Find" for 1945, was published. In the summer of 1947 she went to Tokyo to act as hostess for her father, who had been appointed independent India's first ambassador to Japan. There she taught English at Mrs. H ni's famous Freedom School. Thereafter, she traveled extensively, particularly through the continent of Asia.

Miss Rama Rau is the author of seven other books, including a novel, *Remember the House,* and many magazine articles, many of which were collected in *Gifts of Passage.* Her dramatization of E. M. Forester's *A Passage to India* was a success on both the London and the New York stage. She makes her home in Bombay.

70 71 72 73 10 9 8 7 6 5 4 3 2